"Am I Ugly?"

"Ugly?" André laughed unsteadily, surprised at the tremor in his voice.

Delphine's body was full and ripe, glowing and golden from the kiss of the sun. Her waist was very slender, but her hips curved sensuously, and the voluptuous swell of her breasts made him wonder how she had managed to hide such beauty.

André stepped toward her, hesitating, then stooped and plucked her cloak from the floor, his hands shaking, and wrapped it about her shoulders. His fingers grazed her collarbone, explored the hollow at the base of her neck, then slid down to caress the soft fullness of her breast. His chest rose and fell with great heaving breaths, and his face twisted in agony; he closed his eyes and turned away, his hands tight-clamped fists at his sides.

"In the name of God," he choked, "go to your cabin, or we are both undone!"

"No," she said softly.

Dear Reader,

We, the editors of Tapestry Romances, are committed to bringing you two outstanding original romantic historical novels each and every month.

From Kentucky in the 1850s to the court of Louis XIII, from the deck of a pirate ship within sight of Gibraltar to a mining camp high in the Sierra Nevadas, our heroines experience life and love, romance and adventure.

Our aim is to give you the kind of historical romances that you want to read. We would enjoy hearing your thoughts about this book and all future Tapestry Romances. Please write to us at the address below.

The Editors
Tapestry Romances
POCKET BOOKS
1230 Avenue of the Americas
Box TAP
New York, N.Y. 10020

Delphine

Ena Halliday

A TAPESTRY BOOK
PUBLISHED BY POCKET BOOKS NEW YORK

Books by Ena Halliday

Delphine
Lysette
Marielle

Published by TAPESTRY BOOKS

An *Original* publication of TAPESTRY BOOKS

A Tapestry Book published by
POCKET BOOKS, a division of Simon & Schuster, Inc.
1230 Avenue of the Americas, New York, N.Y. 10020

ISBN: 0-671-46166-4

First Tapestry Books printing July, 1983

10 9 8 7 6 5 4 3 2 1

POCKET and colophon are registered trademarks
of Simon & Schuster, Inc.

TAPESTRY is a trademark of Simon & Schuster, Inc.

Printed in the U.S.A.

Delphine

Chapter One

THE SAVAGE GRINNED AS HE BENT OVER ANDRÉ, HIS TEETH as white as the feathers in his raven hair, his dark eyes glinting in triumph. The red-skinned body was sleek and pungent with bear grease; André strove in vain to grip the shoulders, the powerful arms that pinned him to the ground. At last, with a loud grunt, André arched his chest upward, easing for a moment the weight of the body that pressed on his. He wrenched himself clear, scrambling to his feet at the same moment as did the savage. They circled the clearing warily, drawing great gasping breaths, each looking for the advantage over the other. André stopped, sweeping a sweat-stained arm across his mouth, then lunged, catching the savage by surprise and flipping him onto the ground. There was a dull thud as his opponent's back smacked against the packed earth; in a second André was upon him, his elbow jammed up to the man's chin, forearm pressed against his windpipe. The savage struggled, gasped, then lay still, but his black eyes gleamed with a crafty light. Without warning his hand snaked under André's upraised arm and clutched the golden beard poised just above his own face, tugging at it

1

so fiercely that André howled and rolled away, sitting up and rubbing his outraged chin.

"For shame, Na-e-Ga!" he said, aggrieved. "A man's beard is his pride! You have used me unfairly."

The savage sat up in his turn, his face split in a sly grin, and stroked his own smooth-shaven jaws. "Have I not told you for all these seasons, my brother, that a true man keeps his face bare?" His voice was soft with the Huron dialect. "If you give me the advantage by going about like some shaggy creature of the woods, it is mine to take!"

André shook his head. "No, I would have bested you, but for your treachery!" He looked up at the laughing man above him. "What say you, Georges? Was the fall mine, by rights?"

Georges de Mersenne frowned, his glance going from one man to the other. "You pose me a knotty problem, André, worthy of a Solomon. For, look you, you return to France today, whilst I stay here in Quebec! Shall I then insult Na-e-Ga by judging in your favor?" The savage smiled broadly. "On the other hand," and here Mersenne pinched at his own neatly trimmed beard and moustache, "a little hair is not such a terrible thing, and not to be mocked, nor used for unfair advantage!"

Now it was André's turn to grin. "Ha!" he said, pointing a triumphant finger at Na-e-Ga.

"On the other hand," interrupted Mersenne, "when I wish to trade with Na-e-Ga next spring, neither André, Comte de Crillon," a polite nod in André's direction, "nor all the bearded gentlemen of Louis's court, nor all of Richelieu's henchmen will avail me if Na-e-Ga will not part with his furs! No, I must vote for Na-e-Ga and his Huron brethren!"

"So be it," said André good-naturedly, rising to his feet to clasp the savage's hand in his own. His blue eyes twinkled, delivering one final shot. "However, his treachery was like that of the Iroquois, the 'snakes that strike without warning,'" he said, using the derisive name—Iroquois—the Hurons and Algonquins used to describe their enemies, the tribes of the Five Nations.

Na-e-Ga laughed and shook his head. "You are a villain, my brother, to turn a man's knife against his own breast!" Georges de Mersenne looked mystified. "I was not born Huron," explained Na-e-Ga. "I was Seneca. Of the hated Iroquois. Born, they say, near that great water to the south. So my name: Na-e-Ga, Thundering Water. My mother and I were captured by a Huron raiding party. The old chief of the Hurons took me for his son, and I have been Huron since, for I have known no other life."

"You never told me!" said Mersenne.

Na-e-Ga looked meaningfully at André. "Men tell many things around a campfire."

"Seneca or Huron, I shall miss you," said André, his voice strained with sudden emotion.

"It is time for you to return to your home and your people. You are no longer the man of madness and black spirits that you were when first we headed our canoe up the River of Hochelaga. I think the solitude has brought you peace, my brother." Na-e-Ga swept his arm about the clearing, encompassing the soft April day. "The green has returned to the trees, and the pain has left your eyes. Is it not time to go home?"

André nodded, unable to speak.

"I wish you a safe voyage," said Na-e-Ga. "My sister, White Deer, will mourn for you a little, I think." He clasped André's forearm, then drew away and scrambled down the bank of the river to the birchbark canoe that waited in the rushes.

André stood in the clearing, waving his arm in farewell

until the small craft reached a bend in the river and was lost from sight. Bending down to retrieve his buckskin shirt, he slung it across one bare shoulder and followed Mersenne along a path to a rough-hewn cabin set on a rise at some distance from the main street of the stockaded village of Quebec. A dark-eyed young Huron woman, her hair plaited into two long braids, hurried out of the cabin at their approach, and waited for instructions from Georges de Mersenne.

"Will you shave, André?" he asked, lapsing into French.

André smiled. How strange it sounded! A whole year! Na-e-Ga had been such a skillful teacher of the Huron dialect that André had almost forgotten his native speech. "Yes," he said, feeling tongue-tied. "For all my brave talk to Na-e-Ga, I have in the past kept my face bare. Marielle—" He stopped and took a deep breath. It was the first time he had been able to say her name in more than a year. "Marielle—Madame la Comtesse—preferred me clean-shaven."

At Mersenne's directions, the girl brought forth a large basin of water that she placed on a tripod near the door, then fetched scissors and razor and a small silver mirror. She propped the mirror, eye level, against the split-log siding of the cabin, and handed André a linen towel, smiling shyly as she did so. Georges frowned and patted her familiarly on her rump as she passed him to reenter the cabin, the gesture comfortable and possessive at the same time. "Eh, bien," he said almost reluctantly, "I should go to Paris with you, André. Quebec is growing. I think we have near to two hundred souls now, and with the Ursuline Sisters opening their school, I should find me a wife and begin a family."

André had begun to clip away at the thick growth of his beard. The golden ringlets fell to the ground at his feet, glinting in the bright sunshine. "When were you last in France?" he asked.

"I came here to New France with my father eleven years ago, in 1628. I was fifteen then. We meant to stay only the year, exploring, bartering for furs. But then the British attacked Quebec and we fought beside Champlain. My father was killed. When Champlain was taken by the British and Quebec fell, I took refuge with the Hurons and Algonquins. There seemed no reason to return to France, even after Quebec was restored to us in 1632. I scarce remember my grandmother. Though her estates will someday be mine, I have no hunger for them. And save for Jean-Auguste, my cousin and your great and good friend, I do not know a soul in all of France." He gestured to the town below, the wide St. Lawrence River beyond, called by the savages the River of Hochelaga. "This is my life now."

"It is a good life," said André, reaching for the razor. "I shall not soon forget my days as a *coureur de bois*, hunting and trapping in the woods. The sight of the Lachine Rapids above Mont Real, the feel of a canoe under me as it glides through the water—"

Mersenne laughed. "And a dark-skinned woman? Will the fine women of the salons seem pale after White Deer?"

André smiled ruefully. "The women of the salons will have little patience with a man who has forgotten how to speak French with any grace or charm!"

"You misprize yourself! Even as a lad I remember hearing of the amorous exploits of Monsieur le Comte de Crillon! What need you for words?"

"And then I am too old."

"Fie! What nonsense!"

"I shall be forty-one at the end of this month."

"And more hale than you were last April when you set

out with Na-e-Ga! You should look more closely into that mirror."

André finished his shave and splashed his face and torso with water, toweling himself briskly and leaning forward to his reflection in the shiny metal. It was true, what Mersenne said. His hair, though it needed trimming to its customary length just below his ears, was still the color of old gold—not a speck of silver, even at the temples. His skin was bronze from the sun, taut and unlined save for the creases at the corners of his wide mouth, long-ago creases from forgotten laughter. His eyes were deep blue and clear, as always. But how could it be so, that his face had not changed in all this time? That his face should stay the same—and his heart so barren—and Marielle lying in her tomb at Vilmorin for almost fifteen months?

"Come," said Mersenne, leading him into the cabin. "You shall see I kept your sea chest well while you were away." He opened a large brass-bound trunk and began to pull out articles of clothing: knee-high stockings, and boots cuffed deep, wide-legged brown twill breeches to tuck into them, a soft linen shirt, and a rust-colored doublet. André exclaimed in delight at the sight of his own garments, and quickly stepped out of his buckskin breeches and moccasins to stand naked in the center of the room while the girl helped him into clothes that felt unfamiliar and wondrously soft against his skin. His doublet was snug across his wide shoulders, the muscles grown hard after a year spent paddling a canoe. He left half of the buttons of the jacket unfastened, to give himself a little ease. When the girl handed him his falling band, a large white linen and lace collar that tied on over his doublet, he allowed himself a moment to admire the crispness of the fabric before tying the band strings. He pulled the cuffs of his shirt down over his hands, then folded them back over the sleeves of his doublet.

"Mon Dieu!" he said. "I had forgotten the look of pristine linen at wrists and neck! Do they still wash it in the Loire, I wonder, and hang it in the sun to dry?" He buckled on his leather wallet, then slipped the harness for his sword diagonally across one shoulder, making a pass or two in the air to test the blade before gliding it into its scabbard. Finally he tied on a short brown cape, tossing back one side so his sword arm was uncovered, and picked up a pair of gray gauntlets.

"You are a gentleman of France again!" exclaimed Georges in admiration. "But hold! Your hat! I did not wish it to be crushed in the chest." He reached up and fetched down a large box that was tucked into the rafters, carefully opening it and pulling out a dark brown beaver hat, dashingly plumed, and handing it to André with a flourish. "Monsieur le Comte de Crillon!"

André set it firmly upon his head, tilted it at a rakish angle, and bowed in his turn. Then he smiled sheepishly and stroked the soft brim. "It is splendid, is it not? I think I have missed my hat more than my sword these past months!"

"What of these things?" Mersenne indicated the pile of discarded clothing on the floor.

"I shall keep my blade, of course," said André, slipping his hunting knife in its scabbard into the top of one boot. "As for the rest—burn them, for aught I care! They are rank with the caulking from the canoes—the women of Paris would not take kindly to the stink of spruce gum and venison fat! Wait!" he said in sudden panic as the girl began to gather up his garments. Snatching the buckskin breeches from her, he rummaged in a small pocket and withdrew a golden locket looped on a blue ribbon, and clutched it tightly in his hand.

"Madame de Crillon?" asked Georges softly.

"Yes."

"Will you—show me her picture now? I have heard so much of her great beauty. My cousin Jean-Auguste would write of it sometimes—and when she danced in the court ballet—"

"Yes. They spoke of it for some years—" André held out the locket to Mersenne, lifting the embossed cover to reveal the miniature portrait. Georges nodded and smiled his admiration, then André looked at Marielle's sweet face for a long moment before closing the locket gently, slipping the ribbon around his neck, and tucking it beneath his shirt. He was surprised that he felt no sharp pain, just loneliness, a dull ache, a longing for his home and his children. For the taste of bread and wine, the sight of the Loire valley, and his château. He felt as empty as he had a year ago, but at least each day was no longer a living hell, where he almost prayed to die. Perhaps— someday—he would be whole again.

Monsieur Maurice Fresnel, master of the merchant vessel *Olympie* out of Dieppe—two hundred tons and a complement of fifty-five men—stood in the waist of his ship and watched the small pinnace, its single sail set to the breeze, ply its way from the landing on shore to the railing where he waited. His passenger, the nobleman whose voyage had been arranged by Georges de Mersenne, stood in the stern of the small boat, face turned toward the *Olympie* and the open sea, arms folded across his chest. A fine-looking gentleman, remarkably handsome, thought Fresnel, though perhaps a bit of a strutting popinjay, to judge by his flamboyant hat. Still, Mersenne had said he was a brave soldier who had served the crown in many a campaign, and was even now returning to France after a year in the deep woods with the Huron. Fresnel shrugged. Popinjay or brave soldier—so long as his gold was full weight! *Le bon Dieu* knew they could use a few extra crowns and livres! It was not easy, being an independent ship owner from Normandy, when King Louis XIII granted a virtual monopoly on fur trading to the Company of New France. The *Olympie* ranged up and down the coast of the New World from the Grand Banks to the islands of the Indies, picking up what trade she could, bartering knives and needles and scissors, watches and tools, in exchange for furs, fish, whale oil, tobacco. A passenger who paid in gold might make the difference between just getting by and a comfortable profit this season! He might even be able to fix up the cottage in Dieppe this fall. Delphine had her heart set on real glass for the window, instead of the oiled parchment and heavy wooden shutters that kept out the elements but so much of the light as well.

The pinnace was now alongside the *Olympie*. The nobleman mounted the rope ladder to the gangway—that space between the railings—and stepped aboard to stand beside Fresnel. He was broad shouldered and tall, taller even than he had seemed in the pinnace. He inclined his head. "Master Fresnel?"

"At your service. And you are Monsieur le Comte de Crillon?"

André nodded, holding out his hand in greeting.

Fresnel indicated his right arm, held unnaturally against his rib cage. "You will forgive me, monsieur. My starboard oar is useless. A Spanish merchantman crossed our bow last summer. We toppled her mizzenmast, but not before the scurvy devils splintered a piece of the quarterdeck railing—and my arm as well!"

"You are prepared to do battle, then."

"If we must. God's truth, we were near blasted out of the water by the Spanish dogs in '35! Sailing off the coast of Darien, we were, and never knew good King Louis had sent a declaration of war to the lubbardly knaves! Well, we have six stout culverins on the gun deck, and my blacksmith can forge shot as well as tackle. As for my bosun here"—and he indicated a jolly-faced giant who ambled toward them, rolling-gaited as though the ship were already under way, and hitching at the wide leather belt that held up his breeches—"we call him Gunner for all the years that he served in the King's navy!"

The bosun scraped off his red mariner's cap and bobbed politely to André. "Monsieur le Comte," he said, "welcome aboard *Olympie!*"

André shook his head. "Nay. If we are to be shipmates for this long voyage—how long should it take, Master Fresnel?"

"Six weeks, by my reckoning, if we have the westerly winds in our favor."

"Well then, Gunner, for six weeks you must call me André! Monsieur le Comte is a burden I need not take up until we reach France." Smiling, he clapped the bosun on the shoulder.

"Well met—André!" The bosun grinned, revealing a wide gap between his two front teeth. "But you look like a Monsieur le Comte! Be hanged if I have seen such a wonderful hat since we left Dieppe!"

André laughed aloud. "Be hanged if I have worn such a hat since I left France!" He indicated the brass-bound chest that a seaman had hauled up from the pinnace and laid at his feet. "Tell me, Master Fresnel, where am I to put my belongings?"

"I have given you the cabin aft, the Great Cabin under the poop deck."

André frowned. "But is that not yours, by rights?"

"I am above you, in the roundhouse." Fresnel smiled. "Closer to the wind, mayhap. I like the sound!"

"Only a madman likes the sound of the wind in a gale! I will take the stillness of a cabin 'tween decks!"

André turned to the man who had spoken. A small man, delicately built, he had come upon them so quietly that André had not noticed him. A thin man, with close-cropped white hair and fine features, he was almost beautiful. He might have been fifty or so.

Fresnel laughed. "Sink me, Copain, but I wonder you come to sea at all!"

Copain waved Fresnel away with an airy sweep of his fingers. "Even a ship needs a reminder of civility! And now, with Monsieur le Comte here, the voyage will be far less tedious! Do you fancy the poetry of Malherbe, monsieur?"

André chuckled. "If you are looking for civility, I shall be poor company. Firstly, I am André on this voyage, and none other! And then I have spent a year with the Huron; I can scarce remember the taste of wine, let alone the sound of poetry!"

Copain sighed. *"Eh, bien!* We must manage as best we may!" He bowed elaborately, his hands making small circles in the air. "At your service, monsieur. I am Robert Copain, master's mate, ship's navigator, scholar, teacher, philosopher *extraordinaire*. I am enchanted to make your acquaintance—André," he finished in disgust.

"Mon Dieu!" laughed André. "A born aristocrat, haughty to the core! Would you trade places with me, Copain?"

"Only if I might have your hat!"

André shook his head. "Never! And now, Master Fresnel, if I may see my cabin—"

"Will you go ashore again?" asked Fresnel. "The sun is still high and we do not set sail until the evening tide—"

"No. I have said my farewells."

"Well then—Gunner!" The bosun nodded, hefted

André's sea chest onto one shoulder, mounted the steps
to the quarterdeck, and motioned André to follow. There
were two cabins flanking the passageway that led to the
Great Cabin in the stern. André imagined they must be
for the other officers, since Master Fresnel eschewed the
Great Cabin, traditionally the captain's quarters, for the
roundhouse above. Gunner set down André's chest in
the middle of the room, then tugged politely at his
forelock before going out and closing the door. André
glanced about him. It was a fine cabin that ran the width
of the ship, its sides curved inward to follow the shape of
the hulk, its beamed ceiling hung with a large brass
lantern. At the stern end of the cabin was a wide bank of
windows, small paned and leaded, with a padded window seat beneath. Tucked between two bulkheads on
one side was a large bunk covered with a thick straw
pallet and several coverlets; on the opposite wall was a
small desk and chair, bolted to the carpeted floor. Above
the desk there were two or three small shelves protected
by a guard-rail, empty save for a pewter flagon, a stout
tallow candle, and a book of prayers. André set his sea
chest beneath the desk, wedging it firmly so it would not
dislodge in rough weather. There was no point in un-
packing; he had few enough belongings—a fresh shirt
and several pairs of stockings, a leather jerkin, his shaving
things, his writing case, a long warm cloak should the
weather turn bad. He slipped the small leather wallet
from his belt, checking the coins within before tucking the
pouch under a corner of the mattress. He nearly took off
his cape and sword and fine hat, then thought better of it.
There would be time enough on the voyage for plain
clothes and sensible attire; he wished to enjoy feeling
elegant for a little longer. He heard Fresnel calling up to
the rigging, the voice so loud that André knew he must be
using a speaking trumpet; then he heard the bosun's

silver whistle piping out commands. There seemed to be
a great deal of stir and bustle on deck; perhaps he would
go topside and watch them loading the ship.

The *Olympie* was buzzing with activity. Gunner stood
in the waist of the ship, at the port gangway, calling down
orders over the side. André strolled to the quarterdeck
railing, the better to see the pinnace, its sail now furled,
drawn up to the hull of the *Olympie*. Close beside it was
the long boat, larger even than the pinnace, and manned
by half-a-dozen oarsmen. Both boats rode low in the
water, weighted down with cargo and supplies which, by
dint of much shouting and barking, Gunner was contriving to have hauled aboard. A score of seamen sweated
with ropes and tackles attached to the ends of the yards,
swinging up to the deck bales of furs—sleek beaver and
seal and otter—and casks filled with dried codfish. There
were provisions for the passage: slabs of salted beef and
pork, pickled meats and fish, peas and beans, and
hardtack—the saucer-shaped dried sea biscuits that
would withstand most vermin on a long voyage. There
were barrels of fresh water and ale, cooking oil and salt,
onions and dried apples, and as much fresh meat and
produce as could be used in the first week or two before
they rotted or turned fetid. There were even cages of
pigeons and several large chickens, flapping and cooing
and clucking. There was lumber for repairs and fuel—in
the galley the cook built his fire in a pit of sand—and a
large tree trunk, newly stripped of its leaves, to replace a
mast, should that calamity arise.

As the supplies were swung on board they were
carried to open hatchways, to be stowed away and
lashed down in storerooms beneath the main deck and
the forecastle, the large cabin in the bow of the ship that
housed most of the men.

At last, the hubbub having died down a bit, André

ventured down from the quarterdeck, joining Gunner, who now stood firmly planted in the middle of the main deck, mopping at his neck with a large handkerchief.

"By my faith," laughed André, "I would rather arm a regiment to do battle than supply a ship!"

"True enough," said the bosun. "Your men can always forage in the countryside! There is no help for it if we should run short on the high sea! Many's the time I've eaten wormy bread, and glad of it too, I'll be hanged!" He smiled and swept his arm toward the men who swarmed about the hatchways, then cast his eyes aloft to the dozens more who clung to the rigging, tying ropes and stays, making last-minute repairs in the canvas sails. "But 'tis a good crew, and Master Fresnel is a fine captain to sail under!" He smiled as a sudden gust of wind ruffled the plumes in André's hat. "Will you stow that topsail when we are under way, André? I'll be hanged if the crew has talked of aught else since you came aboard!"

André bristled, defensive at the unending jibes directed toward his hat. "I shall wear it as it pleases me!" he said a little pompously.

Gunner tugged at the grizzled curl that hung over his forehead. "Begging your pardon, Monsieur le Comte. Master Fresnel and Copain are on the poop deck, reading the charts. Mayhap you will find their company more to your liking."

"Indeed," said André coldly, feeling rebuked, yet unwilling to let go of his pride so easily. He moved away toward the aft ladder, meaning to join Fresnel.

"I'll be hanged," muttered Gunner half to himself. "Where is that lout Michel? Half the day to fetch a coil of hemp—" He looked up at the main mast that towered just above him, squinting his eyes at the bright sunshine. "You! Michel!" he shouted. He had no need for a speaking trumpet.

About to climb to the quarterdeck, André turned, looking toward the main topsail. Above the crow's nest, the basket-enclosed landing at the very top of the mast, appeared a dark head of hair.

"Blast you, Michel, I want you now!"

Michel scrambled out of the crow's nest, waving to Gunner and making his way down the rigging as fast as he could. André took him to be a lad of about sixteen, no more, his face scarred by the blemishes of youth, his hands and feet too large for his body. He looked frightened as he stood before Gunner, but when the bosun merely cuffed him on the side of the head and sent him on another errand, he grinned in relief. He smiled slyly at André as he passed, and looked up at the mainmast.

"Gosse!" he shouted.

Another head appeared in the crow's nest, shaggy and yellow as hay on a midsummer's day. The lad who climbed out of the basket seemed to André to be even younger. Fourteen at the most, and clad in a white shirt and breeches that were far too voluminous for his gangly frame. He waved back to Michel, and called something to the seamen who were strung out across the main yard-arm. Then, without warning, he wrapped an arm around a boarding rope and leaped clear, a hundred feet above the main deck, landing in the rigging of the mizzenmast, which rose up through the quarterdeck.

There was a loud gasp from Gunner. "Gosse! You blasted fool! Would you kill yourself?" The bosun's cheery face had gone white, and he looked in panic toward Master Fresnel.

Safe on his new perch, Gosse grinned. Then, boarding rope still in hand, he launched himself through the air and swung directly toward André, the movement so sudden and unexpected that André had no time to duck before the figure swept past him, kicking off his glorious hat and landing lightly on the deck some paces beyond him. There were cheers from the sailors in the rigging; Gosse, his back turned to André as though the man scarcely existed, waved triumphantly back.

Gosse, thought André, his blood boiling as he surveyed his hat—the crown now soiled and crushed—lying before him. Gosse. The boy was aptly named: Brat. "Pick up my hat, boy," he said, the voice quiet, deadly. For answer, Gosse spit on the deck. Michel snickered. "My hat!" André growled. Gosse, still turned away from André, stuck out his backside and wiggled it insolently. There was more laughter from the seamen who had begun to gather around. André sputtered in outrage. "By my faith!" he roared. "I'll box your ears!" He advanced menacingly toward the boy.

"Well, Gosse, you heard the gentleman!" Michel could hardly contain his laughter.

Even Gunner had begun to grin, the color returning to his face. "Come, boy. Do your duty!"

Gosse shrugged and swaggered to André's hat. He stooped down and picked it up; then, with a sudden gesture, skimmed it across the railing and into the water. There was a chorus of hurrahs from the rigging.

"Now, by God!" said André. "You will fetch it!" He strode to the boy, picking him up by the scruff of the neck and the seat of his pants, and marched to the railing. Gosse squirmed and squeaked, his voice a high soprano.

"Hold!" cried Fresnel, rushing from the poop to put a restraining hand on André's arm just as he would have pitched the boy into the water. "I beg mercy for my daughter! Pray do not drown the maid!"

"Maid?" André put down his struggling burden, setting the creature on her feet. Gosse snarled and wheeled away, but André set his hands firmly on her shoulders and turned her back, his blue eyes traveling over her in amazement. He saw now that what he had taken for the soft, unformed features of a young boy were, at close view, unmistakably those of a girl, some years older, though obviously still a child. She was tall and thin; whatever feminine shape she might possess was swallowed up in the looseness of her shirt and breeches, so her bare arms seemed to dangle awkwardly beneath the rolled-up sleeves and her ankles appeared almost fragile in contrast to her drooping stockings and coarse shoes. Her sun-bright hair, without a hint of curl to it, was jaggedly cut and hung—lank and matted—over her forehead and just below her ears. Her skin was rosy and alive. Indeed, the vivid pinkness of her flesh and the clear yellow of her hair made her seem an innocent cherub, like some dimpled angel in a painting in the Louvre Palace—until one noticed the malevolent gleam in her amber eyes. Cat's eyes, crafty and mischievous. She was incredibly filthy.

Fresnel smiled sheepishly. "Monsieur le Comte, you must forgive my daughter Delphine. She did not mean—your hat—it was an accident—"

"Ha! Sink and scuttle me, father, if I did not mean to do it!" Her eyes twinkled merrily, sending out golden sparks. "For look you, says I, there's a hat that should be fed to the fishes!" André glared at her. "Be of good cheer, my fine cockscomb," she said. "Michel will fetch your hat!" She snapped her fingers in command. The boy picked up a grappling hook, leaning carefully over the railing and fishing in the water until he had snagged a corner of André's hat. He hauled it, dripping and bedraggled, onto the deck, and handed it to Delphine. She marched to André and plopped it unceremoniously at his feet, so it sent up little splashes onto his boots. At André's scowl she grinned, then bent down and ripped one of the plumes from his hat, straightening and fanning herself delicately with it. She threw back her head and laughed. "Ah, Monsieur le Comte, you look as sour as a man whose whore, legs spread to the points of the compass, has—"

"*Nom de Dieu!*" interrupted Fresnel quickly. "Hold your tongue!" His voice was almost pleading. "Please, Delphine—"

She whirled to her father, her eyes filled with sudden fury. "I am Gosse!" she shrilled. "Gosse! Delphine is a fool's name—fit only for mincing ladies who go about with faces like dead mackerels!" She sneered at André. "The kind of ladies favored by monsieur, no doubt!"

André's lip curled contemptuously. "I have spent a year with the Huron savages and their women and children. And never a one so foul tongued, foul tempered," his nose twitched, the wide nostrils flaring in disgust, "foul smelling, as you. By my faith, I should have pitched you into the river, to see if you could come clean!"

Delphine squeaked in anger and swung back a tight-clenched fist, meaning to strike André, but Fresnel clutched at her arm. "Come, come, Gosse," he said, his voice soft and conciliatory. "There is time before we set sail. Remember the creek where you and Michel swam when last we were in Quebec? It is a warm day, and you have worked so diligently all the morning in the hold—a refreshing swim—" He smiled thinly.

"No." Stubborn chin thrust forward.

"I shall send Gunner for fresh things from your cabin. The pinnace is below, and ready—"

"No!"

"If we are to read Ronsard this evening, you cannot come to my cabin smelling of bilge water." Robert

Copain's voice was low and mild, but Delphine turned at the sound of it, looking suddenly shamefaced.

She shrugged, pretending indifference. "I suppose it is a fine day for a swim, and the creek is pleasant. Come, Michel!" She made for the gangway and swung herself over the side, her feet finding the rope ladder. She hung there for a moment, head and shoulders above the deck. "And then," here she waved the plume insolently in André's direction, "I have had my sport with yon prancing puppy—"

André strode to the edge of the deck and knelt in front of her, his face close to hers, sapphire eyes burning. One strong hand clamped about her wrist; with his other hand he pulled the plume free from her fingers and tossed it into the water. "Take care," he said quietly. "The puppy is an old dog!"

She struggled for a moment against the hand that clasped hers, opened her mouth to curse him, then kept silent. Something in his blue eyes held her transfixed, shaken as she had never been in all her life, imprisoned in those azure depths. A look that was almost fear flitted across her face; her own glance faltered and she looked away.

"Damn your gizzard, Michel!" she growled. "Are you coming, or must I stand in for shore alone?"

Chapter Two

DELPHINE SCOWLED UP AT THE TREETOPS, HER ARMS crossed in front of her, rigid jaws chewing ferociously on the last piece of dried apple. She swallowed, then dislodged a bit of fruit from between her teeth with one grimy fingernail.

Seated beside her on the bank of the small creek Michel sighed, glancing at her surreptitiously out of the corners of his eyes. At last he spoke, his voice petulant. "You have scarce said a word since we left the *Olympie*. I stole the apples for you this morning! If we are found out, it is I who will get the beating! You might at least talk to me, Gosse!"

"Pah! Who taught you to steal so you would not be found out? I am minded of the first day you came aboard, all runny nosed and whimpering! Who showed you the secret trapdoor into the galley? Who listened to you crying all that night and fed you with the cook's best cheese? Sink and scuttle me! I had not thought a ten-year-old boy could be such a mewling babe!"

Angrily Michel jumped to his feet. "I am a babe no longer! I am almost a man!"

She smiled up at him, her face twisted in a patronizing smirk. "Sixteen?"

"Near seventeen!"

"You lie! You shall not be seventeen until January next! Whilst I—" She dismissed him with an airy wave of the hand. "I have been eighteen for ages!"

"Since last month!" Michel laughed, then ducked as Delphine hurled a clod of dirt at him. "Are you coming in to swim?" he asked, and kicked off his shoes. She turned her head away, nose in the air. He pulled off his stockings. "I know the why of your black mood," he said mockingly. "The great monsieur frightened you!"

Her golden eyes glowed in anger. "God rot your bones for such a lie!"

"He is a man to be reckoned with!"

"Pah!" She threw herself back on the bank, hands behind her head, and stared up at the treetops and the deep patch of blue April sky beyond. Blue. Like the color of his eyes. Glowing sapphire. The sea in the shallows of the Bermudas. She had felt as though she would drown when she looked into them, reading strange secrets in their unknown depths. Perched on the ladder of the *Olympie* she had shivered, a trembling that had seemed to begin deep in the pit of her stomach, yet was not so much trembling as the fluttering of wings, a gossamer creature trapped somewhere within her vitals, frantic to be released.

"Come on!" said Michel, tugging at the lacings of his breeches. Delphine sat up, idly watching him shed his clothes. How strange to look at was the male body! Though her own body scarcely pleased her—the more it took on the contours of womanhood, the fuller became her garments to cover it—still, there was a certain pleasing rhythm in the rounded form of a woman. But a man's body—ugh! She had seen them all at one time or another: the fat cook, bare rumped, squatting in the scuppers (that open grating that hung over the front of the ship) to relieve himself; the sturdy seamen naked on the deck in the middle of a summer storm, stripped bare while they rinsed their salt-stiff garments in the soft rain; the drunken blacksmith behind some seaside tavern, perched above a frowzy wench, his thin backside contracting violently as he pumped in and out, in and out.

She had not been as open with them. Her father had been uncharacteristically stubborn about her guarding her modesty, and her own disgust at her developing body had kept her well covered in front of the crew. But Michel was different; they had grown up together. Now she watched him in amusement. What a bother it must be to carry around such a drooping ugly thing! She must ask him one day if he noticed it when he walked!

Unselfconsciously she pulled off her own clothes, kneeling at the bank and swishing the garments through the shallows to loosen some of the dirt and grime that fouled them. When she was satisfied, she spread them out on a low branch in the sun, then eased herself into the creek and swam toward Michel, challenging him to a race. They raced and splashed and cavorted, and once Michel wrestled her under the water, holding her struggling head beneath the surface until she jabbed an elbow into his midriff and he released her, gasping for air. At last, winded, she made for the shore and a soft patch of grass, stretching out and luxuriating in the feel of the warm sun on her naked body. Sighing contentedly, she sat up and ran her hand through her yellow hair, then cursed as her fingers caught on a knotted tangle.

"Copain says I should comb it sometimes."

Michel had been practicing a series of small dives on

the surface of the water, submerging and reappearing again. Now he stopped and looked at her.

"Do *you* think I should comb it?" she asked, her face suddenly troubled.

"Does it matter what I think?" he said sourly. "If *Copain* says, then surely you will do it! Copain says comb your hair! Copain says come and read poetry!" He made a face and blew bubbles in the water. "Poetry!" he scoffed.

She bristled. "Poetry is beautiful! If you were not such a fool, you would have tried to learn to read when my father wished to teach you. Now you'll be a stupid lout forever!"

"You were always putting on airs," he sulked, "and now, with Copain, you are even worse. Rot and damnation! I wish he had never come aboard." He slapped sullenly at the water.

"I have not been sorry these past two years, since Copain."

"You know nothing of him. Brise, the carpenter, says he has been in prison!"

"I know he is gentle and kind! I can talk to him—tell him things that—" She stared away into the distance, her eyes suddenly wistful. How she had suffered with the shame of her first sign of maturity, the bloody badge that had marked the gulf between her and the crew— between her and childhood. Red with embarrassment, her father had explained how the women of the towns used wads of rags and rinsed them out when they were soiled. Disgusted, she had for years burned her linens when she was ashore, or cast them to the stormy ocean when aboard ship. Then Copain had appeared and talked gently, reassuring her that she need not feel ashamed. The first flowering of your womanhood, he had said, making it seem a kind of benediction. "I never had a mother. Copain has been like—like a mother to me."

Michel snickered. "A mother! Soft and weak like a woman! Always with his books. He never goes aloft, never mans the capstan! Hides behind his charts—just because he can read. He never looks for a woman in port either!"

Delphine jumped up in anger, glaring down at him in the water, her hands on her bare hips. "Damn your eyes! There are better things to do, I'll wager! It makes me sick, the way the men always talk about it—as if going down on a woman is all they live for! Pah! I cannot imagine any joy in it!"

Michel looked smug. "That's because you know no better."

She sneered. "Be cursed, but you never had a woman!"

"I did!" he bragged. "When we made landfall two weeks ago—there was a girl—"

"Aah!" she said, annoyed at his superiority. "Well, no man will ever touch me—tap at my door—suck at my breasts!" She looked down at the rounded swell of her bosom, her mouth twisted in disgust. She looked up. Michel was standing immobile in the water, staring at her. She threw back her head and laughed uproariously. "Sink me for a bilge rat! Is it happening again?"

"Shut up!" he growled, his face tight.

She giggled. "Is your poor prickle standing up, there under the water?" She motioned him ashore. "Come show me how you salute me!" Michel turned away in agony. Delphine plucked her clothes—now nearly dry—from the bushes and began to put them on. "Sometimes," she muttered, "I'm glad not to be a man after all."

Still burning with anger and humiliation, Michel hauled himself out of the creek, taking care to keep his back to Delphine as he dressed. "How do you know you wouldn't like it if you don't try," he said at last.

"With you?"

"Pourquoi pas? Why not?"

"My father and Gunner would skin you alive for talking like that!"

"Then let them skin me for the doing!" he cried, and clutched fiercely at Delphine. She exploded in fury, pummeling him about the head and shoulders until he tripped and fell backwards onto the grass. She kicked him once in the ribs with her bare foot, then stood looking down at him, feeling her anger drain away at the sight of his forlorn face.

"Why do you spoil our comradeship?" she asked sadly, and held out her hand to help him up.

"It's just—when I see you—I can't—" He looked as though he would cry.

"Poor Michel," she said, stooping down to pick up her shoes and stockings. "We shall not swim again, I think." They walked along the bank in silence, mourning the loss of something they could not even name.

"Has it never happened to you?" he said at last. "A strangeness—when you looked at a man?"

She shrugged. "Men, women, sea-oxen—they're all the same to me!"

"It will happen to you."

"Never!" And yet—she recalled clear blue eyes in a handsome face, deep golden hair, smooth bronzed skin that she ached to touch, to see if it felt as cool and sleek as it looked. "Never!" she cried again, and stamped her foot to drive away the tantalizing image.

*   *   *

André emerged from the Great Cabin, noticing that the doors of the two cabins that flanked the passageway were open, the cabins beyond empty. Copain and Gosse must already have gone to supper. He had put aside his fancy trappings—sword and cape and lace falling band—and removed the heavy doublet. His shirt, with its small neat collar, was covered with a sleeveless leather jerkin. After a year of buckskins, he really felt more comfortable dressed thus. Feeling the gentle sway of the ship beneath him, he made his way down the aft companionway, the interior ladder that led from the quarterdeck and his cabin to the messrooms and galley below. There was another companionway to the roundhouse above on the poop deck; Master Fresnel and the crew could move through the ship in foul weather without going out into the storm.

He was not looking forward to this voyage. When he'd left France a year ago it seemed as though the war with Spain and the Holy Roman Empire was drawing to a close. Indeed, though Richelieu always needed the services of his generals, the cardinal had been sufficiently optimistic about the future to allow André to leave for New France, even going so far as to charge him with restrengthening France's ties with the Hurons, that full trade might be resumed when peace came again. And then, perhaps, the cardinal had read the grief in André's eyes, and knew that a man who courted death would be useless on the battlefield.

But much had happened in a year. André had spent hours with de Mersenne, catching up on all the news. There was the joy, of course, at the birth of the Dauphin, *Louis Dieudonné*, Louis the God given, and an end, at last, to the plots and cabals against the throne when King Louis XIII and his queen had been childless. But the Prince of Condé, under whom André had served at Dôle, had been routed at Fuenterrabia on the Spanish frontier. There were whispers of treason. Condé's second-in-command had fled to England, and had been tried in absentia and executed in effigy. There was the loss of Saint-Omer in the Netherlands and the defeat at Vercelli in Italy. It was clear there would be more fighting before this war was done! André would arrive home in time to mobilize his own men for the summer campaign. He had welcomed this sea voyage and the last weeks of tranquillity it would provide before the press and tumult of battle. But—farewell serenity! That young hoyden of Fresnel's would surely give him no peace! He frowned in disgust, still half disbelieving that such a coarse creature could possibly be female. A disagreeable child—full of fire and temper when *she* was crossed, but content to torment others. He rubbed his tender kneecaps. Damn the little savage!

They had sailed on the evening tide, their yards braced round to catch the wind, the sun an orange blaze on the water. André had strolled the deck, watching Quebec vanish in the setting sun, threading his way past the jumble of ropes and shrouds that hung from the rigging. The seamen had begun to disentangle the lines and coil them into neat piles on the deck. André had not noticed the line that had suddenly gone taut at his ankles; he had pitched forward, his soldier's reflexes breaking his fall a bit at the last moment. Pulling himself up, his knees and palms smarting, he had seen Gosse sitting on a large coil of rope, grinning like a cherub, her eyes wide and blameless. Gulled by that innocent face, he had almost thought it an accident, until Gunner had hurried to his side, all humble apology, and cast a reproachful look at Gosse. But when she frowned, Gunner had smiled sheepishly and turned away. *Nom de Dieu!* thought André. It was beyond him why they should be afraid of a little chit of a girl—even if she *was* the master's daughter! Perhaps it was just habit to defer to her—but she wanted a bit of taming, that one!

He sighed and opened the door to the captain's mess. The voyage was just beginning. And unless he sulked, played the haughty nobleman, and supped alone in his cabin (with too much time to dwell on Marielle), he would have to take his meals with her and swallow his displeasure at her behavior. Damn! he thought again, feeling himself bedeviled.

Gosse was laughing, her voice deep and throaty, as he entered. André was struck by the vibrant timbre of it, so surprising in a young girl.

"Split me!" she exclaimed, taking a swig of ale from her tankard and wiping her mouth on her sleeve. "But here is your passenger, father! Did you mind the way he danced on deck?" She took another drink and laughed again, ignoring the dribbles of ale on her chin.

Master Fresnel arose, indicating with his lame arm André's chair at the long table; Gunner, sitting next to Gosse, tugged politely at his forelock and nodded in greeting.

"How kind you are to our guest, Gunner!" Delphine smiled across at André, the devil peeping out of her eyes. "Did *you* like his dance, bosun?"

Gunner looked at her fondly. "That was wicked of you, Gosse."

"*I?*" she said. "What had *I* to do with it? Ah, Monsieur le Comte! You will ruin your pretty face if you do naught but frown!"

"André!" said Gunner, emphatically. "You must call him André on the voyage. He is as any other seaman on this voyage—no different!"

She snickered. "I wonder—will he know well enough not to piss into the wind?"

"We need not wait for Copain," said Fresnel quickly, indicating the wooden trencher piled high with roasted pigeons. "Come, monsieur, while the meat is fresh and the voyage is young."

André reached for a bird, but Delphine was there first, snatching it from his grasp and biting savagely into the tender meat. He helped himself to another pigeon, disjointing it on his pewter dish, stripping each savory morsel from the bones with his fingers before putting it in his mouth, carefully licking the sauce from his hands. He tried not to look at Gosse as he ate. It was enough to make his stomach churn, the way she gestured with the carcass in her hands and belched noisily and let small crumbs of food foul the front of her shirt. But once he caught her eye and was surprised to see her blush, as though she were embarrassed at his obvious disapproval. But surely he was mistaken: after that her eating seemed to grow even more crude. Indeed, when she toppled her tankard in his direction and the last drops of ale spilled on him, he was convinced she had done it deliberately.

"Nom de Dieu," pleaded Fresnel. "Mind your manners, Delphine!"

She picked up her empty tankard and slammed it down on the table. "Why must you call me Delphine? Sink and scuttle me, but I hate the name!"

His face twisted in distress, Fresnel opened his mouth to speak, but André interrupted him smoothly.

"You must be more understanding, Master Fresnel. I would say that Gosse minds her manners—though there be those who would vow that there are all kinds of manners: for men and ladies, and savages in the New World, and pigs in their sties!"

Delphine gasped in outrage and rose to her feet, swinging back her arm to toss the mug at André; Copain's gentle voice stopped her.

"Have you left me aught to eat, Gosse?"

Her rosy cheeks turned a darker shade of pink and she sat down, unable to look at Copain.

"You must forgive my daughter, monsieur," said Fresnel. "She never learned gentle ways. Her mother died when she was just a babe. I had no sisters nor cousins to tend her ashore. And so we raised her aboard ship, Gunner and I."

Gunner beamed proudly. "And a fine sailor she is! You'll not find a better hand in a storm, I'll be hanged, nor a braver one when the wind is northerly and the lines are frozen!"

Gosse grinned at André. "Have you ever been up in the rigging, landlubber? Mayhap before this voyage is done we shall see how brave a soldier you are!"

"There is not a man faster than she in the shrouds!" Fresnel smiled fondly at his daughter. "She has been climbing for almost all of her eighteen years!"

André looked at her. Eighteen years. She seemed so much younger. Eighteen. Marielle had been nineteen when he met her. He felt suddenly old and tired. He rose to leave.

Gosse laughed, that rich, musical sound that was so unexpected. "Split my gut!" she said. "Have we chased you away, my proper gentleman? With all this talk of climbing?"

He turned to her, his blue eyes cold. "Perhaps it is a pity you did not have the gentling company of women." He left the room.

Copain sighed. "There is a man who has known torment." He smiled at the look of surprise on Delphine's face. "There is no torment in your sunny world, is there, *ma petite*? And now—shall we read Ronsard?"

They mounted the companionway to the quarterdeck cabins. André's door was closed. Copain led the way into his small cabin, striking a spark with his flint and lighting the lantern that hung from a beam. The sudden flame shimmered on his silver hair. Taking a small book from his sea chest, he set it on the table in the center of the cabin, and pulled up a long bench, that he and Delphine might sit side by side. She looked from the book to Copain, her eyes troubled.

"Think you he is unhappy?" Copain nodded silently. Delphine bit at a fingernail, lost in thought. "I like him not," she said at last.

"Why?"

"I know not."

"Are you afraid of him?"

"No, God rot!"

"Is that why you tripped him on deck? To prove that you fear him not? And you would have bounced your tankard off his skull had I not stopped you. Wherefore?"

There was a catch in her voice. "Oh, Copain! His eyes—" Then, "I wanted to hurt him!" she cried fiercely.

"When you have words at your command, you can bank your fires a little. Words can be the greatest weapon. Now, to our book," he said, turning the pages with delicate fingers.

Delphine saw the scars of shackles on his thin wrists. She had accepted them in the past; now, remembering Michel's words, she was filled with curiosity. "Why did you come to sea? You scarce belong in this rough life."

"There was—nothing left," he said, his mouth pinched in a sad smile. "The last refuge."

"Are you a ruined nobleman?"

He laughed. "You are more the romantic than you know! But—no. I have been many things, but not that. Teacher, churchman, fugitive," he sighed, "until I am weary of remembering—weary of life. Far more weary than our monsieur next door. He will live again, whilst I—" He shook away the thought. "Come! Ronsard!" He lit a pipe and turned to the book.

They read for an hour, sometimes silently, sometimes saying the verses aloud to hear the melodious roll of the words. Occasionally Delphine would ask the meaning of a line, an unfamiliar word.

"I am *not* a romantic," she said at last, jabbing at a page with her finger. "Look here. 'Amours de Cassandre.' This verse. Comparing his love to a rose. Pah! What nonsense! I like this one far better—'Amours de Marie'—where he tells his lover Marie to get up and enjoy the day." She turned to Copain, her amber eyes sparkling. "*There* is joy! In life! In the moment!"

"But look you," he said gently. "See what follows: 'Sur la Mort de Marie.' She dies. Like the rose, all things fade."

"No! Nothing shall change! The sun shines forever!"

"But life goes on—"

"No—" more softly, the eyes dark with sudden pain. "I shall not let it change."

"But even you—since I came aboard *Olympie*—you have changed."

"No! I am Gosse still—and always! Never Delphine!"

"Delphine will cry to be set free some day, and there will be tears, and clouds that cover your sun—"

She jutted out a determined chin. "Then you and I shall laugh together and play skittles on deck and send the fool Delphine away!"

"Shall *we?*" he asked sadly. "Here. One more verse. My favorite, I think. One of Ronsard's last. Where he

welcomes death." Copain pushed the book toward her.
She read it silently, then looked up, her eyes filled with
tears. Copain smiled gently and recited the last two lines
aloud.

> Pass on, say I, and seek your fate,
> Nor trouble my repose. I sleep.

"You cannot mean that!" she cried. "You cannot."

He shook his head. "Of course not, Gosse. It is just a
poem. Now smile, and I shall give you a pretty trifle I
came by in Quebec." He reached into his pocket and
pulled out a long pink ribbon which he handed to
Delphine.

"*Nom de Dieu!* What do I want with a ribbon?" She
nearly threw it down, but he stopped her, his thin hand
on hers.

"It's a pretty thing," he said. "Keep it—just to look at.
What harm?"

She shrugged and bid him good-night, crossing the
passageway to her own cabin. She did not bother to take
flint to her lantern; though neither moon nor stars shone
through the small porthole, there was enough light
streaming under her door from the large lantern in the
passage to see her to her bunk without tripping. She
kicked off her shoes, unfastened her wide leather belt
with its sheathed knife, and cast it down. On an impulse,
she pulled her shirt free from her breeches, so it hung
loose and full to her thighs. Carefully she tied the pink
ribbon about her waist—fluffing out the skirtlike peplum
that it formed—and, very softly, very tentatively, she
began to dance, around and around, humming a sweet
melody under her breath.

Chapter Three

THE FIRST SQUALL HIT THREE DAYS LATER, JUST AS THEY had seen the last of land, the islands of St. Pierre and Miquelon off the Grand Banks. Delphine, her red cap pulled well down on her ears, gloried in the storm, moving through the ship with a happy swagger, her rolling gait more pronounced as the *Olympie* heaved ever more violently in the swells. She had been the first topman up in the rigging, furling the sails against the wind so they should not split. Now she sat below decks, braiding the lines that threatened to shred, helping to stir the black pitch that would keep the salt water from corroding the ropes, patching the spare sails.

After a day spent clinging to the railings, clutching the hand ropes that lined the passageways, staggering from the quarterdeck to the messroom and back again, André took to his bunk, deathly ill. He retched into the basin that Michel had brought, until there was nothing left in his stomach; then he retched again, great dry heaves that pulled at his chest and belly until the muscles were sore. On the second day he woke in his bunk, soaked with sweat, his stomach still queasy though the pitching of the ship had abated. He lifted his pounding head from the pillow and saw Gosse perched on the foot of his bed, cross-legged, drenched with salt water that left a wet patch on his coverlet. She was munching a sea biscuit and grinning.

He groaned. "Surely I have died and gone to hell, and you are the imp that Satan has sent to torment me!"

She popped the last crumbs into her mouth and scraped off her hat, leaning over the edge of the bunk and wringing the cap out onto the carpeted floor. "I have been watching your face as you slept," she laughed. "Gunner says he thinks you have had many lovers swooning over you, you are so handsome! Sink my bones, but they would not find you so handsome now, with your skin as green as a bullfrog's!"

He closed his eyes wearily. "Go away."

She bounced off the bunk and came close to him. "Curse me, but you are helpless! Sit up." While he slid his aching body into a more upright position, she arranged the pillow behind his back. "I stole an extra ration of water for you," she said, producing a small flask from under her wet jacket. "Drink it slowly. And here's a ship's biscuit, if you can manage it." She laid the biscuit on the coverlet, took off her jacket, and returned to her spot at his feet. "Have you?"

André took a sip of water, rolling it around for a minute in his mouth, letting his tongue spread it across his parched lips. "Have I what?" he asked.

"Have you had many lovers?"

"By my faith, but you are bold!"

She giggled. "When I have you at the advantage, why not? How old are you?"

"I shall be forty-one next week."

"My father is older. And Copain. Are you married?"

"No."

"Any children?"

"I have two young sons—by my late wife." He took another drink; then, encouraged by the stability of his stomach, he nibbled a corner of the sea biscuit.

"And bastards?"

"*Mon Dieu!* None that I know of."

"Are you wealthy?"

"If my estate has not fallen to ruin whilst I have been away—yes." His eyes grew distant. "My château is in the Loire valley, near Vouvray, nestled amid sweet vineyards and rich earth."

"A farmer as well as a soldier," she said.

He put his hand on his aching forehead. "Surely not a sailor!" He smiled warmly at her, the first time she had seen him with anything but a scowling face. It set her to thinking.

"Copain says you are a man in torment. Is it so?"

The smile faded. "You go too far."

She bristled. "How so? If your soul is troubled, may I not ask?"

"My soul is my own affair," he growled. "Concern yourself with things you understand—or should! Practice the arts of womanhood and leave me in peace!"

She jumped from the bunk, her eyes burning with anger at his rebuff. "Damn your liver!" she cursed, then smiled maliciously. The voice dropped to a catlike purr. "I shall go to the galley. Cook has promised to make me a porridge. The beans are a trifle old; as the maggots rise to the surface he must skim them off. There are those who find them a delicacy, but not I! They crunch most horribly in your teeth. If he has caught a rat, he will add it to the pot. I think it a tasty bite—though the tail is smooth and slimy, rather like eating worms. I like the thin red ones that live in the old cheese. Weevils, on the other hand—" She stopped. André had begun to gulp and clutch at his stomach, pushing the hardtack and water

flask quickly away. Gosse stooped and picked up the
basin from the floor, shoving it in front of his face.
"Here!" she cried. "Puke your guts out!" She whirled
about, snatching up her hat and jacket, and stamped
from the room, hearing behind her the sound of André
being sick once again.

In a day or two he felt better. The sea had calmed, and
shimmered like glass under a glorious sun. There was a
steady breeze that puffed *Olympie's* sails and blew fresh
and sweet in his face when he strolled the quarterdeck.
He found he was able to eat his meals with gusto, as
though his stomach, having made its initial protest to a
sailor's life, had decided to accommodate him. At first he
was cool to Gosse when they passed on deck or supped
across the table from one another; his sense of outrage
(or perhaps his wounded pride) over the scene in his
cabin was not yet assuaged. But Gosse was as sunny as
the weather, bright as though nothing had ever
happened. André was astonished. Her storms were
fierce, raging tempests, yet they blew away and were
forgotten. What a strange imp! It was impossible to stay
angry with her—her joy was infectious. Perhaps that was
why her father had never managed to curb that fiery
temper.

Coming down from the quarterdeck one sunny afternoon, his thoughts filled with Marielle, he heard Gosse's
laughter with its vital ring even before he saw her. She
was perched on her knees on a coil of rope, playing
backgammon with Copain, the board set between them
atop a rain barrel lashed against the mainmast. It was the
kind of day a sailor welcomed: The sails well-trimmed to
the brisk breeze, the canvas billowing full, the bow
cutting a clean swath through the gentle swells. Their
chores done, many of the crew lolled on deck enjoying

the sunshine, and whittled away at pieces of wood or whalebone, graceful objects taking form under their skillful fingers. Brise, the carpenter, had sent a small crew aloft to look at the main yardarm; the last topman up had complained that it seemed to be bowing slightly.

Casting down her dice on the backgammon board, Gosse looked up as André approached. "Ah, Monsieur —André," she said, "have you come to watch me defeat poor Copain at trictrac?" She counted out one of her colored stones on the board, grinning as Copain made a face in mock dismay. André leaned up against the mast, arms folded across his chest, and watched the game progress. Gosse laughed again. "Split me, Copain! What are we to do with such a sour-faced monsieur? Do you never smile, André?" She threw her dice and crowed in triumph. "The game is mine, Copain! Another?"

Copain shook his head and stood up. "You have bested me twice today, and that is enough. I have my charts to attend. Play trictrac with André. Mayhap that will bring a smile to his face."

The golden eyes flashed wickedly. "Only if I let him win—which I shall never do!"

André grinned in spite of himself, and sat opposite her. "You speak bold for such a sprig! I am not so helpless as I was but a few days agone!" He arranged his stones on the board.

"What matter? One does not play the game with one's gut, queasy or no!" She dimpled mischievously and tapped at her forehead.

He laughed. "You dare challenge me thus? I shall have you now!" And cast down his dice.

They played enthusiastically for the next quarter of an hour, trading merry jibes and taunts. André was surprised at her keenness; it was so easy to dismiss her

merely as a difficult child. But she played with intelligence
and skill, fiercely intent on winning despite her light
words. He was almost sorry when the final throw of the
dice gave the game to him. He smiled at her, meaning to
make light of it so as to console her, but she leaped up in
anger, muttering a foul curse and upsetting the board
with an impatient swipe of her hand.

He stood up in his turn. "Can you not lose with grace?
Small wonder they named you Gosse—Brat!"

"Be hanged for a scurvy dog!" she spat, and swirled
away, then gasped as she felt him thud against her back,
knocking her to the deck. Even as she struggled to
extricate herself from beneath him, she was aware of
noise and hubbub among the men. Pulling clear of
André, she sat up, and saw that a large piece of the
yardarm had cracked and come crashing down on that
portion of the deck where she had been standing but a
moment before. André himself was half covered by the
rope and tackle and torn bits of sail; when the men pulled
away the debris Delphine winced to see his upper arm
bloodied, the soft flesh pierced with more than a dozen
splinters and sharp pieces of the yard. She helped him to
his feet and led him, still shaken, up the ladder to the
quarterdeck, where the light would be better for the job
at hand. She seated him on a barrel, his arm propped on
the railing. While the crew set to work with hatchets,
freeing the broken yardarm and torn shrouds so a
sudden tug of wind should not snap the mainmast,
Delphine sent Michel to the galley for some beer for
André, and rolled back his sleeve to assess the damaged
arm.

"*Merde!*" she swore, "What a mess. They are deep,
some of them." She looked at him, her eyes soft with
compassion, and drew her knife.

"If you must cut, then do so," he said firmly, his strength returning. "You need not be timid. I have suffered worse in many a campaign!"

While Copain watched, offering advice and encouragement, she began to draw out the splinters of wood, using the point of her knife to probe when a piece, deeply imbedded, had snapped off beneath the surface of André's flesh. Once or twice he gritted his teeth as the blade dug deep, but otherwise he was silent. She was conscious suddenly of his eyes on her as she worked—those intense blue orbs that turned her knees to water—and the tanned and strong-thewed arm beneath her fingers. Her hands began to shake.

André chuckled. *"Nom de Dieu,"* he teased, "are you losing your nerve? Can it be that Gosse the brat is filled with tenderness toward the man who has just bested her at trictrac?"

"Son of a dog," she growled, to hide her agitation. "But I cannot do it! Here, Copain. Your fingers are thinner than mine—you do it! I'll fetch water to rinse the wounds." By the time she returned with a large bucket, Copain's job was done. Delphine hesitated for a moment, then poured the water onto André's arm. He flinched and gasped, surprised eyes flying to her face. Copain dipped a finger into the last of the water in the bucket, put it to his mouth, then made a face at the sharp taste of the salt. Delphine shrugged, her eyes hidden once again behind a curtain of indifference. "Why waste fresh water on such trifling wounds? Has not André told us what a brave soldier he is?"

"By my faith," muttered André, rising to his feet and making for his cabin, "there will be a reckoning!" He disappeared down the passageway.

Copain glared at her. "Why did you do that?" he asked, his voice unusually harsh. "He saved your life! I have never seen you behave more vilely than you do with that man! You have lost at trictrac half a hundred times, yet never raged so before!"

"Leave me alone," she said, her eyes cloudy with dark uncertainty. "Damn you, leave me in peace!"

But Copain wondered if the words were meant for him.

The weather remained fine, the days sunny, the nights cool and comfortable. Master Fresnel was more than satisfied at the progress of the *Olympie;* if the westerly breezes held, they might make landfall sooner than they had expected.

André was surprised that this piece of news did not afford him much pleasure; in a strange way he had begun to enjoy the voyage. Perhaps it was that quicksilver Gosse. As often as she angered him with her coarse ways and fiery temper, made him want to shake the willfulness out of her, so often did she make him laugh, delighting in her exuberance, the happy innocence that scarcely hid the sharp mind. He had not thought he could ever laugh again.

It was a clear night, crisp and fresh. Fastening his doublet, André stepped out on deck, meaning to climb to the poop and stand with the watch beneath the great lantern; Gosse's laughter from amidships made him stop. In the waist of the ship—on the main deck—a dozen or so of the men were gathered about a brazier of burning coals, laughing and joking while they warmed themselves at the fire. Gosse's voice, rich and deep and musical, rose above the rest. If he did not listen to the foul language, the crude jokes, it was a beautiful voice, smoky and resonant, its depth attributable perhaps to the child growing up to the sound of masculine voices only.

"You!" she said suddenly, her voice deeper still. "Do

my bidding, if you please!" There was a chorus of laughter from the men, then a moment's silence followed by another burst of merriment. André made his way quietly down to the main deck. "By my faith," growled Gosse, "dare to make faces at me—a great and wondrous soldier?" André could hear Michel's snickering laugh. Creeping closer, he saw that Gosse was swaggering among the men, parading about with exaggerated bravado. And on her head was André's plumed hat.

Damn! he thought, remembering with what care he had stowed it in his cabin. The brazen little devil must have stolen it! Then he began to chuckle. Her imitation of his own long-legged stride was so sure, so accurate, that he found it hard to sustain his anger, resigning himself to the fact that his hat would be the source of torment for him until this voyage was done. He stepped forward into the light of the brazier. "Monsieur le Comte?" he said smoothly.

She turned, not a flicker of embarrassment, a shred of uneasiness crossing her face. She swept the hat from her head, waving it in the air with all the fussy obsequiousness of the worst lickspittle in Louis's court, then bowed deeply. "Monsieur de Crillon. *Enchanté!* Will you take a turn about the deck with me? I cannot be sure, of course, but I think there will be no ropes this time to make you dance!"

He bowed in his turn. "You make a fine gentleman. But—can I trust you? No, if I must dance"—and here he indicated a young sailor tootling quietly on a reed pipe—"let it be to music! Come, lad, can you play us a tune for dancing?"

The sailor struck up a cheery air and the rest of the men paired off, dancing a variation of a folk dance that André had seen many times in his own village—but with the lighter, younger seamen taking the women's parts.

André danced with Delphine, surprised at first that a girl who could climb the rigging with such grace was so clumsy and heavy-footed; then he looked around him and saw the only examples she had ever known. "Come," he said gently, "if you are to dance the woman's part, you must dance it like a woman!" Patiently he led her through the steps and they began again, though she seemed suddenly tense and unhappy. "Dance it as you wish," he said at last, "if it pleases you." He smiled to see her brighten immediately, throwing herself with renewed vigor into the lively dance. At the last piped-out notes, André laughed and swung her into the air, his hands about her waist. As he let her down again, he frowned, surprised to feel the soft and yielding body beneath her bulky clothes, shocked at the sudden stirring that trembled within him. With her chopped hair and boyish manner, it was so easy to forget she was female.

"Do you never dress your hair?" he growled, and pushed her away, feeling a sudden hatred for her he could not even explain.

"Damned pismire!" she cursed, and struck him on the face so he staggered back. She whirled and ran toward her cabin, but he followed her and grabbed at her arm, swinging her around to face him.

"Gosse," he said, his voice deep with remorse. "Forgive me. That was cruel."

She looked at him with narrowed eyes, her face hard. "If I had words—" she said softly. "If I had words—I would leave you bleeding on this deck!" She almost seemed about to cry; then she was gone, leaving him to curse himself for a thoughtless fool.

In the morning she revenged herself by wedging a block of wood under his cabin door to keep him trapped inside, having first tossed in a dead and stinking rat. It was not until the stench had nearly overpowered him that he thought to see if one of the panes of his large window were hinged; picking up the rat gingerly he brought it to the casement and tossed it out into the ship's wake. It took another twenty minutes of shouting and pounding at the door until someone heard him and set him free; by that time his hoarse voice and sore knuckles had nullified whatever remorse he had felt the night before.

He was determined to ignore her at supper; a chance remark by Copain about the battles for the Valtelline, the Alpine valley so vital to both France and Spain, gave him the opportunity. The man had obviously been a soldier, and they spoke at some length about tactics and generals and the merits of various campaigns. Piqued at being ignored, Gosse interrupted them, her chin jutting out belligerently.

"You never told me you were a glorious soldier, Copain!"

He smiled indulgently at her and turned to André. "You see, the child knows nothing save life at sea. There is much to teach her." He sighed. "War is not glorious, Gosse. I have killed more men than my soul can contain—even shriven. I took part in the siege of La Rochelle—out of every hundred men and women and children not eighteen survived to surrender. There were no animals left in the city—they had eaten them all: dogs, cats, donkeys. They scarce had shoes left; they had boiled the leather with tallow for a delicacy! I could go to battle no more after that."

André glanced at Copain's scarred wrists with their marks of chains, his blue eyes dark with understanding. "Were there years of peace, at least, between La Rochelle and—" He left the words unspoken.

A gentle laugh. "There is no peace, save only in God's

heaven, but 'Father' Copain found serenity for a time—"
A long silence. "Did you fight at La Rochelle, Monsieur le Comte?"

"No. I was at La Forêt, in the Languedoc campaign. Marielle used to say it was a happy circumstance of fate." He stopped in surprise, the name still strange on his tongue. "She—my late wife—was born in La Forêt. We met in the midst of the battle."

Copain nodded. "The spring of '29."

"Yes. We were married for nearly nine years. Two fine sons she bore me."

"And then—?" Copain's voice was soft and gentle, urging him on.

André sighed. He had not thought he could talk so freely of those times; now it seemed as though a weight were being lifted from his heart. "We had begun to drift apart, as so often happens, I suppose. And then—she was captured by brigands, held for ransom. She suffered a miscarriage and we thought she would die. Then, wonder of God, she recovered. It was a gift. Six months almost we had, as sweet as any we had ever known together, even in the first years of our marriage." He stopped and took a long drink from his flagon, fighting back the emotion that threatened to unman him. "A winter fever carried her away. She was a gentle woman; she died as she had lived—softly, sweetly."

"What was she like?" asked Delphine sharply, suddenly filled with an aching need to know this woman.

He smiled at her indulgently. "She was, above all women, most fair, chaste, and pure. A woman of modesty and grace, who blushed to hear my grooms swear."

"And what did she look like?" It was almost a desperate cry. Copain put a restraining hand on Delphine's arm, but she shook him off, her eyes burning into André.

"She was the most beautiful woman that Paris has

ever seen—I shall not find her like again in this world!
She danced once in the court ballet; the king himself did
her honor, entering the tableau to salute her beauty."

"I heard of such a woman," said Copain. "I had
thought it court gossip, meant only to bedazzle us in the
provinces."

"See for yourself if I tell the truth." André pulled the
locket from his neck and proffered it. Delphine snatched
it quickly and held it in the palm of her hand. It was an
embossed oval case, some two by three inches, with a
hinged lid. Opening it with trembling fingers, she gazed at
the portrait of Marielle.

It was the picture of a stately woman, elegant and
serene—and breathtakingly beautiful. Her skin was pale
and creamy, the hazy green eyes modestly cast down;
her features were fine-chiseled and delicate, save for the
sensuous fullness of her red lips. Her hair, like a brilliant
halo of burnished chestnut, hung full and loose about her
face, curling in gentle ringlets on her shoulders, caressing
the soft bosom.

Delphine pressed the locket quickly into Copain's
fingers and jumped to her feet. "She would blow away in
the first gale," she sniffed. She slapped at her forehead as
though a sudden thought had struck her. "Split me for a
sailor's whore! But I have forgot that Michel was to do a
chore for me tonight! If that lout has gone to sleep, I shall
kick his lazy backside out of his hammock, though his
howls wake the whole fo'c'sle!" She hurried from the
messroom and onto the deck, where she knew the men
would be gathered swapping stories, and tugged urgently
at Michel's sleeve. "Come," she said quietly, and led him
up the ladder to her cabin on the quarterdeck. He
followed in silence, waiting until she had lit her lantern
and closed the door before giving way to his curiosity.

"What's in the wind?"

She turned and rummaged in her sea chest, pulling forth a pair of scissors. "Here," she said. "I want you to cut my hair."

"God's blood! Why?" He fingered his own dark curls. "'Tis shorter even than mine, as it stands now!"

"Damn your eyes—cut it!"

"Gosse—*nom de Dieu!* I am no barber. You will look like a shorn sheep."

She forced the scissors into his hand. "Cut it!" she raged.

Hesitantly he took them from her and clipped a small straight lock beside her ear, leaving the edge more jagged than ever; then, with a curse, he threw the scissors down. "I cannot!"

She began to cry. "Please," she said. "I hate it so." She turned away, sniffling deeply, then turned back to him, impatiently scrubbing away the tears as though he had no right to see her weep. "Do you want to kiss me?" she asked suddenly.

He gaped, then nodded and shuffled toward her, putting his hands up to take her by the shoulders. She pushed him aside.

"I said kiss me, don't touch me!"

He shifted uneasily, then bent his mouth to hers, closing his eyes and pressing as hard as he dared, intoxicated with his good fortune. At last he lifted his spinning head to see her smiling at him, the smile of a queen, regal and proud.

"Good-night," she said, and watched him stumble to the door and go out. She stood, motionless, for a long time; then, her lip curled in disgust, she wiped her hand across her mouth again and again, and kicked violently at the pair of scissors on the floor.

Chapter Four

THE WEATHER TURNED COOL, AND ROLLING CLOUDS OB-
scured the warmth of the sun for days at a time. André
wrapped himself in his heavy cloak to stand on the
quarterdeck and watch the darkening sky that seemed
always on the brink of storm. When the rain came at last,
the ship was damp and cold, and the men shivered as
they came below, their clothing drenched from standing
the watch for hours. Fresnel had a fire built in a passageway between decks, and it helped to ease the discomfort
brought on by the steady downpour. A spare canvas was
stretched on deck to catch the precious rainwater. The
wind was fresh and they made good headway despite the
rain.

But the next day the storm began in earnest, with a
howling that made the yardarms rattle in their chains, and
sent great waves crashing into the bows. Fresnel sent a
crew of topmen aloft to inch their way across the
treacherous footropes that hung just below the yardarms.
Leaning precariously over the yards, their hands numb
with cold, the men gathered in the flapping sails and tied
them securely to the yardarms by means of those short
ropes called buntlines, taking care lest a sudden gust of

wind should snap a corner of the sail and send a man plunging to the deck below. The three topsails were furled—fore, main, and mizzen—as well as the lower course of both the foremast and mizzenmast; only the mainsail was left as a storm sail to steady the ship.

By the next day the tempest had increased its fury. The masts creaked dangerously, their stay lines stretching with each pitch of the ship, and the men worked furiously to take up the slack with tackles. If the lines were too loose the masts might crack; too tight, and the tackles might burst or the stay lines snap. Fresnel was reluctant to pull in the storm sail because it helped to stabilize the roll of the ship, aware, however, that a sudden burst of wind could split the sail or pull the whole mast down. He waited for half a day, hoping for an end to the storm—while the wind roared and the timbers shook—before ordering the mainsail to be furled. Now they rode under bare poles.

The storm became more terrible still. The ship tossed on the wide ocean with such violence that the fires were doused for fear a stray ember, thrown from its sandpit, would ignite the decks. Already miserable from the wet and chill, the men ate cold food. They made their way on the slippery deck from one handhold to another, while the waves hissed and foamed around them and the water sloshed into the hatches. The kegs and barrels of food had to be checked constantly for leakage, and lashed more securely into place as the turbulent pitch of the ship increased. The crew stood on a catwalk above the stinking bilge water, the rats squealing frantically underfoot, as they manned the pumps around the clock to keep the constant torrents of water down the hatches from sending them to the ocean floor.

After two days with no sleep, they were exhausted and snappish, growling sullenly at one another. Despite the tossing of the ship, André's stomach had held, and he had insisted on taking his turn in the bilge with the rest of the men. He had been astonished at Gosse's fortitude. The work was obviously exhausting for her, despite her young strength, but she never complained, heartening the men with her jokes and buoyant laughter.

At last the storm eased a little, the rain slackening and the seas calming, though the fierce wind showed no sign of abating. Master Fresnel came to the bilge to tell Monsieur le Comte that the cook had managed to start a fire and there was hot food waiting in the messroom.

André straightened, feeling the ache in his shoulders from the long hours at the pump. He smiled warmly at Gosse working beside him, noticing for the first time the pale lavender shadows under her eyes. He felt an irrational urge to pick her up and cradle the foolish child's head on his shoulder. Whatever possessed Master Fresnel to allow his daughter to toil for so many hours without rest?

"Come, Gosse," he said. "Have you not had enough of this stinking place?" And held out his hand to her.

She laughed, deep and vibrant. "Landlubber! Sink me, father, you should see André's face sometimes! For whilst the bilge is a singularly unlovely place"—and here she indicated the fetid water below them, foul with dead rats and excrement, garbage and vomit—"only a land-lubber would make faces the way André has!"

"'Tis true enough," said André, "and no denying it! I could not live aboard ship, I think. I have been spoiled by life ashore."

The three of them clambered up the aft companion-way, stopping at the steerage—a smelly little hole below deck—to see how the helmsman had weathered the storm. There had been a time, in the height of the tempest, when the whipstaff—the long steering pole that emerged from the floor and was attached to the tiller below—had swayed and vibrated so violently that it had sent the helmsman crashing against the bulkhead, and required six men to hold it steady. Now the seas had begun to calm enough so they could hear the creak and groan of the swinging rudder far below, and Copain, navigating from the poop, three decks above them, could be heard calling down directions through his speaking tube. Gunner was with the helmsman, peering at the compass set into its binnacle.

"What's the course?" asked Fresnel.

"East, northeast."

"Hold her steady until the storm passes," said Fresnel. "We shall not know until tomorrow, when Copain can take a reading with the quadrant, how far off course we have been blown."

"Think you that—" began André, then stopped, as the *Olympie* gave a sudden shudder. Master Fresnel frowned. It was a stronger shock than usual, even for a storm of this magnitude, and he turned about, minded to send Gunner to seek out the reason.

Michel burst into the steerage, his eyes wide with dismay. There was almost a flicker of panic in them as he glanced briefly at Delphine. "Bosun," he said to Gunner, "come quick!"

"What is it, lad?" said Fresnel.

"The foremast—the brace snapped and the yard was shaking and twisting—and some of the buntlines on the topsail broke—half of the sail is flapping free and one of the buntlines is twisted into the broken stay—" Michel panted heavily and wiped the salty spray from his face.

"I'll be hanged," growled Gunner. "Would you waste the time to tell me this? Did no one go aloft?"

"Yes."

"Who?"

Michel looked shamefaced. "All the men are tired—
and he never works hard—they dared him—" He looked
uneasily at Gosse. "Not me, of course, God rot!"

Delphine turned white. "Who?"

"Copain."

"Mother of God," she whispered, and pushed past
him to race to the main deck. The men followed her.

The wind whipped at their garments and the seas still
washed across the decks. Holding firmly to a brace,
Delphine shielded her face from the rain and looked up
into the rigging. Copain had managed to work himself
out to the end of the yardarm that, freed from its stay,
wobbled precariously. He had taken up a fresh line that
he had contrived to fasten to the arm, and had dropped
the other end to the men on deck, where they were
threading it through the tackle and belaying it to the pin
set into the railing. Now he was attempting to disentangle
the buntline from the broken stay, for if the topsail was
allowed to flap free it would soon split in this fierce wind
or pull down the mast. Already the violence of its shaking
had carried off the top lantern, and the canvas slapped at
Copain as he frantically worked to pull out his knife and
cut the twisted lines that hung in a jumble all around him.
Just as he severed the cords, there was a sudden gust of
wind and the sail struck at Copain, knocking him from his
slippery perch. The tangled buntline, still attached to the
sail, twisted around his leg as he fell, and he hung, upside
down, a hundred feet above the deck. His body tossed
brutally back and forth in the wind, the rope cutting ever
more deeply into the flesh of his leg until the flapping
topsail was spotted with his blood.

Delphine was up in the rigging before Fresnel could
stop her, making for the yardarm of the lower sail,
working her way across the footrope until she could
reach up—one hand on the yard, one for Copain—and

clutch at his arms as the pitch of the ship swung him in her direction. She had him once, lost him in a sudden toss of the ship, clung to him again. She was trying to figure out how she could release the rope that held his leg when the sail tore, dropping him several feet below her. She wrapped one arm firmly around the yard and reached down with the other; he managed to take hold of it. She closed her eyes against the strain of his weight as he hauled himself up, but at last he was beside her, gasping, leaning against the yardarm, balanced precariously on his good foot on the swaying footrope. Delphine drew her knife and bent over to slash off the line that held his leg, then bit her lip and turned away as she straightened. The rope had cut so deeply into the flesh in some places that the muscles of his calf gaped wide, flaccid and useless. If he were lucky, he might be crippled; if he were not, the leg would have to be removed. Delphine motioned frantically at the half-dozen men who were already swarming into the rigging, some to refurl the sail, some to help Copain. Then she looked at him. The rain pelted his delicate features, dripped off his snowy hair, plastered his shirt to his thin body. He glanced once at his useless leg, then smiled at her—a weary, sad smile—and closed his eyes. In the next roll of the ship he was gone, slipping gently off his perch as though he had planned it. She saw his body sprawled below for a moment or two, then a great foaming wave swept across the deck, bubbling and hissing. When it departed, cascading over the railings, the deck was empty.

Numb with disbelief, she made her way down the rigging and staggered to her cabin, deaf to the comforting hands and voices that reached out to her. She slammed the door on them all and threw the bolt with a savage swipe of her hand, throwing herself on her bunk and holding the pillow tightly against her ears. To keep out their voices, the storm, reality.

André groaned and stirred in his bunk, dragging himself reluctantly from the depths of sleep. He wondered at first what could have wakened him—he had thought a battle cannon could not have disturbed his slumber! He sat up, groping on the small shelf above him for his tinderbox and a tallow candle, then lit the candle and set it back on the shelf. He swung his long legs over the side of the bunk and pulled on his boots, grimacing as his stockinged feet came in contact with the cold damp leather. It could scarcely be near morning—the boots had had little time to begin drying out from the soaking rain. He was aware for the first time of the noises that had disturbed him: a loud pounding outside in the passageway, the sound of frantic voices, and an occasional muffled crash. He thought at first that the sound was coming from Gosse's cabin—she had stayed locked in her room all afternoon and evening, not even emerging when Fresnel led the company in prayers for Copain and the end of the storm—but when he opened his door he saw that Gosse's door was ajar, the room empty. Across the way, Fresnel and Gunner were at Copain's closed door, alternately banging furiously, then wheedling and pleading with Gosse through the heavy timbers. There were shrill curses from within and the sound of breakage as some object or other crashed against the bulkhead or the door.

"*Nom de Dieu!*" cried André. "What is it?"

Fresnel rubbed at his crippled arm and sighed tiredly. "'Tis Gosse. She's in a rage. Locked herself in Copain's cabin and won't come out—and now it sounds as if she's breaking everything she can get her hands on!"

André shook his head in annoyance. He would never

understand why they allowed her childish tantrums. "Why not let the hellion spend her anger undisturbed? What matter if Copain's cabin is ruined?"

"She has been drinking, I think. I had a bottle of distilled spirits in my cabin—very dear, and only for when we must cut a man. I think she took it." Fresnel turned back to the door. "Delphine—child—please, I beg of you, open the door!" There was a metallic clank as something struck the other side of the paneling.

"Come, Gosse!" Gunner's voice was bright with false cheer. "Remember that perspective glass you doted on? Sink me, but your father wants to give it to you now!" He looked quickly at Fresnel, who nodded in agreement. "Come! Here it is!"

André muttered under his breath and turned away. "Mayhap it is her way to grieve for Copain. Why can you not leave her in peace?"

Fresnel's shoulders sagged wearily. "Because she has taken the compass and the backstaff and every chart aboard ship! And the hourglass as well! I have men who can navigate—but not with empty hands! We have put out several sea anchors to keep us from straying further off course, but the sea is choppy and I must set some sail lest we capsize! But how are we to navigate? I can put the men to searching the ship, but *le bon Dieu* alone knows where she has hidden the things!"

André frowned. "In the cabin with her?"

"Mayhap. But if not, and we batter down the door, she will be in such a rage that she'll never tell us!"

André thought a moment. "Perhaps I can serve you. Can the ship hold for another half an hour or so?" Fresnel nodded. "Then leave me alone with her. I think I can soon find out where she has hidden everything."

"Why should you succeed where we have not?"

André laughed ruefully. "Because she is not overly

fond of me." He waited until the two men had mounted
the companionway to the roundhouse, then stood very
close to Copain's door. "Gosse," he said softly, "it is
I—André. Can you hear me?" There was a shrieked oath
from within, and a loud bang (he thought she might have
kicked the door) on the inside of the paneling. "Good!"
he said placidly. "Now listen to me, you sour-tempered
little savage. Do you think, because you crash about in
there and scream foul curses, that I fear you? I am not
your father or Gunner to tremble at your childish furies! I
shall stand here outside your door—all the night, if need
be—and tell you that you are a little whelp who cannot
even behave in a civilized manner, nor speak save with
curses, nor—" and here he racked his brain to think of
insults that would enrage her without causing unnecessary
pain when she were sober again "—nor play a worthy
game of trictrac, nor—" He stopped, hearing a gentle
squeak as she cautiously pulled back the bolt. He braced
himself, anticipating the assault. As the door flew open he
instinctively ducked and heard the sound of crashing
glass behind him. In a moment the passageway was filled
with the pungent smell of liquor. Before she could slam
the door again he pushed against it with all his might,
sending her flying backwards onto Copain's bunk. While
she lay there gasping, he closed the door and surveyed
the cabin. It was in chaos. All of Copain's books lay torn
in shreds and scattered about the room, a small tobacco
box had been smashed against one wall, and half a dozen
clay pipes seemed to have been stamped to powder on
the floor. A bottle of ink had been tossed against the
bulkhead, and still oozed its black stain down the wall.

Delphine staggered up from the bunk, her eyes glowing with fury, yet slightly unfocused. It was clear she was
very drunk. "Stinking bilge rat!" she shrieked, and began

to throw things at him, her hands clutching at boxes and tankards within her reach.

He warded them off as best he could and advanced on her, fighting back his anger, remembering that Copain had always been able to control her behavior with quiet calm. "Gosse," he said, "you must return the charts and compass. 'Tis foolish to carry on so."

"Devil take you for a scurvy whore's son! Go away and leave me alone!"

"Why are you doing this? When the ship could sink?"

"Let them all die," she cried, "every whoring one of them! Always tormenting him—sending him aloft to his death—let the ship go to the bottom, with every lousy knave aboard!"

"And would you kill yourself too?" he snapped, feeling his impatience growing in spite of himself. "I cannot believe that! Give me the compass. The charts."

She glared at him. "Sniveling cowards! They shall have their charts when I am ready to give them! Go away!"

He took a step closer, frowning down at her. "I shall not leave until I have them."

She stamped her foot. "You shall go now! And empty-handed! With a present from me to see you on your way!" She drew back her hand and slapped him across the face, snapping his head back with the force of the blow. She made a fist and went to strike him again, but he caught at her arm and spun her around, grabbing her shoulders from behind. She tore one arm free and reached for the knife in her belt, swinging it over her shoulder toward him; he saw it coming and released her, jumping back at the last moment from the murderous swipe of the blade. His hand shot out and closed around her wrist, squeezing the delicate bones until she cried out and dropped the weapon. Her hand still imprisoned by his steely grip, she tried to kick him, and cursed as he sidestepped and dodged her heavy shoe. Suddenly she darted toward him and clamped her teeth around the hand that held hers. She could taste blood in her mouth as he yelled and leaped back, his eyes burning in fury.

"Damned savage!" he swore, and raised his hand to strike her down. He caught himself at the last moment, and took a deep gasping breath, forcing his anger to drain away. He watched her as she stood, swaying slightly, her amber eyes glowing with the challenge. He raised his bleeding hand to his mouth, staring at her beneath beetled brows as he sucked the blood from his wound, afraid to speak until he had mastered his emotions again. "And still Copain is as dead as he was this morning," he murmured at last.

Gosse the brat vanished in an instant. Her face contorted in sudden pain and she crumpled to the floor, all the fury gone. She huddled there, clutching her arms tightly, as great racking sobs shook her body. André knelt by her and picked her up in gentle arms, crossing to the bunk and sitting down, Delphine cradled in his lap. His own anger forgotten, he held her and rocked her as she moaned and sobbed, feeling a tenderness for the poor child he had not thought himself capable of. At last, with a long shuddering sigh, she quieted. Still holding her, André crossed the passageway to her cabin and laid her on her bunk, smoothing back the damp hair from her forehead and stroking her tear-ravaged face until her eyes began to close sleepily.

"Gosse," he said quietly, "where are the charts?"

She sighed, her voice soft and little-girl sweet. "I put—Copain's sea chest—under his bunk." She sighed again, closed her eyes and slept.

Blowing out the lantern, André tiptoed from her cabin

and returned to Copain's room. He retrieved the compass and the rest from the sea chest; about to quit the cabin, he stopped, struck by something rather curious. Every book of Copain's had been ripped to shreds—except one. On the table one book lay intact, opened to a page. Coming closer, he saw that someone had taken a pen to the page and enclosed two lines from a verse, circling around and around until the lines, hemmed in by their black wall, seemed to leap off the page:

> *Pass on, say I, and seek your fate,*
> *Nor trouble my repose. I sleep.*

Chapter Five

IN THE MORNING SHE WAS MISERABLY ILL. STAGGERING onto the deck, her hand across her eyes to shield them from the bright sun, she leaned over the railing to vomit into the sea. André tried to tease her gently, reminding her of his own seasickness, hoping to ease the pain that turned her golden eyes black and despairing. But she snarled at him and cursed him foully, as though she were humiliated that he should have been a witness to her frailty. That day and the next she spent hours in the crow's nest, driving Michel away when he tried to intrude on her solitude; for weeks afterwards she moved about the ship like a wraith, until it near broke André's heart to see her lively spirit brought so low.

But gradually she began to return to her own self, laughing with the crew, lashing Gunner with her tongue until the warm-hearted giant crept away, red faced. And one day when André was on deck—a brisk breeze blowing—and the cook had given Gosse a bucket of watery, rancid oatmeal to heave over the side, she stood deliberately upwind of him as she tossed the foul mess, and André was splattered from head to toe. He roared his outrage and went to rap her ear, but she made a face and scrambled into the rigging, daring him to follow. He considered it for a minute, then changed his mind. In this wind he'd probably be blown into the sea. He stormed to his cabin, more furious with himself than with her. This was the second time he'd nearly struck her. Damn the imp! How had she managed to rouse such passion within him, strip away his civility and sense of chivalry, strike at the rough core of him?

At supper that night, when she lost her temper at some trifling thing that he said, and had to be restrained by Fresnel from hurling her plate of stew at the bulkhead, André determinedly ignored her, biting his tongue against the angry words that choked him, swallowing the urge to shake her until her teeth rattled in her head. Perhaps it was her way of dealing with the loss of Copain—to throw herself more fiercely into her deviltry. And truly her pranks and tantrums seemed to have less exuberance in them, more unreasoning fury hovering just below the surface, as though she were taking revenge on him—on the world—for the death of Copain. And sometimes, when he caught her staring at him with a look that was dark and brooding and unfathomable, he wondered if it was something more, something that went beyond Copain.

The weather turned surprisingly hot, the May sun baking *Olympie*'s brine-soaked timbers. The stench of the bilge was worse than usual. André found that even the Great Cabin was stuffy, the air tinged by the fetid water below. There came a night when he could no longer stay within, tossing on his straw pallet; if he could not sleep, he could at least breathe! It was a beautiful night. The moon had set and the stars twinkled brightly in the heavens, glittering pinpoints in the vastness of sea and sky. He went to the forecastle in the bow of the ship, mounting the ladder to stand beneath the great running lantern that hung from the foremast and creaked rhythmically in the soft air. The sound was punctuated by the gentle plashing of the waves and the faint squeak of taut ropes and lines.

André leaned against the mast and breathed deeply, tasting the beauty of the night. The air was sweet with spring, stirring vague but familiar longings within him, yet salt tanged and filled with the promise of adventure and the unknown. There was a sudden sound behind him. Peering closely in the gloom, he saw Gosse perched on a coil of rope.

He laughed warmly. "It would seem I was not the only one who found the night enticing."

She rose from her seat and moved past him to stand at the rail, her eyes turned to the heavens. "Did you know that there are pictures in the sky? Copain used to show me. See? There!" Her pointing finger drew the shapes in the air. "The crow sipping from the cup of wine that has spilled at his feet. And there is a lion—do you see? Below the bear—those stars are his tail!" Her voice was filled with childish wonder and delight. "When we sail in the Southern Hemisphere, near Tierra del Fuego where the storms are so fierce, the stars are all different. But when the stars appear—*mon Dieu!*—they are so close—as though God himself is near!" Her voice caught, halfway between a sob and thrilling sigh. "Why should that be, do you suppose? We are no nearer to heaven there, and yet—"

"You love the sea," he said quietly, moved by the passion in her voice.

"Yes! Oh yes! In the winter, when the foam is frosty on the green waves, and the sky is gray—and the summer— Oh!" she burst out impatiently. "If my unschooled tongue could only say what my heart feels. Copain would chide me for spending too little time with books." She sighed and stared into the night. "I shall have my own vessel someday," she said at last, "and the sea shall belong to me—"

"And you would be content thus forever?"

"Yes! No—I know not!" she cried in anguish. "When we harbor in a strange port, with strange people, new sights, I want to see, taste, have—*Ah Dieu!*" She threw her arms wide in the night air, clenching her fists as though she were grasping all of life and fiercely drawing it down to her breast. She turned to André, her eyes shining, yearning, in the light of the lantern. "But on a night like this—" Her voice was suddenly soft and wistful. "I think I would be content if the voyage went on forever, and nothing changed. Why should that be so?"

Dear Mother of God, he thought, turning away so she might not see the look of pain on his face. How could such sweet innocence still exist in a world that was—to him—cold and barren, old and tired? He laughed unsteadily. "You are so young, child. I can no longer remember when life held such joy, such promise—"

"Curse your gizzard!" she cried out. "I am not so young! I am eighteen!"

A heavy sigh. "I can scarce recall when I was eighteen."

"My mother was dead at eighteen—and I a babe of two." She thrust out a belligerent chin. "How old was your—Marielle?"

"Nineteen when I married her."

"Yet you call *me* child!"

He laughed softly. "It was a long time ago. I did not feel so old, and so, mayhap, she did not seem so young! And then—you say you are not a child, yet you behave like one. What are you? Child or woman?"

"I am what I am!" she exploded. "I am Gosse! And content to be as I am!"

"But how long can you pretend to be what you are not, nor ever will be? For all your false show and bluff manner."

"Which is—?" The voice was heavy with scorn.

"A lad."

"Damn you!" She raised her fists to pummel his chest, but he grasped them firmly in his two hands, pulling her close to him so she was suddenly aware of how he towered over her, of how the width of his shoulders blocked the stars from her view.

"No, Gosse," he said gently, as though he were chiding a child, "the time will come when you must be a woman, willy-nilly. However much you rage against it."

Copain would have said the same, she thought, feeling herself defenseless. Damn the man! What a fool she'd been to open her heart and soul to him—doubly the fool to tremble so at his nearness. "Blasted whore's son!" she swore, shaking free of his grasp. "Not all women must have chestnut hair and helpless eyes and priggish manners!"

He fell back a step—hands clenched at his sides—as though she had struck him. When he spoke at last his voice was cold and hard, the words hissing through tight-held jaws. "Foul-tongued viper," he growled, then steadied himself with a deep breath. "For me, Marielle will always be the perfect jewel, the mirror against whom all others must be held. Had you but one particle of her womanliness—" He swung about on his heel and strode away.

She started to call after him, then clasped one hand over her mouth and turned away in anguish. For was it not so, what he had named her? Foul-tongued viper. And the only words she had thought to hurl at his retreating back had been ugly curses. Ugly and unwomanly.

* * *

May was drawing to a close. Under a fair breeze and a clear sky *Olympie* neared the coast of France. Fresnel reckoned that they would make Dieppe in three or four days, thanks be to God. It had been a good voyage, save for the loss of Copain: enough food and water, minimal damage to the ship from the storms, the cargo still safe and dry below. Until they reached the Channel, there was very little work to be done; most of the crew was on deck playing cards or dice, or washing and patching their clothes to be ready to go ashore.

André spent the morning writing to Georges de Mersenne; he could post the letter at Dieppe to be carried back to America on the first westward vessel. He had put aside his leather jerkin, for the day was warm; now he unbuttoned the top of his shirt and rolled the voluminous sleeves above the elbows for added comfort. He yawned and stretched contentedly, then closed his writing case and stood up. It was too fine a day to stay in his cabin; he descended to the main deck—half anticipating, half dreading some new deviltry from Gosse.

He was greeted by the sound of steel clashing against steel. Gosse, her bright yellow hair caught by a twist of red bandanna around her forehead, was brandishing a slender rapier, leaping and thrusting at Fresnel while he, a long dagger held in his uncrippled left hand, fended off her attacks with some difficulty.

"Good!" he cried. "Remember what I taught you, Delphine. On the *passado* you must thrust at the same time you advance. At the same time! Good!"

André leaned against the railing, nodding his head in admiration. Damn, she *was* good! A little crude perhaps, the movements needing a certain refining, but better than half the young gallants he'd seen at Pluvinel's Academy. Fresnel had obviously taught her well. It was a pleasure to watch her skill as the blade flashed in her hand, the supple wrist original and inventive in its response to Fresnel's varied feints and parries. At last she stopped and grinned at André, her eyes shining, breast heaving with the exertion.

"Well?" she challenged. "What think you?"

"Your *stoccado* is superb. Each thrust is sure and accurate. But can you defend? What of your *parades*? Your *volts*? Can you parry? Leap to avoid a thrust?"

"Of course!" she snapped. "Sink me, but the man is a fool!"

"I am to blame," interjected Fresnel quickly. "I taught her all the defensive positions: *prime, seconde, tierce, quarte*—and variations besides. But with this lame arm," he rubbed his crippled right limb, "she no longer is able to practice the skills."

"Can *you* fence, monsieur?" she sneered at André.

"I have had my share of bouts," he said mildly, refusing to be drawn into a show of anger.

"Then perhaps you will show me *your* defense! *If* I give you the opportunity to attack, you will see mine!"

"I would not speak so boldly, if I were you," he said, sending Michel to his cabin to fetch his sword and gauntlet. "I have the experience of years, if nothing else. And combat. Whereas a sapling like yourself can scarce have had many occasions to run a man through!" He smiled good-naturedly, trying to defuse her temper before it should build.

"But I shall let my thoughts dwell on it!" she hissed.

"Come, come, Gosse," he said, slipping on the gauntlet Michel had brought, and pulling his rapier from its leather shoulder sling. "Let us fence as friends, for the joy of the sport." He made a pass in the air with his sword, enjoying the unfamiliar heft of the blade. "I have not held a rapier for more than a year; I fear me I am soft! I shall need your indulgence, not your enmity. Come." He urged her forward with a movement of his hand. "Have at me."

While Michel watched in rapt attention, his eyes never leaving her, and Fresnel smiled his approval, Gosse launched her attack, darting forward to thrust at André. He parried the blow neatly and without too much effort; despite her skill he had, after all, been fencing for longer than the child had years. He let her take the offensive for awhile, murmuring an occasional *"Bon!"* or "Well done!" when she was particularly adroit. And when he caught her blade in a parry and returned it with an unexpected thrust, he was delighted to see her respond instantly with a finely executed *volt,* leaping neatly to one side while she deflected his rapier point. He attacked again. Again she parried, turning her defense into a smooth *passado* that caught him by surprise for a moment so he was forced to back away. As they fenced, he was pleased to discover that her skills were sharp enough to challenge him. But after ten minutes or so, during which she grew more intense, clenching her teeth in concentration, her faults were becoming obvious.

"Wait," he said at last, pausing to dab his forehead against his rolled-up sleeve. He smiled warmly. *"Mon Dieu,* but you're remarkably good, Gosse! What you need now are the subtleties, a little refinement. You are too direct in your attack and defense—you give the game away. Mayhap it is in your footwork. A little more grace and I would not so easily see you shifting from *tierce* to *quarte* and back again."

"Sink me, what bilge is this?"

"Not bilge," said Fresnel sharply. "Monsieur has a

good eye. I should have seen that myself! What more, André?"

André looked questioningly at Delphine. "Shall I go on, Gosse?" She frowned but said nothing. "Well, then—you are too intense. Your step is heavy to begin with, not nearly agile enough, but when you begin to concentrate so fiercely on your sword arm you lose all nimbleness. It makes you vulnerable—especially in retreat."

"Retreat? Damn your gizzard—I never retreat!"

"Nom de Dieu!" he burst out, his voice rumbling with exasperation. "I do not mock your skills. Say rather 'backstepping,' not 'retreat!' But if your footing is clumsy, you have lost the match on one pass. Can you not move thus, lightly on the balls of your feet, your steps smaller, closer together?" He demonstrated the movement for her.

"Rot and damnation," she sneered. "Are you dancing again, my pretty popinjay, your soft hand wrapped in its glove lest it blister?" She stamped her foot resolutely. "I shall fence as I please—there is nothing you can teach me!"

"Name of God," he muttered, surprised at his own forebearance in the face of her bad temper. "Must I prove it to you?" He raised his sword determinedly. "Defend yourself."

He waited until she had put up her guard, then pressed his attack, deliberately forcing her backward with more speed than he had shown before. Her feet, caught in their clumsy anarchy, tripped one upon the other and she stumbled and fell to the deck, sprawled flat on her back. André put his foot lightly on her wrist, pressing gently until she had loosed her grasp, then hooked his sword point in the looped quillion of her blade and drew her

rapier toward him. He put it aside on the deck and
reached down to her, holding out a friendly hand to help
her up.

"Do you see what I mean? If you would use the
feminine grace with which nature has endowed you, you
would not trip so easily. Come—will you try it again?"

Her eyes burning with fury, she sat up and slapped
aside his hand, muttering a curse under her breath.

He shrugged. "I knew that you were a stubborn child,
but I am surprised to find you such a fool in a matter
where your head should rule!" He turned away in
disgust, sheathing his sword in the scabbard that lay
across one of the kegs on deck. A belaying pin, hurled
savagely through the air, caught him on the tip of his left
elbow. He gasped in shock as the pain shot through his
arm, and nearly sank to the deck, his face drained of
color. Mouth twisted in a painful grimace, he clutched at
his arm, kneading it to ease the searing fire that radiated
from his elbow. He turned to Gosse as he shook his hand
to relieve the numbness that had followed the fierce pain.
His eyes were like two blue flames, burning with rage.

Delphine stood her ground, hands on hips, glaring
belligerently at André, ignoring the angry scowl on her
father's face. André pulled off his gauntlet and slammed it
down on the deck. "Now, by my faith," he growled, "this
child has tried my patience once too often!" He strode
menacingly toward Delphine; too late she read the
danger in his eyes. She yelped in surprise, her mouth
agape, as he grabbed her wrist and pulled her to a low
keg. Sitting down and slinging her roughly across his
knees—face downward—he turned his attention to that
portion of her anatomy that lay beneath his broad, flat
palm. His hand rose and fell; she squeaked in outrage
and tried to wriggle free of his firm grasp. Behind them, a

horrified Michel would have rushed to her rescue, but Fresnel, his face grim, held him back.

Delphine began to kick and swear in earnest, pouring forth a stream of foul sea oaths that might have shamed a pirate, calling him whore's son, bloodthirsty bastard, filthy scum, and worse, until even André was shocked. Grunting in anger, he held her more securely on his lap. If he did nothing else, he would thrash the brat soundly! He could feel, through the thin cloth of her sailor's breeches, the firm young flesh of her buttocks; from the way his own hand had begun to tingle and sting, he knew he must be inflicting some damage on those tender mounds, despite her brave curses. The thought gave him a certain degree of satisfaction and he smiled grimly as he smacked away. She would not mock his "soft" hand after this!

Suddenly she choked on a curse and the choke turned to a sob. Knowing her well chastened, he flung her away and stalked to his cabin, borne on a tide of righteous anger. Behind him he could hear the mocking laughter of some of the crew—Gosse would not so easily intimidate them with her temper now!

Crying, Delphine struggled to her knees and spit after him as he vanished to the passageway, humiliation as much as pain the source of her tears. Fresnel had released Michel and he rushed to Delphine's side, helping her to her feet, his face awash with sympathy. But as soon as she was standing, she cursed fiercely and swung a tight-clenched fist at Michel's jaw. The poor lad crumpled to the deck, stunned, as Delphine limped to her cabin—conscious of the snickers of her shipmates. There she threw herself on her bunk (face down, of course), to gently rub her outraged rump, and to curse André for a brute and a villain.

* * *

André sipped the last of his cider, gazing morosely across the table to Gosse's empty chair. His mind was filled with restless thoughts. God knows the little devil had deserved a beating long since, but it was his own intemperate behavior that disturbed him. He had thought himself wise enough—and old enough—by now to deal with her in a more rational fashion. But in spite of his fine resolve, she had managed to stir his basest passions, plumb emotions—anger, tenderness, unreasoning fury, remorse—that he thought had died with Marielle. It was small comfort that Fresnel and Gunner had spent the meal beaming at him. Curse them both for making him do their work!

The door opened cautiously and Delphine peered in. She seemed disconcerted to find them still there, and she hesitated for a moment before coming into the mess-room. Head held high, she sailed around Fresnel's chair and found her own seat, flinching almost imperceptibly as she sat down. The slight movement, however, did not escape Gunner, who grinned with delight. She ladled out a bowl of broth—thick with bread sops and onions and the last of the dried peas, and enriched with a large dollop of lard—and ate quietly, making a conscious effort to refrain from slurping so as not to earn André's disapproving scowl. Cold and silent, stiff with injured pride, she ignored him across the table. Once, when he reached for the straw demijohn to refill his cup with cider, and she saw—beneath his still rolled-up sleeve—the terrible bruise on his elbow, purpling under his tanned flesh, her eyes locked with his for a moment until she blushed and turned away guiltily.

Almost as though it had been planned, Gunner and Fresnel left the cabin together, abandoning her to André. He picked up his cup and came around the table to sit beside Delphine. Spearing pieces of dried apple on the

point of her knife, she chewed and swallowed as though
André did not even exist.

"Gosse," he said gently, "it was not my place to treat
you so cruelly today, and I beg your forgiveness." He
gave a soft laugh. "Which is not to say that you had not
earned it, God knows! But I am sorry, and would take the
moment back if I could. Will you forgive me?" For
answer, Delphine slammed down her knife and took a
long draught of cider. "You will be a woman someday,
mayhap a wife and mother," he went on, ignoring the
sudden sharp look she shot at him. "Such an unbridled
temper is unseemly—by my faith, your husband will be
forced to beat you every week if you play the shrew!
'Tis a pity you had no woman to teach you softness,
but you are a clever child—surely you can see the
folly of your ways!" At his words Delphine spat her
mouthful of cider onto the floor, her face twisted with
contempt.

André sighed unhappily. "We shall soon be in port.
Can we not part as friends, remembering the times
we laughed together? *Nom de Dieu*, Gosse! Look at
me!"

Defiantly she banged down her cup, and turned to
stare him full in the face. And then she was trapped,
drowning in the blue of his eyes, helpless and tormented.
Sweet Jesu, she thought, he is so beautiful! Like a golden
god in the stories Copain had told to her, with his strong
face and clear eyes. She began to tremble, soft lips
quivering, eyes sparkling with the beginning of tears, her
whole body on fire with a feeling so foreign and new as to
be scarcely understood.

He looked startled, then he frowned, as though he
were seeing her face for the first time. "Gosse—" he said
softly, questioningly. He leaned forward and put his hand
on her bare arm, sending shivers through her body. As

he bent toward her, the locket around his neck slipped out from under his shirt and hung suspended between them. The locket with *her* picture. A woman of modesty and grace, he had called her.

Damn him! she thought. "Take your scurvy hand off me," she snarled, reaching for her knife and holding it poised menacingly above his arm. The magic moment had vanished; now he glared fiercely at her, his eyes daring her to strike. Her hand and eyes wavered at the same time; with an ugly curse she drove the point of her blade into the soft oak just to one side of his arm.

"It would take a hundred beatings to tame an uncivilized whelp like you!" he spat in disgust, and stormed from the cabin.

She jabbed her knife into the table again and again, making little nicks on its smooth surface. She would hate him forever—for everything he was, for everything he said and did. She would hate him until the day she died.

Then, why did his eyes haunt her? Why—even when he was being kind—did she drive him away with her ugly ways? He had been right about her fencing; had her father spoken the words she would have heeded them. Ah God, she thought, and groaned aloud. What was happening to Gosse?

She hated André. No. No. She feared him, as Copain had guessed—feared him enough to torment him constantly, though she could not even begin to understand why. But when he was near, when he spoke to her, smiled at her—*Dieu!* Why did she ache inside with a longing for something that had no name? He called her child, he scolded her for being unwomanly, graceless— and his words stung more than the beating she had finally goaded him to by her childish cruelties.

What are you, child or woman, he had asked. And she had answered him every day of this accursed voyage by behaving like a child. But I'm a woman! I *want* to be a woman! Oh, Copain, she thought in anguish, why must Gosse die that Delphine may live?

With a tormented cry, she cradled her head on her arms and began to weep, giving herself up to the heartbroken sobs that racked her body, to the agonizing conflicts that shook her to her very soul.

Chapter Six

THE SOFT CLANGING OF THE HARBOR BELL DRIFTED through the night air, reverberated against *Olympie's* gunwales, swirled among the fingers of mist on her decks. André's heart gladdened at the sound. Somewhere beyond the fog was the stone *quai* of Dieppe, France. Home!

They had sighted the coast just at twilight, and then the fog had closed in, so thick that Master Fresnel was afraid to advance any further, lest the ship collide with other vessels in the harbor. The crew had let go the anchor and furled the topsails, leaving the lower courses unfurled, as the wind was light. In the morning they could stand in for shore under sail, or use the pinnace and longboat to tow *Olympie* closer in; for tonight she rocked gently on the tide, sighing and whispering, as though she too were glad to be home.

Home. André smiled and murmured the word aloud. Vilmorin's rolling fields, the smell of the grapes on the vine, the amber stones of the old château. Home—to the lads who waited for him: sunny, golden-haired François and quiet, shy Alain with chestnut curls that echoed Marielle's burnished glory. He had seen so little of them through the years filled with wars and campaigns; now he ached to stay at home and watch them grow, and hunt and ride with them, and teach them to love the land as he did. God willing, there might be a few weeks to spend with his boys, while he mobilized his troops and waited for orders from Paris.

Paris. If *le bon Dieu* smiled on him, and he survived the summer's battles, he might go to Paris during the winter. What a pleasure it would be to rediscover the theater, the glittering and erudite salons where wit and intelligence ruled, the mindless pleasures of court life, dancing and jousting and endless fêtes among perfumed courtiers and their ladies. *Ah, Dieu.* Their ladies. He leaned against the ship's railing and stared into the fog-gray night. What a reckless libertine he'd been in those years before Marielle had taught him to love, taught him that love went far beyond the pleasures of the body. How she had stirred him with the strength of her devotion, so he could not even relieve himself with an unblushing wench as so many of the soldiers did while in the field. The rake-hell had become a devoted husband, needing no lover save the one who waited for him at home. For all those years—no one but Marielle.

And after Marielle died—he felt himself burning with shame to recall it—he had gone to the town of Vouvray, and had drunk too much and tried to rape the tavern maid, though her always-worshipful eyes made it clear that she was willing enough. And he had fled from her, howling into the night air, leaving her waiting on the floor, her skirts pushed up above her bare hips, her bosom heaving in anticipation. Fled from her, lest she discover his dark secret.

And White Deer. She had swum naked in front of him, and leaned toward him around the campfire so her loose tunic fell away and he caught glimpses of her rounded breasts. Sometimes he had wondered if she were deliberately trying to seduce him. Poor White Deer. She must have thought he did not care for her. But how could he tell her—tell anyone—that since Marielle's death he had no manhood left? He was too old perhaps, too jaded, to be moved by the sight of a woman, to feel the blood coursing in his veins, the stiffening, the hardening, as though all the essence of life flowed to his impatient loins. Let the young men dally with the married women, fight the clandestine duels of honor, know the joy of seduction and conquest. He was content to go home to his children and live out his remaining years.

But—Paris. He felt a twinge of dismay. He could hear the gossips now. De Crillon? they would scoff. That impotent old man? Damn! he thought. How they would laugh when they learned the great lover was no more! Yet the pain of that humiliation was nothing compared to the deeper pain in his heart, however much he tried to deny it, of knowing that he had lost forever one of life's sweet blessings, the joy that a woman's body could bring. He sighed heavily. Best to think of the morrow, not the sterile years of his dotage. If there were a coach leaving Dieppe for Paris, he could be home within three or four days. He yawned and moved toward the quarterdeck. His only regret was parting with Gosse so unhappily. Since the day he had beaten her she had avoided him, taking her food to eat alone in her cabin, scorning all his attempts at reconciliation, strange and distant and—He frowned. He could scarcely fathom what he had read in her eyes. Grief? Confusion? Torment? And several times in the last few days he had come upon her and sworn she had been weeping. He moved down the passageway to the Great Cabin. Perhaps, if a light still showed under Gosse's door he would speak to her, try once again to part as friends.

Gosse's cabin was dark; she must be sleeping by now. He was surprised to see the light under his own cabin door. Odd. He thought he had extinguished his lantern before his stroll on deck. He opened the door and walked in.

Gosse was sitting at the window seat, wrapped in her boat cloak, gazing out at the misty night. André closed the door softly; she scarcely stirred, so he thought at first she had not heard him enter.

"Gosse—what are you doing here?"

She continued to stare out the window. "Waiting for you."

"But—wherefore? It is so late—and so much to be done on the morrow!"

"I want to stay here tonight." Her eyes flicked nervously to his face, then back to the window.

Mon Dieu, he thought, she sounded almost afraid! Could it be some superstition that frightened her on this last night of the voyage? Or a childish nightmare that had driven her to seek solace with him? "Would you spend the night at my window?" he asked gently.

She stood up. He was surprised to see that, below the heavy cloth folds she had drawn about her body, her feet were bare. "No," she said, and now her eyes met his. "In your bunk."

He fell back a step. "Name of God, you cannot mean—"

She rushed on, as though to stifle his objections before they could be uttered, her trembling chin belligerent and vulnerable all at the same time. "I washed my feet! I even combed my hair!"

"Gosse. Don't be foolish—" He stopped. What was he to say now? How had he failed to see what was happening, failed to read the light that now shone in Gosse's amber eyes? Had he not broken enough hearts in his time to recognize that look? He took a step toward her. "Please, Gosse—"

"Don't you want me?" she asked, her eyes almost pleading.

Dear God, how difficult this was! "I—I shall not soon forget you, Gosse. Had I daughters, I could wish them to be as—spirited a child as you are—"

"Damn your gizzard," she growled, her eyes narrowing. "I am *not* a child! I am a woman!" With an impatient gesture she threw down the boat cloak. The swinging lantern cast flickering shadows over her naked body.

"Mon Dieu," he breathed, feeling a sudden tightness across his chest.

"What is it?" she whispered, her voice soft and pathetic. "Is something the matter? Am I ugly?" She wrapped her arms self-consciously about her waist and hips.

"Ugly?" He laughed unsteadily, surprised at the tremor in his voice and the sudden quivering that seemed to shake him from head to toe. "Ugly?" He gulped, his mouth dry.

Her body was full and ripe, golden from the kiss of the sun, glowing and golden save for the dark triangular patch above her thighs, and the deep pink of her rosy nipples. Her waist was very slender, but her hips curved sensuously, and the voluptuous swell of her breasts made him wonder how she had managed to hide such beauty, such—womanliness—beneath her garments. He stepped toward her, hesitating, then stooped and plucked her cloak from the floor, his hands shaking, and wrapped it about her shoulders. His fingers grazed her collarbone, explored the hollow at the base of her neck, then slid down—almost with a will of their own—to caress the soft fullness of her breast. Beneath his shirt, his chest rose and

fell with great heaving breaths, and his face twisted in
agony; he closed his eyes and turned away, his hands
tight-clamped fists at his sides.

"In the name of God," he choked, "go to your cabin,
or we are both undone!"

"No." The voice soft, yet stubborn.

He turned back to her. She had cast off the cloak once
again, and stood tall and proud, her chin held high, eyes
glowing with defiance. Then she smiled, her lips warm,
inviting, beguiling. Eve and Salome and Jezebel peeped
from her gold-flecked eyes, sighed through her rosy lips.

With a tormented cry he crushed her in his arms,
taking those lips for his own, tasting their sweetness as
she yielded to him, her mouth opening to his searching
tongue. He kissed her fiercely, hungrily, never wanting to
stop, feeling his youth return to his body.

For this! thought Delphine, enveloped in his embrace.
Sweet Mother of God—for this! All the weeks of misery,
of aching, of confused longings and dark shadows—for
this! It was like coming home to port after she had been
lost at sea, knowing that this was where she belonged, the
snug harbor that had awaited her all this time.

At last he lifted her in his arms and placed her gently on
his bed, reluctant even to be parted from her for the time
it took to pull off his clothes. Nestled on the straw pallet,
she watched him shed his garments—shirt and boots and
breeches—and cast aside the locket as though it meant
nothing to him. She could feel no fear, only anticipation,
joy, her lips still burning from his kisses. She had watched
the men with their harlots, heard them talk of the brothels
in port—she knew what was expected of her. She let her
knees fall wide, smiling at him, watching, waiting. The
men had talked of the wonder of it, the ecstasy—
however crude and clumsy their words—and how could

it be aught else, with this beautiful man trembling above her, with his hard-muscled body lowering onto hers?

And he would not hurt her. She knew that much from her talks with Copain, remembering the day she had slipped on the rigging and fallen spraddle-legged to the deck and felt a sudden sharp pain. Copain had teased her ("Your husband will think you are not a virgin," he had laughed) and she had raged at him, but now she was glad. She did not want even a moment's grief to spoil this beautiful night. Let him use her body as he wished—he could bring her nothing but joy. She sighed contentedly as his lips covered hers again, abandoning herself to him totally, trusting in his instincts. To her surprise he did not mount her at once, but let his hands roam her body, caressing her breasts and flat belly; she gasped at the flames that seemed to shoot out from his fingertips, tormenting her flesh wherever he touched her. When his mouth followed the path of his hands, moving down to her breasts, his lips and teeth teasing her nipples to hard points, she cried aloud and tangled her fingers in his hair, pulling his mouth back to hers, unable to endure another moment of such exquisite agony.

With a grunt, he dislodged her hands from his hair, rubbing his tender scalp and glaring down at her with a look that was part passion, part annoyance. "Are you so impatient, you little savage," he growled, "that you must scalp me? So be it!" He positioned himself above her, entering her, filling her, lifting her senses to heights undreamed of till now. She moaned and writhed as he thrust deep, her fingernails digging into his shoulders, her thoughts spinning out of control until there were no thoughts left, only sensations, only the throbbing of her heart, the pulsing spasms in her loins.

"Gosse!" he gasped, and shuddered against her,

wrapping her in his arms while she drifted down from the heights. *Ah, Dieu,* she thought, holding him close, unwilling yet to have him withdraw. How could it be so? A part of her body that had mortified her, that had been the symbol of her feminine weakness, her *differentness* from the crew—how could it be so? That it should bring her such pleasure—unknown, unimagined until now?

She opened her eyes to see him smiling down at her. "Am I a woman?" she demanded.

He stroked the side of her cheek, marveling at the delicate curve of her jawline. "By my faith," he said, his voice husky in his throat, "you are indeed! I am the blind fool, not you. Not to have seen, not to have known." He kissed her softly and rolled away from her, lying on his back, eyes closed, letting contentment fill his being.

She sat up, cross-legged, close to him that she might look at him as he lay. It seemed as natural to be naked with him as it was to swim with Michel, though different. Vastly different! "And am I—" she hesitated, afraid to say *beautiful,* lest he mock her "—pleasant to look upon?"

He opened his eyes and grinned. "Little minx! Yes. You are—pleasant to look upon!" He lifted up a lazy finger and touched her bosom, then stroked the inner edge of her thighs, so enticingly presented to him by her seated pose. She gasped as a shiver ran through her. He laughed aloud, delighted at her sensuality. *"Mon Dieu!* How did you keep all that passion hidden?" He smiled ruefully and rubbed his elbow, still discolored from the blow of the belaying pin. "But then, mayhap, you did not *truly* hide it!"

She dimpled prettily at him. "Do you like me better thus?"

"Without a doubt! And most assuredly without your lumpish clothes!"

"Damn your eyes! I could scarce climb the rigging in a skirt!"

"Hold your fire," he laughed, pulling her down into his arms. "I meant merely that I preferred you with no clothes at all!" He kissed her roughly, while his hands played up and down her spine and she twitched and shivered, astonished at the sensitivity of her own flesh. Had it always been so, that—all unaware—her body had waited for the touch that would awaken it? Or was it only André's touch that brought forth feelings that had *never* been there before?

Breathing raggedly she broke from his embrace at last and sat up, letting her eyes sweep his naked body laid out before her. "I think—that I prefer *you* thus, as well."

"Indeed?" He smiled quizzically, unsure if the words came from Gosse the woman, or Gosse the innocent child.

"Yes." She nodded emphatically. "You have a finer body than any of the crew, even Michel, though he is young and strong." She touched his broad shoulders, pocked with a dozen or so small scars. "His skin is smooth. Were you wounded many times?"

"Not so many," he said testily, vaguely annoyed that she should talk of other men's bodies while she lay with him. "'Twas shrapnel from a cannonball."

She frowned, mystified. What had she said to earn his sudden displeasure? "No matter," she said quickly, "you are not one whit less handsome!" She curled, kittenlike, in the crook of his arm.

Placated, he turned sideways and stroked her hair, then smiled at her, his eyes already heavy with sleep. In a few minutes his eyes were closed, and his chest rose and fell with the gentle breaths of slumber. Delphine dozed sporadically, but she was filled with far too much excite-

ment and wonder for deep sleep. At last she pulled away
from his arm, that she might lie beside him and watch
him as he slept, filling her eyes—her heart—with the sight
of his long-limbed frame: bronzed and beautiful, flecked
with golden glints from the fine hairs that covered his
arms and chest, darkening to a reddish gold at his loins.
Even in repose his muscles were hard and strong beneath
the taut flesh, and his shoulders were extraordinarily
broad. It made her tremble just to look at him. Softly, so
as not to disturb him, she ran her fingers over his body,
his chest, his hard belly, reveling in the feel of his cool
skin under her hand. *Ah, Dieu!* she thought, feeling her
heart begin to pound again, what a wondrous thing a
man's body could be! She hesitated, fascinated but
uncertain, her hand poised above his flaccid member,
before working up enough courage to touch him there.
When she felt a sudden quivering beneath her hand she
held her breath, her eyes darting to his face. He was
awake, watching her through those warm blue eyes,
heavy lidded and smoldering with desire. Embarrassed,
she started to pull her hand away, but he held it there, his
strong fingers about her wrist, until she had caressed him
to a hardness. Delighted at her accomplishment, Delphine giggled and sat up, then composed her face to a
more restrained mien. Mayhap it was not ladylike to
seem so forward and eager. "If you please," she said,
very proud, very proper. "I should like you to do it
again."

A small smile played around the corners of his mouth.
"Would you now?"

"Yes. But would you—contrive to take a little longer at
the doing? I would you were not so abrupt this time."
Surely a lady would behave thus.

Now he was grinning broadly. "I will contrive as best I
may, but 'tis not such an easy matter!" He laughed aloud

and rolled onto his back, his arms flung wide beside him. *"Mon Dieu!* What a wondrous creature you are, Gosse!"

Her amber eyes flared with sudden anger. "Damn you, you shall not make sport of me!" She leaned over him, her fists poised to smash down onto his chest, but he grabbed her hands and rolled over with her, pinning her under his body. She struggled fiercely beneath him, her eyes shut tight with humiliation. Then, knowing herself trapped and helpless, she lay still, her eyes still resolutely closed, fearing to read mockery in his face.

His voice was gentle, caressing. "Come, open your eyes, Gosse. Please." He kissed her softly, his mouth sweet on hers, until, relenting, she looked at him. She saw no scorn in his eyes, only tenderness. "I do not make sport of you," he said. "You have given me back my life tonight. If *le bon Dieu* gave me the strength, I would make love to you all the night through." He kissed her again, his mouth less gentle now, then laughed at the look of naked desire on her face. "Would that please you, my little savage?"

For answer she twined her arms around his neck and pulled his mouth down to hers, nipping at his lip with her teeth, holding him fast, possessing and possessed, wanting nothing more than his mouth, his arms, his body—forever. When he took her, she clung to him, writhing beneath him, crying out in rapture, her nails raking across his back in violent and uncontrolled testimony to the fierceness of her passion. Their bodies moved together like a storm at sea, surging and swelling, wild as the tempest, the pounding surf; with a roaring crescendo the waves crested and they stilled at last, lying spent and exhausted in one another's arms, like driftwood cast upon the shore.

After a long time, Delphine roused herself. André was sleeping again; she moved softly so as not to disturb him.

There was much to be done. Swiftly she wrapped herself
in the boat cloak and tiptoed to the door; then, filled with
a sudden burst of emotion, she hurried back to his
sleeping form and, bending, kissed him softly on his lips.
You were wrong, Copain, she thought. You said that
Delphine would come with tears—and lo! Here am I, my
heart overflowing with happiness! Smiling down at André
as he slept, she extinguished his lantern and quit his
room. When she regained her cabin, she was aware that
the fog must have dissipated, for the full moon streamed
in through her small port; there was no need even to light
a candle. She opened her sea chest and rummaged
about until she had found what she was looking for: a
dark green homespun skirt, cut short above her ankles in
the peasant manner, and a linen petticoat. Smoothing
them out with gentle hands, she laid them across her
bunk while she cast off the boat cloak and donned her
shirt. Son of a dog! Why had she left her only chemise in
the cottage at Dieppe? She put on the petticoat and skirt,
nervously wondering if he would think they looked silly
with a man's shirt. No. She would not think of that. There
would be time enough for chemises—and gowns as well,
when they were in Paris together. She was almost certain
he would want her for his mistress—it had always
sounded like a grand life when she read about it in
Copain's books. But, failing that, she would be content to
be a servant in his household. She was young and strong;
she did not fear hard work. And as long as he took her
into his bed, what did it matter? Mistress or servant, she
would please him so that, sooner or later he would surely
ask her to be his *comtesse*.

She took her few belongings from the shelf and stowed
them in the chest, that she might be prepared to go
ashore in the morning whenever he was ready. Then she
yawned. It was still several hours before dawn; she could

sleep a bit before it would be time to say good-bye to her father and Gunner. She stretched out on her bunk, spreading her skirts around her, and fell asleep, her mind filled with happy thoughts of beautiful tomorrows.

When she awoke the sun was high in the sky and *Olympie* was creaking into the harbor. She could hear the cheery yo-ho-ing from the men on deck as they braced the yards around and let go the anchor, and the voice of Gunner roaring his commands. Smiling, she sat up and opened her small porthole, filling her nostrils with the familiar harbor smells of pine tar and pitch, of rotting seaweed and fishnets hung to dry in the morning sun. André's door was still closed; she nearly tiptoed in, minded to tickle him awake, then thought better of it. She had not seen Dieppe for nearly six months; there would not be time later, amid the bustle of farewells, to take a last look at her beloved port. She steeled herself for the jibes the men would direct at her skirt, then shrugged, determined to ignore them. After all, had she not many times donned her skirt when the work was through, and gone ashore with the crew in some foreign harbor? And just because her heart was fluttering in anticipation did not mean that—to watching eyes—she appeared any different than she had in the past. Sure enough, only Michel, grunting under the burden of a heavy bale of furs, took note of her skirts and accused her sulkily of avoiding her share of the work by dressing like a helpless woman.

While the pinnace and the longboat were lowered into the water to begin the ferrying of cargo to shore, Delphine leaned against the railing and drank in the morning. The stone *quai* and the chalk cliffs beyond the beach had never seemed more white and clean, the sky never more blue, the sea sparkling and sun-kissed. She could scarce tell if she saw with her eyes or her heart, but she nearly wept for the beauty around her. Oh, André, she thought, awake and see the day that God has fashioned for you and me!

After half an hour had passed, she could no longer contain her impatience. "Sink me, father," she laughed lightly as Fresnel passed her on deck to speak to Brise, the carpenter, "but our fine gentleman will sleep the day through!" Would her father hear the tremor in her voice?

"Not he," said Fresnel, turning. "He has gone long since. He feared to miss the coach to Paris and would not wait for us to drop anchor. Thanks be to God a fishing vessel was coming in to port just at dawn, and we were able to transfer Monsieur le Comte and his belongings to be taken ashore." Fresnel patted the leather wallet at his belt. "I wish him a safe journey home. He was more than generous. I could hope for such fine passengers every voyage."

Delphine gripped the railing tightly until her knuckles gleamed white. "Pah!" she sneered, her face twisted in contempt. "The scurvy whoreson had naught to give but his gold! Good riddance, says I!"

"Fie, Delphine. Fie! He took special pains to wish you good-bye. He was loath to disturb your slumber, but he charged me to bid you farewell as a fond friend."

"Did he? A fond friend, say you?" Her lip curled in disgust, tasting the last bitter dregs in her cup. "A fond friend! D'you hear, Michel? D'you hear, Gunner? Sink and scuttle me! I'll see him upon a Spanish rowing hell ere I call that knave friend! Eh, Michel?" She tossed back her head and roared with laughter.

"Aye!" he agreed, laughing in his turn. "Good riddance! I liked not the man from the first day he came aboard."

"A loyal comrade and true, Michel," she said, throwing her arm familiarly about his shoulder.

He grinned, emboldened by this sudden show of warmth. "To be sure, you had more cause than I to hate the man! Eh, Gosse?" And slapped her on her rump.

She whirled on him, her eyes glowing. "Damn your liver! Don't you touch me! Don't you ever dare!" Growling in anger, she pushed him away so he toppled over a barrel.

"God's blood, Delphine," sighed Fresnel. "Can you not—"

"Damn you!" she shrieked. "I am Gosse! Do you hear? *Gosse!* I shall *never* be Delphine! Never!" And fled to the refuge of her cabin and the release of burning tears.

Chapter Seven

"BY NEPTUNE'S TRIDENT, FATHER, I SHALL NOT STARVE!"

Fresnel frowned and stomped to the open door of the cottage, leaning against the jamb and scowling past the grassy dunes to the sheltered cove beyond. "I like it not," he growled. "You have never stayed behind when *Olympie* called!"

"God's blood! We have scarce been ashore for two weeks! Why must you sail so soon again?"

He turned to her, his eyes dark with accusation, his arms gesticulating excitedly as he talked. "Monsieur Ramy offers to underwrite a short voyage—it is June, name of God, and there are no storms! We shall take lumber to the Levant and return with silks and wax and leather. Three months! Three months—and shall I tell him I do not wish the commission because my daughter Delphine has not had her fill of being ashore?"

Delphine rubbed her hand tiredly across her eyes. "Must I implore you again, father? Sail without me! You have a new navigator in Copain's place, we have patched and caulked until I think I will choke from the smell of pine tar, and my fingers refuse to shred another rope end to make oakum to seal *Olympie*'s seams! Why do you

need me on such a short voyage? If you will prick that
sluggard Michel, you will scarce miss my hands!"

"But why, Delphine?" he asked softly.

"Because I am tired!" she snapped. "Because I wish to
stay ashore, because I wish to be alone, because—" her
voice faltered, caught on the edge of a sob, "because I
have no heart for it." She bit her lip and turned away.

"Delphine—child—what is it that torments you?" He
put a gentle hand on her arm.

She shook her head, unable to speak, fighting back her
tears. "Please, father," she whispered at last, "let me
be." She sniffled, then smiled brightly. "You'll see—
when you return in September you shall find your old
Gosse again, as hearty as ever! Did I not leave my gear
aboard *Olympie* to prove to you I shall go to sea again?"

"Well, it does not please me, but—Will the coins I gave
you be enough to see you through the summer? Thanks
be to Monsieur le Comte, I was able to pay back the
moneylender with interest for last year's loan for supplies
and cargo. If you husband the money carefully, we might
still be able to glaze the window before Christmas."

"There is little that I shall need." She ticked off the
items on her fingers. "We have planted leeks and
cabbages and other potherbs. In a few weeks I shall have
fresh vegetables for my soup. And I found some turnips
still in the ground from last winter. There are mussels and
oysters along the shore, and fish, if I am so minded. I
have a small piece of salted pork, two *litrons* of dried
peas, and a boxful of ship's bread. If I want fresh bread,
there is a bit of flour left in the bin, and when the pears
ripen on the little tree I shall make perry and trade it for
some milk and butter. What more will I need? I have my
books—and I shall welcome my solitude." She smiled
and put her arms about his neck. "Now be off with you,
and trouble yourself no more over your foolish Gosse!"

He kissed her on the cheek, then frowned and stood back, taking her hands in his. "You are so young, so innocent, so—trusting. Do not—trust—too much, Delphine."

She swirled away from him. "I shall not spread my legs for any man, if that's what you mean, father! You may have raised a fool for a daughter—but not a whore!"

"You are not a fool, and you are very dear to me," he growled, and, stooping, swept up his sailor's bag from the floor and went out.

"God be with you," she cried. "And a safe voyage!"

He stopped at the rise of a dune that led to the path and the wide harbor beyond. "God grant you peace," he murmured, and cresting the dune, was soon lost from sight.

The lonely weeks passed slowly. They had never stayed long enough on shore to have many friends in Dieppe; *Olympie* had been Delphine's whole world. Now she tended the small garden and fetched buckets of water from the rill behind the cottage. She watered her vegetables and soaked the salt out of the bits of pork she cooked with the peas or turnips for her suppers. She scrubbed the small cottage until her hands were red and sore, and strewed the coarse planks with fresh-cut rushes. Then she swept it clean after a few days and scrubbed it again for something to do, pausing sometimes to study her reflection in the pail of water. Child or woman? she thought. *He* had wanted a woman, with long flowing chestnut curls, and sweetness and grace. Not a ship's brat with lank yellow straw for hair and a face as plain as earth.

She walked on the beach from time to time, but most days she felt too lethargic even for that, and sat instead on a small bench just outside her door, reading Ronsard and Malherbe, finding the verses flat without Copain to share them with. And sometimes she took out her knife to whittle away at pieces of driftwood washed up on the beach, fashioning with some difficulty a small comb embossed with flowers to hold the fast-growing hanks of hair that had begun to fall over her eyes.

And one day, wrapping a shawl about her cropped hair and shoulders, she ventured to church, huddling in a dim corner, watching in agony as the women came down the aisles—graceful, charming, surrounded by handsome young men. Holy Mother, she prayed, make me beautiful! Then she sank to her knees, hands clasped together, to beg forgiveness for her sinful vanity.

She looked up. Across the aisle a man was watching her. He seemed to be about thirty or so, and was dressed in the somber clothes of a merchant—dark doublet and breeches, unadorned falling band, the silver buckles on his low shoes the only indication of his comfortable circumstances. His face was pleasant and boyish, crowned with a head of curly brown hair. She frowned at him and bent more diligently to her prayers. When she looked again, peering cautiously out of the corner of her eye lest his glance be still on her, he was gone.

At last she rose, moving quietly up the aisle to the front portal of the church, aware for the first time of the clumsiness of her gait, as though she were still aboard ship. She stopped at the font to dip her fingers in the holy water, the movement a hollow gesture; her soul was more troubled by her inadequacy as a woman than it had been before she came to church.

"Mademoiselle?"

He was standing there, smiling, offering her holy water that he had cupped in the palm of his hand. She hesitated, feeling the hot flush stain her cheeks, wondering if it was sacrilegious to refuse such a Christian gesture.

"Please," he said, his dark brown eyes soft on her. "The water will be doubly blessed for me."

Modestly she averted her gaze while she touched her fingertips to the water he proffered, making the sign of the cross before escaping into the bright sunshine.

"Mademoiselle!" As she reached the bottom of the church steps, he caught at her hand and would have brought it to his lips. She wrenched her fingers away and raced down the narrow lane next to the church, twisting and turning through the cobbled alleys and byways, never looking back or stopping until she had reached the safety of the dunes and her own cottage. She leaned against the doorway, gasping for air, unable to rid her mind of the pleasant face, the warm brown eyes. How dare he presume to be so forward, she thought self-righteously—but she could not prevent her lips from curving upward in a shy smile.

The next day—and the next—she wandered through the streets of Dieppe, pretending to herself that she was only out for a stroll, but she did not see him again. It didn't seem right to seek him openly in church, and she went instead to early mass, that she might not profane God's house.

By the beginning of July the weather had turned hot, draining her energy, making her feel sluggish and sleepy much of the time. And though she resolutely swept her waking hours free of André—dismissing him as a dark cloud that had caused her a moment's pain, and no more—her dreams were haunted by his blue eyes, and she awoke filled with longing and grief and an all-consuming hatred. Restless, she wandered down to the bustling harbor at the mouth of the Arques River, feeling a little more at home among the ships and sailors. Then she climbed the chalk cliffs that sheltered Dieppe and gazed out at the open sea, almost regretting her decision

to stay in port. *Olympie* might torment her with
memories of André, but could her despair be any greater
than the misery she suffered every day ashore, knowing
herself different from all other women?

There was to be a great fair in Dieppe, with merchants
and artisans coming from the surrounding towns and
regions to sell their specialties. Delphine had learned of it
one sunny afternoon when, yearning for a sweet pastry,
she had caught a few extra fish and traded them to the
baker for a cherry tart and the latest gossip. A fair! She
had seen many a foreign and exotic market, but never a
fair in her own country! She hugged herself for joy, filled
with excited anticipation, planning what to wear with as
much care as though she were a great lady going to a
ball. She washed her best apron and folded it carefully
while it was still wet; when she shook it out to wear, it
would be embossed with neat squares from the folding.
She had never bothered with garters before, letting her
stockings droop as they wished; now she undid a length
of hemp, pulling out a few strands and braiding them into
a fine string to tie up her stockings just below her knees.
She washed her chemise and dried it in the sun, and beat
the beach sand from her green skirt. She would wear an
extra petticoat—a heavy, cream-colored flax one—so
she could tuck up one side of the green skirt and let the
petticoat show. She even managed to whittle another
comb for her hair.
   On the day of the fair she dressed carefully, wrapping a
large white linen neckerchief about her shoulders and
tucking the ends modestly into the bodice of her low-cut
chemise before donning her rust wool jacket. The day
was warm, but only a common peasant would go to the
fair without a jacket! She parted her hair in the middle
and pulled the tresses away from her face, fastening them

at her temples with the two combs. She peered into her small mirror to study the effect; she could pass for a woman from the front, but the moment she turned her head the chopped sides and back of her hair made her look like a street urchin. If only she had a little cap of linen—She sighed unhappily and picked up the pink ribbon Copain had given her. Tied about her waist, the long ends hanging down over her snowy apron, it gave a very fetching look to her costume, and she smiled, feeling heartened again. She counted out the few coins she would allow herself to spend, and put them in her pocket along with a piece of ship's bread in case she were hungry.

The fair had been set up on the opposite side of the town from the harbor, in a broad meadow just within the ancient and crumbling walls of Dieppe. With the advent of gunpowder and cannon, the old walls of almost every town—except the most heavily fortified—had become well-nigh useless, and had been allowed to fall into ruin. Dieppe's old stones were overgrown with ivy and mosses and meadow flowers that ran riot in the fields beyond the walls—bright patches of red, pink and yellow that danced among small groves of dark green trees.

Delphine clapped her hands delightedly at the sight that greeted her. There were scores of small booths set up, trestle tables gay with colorful cloths, canvas tents painted and adorned with many-hued pennants and banners. In the shade of a large elm tree a man in a scarlet gown was swallowing fire, extinguishing flaming fagots in his throat to the breathless "aahs!" of the crowd. Delphine watched for a while, her eyes wide with astonishment, then moved on to a troupe of actors performing a ribald comedy on a makeshift stage. One of the men, a large goat's horn tied to his groin, pranced and capered about in pursuit of a young girl. She threw up her hands in pretended horror before allowing him to cast her to the stage floor and perch over her, undulating and bobbing in a crudely pantomimed gesture that was not lost on the squealing throng. Delphine frowned and turned away, strangely offended by the sight; it was easier to watch a man go down on a whore than see the ugliness of this mock show. She carefully avoided the young boy who passed through the crowd, holding out an upturned hat for contributions. Rot and damnation, but she would not pay to see such a thing!

She moved through the meadow, drinking in sights and sounds that were new to her: a team of acrobats, balancing one upon the other to dizzying heights; a group of country dancers swirling to the shriek of a bagpipe; itinerant vendors, hawking their wares to every passerby, crying out in song and monotone their varied offerings. There were pastry sellers and women with baskets of onions and oysters, hot chestnuts and oranges and lemons. A man in rags implored the folk to buy his twig brooms, and an old crone moved through the crowds with a jug of milk balanced on her head. A young barefoot peasant lad, dressed in oversized clothing that seemed to be the castoffs of some aristocratic master, pushed a heavy wheelbarrow containing a grindstone, his singsong cry promising a sharp blade and a good future to all who availed themselves of his services.

The buyers were as interesting and varied as the sellers. Haughty aristocrats rubbed elbows with the lowest urchins, and the somber garments of the merchants and other bourgeoisie punctuated the colorful scene with dots of brown and black and gray. The pickpockets might have had a field day, save that the Town Council of Dieppe, seeing a golden opportunity for a moral lesson, had taken the occasion to hang several thieves and murderers in the midst of the festivities. The corpses dangled from an oak tree, with signs about their wrung necks to warn others away from a life of crime.

Clutching her coins in one tight fist, Delphine moved past the booths that dealt in regional specialties: linen collars and handkerchiefs from Brittany, flints and steels from Lorraine and the Savoy, laces from Alençon. There were hats from Paris and kid gloves from the region near Bourges, and glass beakers and goblets—*à la façon de Venise,* in the Venetian style—from Orleans and Nevers. There were several booths set up to display the speciality of the Dieppois: delicately carved objects of ivory—combs and statuettes, hunting horns, handles for swords and daggers and table knives, chessmen, and embossed seals.

Hungry at last, Delphine stopped on the edge of the meadow to eat her piece of hardtack and wash it down with a mug of perry—the Norman cider made from pears—that she had bought of an old woman. Though she was still hungry, she refrained from spending her money on more food, tempting as was the abundance and variety about her. She had been hungry before, and there was a well-stocked larder at home if her pangs became too severe, but she might never again have the opportunity to purchase something unique and wonderful for herself. She shopped carefully, unwilling to part with her coins until she was sure of her own desires.

At last she stopped at a stall presided over by a fat little man with a luxuriant head of black curly hair that fell to his shoulders, nearly obscuring his linen falling band. Before him on the counter were several wig stands, each crowned with hair as abundant as that on his head. As she watched in amazement, he plucked the wig from his head—his skull as naked and shiny as an eel—and replaced it with a bright red *perruque.* Self-consciously Delphine patted her own cropped hair, then shook her head as the man turned to take a ladies' wig from the shelf behind him.

"No," she said, "it will grow soon enough. But perhaps—" She fingered a small glass vial on the counter, holding it up to examine the ebony liquid inside.

"Not black," he said emphatically. "Not for you, mademoiselle!"

"No. I thought—mayhap—brown, with a touch of red. I have always favored—chestnut curls—"

"Would you abandon Apollo's treasure when you have captured it for your very own?"

Delphine whirled in surprise. The man from church was smiling down at her, brown eyes twinkling merrily. At the sudden look of apprehension on her face he put a gentle hand on her sleeve. "I beg you, my charming little bird, do not fly away again! And never change the color of your hair. It glows with all the sun's radiance—you cannot think to alter one single tress!"

"Go to the devil," she said softly, uncomfortable with his unexpected flattery, unable to put anger into her voice. She moved away into the crowd.

"Did you know," he said, keeping pace beside her though she ignored him, "that the women of Florence suffer the most horrible torments to have hair the color of yours? They dab their curls with foul-smelling salves and put on great wide hats with open crowns through which they draw their tresses. Then they sit in the sun for hours on end—with flies buzzing around their stinking pates— and if their hair does not fall out, nor their skin break out in festering sores and boils, they may flaunt golden hair for a month or two! Ah, there!" he said, as she began to laugh in spite of herself. "I had begun to think you could not smile."

"Do they really?" she asked. "Do they really do such terrible things to their hair?"

"Indeed they do! And what did you do to *your* hair? Or were you ill?"

"Damn your eyes!" she spat. "It was a bother and I cut it!"

"No matter. It wants a bit of curl, that's all. And a little cap to cover it until it grows long again."

She snorted, taking in his fine doublet and breeches, his silk hose and linen collar, his wide-brimmed hat. "*You* may spend your money on fripperies—but I shall not, God rot!" Then blushed, remembering the bottle of hair dye she would have bought.

If he was thinking of it too, he did not let his face betray him. "Come," he said, "it would please me greatly if you would allow me to buy you a cap."

"Why should you?" Her amber eyes were dark with suspicion.

"Because I have money to spend on fripperies. And because you would look charming in a cap. And because it was a cheerless day until I saw you, mademoiselle. Mademoiselle—?"

"Delphine. Delphine Fresnel."

"And I am Gilles Despreaux."

"Without a *de?*"

"Alas! I am but a simple craftsman, an upholsterer by trade. Do you fancy a nobleman with *de* to his name?"

"Not I, God rot! Let them all be damned to hell, says I!"

He laughed. "Leave a few to buy furniture of me! Come"—slipping a hand beneath her elbow—"there are dainty caps over here."

She frowned and shook free of his grasp. "I am not a fool to be beguiled so easily. I shall not go down for you for the price of a cap!"

"No. I thought not," he said, suppressing a smile.

"Then why do it?" she asked, striding along beside him.

"I told you. I should like to see you in a cap. You are a charming young woman—so different from most."

She stopped for a moment, searching his face for any traces of mockery, before continuing, heavy-gaited, at his side.

"Do you live in Dieppe?" he asked.

"Yes. No—mostly on shipboard, but there is a little cottage for when we are not at sea."

"Ah! Shipboard! The source of your singular charm."

"Damn you!" He *was* mocking her. "Be cursed for a scurvy dog!" She tried to turn away, but he held fast to her arm.

"Name of God," he said, "but I meant it for praise." He looked at her oddly. "Do you *want* to be as other women?" She bit her lip but said nothing. "Well, then," he continued, "to begin with, you must contrive to walk as though you were ashore, not still at sea. You need not match me step for step—take two dainty steps to my one. Mademoiselle?" He held out his elbow for her to take; blushing, she slipped her hand through his arm and minced along beside him, feeling awkward and foolish and ladylike all at once.

He bought her a little Flemish cap that fit snugly at the nape of her neck, fanning out into graceful wings on either side of her face, the whole edged with dainty lace. She curtsied a thank you and held out her hand; thinking merely that he would grasp her fingers, she was surprised and flattered when he brought her hand to his lips. He turned her hand over and stroked her palm—rough and calloused from the work aboard *Olympie*—smiling warmly when she would have pulled away in embarrassment.

"I shall buy you creams and orange-water. You will have the loveliest hands in all of France!"

Despite her protests ("What shall I do when I must hoe my garden? Willy-nilly, I must toil with my hands!"), he bought her a tin box of sweet-smelling cream and a vial of orange-water, insisting that she use some at once, and stroking the softness of her fingers approvingly when she was done. She had never felt so flustered and disarmed by a man's kindness, though a small voice whispered within her to beware. Giggling, and a little bit frightened, she allowed him to lead her to a fortune-teller who had set up a dim tent on a quiet corner of the fairgrounds.

The old crone, a gnarled woman with a large red wart on her nose, pocketed Despreaux's gold, then looked into his hand. "I see fortune for you, monsieur. Happiness, good fortune, riches." She droned on, the words mechanical, as though she had said them a hundred times.

Despreaux glanced at Delphine, then back again at the old woman. "And love?"

She hesitated. "Who can say what is love, monsieur? If your heart is open, love may enter. But—desire—may come in the guise of love—" She closed his fingers into a fist and pushed his hand away. "Your palm does not tell me. Come, mademoiselle," beckoning to Delphine, "let me see your hand."

Nervously Delphine sat before the old woman and held out her palm. The fortune-teller ran her fingers along the creases of Delphine's flesh and began her ritual once again: happiness and riches and good fortune, love and a handsome man.

"And joy always?" It was almost a plea, Delphine's voice hopeful and fearful all at once.

The old woman smiled at such innocence, then looked into the amber eyes, so filled with trust, yet dark and troubled with some deep sorrow. The smile faded from her face. "No. Much grief, I think. Grief and pain. I see it in your—" she recovered herself, glancing quickly down at the young hand still within her withered two "—in your palm."

"Alas!" whispered Delphine.

"Stupid old woman!" growled Despreaux, and gave the crone a cuff to the side of her head that sent her sprawling to the ground. "Would you frighten mademoiselle with your foolish talk? Come"—pulling Delphine to the tent's entrance—"let us be quit of this lying old fool!"

"Wait!" The fortune-teller raised a shaking finger and pointed it at Delphine. "You may have need of me again. The little alley behind the Church of Saint Jacques. You must ask for La Sorcière."

Though Despreaux scoffed at the fortune-teller's words, Delphine was unhappy and distracted, feeling herself suddenly cursed. To cheer her, Despreaux bought her a meat pastry; they sat together in the shade of a tree, eating and drinking from the large demijohn of wine that Despreaux had also bought. Delphine noticed the way he took small bites from his pastry, and restrained herself from downing her own pie in two or three large mouthfuls. The wine was very good—rich and strong—and she found herself growing quite giddy, reveling in the unexpected luxury of such fine food and drink. She did not protest when he proposed a stroll in the grove of trees beyond the walls of Dieppe; indeed she felt as free and light as the butterflies that danced among the wild flowers. And when he suggested that she take off her heavy jacket, she was delighted to comply, the warm day and the wine and the jacket having conspired to make her feel uncomfortable and constrained. She sighed contentedly and lay down on a patch of moss beneath a tree, throwing her arms wide to the lovely day.

Despreaux sat above her, a curious smile on his face,
watching her with an intensity that he scarcely hid. At last
he leaned down and kissed her full on the mouth; she
was startled for a moment, then relaxed as she found
herself enjoying the feeling of his lips on hers, the small
tingling that had begun somewhere deep within her. He
sat up and looked at her again, surprised at her warmth,
the way her mouth had responded willingly to his kiss.
Pensive, he allowed his eyes to travel the length of her
body, arrayed so temptingly before him; then, deliberately, he pulled off her neckerchief and slipped his hand
down the front of her chemise to fondle one soft breast.
She trembled and drew in her breath sharply. Emboldened, he loosed the drawstring on her chemise and
pulled it low so her bosom was exposed, deriving as
much satisfaction from her quivering response as from
the feel of her breasts beneath his roving fingers.

"Do you like that?" he asked, his voice low and
throaty.

A flicker of apprehension in her golden eyes.
"Shouldn't I?"

He laughed. "Aren't you afraid I'll take advantage of
you?" Unexpectedly his hand reached up under her
petticoats to stroke her knees, her thighs. To search for
what lay beyond.

"Damn your liver!" she shrieked, leaping to her feet
and backing away from him, her eyes burning. "I am no
whore! Did I not tell you I would not go down for you?"
She clutched at her chemise, shaking fingers attempting
to restore modesty. "Filthy scum! You shall not put
yourself in me! I am no whore! I am no whore!"

Without a word he arose, turning his back resolutely
on her and striding off in the direction of the fair. His
coldness made her feel like a fool, and she ran after him,
feeling shamed and humbled all at once. "Please," she

said. "Please, Monsieur Despreaux," clutching at his
sleeve, "forgive me. I am so clumsy—I cannot say what I
mean—the words—it is only that—I swore to my father—
to myself—that I would not—ever!" He stopped and
turned icy eyes to her. She bit her lip, then pulled the cap
off her head and handed it to him. "Here!" she said, near
tears. "I am not worthy of your kindness."

"Keep it," he said, still frowning as though her behavior angered him—or mystified him. But he turned about
and retraced his steps to the grove, walking slowly
enough so that Delphine might move daintily beside him.

At last she sighed. "Why would you want to take
advantage of me? You are a fine-looking man—there
must be a score of charming women who would welcome your attentions! Whilst I—clumsy—ugly—foolish—
not like a lady should be!"

"Because you are a very beautiful young woman."

Delphine stopped, her jaw dropping open in surprise.
"Sink me, but you cannot mean that! God's blood, I
have a mirror—"

Despreaux turned and took her by the shoulders. "I
have a friend who deals in rare gems. He has shown me
rough stones, and taught me to see the sparkling jewel
within. I saw you in church, your face shining with
holiness—do you think it mattered that you did not move
with grace when the church was lit with your sweetness?
And when I offered you the holy water—*mon Dieu!*—do
you know what it does to your coloring when you blush?
You bloom like a rose—and you talk about what a lady
should be! Stuff and nonsense! Now, do you want to be a
lady?"

"Sink me for a bloody bilge rat! Of course I do!"

He threw back his head and roared with laughter.
"Then you had best not let anyone hear you talk! Ladies
do not blister the ears of their listeners!"

"Damn you!" She raised her hand to strike his face, but he grabbed her wrists, putting his arms around her and pinioning her hands behind her back. They struggled for a moment until, unexpectedly, he kissed her, and she melted in his embrace, abandoning herself to the pleasure of his mouth once again. He let go her wrists and stroked her back before bringing his hands around to cup her heaving breasts in his firm grasp. When she trembled and twitched at his touch, he released her and stepped back, his laugh a soft growl.

"Mon Dieu! What a sensual creature you are! Now, if you behave yourself, I might kiss you again. To begin with—if you would be a lady—you should not walk alone in the fields with a strange man. The gossips will find plenty to talk about, and your family will not be pleased!"

"I have no family. Only my father, and he is at sea."

"Indeed?" He looked at her, his eyes thoughtful. *"Eh bien*—it still is not wise. A man could take advantage, seduce you, rape you, even."

"Is that why you asked me to come for a walk? To seduce me?"

"I know you like me to kiss you—but do you *want* me to seduce you?"

"Sink and scuttle me! Of course not! I'd as soon slit your blasted throat as—" She stopped, seeing the frown on his face, hearing the coarseness of her own words. "No," she said, suddenly shamefaced.

He drew himself up, very cold, very proper. "If you want me to kiss you again, you would do well to guard your tongue!" And he led her back to her cottage as she directed, the few words he could not avoid crisp and cutting and disapproving.

Chapter Eight

DELPHINE KICKED AT A SMALL PEBBLE ON THE BEACH. FIVE days, she thought miserably. Five days and he has not come to see me! He had called her beautiful, had kissed her, had made her forget for a moment that André had found her unworthy. And then he had not come to see her. She cursed her ugly tongue, the coarse speech that had driven him away. She looked up at her cottage; he was standing in the doorway, smiling at her. She resisted the impulse to run like a carefree hoyden to greet him, managing to step gracefully the way he had shown her.

"Mademoiselle Delphine?"

"Monsieur Gilles?" She started to curtsy, then thought better of it and held out her hand instead. She had been diligent in her applications of cream and orange-water; he beamed his approval at the softness of her skin.

"Come," he said, pulling her into the cottage, "see what I have brought you!"

Her eyes opened wide with excitement. "Rot and—" She bit her tongue. "What have you brought?"

He appraised her coolly, wondering how far he could go. "No," he said. "You must buy it with a kiss." She smiled and moved into his arms, putting her hands about his neck, offering her lips willingly. He kissed her gently, then took her mouth with more passion, allowing himself the pleasure of stroking the hollow of her back, feeling the lissome waist beneath his hands, holding her body close to his burning loins. Damn! but the wench excited him! Since the day he had first seen her in church, he had tried to imagine what it would be like to go down on her, to strip away her coarse clothes and hold her naked body in his arms. And the tantalizing sight and feeling of her breasts that day in the meadow—he had almost raped her, he had wanted her so badly! And then she had spurned his advances. It was a challenge he could not resist. It suddenly seemed important to have her come to him willingly, however much cunning it might take.

But she was such a strange creature! Angel and devil in one: defending her virtue with fire, yet melting sensuously in his arms like a practiced courtesan, allowing his hands and mouth to do things an innocent maiden would view with horror. Was she really unwilling to lie with him, or did she just need a little more persuasion? He had deliberately stayed away from her for days; her obvious joy at seeing him now proved the wisdom of his action. And surely she meant to please him with her soft hands and newly graceful walk. It gave him a feeling of power over her: what else might she be willing to do to please him?

"Do you know how I've missed you?" he said, his hands—still about her waist—bunching up her skirt and petticoat so he might touch the bare flesh of her thighs. Then he cursed to himself as she stiffened and pulled away.

"Damn you," she said, more hurt than angry. "You shall not."

He contrived to look pained. "Are you so unfeeling

that you can deny me? Do you know how I ache for
you?"

"No! No and no and no!" She stamped her foot, then
turned away, her voice catching on a sob. "Please,
monsieur, I do not wish to send you away, but—"

He shrugged, seeing the game lost for now. "Forgive
me, *ma chère,*" he said smoothly, "your mouth is so
sweet that I forget myself. Come"—as she smiled shyly at
his words and turned back to him—"here is what I have
brought you." He indicated a shallow brass saucer on a
tripod that he had placed on the table, filled with small
lumps of charcoal. Taking out his tinderbox and striking
flint to steel, he soon had the embers glowing. He pulled
from his pocket a small tool which he set into the middle
of the red-hot charcoal.

Delphine could contain herself no longer. "*Nom de
Dieu!* What is it?"

He grinned. "A curling iron for your hair! All the fine
ladies of Paris dress their hair with little wisps and tendrils
about faces that are so ugly they should be masked!" He
cupped her chin in his palm. "But you, my lovely
Delphine—" He kissed her softly then indicated a chair.
"Sit you here."

She refused to look in her mirror until he was finished,
biting her knuckle in concern each time the hot iron
sizzled about a lock of hair. When he had twisted the last
curl in the iron he placed her lace cap back on her head
and handed her the mirror. She gasped at her reflection,
seeing the way each dainty tress clung softly to her cheek
and forehead, the straight straw changed to delicate
yellow curls that accented the fine bones of her face, the
graceful line of her chin. She felt a sudden pang. If André
could see her now. Then she jumped resolutely to her
feet. Damn André! She smiled at Gilles. "Surely I owe

you another kiss for such a gift!'' And she suited the
action to the words, pretending to herself all the while
that the momentary thrill she felt at Gilles's touch, at the
taste of his lips, could drive out the memory of André's
kiss.

In the days that followed, he brought her ribbon
garters to replace the string, bits of lace for her chemise, a
sleeveless jerkin that laced snugly about her ribcage and
waist, accenting the womanly curve of her body. He
insisted that she lengthen the green skirt to her ankles
(''Only a common peasant wears a short skirt!''), and
chided her when they supped together and she grew
careless of her manners. He frowned when she swore
and turned cold when she lost her temper, until she
found herself tense and on edge, trying constantly to
please him and wondering what kind of fool she had
become to let him rule her so. But when he was pleased
with her, he praised her until she glowed, and bought her
little presents, and kissed and caressed her so she
trembled in his embrace and knew that it was all worth-
while.

One day he took her to see his shop—a large airy
cottage abustle with apprentices—with his fine house set
just behind it and surrounded by a lovely walled garden.
Proudly he showed her his Certificate of Mastership in
the Upholsterers' Guild—his *Lettre de Maîtrise*—that had
cost him a great deal of money and many years of
studying to earn. The young boys under his tutelage
gathered around to be introduced; one lad, obviously
smitten by Delphine, gaped and stammered until Despreaux fetched a blow to his face that nearly sent him
flying. His freckled cheek red from Gilles's fingers, the
boy hurried back to his bench where he had been cutting
a piece of leather for a stool, then gasped in fear and

dismay as the knife slipped in his grasp and dug an ugly channel into the smooth leather.

"By God," growled Despreaux, reaching for a stick, "but you shall pay for that with your hide!"

Delphine frowned, surprised at Gilles's harshness, almost ready to intervene. Gunner had been a fierce taskmaster, but he had never beaten the cabin boys needlessly, and had forgiven many an accident brought about by fear or haste.

Just then the door opened and an elegantly dressed gentleman entered. Despreaux threw down the stick and swept his hat from his head, bowing with a flourish while he motioned the boys back to their work. "Monsieur le Marquis! You do me honor! Have you come to see if your chairs are ready? *Voilà!*" Despreaux indicated half a dozen arm chairs covered in a rich brocade. "The boy is tacking on the last fringes. If you send a wagon around in the morning they shall grace your bedchamber by night-fall!"

The *marquis* nodded in satisfaction, rubbing his hand across the fabric of one chair, then peering more closely at the padded armrest. Despreaux's face was frozen in an obsequious smile. "Delphine, my lovely, show Monsieur le Marquis how charming a young woman will look in his chair."

"But certainly." Remembering Gilles's lessons, Delphine spread her skirts wide and sat gracefully in the chair.

"Beautiful!" exclaimed the *marquis*. "The chairs are beautiful, Monsieur Despreaux." But his eyes never left Delphine's face.

Despreaux pressed the advantage, pleased at the distraction Delphine provided. "Do you fancy a footstool, monsieur? Think of sitting in front of your fire—

mayhap with a lass as charming as this one—would it not
be fine to have a footstool upon which to rest your feet?"

"Yes. Yes, a footstool." The *marquis* smiled at Delphine and pulled her from the chair, keeping her hand in
his. "Would you sit at my feet, mademoiselle, if I had a
footstool?"

She smiled grandly, but her amber eyes flashed. "No,
God rot! You would sit at mine!"

There was a moment of silence, during which
Despreaux held his breath. Then the *marquis* began to
laugh. "By my faith, but this is a spirited wench! I shall
have the footstool, Monsieur Despreaux. Send one along
with the chairs tomorrow." He kissed Delphine's fingers
and made for the door. "There will be an added crown or
two if the girl comes with it!"

"I have a fine leather one," said Despreaux smoothly.
"The boy is finishing it now. You shall not find the price
untoward."

Delphine turned to Gilles, struck with a sudden
thought. "He will not use the damaged piece of leather,
of course?"

Despreaux's eyes flickered for a second but he smiled.
"Certainly not!" He bowed again. "I bid you good day,
Monsieur le Marquis." The smile held until the *marquis*
had left the shop. "You will oblige me, Delphine," he said
coldly, "by allowing me to conduct my own affairs."

"But—I—" she stammered. "But surely you would
not have sold him the footstool with the hide damaged?"
Her face wore the expression of innocence assaulted.

"*Mais non.* Certainly not. But it was *my* place to speak
of it—not yours! Come along," he said, as she continued
to look troubled, "and I will show you my house."

His house was beautiful, far grander than anything that
Delphine had seen before. They had supper in a
handsomely appointed salon on the main floor, and the

next night when she came again to dine he arranged to have their food served at a small table in the secluded garden, under the stars.

He smiled at her across the single candle that was the only light, noting the way she had begun to tilt her head coquettishly when she spoke, the way she used her hands with a grace that had not been there when first he met her. Each day brought changes in her—she seemed almost pathetically eager to please him. Except for her temper that flared from time to time (and he resolved to put a stop to *that!*), he found it surprisingly easy to mold her to a woman of his own creating, much as he created a fine piece of furniture. And she was useful. She had distracted the *marquis*, kept him from examining the chair where the brocade had begun to fray, allowed him, Despreaux, to sell the footstool he had been eager to be rid of—though it had cost him an additional piece of leather and he had beaten the boy soundly for that!

Despreaux leaned back in his chair, sipping his wine, feeling the cool night breeze on his face. Yes, all would be well—except for one thing. He was going mad for the wanting of her. She was a woman of fire, of passion held in check; he ached to release that flame. She allowed him to kiss her, to fondle her breasts while she gasped in sensuous delight at his touch, to hold her quivering body tightly against his own—but that was all. His tricks, his guile—useless! She was adamant. She was not a whore; she would go down for no man.

She was laughing at something he had said, her deep, musical voice rolling over his senses like waves on the shore. Oh God! he thought, what exquisite pleasure it would be to take her. "I want to bed you!" he blurted out, his voice ragged.

She shook her head, her eyes full of pain. "No, Gilles, please. Not for you. Not for any man."

"Not even for a husband?" he growled.

"That would be different, of course."

"Then marry me!" He felt reckless, driven by his hunger.

She jumped up from the table, unable to speak, shaking her head from side to side. "No," she whispered at last. "No. No." He clutched at her arm, half tempted to throw her down to the grass and rape her here in the garden. "Let me go, Gilles, please. Is your carriage waiting to take me home? Let me go." She fled through the garden gate to the coach that waited in the silent night.

She tossed and turned on her straw pallet, unable to sleep, hearing the soft plash of the waves against the beach. How could she marry him? She did not love him. It was flattering to have his attentions, and she was grateful for all the ways he had helped her to become a lady—the lady who would someday break André's heart —but that was all. She knew she was a sensual woman— one night with André had taught her that. She delighted in Gilles's kisses and caresses, her body trembling, her senses aroused, but the passion she had felt with André was missing. Damn his blue eyes, she thought, punching her pillow with tight-clenched fists. He had ruined her for any other man. If it weren't for him, she might be able to feel more for Gilles than superficial fervor. Damn him! Damn him! She would hate him forever!

Delphine glanced up at the lowering sky and shivered, wrapping her shawl more tightly about her shoulders. It was cold for mid-August, and if the rain should catch her she would in all likelihood take a chill and be forced to spend the next few days in bed. What had ever possessed her to come on such a fool's errand? She was half minded to retrace her steps and seek the warmth of home and hearth; then she turned down a cobbled street and saw the Church of Saint Jacques before her. Well, she had come this far, and she had no one else to talk to. The streets were narrow, the old half-timbered houses crowding close, their upper stories cantilevered out so it seemed they must surely fall of their own weight. The lane behind the church was dark, its rubbish-strewn gutter rank with all manner of foul things. Delphine nearly gagged, pulling her shawl across her nose and mouth to keep out some of the odor.

An old man was hobbling toward her, leaning on a gnarled stick. She pushed back her shawl and managed a friendly smile. "If you please, monsieur—I am looking for La Sorcière."

He grunted and lifted his stick, pointing to a door in a crumbling hovel. "You'll find the witch there—may she be cursed. She will not tell me how soon I shall be rid of my shrewish wife. A pox on her!" Still grumbling, he moved off down the lane.

At Delphine's timid knock, the fortune-teller opened the door. "I knew that you would come," she said.

Delphine looked surprised. "How could you know? I did not know it myself until this morning!"

The old woman indicated a small bench by the fireplace where Delphine was to sit, and pulled up a three-legged stool for herself. "I read it in your palm." Her shrewd eyes searched the troubled face before her. "And now you have a question for me."

Delphine stirred nervously in her chair. "No. Yes. I have brought three sols. Will that do?"

The fortune teller nodded and took the coins from Delphine, holding the girl's hand in her own and peering intently into the soft palm. "Your question, little one."

"If—if a—person suffers from—the sickness of the
sea—day after day"—Delphine made a rocking motion
with her hand—"and she is on dry land, does that
mean—that the sea is calling to her, and she must
return?"

"Is there a lover who waits—at sea or ashore?"

"No!" A vehement cry.

"But there was a lover, was there not? In the spring,
mayhap."

Delphine gave a little gasp. "How did you know?"

"Your hand does not lie." La Sorcière frowned, remembering the look on Gilles's face. She had not liked
that one! "Was it the man at the fair?"

"No."

The fortune-teller hesitated. How could she be eva-
sive? She pretended to pore over Delphine's palm,
making a great show of tracing the lines that ran from
fingers to wrist; then she sighed heavily. "There will be a
child," she said at last.

Delphine's face went white. A child! *Ah Dieu!* What a
fool she'd been! There was much she did not know about
being a woman, but she remembered many a whore
counting out a nine-month on her fingers and heaping
curses on one or another of the crew. It was just that the
night with André had been like a dream; it had nothing to
do with the reality of children. She buried her face in her
hands, yearning for her father, for Gunner, for someone
to trust. But *Olympie* would not return for at least a
month, and if it was true—that she carried a child, a seed
that had been planted more than two months ago—she
could not wait so long.

La Sorcière put a sympathetic hand on Delphine's
shoulder, waiting for the tears. Instead the young woman
raised her head and smiled, a brittle smile, a smile of
determination. The fortune-teller sighed. She did not

need palm reading or a magic crystal to know that
innocence had just flown out the window.

"*Merci*," said Delphine, rising to her feet and wrapping
her shawl around her. "Thank you for your kindness, old
woman." She hurried from the cottage and made her
way down the cobbled street in the direction of Gilles's
house, all the while rehearsing what she would say to
him: she could not live without him, she yearned for him
with a passion that would not be satisfied until she was his
wife. She might even manage to say all that without
choking on the words. *Ah Dieu!* she thought suddenly,
fighting back her tears. *Gosse* would never have lied! She
turned her tortured eyes to the dark sky.

"The list grows long, André," she whispered, her voice
sharp and bitter. "The list grows long!"

They married as soon as possible, Delphine's impatience matched by Gilles's, though for vastly different
reasons. They supped in the garden in the last pale glow
of twilight; then the housekeeper, a thin old woman with
a kindly face, led Delphine to her bedchamber. Because
the night was warm, the straight bedhangings had been
folded back to reveal a mound of soft pillows and a fluffy
coverlet on a bed so enormous that Delphine could
scarcely imagine that it was meant for her alone. She
trembled suddenly, caught between fear and anticipation, remembering that Gilles would share it sometimes.
It seemed strange to stand and do nothing while the
housekeeper helped her off with the white cambric falling
band and black silk gown that Gilles had bought her for
the wedding. That, at least, was something to be pleased
about: as the wife of a bourgeois merchant she would be
expected to dress in somber colors, and black accented
her high coloring—the rosy complexion, the yellow
hair—as nothing else did.

Clad at last in a soft linen nightdress, her bare feet luxuriating in the fine carpets that dotted the tiled floor, she padded about the room and waited uneasily for Gilles. But why should she feel such trepidation? She enjoyed his kisses, and when he caressed her breasts she had only to close her eyes and concentrate on her tingling flesh—she supposed that any man could arouse her if he touched her so. But—sweet Jesu!—when she looked in his eyes she felt nothing, when she saw him her heart did not cease beating. It was only her body that responded to him, and nothing more. She extinguished the candles that stood on a small table near the bed, leaving only one light on the mantel; she did not want him to see her eyes when he made love to her.

She turned toward the door. He had come quietly into the room and was watching her, an odd expression on his face. His shirt was unbuttoned and pulled carelessly out of his kneelength breeches, and he wore neither shoes nor stockings, though the lower edges of the wide breeches were still cinched with black silk garters. It was as though something had stopped him in the very act of undressing; some thought, some—need had sent him to her chamber in disarray. He stepped back to the door to close it, then turned to face her again. God's blood, she thought, seeing him sway slightly, he has been drinking.

His eyes bored into hers, burning with fever. "What are you?" he said at last, an edge of torment in his voice. "An angel or a devil?"

She frowned, mystified. "I am Delphine. Your wife."

"Take off your gown and let me look at you."

"Gilles—"

"Take it off!"

She bit her lip and did as he asked, unbuttoning her nightgown and sliding it down over her shoulders to fall at her feet. There was no point in arguing with him if he was drunk.

His eyes raked her body—the lush contours of her breasts and hips. "God, I've waited for you!" Then, "Are you a virgin?" he growled.

She bristled, feeling suddenly defensive. "You never asked before—why should you ask now?"

He paced the room, a man bedeviled by thoughts that overwhelmed him. "Because my mind's image plagues me!" he burst out at last.

"Enough to drink yourself into folly?" She stamped her foot in anger, ignoring the scratchings of her own conscience. "My life—my body—were my own before I met you! Why must I tell you aught?"

He stopped pacing and smiled suddenly, the brown eyes filled with cunning. "I'll know, of course," he said softly. "You kiss like a whore and defend your virtue like a holy sister—but I think you are far too artless to counterfeit a maidenhead that is gone. I'll know!"

"Damn your eyes, you poxy whoreson! You shall *not* know! I fell from the rigging years agone. There will be no show of blood tonight! And, sink me, *I* shall not tell you what you want to know!"

"You tormenting bitch!" he said, pulling her suddenly into his arms and grinding his mouth on hers. She could smell the wine on his breath and she pushed him roughly away from her.

"Go to the devil," she said in disgust, wiping his kiss from her mouth.

He turned and, weaving slightly, stalked from her chamber. When she knelt to retrieve her nightgown, she was surprised to discover that her hands were shaking, as though her very body protested against the deception she practiced.

He was gone all the next day. She sought for him in the shop and sent in vain for the housekeeper, inquiring of his whereabouts. She ate a lonely supper, growing more and more frightened and uneasy. Who would have thought he would care whether she was a virgin or not? She was almost tempted to blurt out the whole truth—André, the child, everything—then thought better of it. If he knew, he might cast her out, and she was unwilling to bring a bastard into the world. It was important to go to bed with him as soon as possible—when the child was born she might still be able to persuade him that it was his.

She had almost given up hope when he came to her bedchamber, clad in a long dressing gown and—thanks be to God—sober. It was easy to wear a mask of contrition—so close to the genuine guilt she felt—and she swallowed her anger even in the face of his deliberately cruel words.

"I trust," he said, his pleasant face twisted in a sneer, "I trust you are in better humor tonight."

She smiled in apology, and put a gentle hand on his sleeve. "As God is my witness, Gilles, I never lay with any of *Olympie*'s crew." It was not a lie. It was *not!*

He pulled her possessively into his arms, scarcely comprehending his own feelings for her. She was his—his alone. He had molded her, created her. And the passion, the fire—it was for him to bring to life. Only him! None other, in the future, nor the past! And though of course he knew he was a skillful lover (hadn't that trollop in Dieppe, Lucie, always flattered him and told him so?), he had had fewer unpaid women in his life than he would have wished, and he suffered to think of Delphine comparing him with anyone in her past. Almost roughly he caught his fingers in her short hair and pulled her head back, covering her mouth with his own, forcing her lips apart, tasting, enjoying, *owning* what was his!

She closed her eyes, feeling his lips on hers, trying not to think of her anger at his abandonment, or her own falseness that poisoned this moment. His mouth was pleasant, his roving hands stirred her senses. When he pulled her down to the bed, his fingers tugging impatiently at her nightdress, she was roused to the point where she was able to concentrate on her throbbing body, anticipating the moment when he would enter her and fill her being with joy and contentment. The way André had done.

But he was not André. He had not the skill, the awareness of her feelings, that André had seemed to have. He took her, grunting, thrusting, lost in his own pleasure, sating his own hunger. She almost cried aloud in frustration, feeling her senses cooling, her anticipation fading away to emptiness. It was like rounding a lush tropical isle in *Olympie,* heart pounding with excitement, and finding an ugly, desolate beach.

At last his body stilled and he moved off her, leaning on one elbow and peering closely at her, his eyes still heavy lidded with passion. She turned her head away, fighting back the tears, hoping he would not read the look of shocked disappointment on her face.

Gilles stirred uneasily and frowned, wondering what had happened, what had gone wrong. Where was the fire he had expected to find, the tiger he had hoped to unleash? Had he imagined a passion that was not there? Or misread her response? Afraid to speak, he rose from the bed and, donning his dressing gown and his tattered pride, left her chamber.

Delphine cursed and sat up, filled with remorse. After all his kindness to her—and now she had wounded him grievously. She threw her pillow impatiently at the foot of her bed. What an artless fool she was! She had not yet learned to compose her face into a mask of deception—but life was proving a bitter teacher.

She would learn, by heaven. By André's lying heart, she would learn!

Chapter Nine

"OPEN THE CASEMENT, ANNE-MARIE. I SHALL STIFLE this morning!"

"Yes, Madame Despreaux." The old housekeeper threw wide the window, brushing away the crisp leaves— flame colored, golden—that had collected on the outside sill overnight. She turned to the large bed, waiting patiently for her orders.

Nestled among her pillows, Delphine motioned the old woman away. "Leave me for a little. I would spend a few quiet minutes abed. I shall ring when I wish to get up." She stretched and yawned, inhaling the sweetness of the morning air, tangy with the crisp scents of fall. Thanks be to God she no longer awoke with her stomach queasy; she had found it near agony to sit every morning and watch Gilles eat a hearty breakfast while her insides churned in protest at the mere sight of food.

Well, she would not breakfast with him today, damn him! She closed her eyes and slipped her hand under her nightdress, stroking her breasts and her belly that had begun to round ever so slightly, drawing comfort from the sensitivity of her flesh, responsive even to her own

fingers. It was her comfort—and her weakness. And that
devil Gilles knew it. For the six weeks of their marriage he
had used it against her—always sweet, always charming,
the hornet hidden in the soft bouquet. ("Delphine, *ma
chère,* if you wish me to come to your bed tonight, you
had best learn to descend the stairs with grace. Not like a
stomping bull! Try it again!" Or, "Delphine, I shall not kiss
you, nor touch you, until you can manage to balance the
household accounts. I do not wish to be cruel, my sweet,
but—") And she would exhaust herself trying to please
him, eager, hopeful that this time—this time, sweet
Mother of God!—when he came to her bed she would
feel more for him than the momentary excitement of his
caresses. She was always surprised by her ultimate
disappointment, making excuses to herself (she was tired,
he was concerned about his trade) that the next time
would be better. She tried to hide her discontent from
him, but an undercurrent of anger nagged at her—anger
that he should so callously use her appetites against her,
anger at his clumsiness as a lover.

And yesterday. Damn the man! He had decided she
should learn to embroider, as all gentlewomen did.
Anne-Marie had shown her how, making the first few
stitches in the work before handing the piece to Delphine.
She had struggled awkwardly with yarn and needle for
the better part of an hour, cursing under her breath,
pausing to suck at a bloody fingertip each time her hand
slipped and the needle pricked her skin. And then Gilles
had bent close, and whispered in her ear, promising a
night of delights if she could finish the piece before
bedtime. She had worked diligently, her shoulders aching
from bending over the needlework, her eyes growing
puffy and tired from the hours of concentration. She
barely stopped to eat supper; at last, weary, stiff fingered

but proud, she had presented the finished work to him and gone to her bedchamber to await him. And he had not come. Damn his eyes, he had not come!

"Will you lie abed when there is work to be done, my lovely?" Delphine's eyes flew open to see Gilles smiling above her. "Or are you dreaming of another lover?" he went on, his words light and carefree. Did she only imagine an edge of steel in his voice?

"Get out of my room, you scurvy whoreson!" she cursed, sitting up in bed and fiercely tucking the coverlet around her. "You are late by several hours!" The golden eyes flashed with anger.

He eyed her coldly, his face twisted in contempt. "I wish you could hear yourself when you swear like an old sea dog. It scarce becomes you—and puts the lie to Delphine the lady, for all your pretty new ways." She squirmed uncomfortably, feeling chastened, ashamed of her own foul tongue. "As for last night," he continued, his voice smooth as honey, "your work was so clumsy I took the scissors and snipped out half the stitches. I did it for your own good, *ma chère*," he said, before she could voice a protest. "When you are a perfect gentlewoman in every way, you will be proud to walk in the streets and know that all Dieppe is filled with envy. 'Look,' they will say, 'there is Monsieur Despreaux's exquisite wife.'"

She glared at him sulkily, the ghost of Gosse strangely disquieted, despite his flattering words. "Will they not say 'There is the exquisite Delphine?'"

His mouth curled in imitation of a smile. "Delphine without Despreaux would still be a coarse hoyden, my love."

She flinched, knowing it was so, her heart filled with remorse for her ugliness this morning.

"And now," he said, "I want you to buy a new lace

falling band for your black silk gown. The mercer's shop
down the lane has many beautiful collars and cuffs from
Italy."

"I scarce need new lace," she protested. "I am quite
content with what I have."

"My beautiful wife must have the finest goods that I
can afford. Now," he said, as she smiled in pleasure, "do
you not regret your sorry greeting?"

"Dear Gilles, I beg your indulgence for my rough ways.
I promise you I shall take up my needle again today, and
make you proud of me."

He nodded his approval and bent down to kiss her,
then put his hand firmly upon her breast.

"Gilles—?" It was a question—filled with hope, anticipation; the expectant smile on her face faded as he
patted her on the head and left her bedchamber. She felt
a momentary pang, then cursed herself under her breath.
Ah Dieu, she thought, what an ungrateful wretch she
was! Save for his disappointing performance as a lover
(and she was not entirely sure it was *his* fault), he was a
good husband to her, indulging her fancies with sweet
gifts, setting her on the path to self-improvement that she
never could have found alone. She had no right to feel
the flicker of uneasiness she sometimes felt at things he
said or did; it was simply the newness of her being a wife
that created difficulties between them. She rang for
Anne-Marie, resolving to herself to make more of an
effort to please Gilles.

With the housekeeper's help, she put on her everyday
gown of gray wool, a simple two-piece dress with a snug
square-necked bodice, cut somewhat low, that ended at
the waist in braid-edged lappets. The gray skirt was
called—after the fashion of the time—*la friponne,* the
hussy. Beneath *la friponne* was an underskirt—*la secret*
—of a paler gray, and beneath *la secret* was a soft lawn

petticoat that matched the chemise worn under her bodice. Delphine turned and eyed her body in the large Venetian mirror, assessing the still-narrow waist. Soon enough she would have to begin wearing *la modeste*, the sleeveless redingote of black wool that would fit over her gray gown and help to disguise her enlarging body. But today she looped up a corner of *la friponne* in the manner of the bourgeoise women so *la secret* would show as well. Anne-Marie tied the white linen falling band about her neck like a high collar, modestly covering the patch of bare flesh. For a more festive occasion she would wear a low lace falling band on the same bodice, baring the first swell of her bosom, or an old-fashioned stiff ruff about her neck. She buttoned on linen cuffs at her wrists, then sat at her vanity table to don gray silk stockings and serviceable leather shoes. Her hair, which she had allowed to grow, now hung almost to her shoulders, though she had had to trim it often to even out the jagged edges. She pinned it quickly with a few hairpins and put on a little cap. If she went out-of-doors she would add a loose hood or a tall stiff hat with a silver buckle. Her hat, her costume, would identify her at once as the wife of a merchant. She briefly contemplated the wispy curls about her face, wondering if she should bother to heat the curling iron, then thought better of it. Her curls would hold for a few more days.

"What is to be done today, Anne-Marie?" she asked, taking the ring of keys from the housekeeper.

"Perhaps you would like to see to the winter stores, madame. September is nearly over, and the harvest as well. If you wish to lay in more fruits or vegetables, it must be done soon, before the farmers have sold all their produce."

Delphine frowned. "You must guide me, Anne-Marie. I know well enough how to lay in stores for a hungry ship's crew, who will eat anything, so long as there is enough of it. But a household of a dozen or so—" She paused, a questioning look in her amber eyes. "How many are we, exactly?"

Anne-Marie counted them out on her fingers. "Monsieur and madame, of course. The cook and the four servants. The coachman and the stableboy—"

"And the six apprentices in the shop. Oh! And you yourself. Two—seven—nine—sixteen in all. Think you we have enough to feed them for the winter, with a little extra for guests? Monsieur Despreaux has indicated he wishes to entertain his friends this season."

"And small wonder!" exclaimed Anne-Marie. "Now that he has a charming wife to show to all his friends!"

"May *le bon Dieu* bless your loyalty. But the charming wife will soon enough have a fat belly, and he will perhaps not wish to show me off then!"

Anne-Marie beamed. "Madame!"

"Hush! Not a word! I shall tell monsieur in my own time. Now—to the kitchen!"

They descended the steps to the large room at the rear of the house, passing through an airy chamber where one of the servant girls was setting up a trestle table and spreading out a tablecloth, neatly embossed with its square folds. While the weather remained warm, Delphine and Gilles took their meals here, but when the days grew cold the large kitchen, with its roaring fireplace, would become the focal point for meals and socializing and domestic small work.

The furniture in the kitchen was strong and serviceable, good Norman oak trimmed with brass fittings. There were several cupboards with diamond shapes carved into their front panels—the very latest style in the provinces; an upholsterer could scarcely furnish his home with old-fashioned castoffs. The table was massive,

with heavy turned legs, and the chairs were upholstered
in plum-colored velvet. Above the cupboards were wall
shelves with thin lath strips that held back the pewter
plates, copper mugs, and porcelain jugs displayed
proudly for all the world to admire. There were several
knife boxes on a small cabinet, and a large *panetière,* a
decorative bread box, that held a week's supply of that
most staple item in the French diet.

The cook, busy peeling turnips at the table, bobbed
politely to Delphine before setting out a large chunk of
crisp bread and a bowl of bacon drippings. While
Anne-Marie poured beer into a mug and mixed it with
sweet fresh milk ("All the better for you now, madame!"
she said with a knowing smirk), Delphine spread pieces of
the bread with the drippings, savoring the pungent
smokiness of the bacon, a rare treat for her until now.
There was no larder aboard ship to keep the oils and fats
from turning rancid, and the salt pork and lard always
tainted the soups and stews, no matter how much the
ship's cook masked the flavor with spices. But here, in
the earthen room carved out in the cool basement, there
was sweet butter and lard, olive oil and walnutseed oil.
The suet and sides of bacon, wrapped in gauze and
nestled in the tubs of dry salt (the tangible sign of a man's
wealth), would give a flavor of meat on those days when
fresh beef or pork was scarce; the oils would enrich the
food when meat was forbidden by the Church for this or
that solemn occasion.

Delphine spent the morning with Anne-Marie, counting the sacks of corn and flour in the granary, the dried
peas and beans and apricots, the barrels of apples. She
inspected the meats—pickled, smoked, salted, dried—
that hung in the cool cellar. She sniffed the herbs that
were freshly picked from the kitchen garden, nodding in
approval as the servant girls tied bunches of the fragrant

greens together and hung them from the ceiling beams to dry. There were barrels of cider and perry, several large hogsheads of wine brought from Bordeaux (the drink the English called *clairet),* and a bottle of aqua vitae, those distilled spirits that warmed the belly and went to the head. *Dieu!* she thought, with a sudden ache in her heart, remembering how she had drunk too much aqua vitae the night Copain died. And André—so tender, so gentle as she wept in his arms. She swayed slightly, feeling the old longing, the old pain.

"Madame, are you not well?"

"Be at peace, Anne-Marie. I am overtaken with weariness, nothing more. I shall sit in the garden for a spell. Finish with the inventory. If there is aught we need more, I shall speak to monsieur for the necessary coins." She made her way to the little garden, and finding a stone bench under a tree she sat down amid the glory of autumn. But her staring eyes didn't see the vibrant reds and oranges of the leaves, only the blue sky beyond. *His* eyes were bluer than that sky—clear and beautiful. The cloudless sky wavered as she gazed, her eyes misted with tears, burning and bitter.

Damn you, André, she thought, will I never be free of you?

"Madame, there is a gentleman here who says he was sent by an old pilot in the harbor."

Delphine wiped away her tears and turned to see Maurice Fresnel.

"Father!" She jumped up, throwing herself into his arms.

"Sink me, Delphine, but had not old One-eye told me you were here, I would have passed you by on the street without recognizing you!"

"And have I changed so much?"

"Only for the better! But they say that you are married!

Is it so?" She nodded. "But why?" he asked. "What possessed you?"

She hesitated. André, the child. No. Let it be her own secret grief. "It was time," she said simply.

"Are you happy?"

"I am—content," she said. "Gilles is a good husband." She took him by the hand and led him back to the bench. "But tell me all of the voyage!"

His eyes crinkling with delight to see her so well and robust, he spun out the tale of the last three-and-a-half months. They had had a successful voyage, with a comfortable profit. Monsieur Ramy had been pleased and had immediately commissioned a voyage to New France and from there to the islands of Guadeloupe and Martinique. *Olympie* needed repairs, but as soon as the work was done, and they could take on new supplies and goods for bartering, they would be off again. Fresnel was sorry to find Delphine married—though he hastened to assure her it was a selfish impulse—for *Olympie* would not return until April or May, God willing, and he was loath to be parted from her for so many months.

They had three weeks together. Delphine spent few hours at the *quai* or aboard ship; Gilles did not like her to share the company of rough seamen. Gunner and Michel came once or twice to the house, but they were uneasy at the changes in her, and sat uncomfortably like strangers while she offered them wine and tried to elicit news of the voyage and their lives. Michel downed his wine in silence, his dark eyes filled with heartbreak and pain; he seemed suddenly so young, so far removed from her life.

Fresnel dined several times with her and Gilles, enjoying the elegance of their menus, the obvious comfort of his daughter's new life. He was a simple man, an uncomplicated man, little given to judging human behavior. He took no measure of Gilles; it was Delphine who concerned him, Delphine and her feelings for her husband.

But he was not a fool, and an uneasy undercurrent tugged at him. "Are you happy, Delphine?" he asked at last, on the day he was to embark for America, remembering that she had never answered the question directly.

"Sink me!" she exploded, in a fury that he should probe her soul, batter at her defenses. "What makes you think I would have been happier aboard that dungheap of a ship?"

The words cut him deeply and they parted in anger, each locked into injured pride. It was not until *Olympie* was well out into the harbor, her sails puffed by the freshening breeze, that Delphine repented her cruel tongue. She climbed the chalk cliffs, seeing the last of *Olympie's* brave banners sink over the horizon, and—a futile gesture—waved a loving farewell.

By November she had begun to thicken noticeably, though not so much that Gilles would be suspicious and begin to count the months. She laced her underbodices (worn more and more now as the weather turned cool) as tightly as she dared, and thanked *le bon Dieu* that she seemed to be carrying a small child; it would be easier to pretend a premature birth when the time came. As for Gilles, he was delighted at the prospect of a child in the spring, a new toy of his own creating, another "possession" of which he could boast. In truth, Delphine had begun to wonder—her heart filled with dismay—if that was all she meant to him. She was a doll, a puppet he dressed and guided and manipulated, a pretty little thing he used to impress his friends and dazzle his clients. She did not like his friends—Monsieur Jacques Charretier, the shifty-eyed *bijoutier* who dealt in rare stones; Monsieur and Madame Vivoin, the draper and his fat wife;

Monsieur Ardoise, the goldsmith, gray faced and old, whose pompous wife claimed ancestors going back to Charles the Fair—but she had learned to hide her dislike and smile and entertain them as Gilles insisted she do. She liked his customers even less, rich merchants and leering aristocrats who were rude and careless, their shameless eyes stripping the clothes from her body, their manners and gestures and words suggestive and lascivious. She had become quite clever in her artfulness, charming them while her soul ached to take a rapier to their guts, to pound them into the ground until they could no longer smile obscenely at her.

It was only with Gilles that she found it burdensome to pretend, hiding her disappointment in his lovemaking with increasing difficulty. Sometimes (if she concentrated hard enough), she could forget for a while that it was Gilles in the bed with her, forget his thoughtlessness, his clumsiness, could begin to feel a certain pleasure in the act of love. The pleasure was small, but it was enough to ease the almost physical ache she felt, the need to be close to someone and to smother the loneliness that sometimes threatened to engulf her. She needed to still the dread deep within her that he had no feeling for her beyond his lust and that sense of ownership that puffed him with overbearing pride. Not that she loved him, but she had hoped that together they could fashion a life of caring and concern.

But as he pleased her less and less in bed, her anger and disappointment became more obvious, in spite of her attempts to dissemble, and Gilles's frustration and humiliation grew apace. He began to demand more and more civilized behavior from her during the day, scarcely hiding his impatience and annoyance at her slightest lapse, as though she were expected to compensate him for the torments of the bedchamber.

By the beginning of December she was forced to wear her loose redingote and set the waistband of her skirt higher up above her expanding girth, although (thanks be to God!) she scarcely appeared to be six months with child. It was the season of Advent, that period before the birth of the Christ Child that was observed as another Lent, with prayers and penance and abstinence. There were countless meals without meat (and joy for the fishmongers), and long hours spent kneeling on the cold stones of the church, while she prayed to be forgiven her deception and, tears streaming down her cheeks, prayed to be free of her agonizing memories of André. His face filled with piety, Gilles announced that, to do honor to *le bon Dieu*, he would not come to her bed until after Advent. But the flicker in his eyes when she passed him—ponderous and heavy-footed with her increasing size—made her wonder if he was merely repelled by her shape, so different now from the perfect woman he wished her to be.

Christmas came at last, with eating and drinking and merriment. The kitchen hummed with preparations for a festive party, and a suckling pig was set to roasting over the open fire. Anne-Marie brushed out Delphine's black silk gown and starched her best lace falling band, dressing her mistress with care long before the guests should arrive. There was a soft knock on the door and Gilles entered. Anne-Marie curtsied and left them alone.

"Let me see how you look," he said, motioning for her to stand up and turn slowly before him. He frowned and tugged at the open front of her sleeveless redingote—set neatly under the falling band—so the edges more nearly came together and hid the rounded swell of her belly. He patted the curls that framed her face, his eyes cold and appraising. "Have you no other cap?" he said at last.

"Of course," she stammered. "But—this is the cap—

you bought for me at the fair—I thought—" She smiled hesitantly at him, and put her hand on his arm. "Gilles— Advent is over—"

"If you have a finer cap, wear it," he said coldly. "Save your foolish sentiment for a time when guests are not expected. And wear these." He held out a gold chain with a large pearl teardrop on the end of it, and pearl earrings. "I would my friends see you at your best. Kindly remember your manners at table—you have become careless of late."

"I wonder you do not stuff me and put me into your shop like one of your chairs," she growled.

His lip curled in disgust. "You were little more than a rough peasant when I married you, *ma chère*. You might show a little gratitude for the changes I wrought, changes that you yourself longed for!" He turned on his heel and left her room.

Delphine sighed and sat at her vanity, pulling the cap from her head. She stared at her reflection in the mirror, her amber eyes filled with pain. It cannot be so, she thought, that I am so little to him! She had worn the cap thinking he would be pleased, that she might stir at least a spark of warmth when he remembered the agreeableness of their first meeting. Perhaps if they could behave as friends, if he could treat her as more than his possession, his chattel, she might find it easier to respond to him in bed.

It suddenly seemed important to discover whether his feelings were moved by Delphine the woman, or merely by Delphine as show. Deliberately she placed the cap back on her head, put on the earrings, and slipped the pearl drop around her neck, then went downstairs to greet her guests. She ushered them into the warm kitchen, now festively garlanded with evergreens, and savory with the scents of roasting meat and pastries. She murmured her thanks at the gifts they had brought, cloves and cinnamon and ground almonds, and indicated where each guest was to sit, carefully ignoring the way Gilles's eyes had narrowed in anger at the sight of her cap.

As she made her way to her own chair at the foot of the table, she allowed herself to lapse—ever so slightly—into the rolling gait that had been her habit before she met Gilles. Madame Ardoise stared in surprise at her gracelessness, then dismissed it as a consequence of her condition. Madame Vivoin, the draper's wife, swathed in yards of brocade that only accented her bulk, jumped up from her chair to offer Delphine her arm.

"May I help you, Madame Despreaux?"

Delphine laughed. "God's blood, why? Do I look like a pisspoor cripple?"

Madame Vivoin blanched and sat down heavily. Across the table from Delphine, Gilles smiled weakly and motioned for the servants to begin serving the meal. While the wine was poured and the soup ladled out, the conversation turned to the peasant uprisings that had taken place in Lower Normandy and Rouen for months now. The homes of the tax collectors had been attacked in protest at the new taxes on salt and wine and dyed cloth (and here Monsieur Vivoin the draper crossed himself), and gangs of peasants, calling themselves the Va-nu-Pieds—Go-barefoots—had roamed the countryside looting and sacking. The king had been forced to send in troops to quell the disturbances, and while the insurrection had not reached to Dieppe and the northern coast, there had been a steady stream of news for weeks that told of the severity and cruelty with which the soldiery had put down the rioting, devastating French towns as though they were enemy lands. And now all of

Normandy was waiting for the king's justice that would fall on all the province, even those towns and villages that were blameless.

Vivoin wrung his hands in dismay. "If the taxes on cloth are reintroduced, they will be made retroactive, God preserve us! I scarce know how I shall survive!" The assembled guests were silent, sympathetic to his distress. In the sudden stillness Delphine slurped her soup noisily. A small muscle worked in Gilles's jaw.

Charretier cleared his throat. "Will your trade not suffer as well, Despreaux? If Vivoin must raise his prices on fabric, will you not be forced to do the same?"

Gilles opened his mouth to reply, but Delphine's throaty laugh cut him off. "You must have no fear, Monsieur Charretier. If monsieur my husband will but tell me how I am to dress, and what to do and say, I shall play the perfect puppet for him and beg from door to door." Madame Ardoise's nervous giggle was cut short as Gilles jumped to his feet, raising his wine goblet and proposing —through clenched teeth—a toast to the season and the Christ Child.

Before the evening mercifully ended, Delphine had spilled her wine, pinched Monsieur Ardoise on the cheek so he blushed and looked shamefaced toward his wife, and suggested that Madame Vivoin's brocaded dress reminded her of a tapestry tablecloth she had seen once in the house of one of Gilles's customers. But as their guests bid them good-night, venturing forth into the frosty evening with torches to light their way, it was clear that they had forgiven Delphine her behavior, content to view her lapses as attributable to her condition, the inherent weakness of the female, or a trifle too much wine, perhaps. Only Gilles's face, hard as granite, was unforgiving, confirming Delphine's worst fears. He took no pleasure in her; she was of no value to him save when he could control her perfectly. Humiliated, she fled to her room.

She was surprised when he came to her room some time later. He dismissed Anne-Marie with an impatient jerk of his head and stared at Delphine with a look of such intensity that she felt stripped of her nightdress and caught her breath, wondering if he would strike her or rape her. Wordlessly he crossed to where she stood in the middle of her bedchamber and tugged at the drawstring of her nightgown, pulling it down over her shoulders, past her waist and hips, until it lay in a jumble at her feet. He took her roughly in his arms and pressed his mouth to hers, while his hands traveled over her body and touched her in places he had never explored before until she gasped in surprise and moved impatiently in his arms, hungry for him as she had never been, her senses roused to a fever pitch.

"Nom de Dieu," he growled suddenly, pushing her away. "I cannot—while my brain reels with thoughts of your behavior tonight—"

She stared in dismay, her body still trembling in anticipation. "But—Gilles—no one noticed, no one cared—"

"I did!" He swung about and made for the door.

She clutched frantically at his arm. "Gilles—please— you cannot leave me like this—"

He shook her off, and now she saw the cruelty in his eyes. *Ah Dieu!* Had it always been there, and she too blind to see it? He had planned this scene, to punish her for disobeying him, and now he was reveling in her weakness, glorying in her agony, her soul stripped as bare as her body. "Mayhap, my sweet," he said, his eyes like knives, "you will remember your lessons the next time!" Then he was gone.

"Damn you!" she shrieked. She snatched up her comb and hurled it at the closed door, then sank to the floor in a quivering heap, shaking in fury and anguish and frustrated passion. She pulled her nightdress about her shoulders, rocking back and forth while she stared at her large bed, so cold, so lonely now. What an accursed thing it was to be a woman, to be a slave to one's body.

André.

He had awakened her senses, had opened a door that led only to pain and grief. She would never forget him. She would curse him every day of her life.

Chapter Ten

THE NEW YEAR DAWNED COLD, AS COLD AS GILLES'S frosty glances. He went about the house in an icy silence, waiting for the apology that usually followed Delphine's errant behavior, her careless lapses. But for the first time she felt no remorse, no wish to humble herself before him. True, she had humiliated him in front of their guests, but she had not wished to hurt him, only to reassure herself that he cared for her whatever her behavior. *He* had humiliated *her* in her bedchamber—and there had been nothing but malice in it. She could not forgive him for that.

She began to retreat more and more to her books, finding solace in words, in ideas, feeling her mind blossoming with the tender tutelage of great poets and philosophers. Sometimes she stared for hours at the face in her mirror, seeing the haunted eyes, flickers of pain in their depths, desperation dancing in the amber lights. She began to be filled with a strange conceit, a fanciful vision that would not vanish.

Once, years before, while *Olympie* lay dry-docked in Quebec for extensive repairs, Michel had captured a wolf cub that he kept in a little cage on deck. Every day Gosse had knelt beside the poor creature, crooning softly to it, feeling the tears well up to see it race frantically about its prison—trapped, innocent, helpless. Snarling in desperation at the hopelessness of its plight, its eyes had been filled with the pain she saw now in her own eyes. She had meant to release it in the dead of night before *Olympie* sailed, but the poor animal had died of despair before she could let it go.

Ah Dieu! she thought. Shall I die in my cage ere someone comes to release me?

In January, Séguier, the king's chancellor, had entered Rouen under a special commission from Louis to exercise extraordinary civil and military powers. The leaders of the *Va-nu-Pieds* were hunted down and executed, and all taxes under dispute were reintroduced. As Monsieur Vivoin had feared, the tax on dyed cloth was backdated to June of the year before, when the protests had first arisen. The citizens—which meant largely the bourgeoisie, since the peasants were penniless and the nobles, being of the aristocracy, were exempt from taxes—were expected to pay an indemnity to the crown, as well as damages to the tax collectors and others who had lost their worldly goods and property during the uprisings.

Gilles had had to raise his prices, and still he complained of the cost of doing business. He insisted that Delphine spend long and wearisome hours in the shop, in the hope that—should a customer enter—her charm, the sweet helplessness of her condition, would make it easier to sell more furniture. And in spite of her protests, he took her with him when he visited the châteaux and fine town houses of the nobility. She had done it in the past, when they were first married, until one disastrous afternoon when she had had to fight off a lecherous *duc*

in his garden while Gilles measured the *duc*'s salon for
new chairs. But now, urged on by Gilles's dire predictions
of economic ruin, she agreed to go.

It snowed late in February, and then the icy rains came
to wash away the snow and leave the cobbles slick and
treacherous. Heavy with her belly's burden, Delphine
made her way carefully through the frozen garden to sit
huddled before the open fire-pit of the workshop, watching the young apprentices—fingers stiff with cold—strip
away old fabric from chairs and settees, cut the new
fabric, tack and stretch and glue it, while their thin bodies
shivered from the cold. When she knew that Gilles would
be away, she had Anne-Marie send down a servant with
an extra kettle of hot soup for the poor lads, cautioning
them to keep it a secret. Though the larder was still
well-stocked with winter stores, Gilles had begun to
begrudge every mouthful that the boys ate.

When I was shapely and pretty and obedient, she
thought sadly late one afternoon, watching Gilles berate
an apprentice for wasting a length of fringe, he valued
me; now he values money alone. She cast her eyes about
the workshop. Despite Gilles's complaints about the
trade, the place seemed as busy and prosperous as ever.
She frowned. What was the boy Pierre doing? She had
watched idly as he stripped a large and worn piece of
brocade from the settee that Madame de la Blache had
sent in to be stuffed and recovered. Stepping outside into
the raw afternoon, Pierre had shaken the dust from the
brocade and returned to the shop to place the fabric,
worn side down, on his worktable, smoothing it with his
hands and plucking small tufts of stuffing from its surface.
Because it was a damask, the pattern was reversible;
Delphine was struck by the vividness of the colors on the
inside compared to the soiled and faded surface that
Madame de la Blache had had to look at for years. Taking

up a template, a kind of thin metal pattern that hung on the wall next to his table, Pierre traced around the edges, following the outline of the template with a sharp-edged knife until he had cut the brocade into patterned pieces for four small chairs. Putting aside the pieces, and sweeping his worktable free of the scraps, he put up a chair, already padded and awaiting its fabric, and began carefully to tack the damask at the four corners of the seat, stretching and smoothing as he worked.

Delphine frowned and stood up. "A moment, Gilles, if you please."

"What is it?" The hard voice was filled with annoyance.

"The chair—Pierre—is that not Monsieur le Comte de Mercier's chair?"

"Of course. Are you blind? You saw it yourself when we were at his château. You remarked on the daintiness of the piece. Has your memory vanished along with your lissome figure?"

Her eyes flashed, but she bit back the angry retort. "My memory has not suffered a whit," she said, drawing herself up coldly. "I distinctly remember that Monsieur de Mercier asked for new fabric!"

Gilles shrugged. "If the damask is serviceable, why not use it? In these hard times—"

"And Monsieur de Mercier *paid* for new fabric!"

A deadly silence, while the apprentices dropped their work and waited, eyes and mouths like round O's, to see what the master would do next. "Go to your room," he said at last, his quiet voice like cold steel. "We shall discuss it later."

She stamped her foot. "You cannot steal from the man!"

"You shall not presume to tell me how to run my affairs," he growled. "Go to your room!"

"Damn you for a grave-robbing whoreson," she hissed through clenched teeth. "I shall go to Monsieur de Mercier!" She held her ground as Gilles, his eyes blazing in fury, snatched up a stick from the basket of kindling. "Will you beat me, you coward?" she challenged. "I can scarcely run from you in this condition. Here!" She thrust out her belly in his direction. "My womb! My child! I piss on your rage! Here! Strike me here!"

A timid hand tugged at her sleeve. She looked down to see the smallest apprentice, whose adoring eyes followed her about the shop each day, gazing at her in dread and terror. "Please, madame," he whispered. "Please go. Do not fret yourself. Pierre will do a fine job—and Monsieur de Mercier will be happy."

Ah Dieu, she thought suddenly, feeling the anger drain from her. She looked about the room at the frightened faces. Gilles would spend his rage on these poor lads. She sighed in resignation. "I beg your forgiveness, Gilles," she said. "It was none of my concern. You must do as you see fit. I am feeling poorly of late—mayhap it is the cause of my intemperate tongue. I shall take supper in my room alone, and pray for guidance from *le bon Dieu,* that he may curb my unseemly temper." She fled to her room, praying that she had placated Gilles enough so that he would not make the boys suffer.

She tossed and turned in her bed that night, unable to sleep, feeling the discomfort of her body as she had not before. And perhaps she had been unfair to Gilles. He was concerned about the cost of new fabric, the additional taxes. Perhaps he felt the need to save a few crowns and livres now and again. And then, Monsieur de Mercier had been in a hurry to have the chairs recovered; perhaps there had been no time to order new goods. Yes. She had been unfair to Gilles.

She slept fitfully, trying not to remember other times,

other instances, that drifted in and out of her consciousness, blended into her dreams. Watching the boys gluing (instead of replacing) a chair frame that had been cracked during the upholstering, or seeing a strip of odd fabric used on the inner edge of bed curtains when Gilles had not bought quite enough yardage to do the job properly. Sitting up suddenly in bed, she came to a decision. She would speak to him in the morning. She would tell him that it distressed her to think he felt it necessary to cut corners, that she knew he did not wish to be less than scrupulous with his customers. But times were hard—she understood that. And so she would do without a new pair of shoes, or scrimp a little more with her household budget, that he might be fair to his customers and still turn an honest profit.

Pleased with herself—surely she could do this small service for Gilles as a dutiful wife, if not a loving one—she lay down again and slept the tranquil sleep of the innocent.

She slept late and awoke still feeling exhausted. Anne-Marie said that Monsieur Despreaux had breakfasted long since, and was in his bedchamber writing his accounts. He eyed her coldly, but listened in patient silence while she explained earnestly how she intended to help him so he should not be forced to—*cheat* sounded too critical; she smiled in understanding and used the word *deceive* instead.

He stood up at his desk and roared with laughter. "What a simple child you are! A pox on them all! What care I if they are deceived?"

She took a step back, shocked at his callous words. "Do you cheat them all the time? Without remorse?"

He sneered. "Why not? The swine—thinking themselves better than I because they have titles! And I must bow and 'Yes, monsieur' and 'No, monsieur'! I shall be rich enough to buy a title some day, and I shall have them licking my boots." He crossed to the mantel and picked up his pipe, taking from a shelf a small silver box filled with tobacco. It was a handsome box, elaborately embossed and ornamented, and strangely familiar.

"Mon Dieu!" gasped Delphine. "I saw that box in the château of Monsieur le Vicomte! Last month, when you hung the draperies in his bedchamber." She looked at him in horror. "Gilles," she whispered, "you did not steal it?"

His eyes narrowed, wondering if he should lie, then he shrugged. "Of course I did. He will not miss it. And do not look so distressed, my innocent sweet. I took it while you were dimpling prettily at the old fool."

She crossed herself hurriedly. "God forgive me."

"Spare me your sanctimony. If I am branded for a thief, you will be too."

She backed away, shaking her head in disbelief. "No—no—no—"

"Yes!" he spat. "Look!" He opened a cabinet and pulled out handfuls of small items—boxes, rings, bibelots —and tossed them on the desk before her. *"This* and *this* and *this*—each time you smiled at a fat monsieur or let him hold your hand! And many more valuables besides! Charretier the jeweler is very good at selling to people who ask no questions."

She was near tears. *"Ah Dieu!* You villain."

"Pah! You ate the food I put on the table, you wore the clothes, the pearl drops at your ears and bosom. You wear them even now!"

"Take them!" she cried, pulling the jewels from her. "They burn my flesh!" She fled his room, his house, stopping only long enough to snatch up a cloak before escaping into the honest February day. She wandered the streets for hours, drifted down to the harbor, paced the long stone *quai*. All that time with Gilles, and she had never known, never guessed. Foolish, simple, trusting Gosse! Do not trust too much, her father had said. Her father! *Ah Dieu!* He would be home again in two months or so. She hurried along the shore, her steps purposeful now. If the cottage had not been damaged in the winter storms, she could stay there until April and her father's return. She could wait until May if need be. She had only five sols in her pocket, but there might be a few supplies left in the cottage from her father's last visit in September. And then, when the child was born, she would have milk to feed it, as long as her breasts were full. She herself could manage with little food.

Thanks be to God the cottage was intact. The pitch-pine caulking (for Fresnel had built his cottage like a ship) was dry and cracked in some places, and the bitter wind blew through the spaces, but the building was sound and she could patch the holes with reeds and mud. The grasses on the floor were tinder-dry and crunched under her feet, but they too could be replaced. There were a few pieces of hardtack and some dried beans and a goodly chunk of salt pork in the box hidden under the straw-palleted bunk where she had slept; more fortunate still was the finding of a small barrel of apples, barely rotted, cached in a corner behind her father's rolled-up hammock. Though the physicians still understood little of the disease, every seaman knew that only fresh vegetables and fruits could stave off scurvy, even ashore. If she could not find a few turnips still in the ground, or a green weed or moist root that had not withered over the winter, she would find her teeth beginning to loosen in her head and sores forming on her body. But with the apples, she need have no fear of scurvy.

She picked up her broom and began to sweep the dry rushes into a large pile in the center of the floor, then stopped and sat down heavily on the single wooden bench. *Dieu,* but she was tired today! She shivered. It was cold. Better to forage for driftwood and start a fire in the open fire-pit. There would be time when she was warm to go about replacing the reeds and fetching a bucket of water for her supper. She searched for a tallow candle and the tinderbox, finding them hidden behind a clay mug on the shelf. The afternoon shadows were lengthening; she left the candle and tinderbox conveniently on the small table, in case she should return after twilight.

The driftwood was plentiful, and though she found herself waddling slowly along the beach—her bulk and the unfamiliarity of walking on shifting sand impeding her progress—she soon had a large armload of wood. She struggled up to the cottage and staggered in with her burden, dropping the pieces of wood noisily to the floor at the sight of Gilles sitting on the bunk and obviously waiting for her.

"Will you come to your senses and return home?"

"This is my home."

"Don't be a fool, my sweet. Are you so naive that you don't think that every man of trade has his own ways of managing? Has your father never mended a broken barrel on the voyage and told his underwriters that their cargo was untouched by seawater? Has he never bought a crate of hardtack and found that the baker had short-weighted the flour, then kept silent because the baker gave him better credit terms than anyone else? Every man cheats!"

"Not every man steals!"

"No. Only if he is clever enough to do so. Now come home."

She stamped her foot. "I shall not!"

He sighed. "I shall not leave this cottage until you are with me."

"Curse your liver," she spat, pulling her cloak more tightly about her shoulders. "Then you shall wait until hell gives up its dead!" And turning, she stormed out of the cottage and down to the beach. The wind blew with a fierceness that cut through her, and the waves crashing onto the shore sent up a fine mist that dampened her skirt hems. God's blood, but she could not stay in the open like this! At some distance from the cottage, she saw a large boulder near the sea's edge, and circled it slowly until she had found its lee side, where she might have some protection from the whistling wind. Sitting down in its shelter, her back against the rock, her cloak wrapped about her shivering body, she leaned back and closed her eyes. The cold made her so sleepy—

It was dark when she awoke. Her hands and feet were numb, and her throat felt raw. I shall take a fever, she thought, if I do not go indoors soon. Surely Gilles would have gone home by now, persuaded of her determination to stay. And if not? There was a seaside inn, half a league distant, where she could at least get a warm meal and a few hours' respite from the cold. It would take nearly all of her money, but in the morning she could return to Gilles's house and collect her possessions. If she were forced to it, she might sell her books and even her finely wrought sea knife. She stood up clumsily, feeling the stiffness in her bones, the dull ache that had begun in the small of her back. She rubbed her fingers briskly together to start the blood flowing again, then stepped out from the shelter of the rock.

She blinked in surprise. Holy Mother of God! Had Gilles built a bonfire next to the cottage? What a fool thing to do, with the dry timbers and the pitch caulking and the rushes just waiting for a spark to ignite them! And such a large bonfire—so large—"No!" she shrieked, and began to run desperately toward the cottage. By the light of the soaring flames she saw Gilles standing helplessly before the burning building; with a great cry she was upon him, assaulting him with her fists, pummeling his face and shoulders and chest. "Damn you!" Her voice was thick with anger and grief. "How could you do such a terrible thing?"

He struggled with her until he had spun her around, her arms pinioned behind her back, while she twisted and writhed to be free of his grasp. "It was an accident," he hissed in her ear. "I meant only to light the candle! *Nom de Dieu*, Delphine. It was only a little cottage!"

She went limp in his arms, overcome with grief. "It was my father's house," she sobbed, then gasped as a sharp pain tore through her. "Sweet Jesu—Holy Mother—" She sank to the ground, clutching her belly, surprised at the fierceness of the onslaught. It was her time—she knew that. But so sudden, so gut-tearing a pain rolled over her in waves that it barely gave her time to catch her breath, to think clearly! She shook her head. No! She must keep her wits about her, play out the last scene of her deception. (*Ah Dieu!* And she had called *him* a cheat!) As he helped her down the beach—half supporting her, half carrying her until they should reach a house, an inn, helping hands—she stopped and turned to him, her eyes glowing by the light of the flames, her voice heavy with accusation.

"Damn you," she panted, "do you see what you've done to me? If I lose the child because it is too soon, I shall never forgive you!"

André smiled and held out his arms to her. Laughing, Gosse scrambled down the rigging and let him swing her onto the deck, his firm hands strong and comforting about her waist. He kissed her gently and led her to the gangway and the pinnace rocking softly alongside *Olympie*. Her silken gown swayed as she walked with dainty steps, head held high and proud. Copain swept his cap from his head and bowed low, while Michel knelt to kiss her hem as she passed. The sun was warm —almost too warm—and she stirred uncomfortably, wishing she could cast off her coverings. She sat in the pinnace, André beside her, and waved farewell to her father, to the crew. André touched her shoulder and she turned, seeing where he pointed to the golden-stoned château set back from the beach. He laughed happily, his blue eyes glowing, his teeth white against the bronzed skin. He laughed—and laughed—and laughed—

Damn! she thought, why must it be so hot? She pushed aside her coverlet and opened her eyes.

"Madame! Thanks be to God!"

She frowned and stared about her bedchamber, dim and cheerless from the murky day. Gilles turned from the rain-streaked window to come and stand at her bedside, peering down at her with eyes that were concerned yet oddly distant. How pale and colorless he was, how devoid of humor or spirit or simple goodness. She cocked her head, squinting at him out of one eye. "Rot and damnation, Gilles," she croaked, hearing the strangeness of her own voice, "do you never laugh?"

"I can see you are getting better when you remember your foul ways. Mayhap in a day or two you will remember your manners as well!" He nodded stiffly to Anne-Marie. "Kindly inform me when madame is well enough to take supper with me again." And he left the room.

Delphine closed her eyes, still feeling trapped in the mists that swirled in her brain. Why should I not be well?

Did not André and I—No—No! André was gone, and
Copain was dead, and the cottage on the beach, and the
cold wind, and the pain tearing at her, the inn and the
house, faces, voices—and the pain. The pain. Her eyes
flew open and her hands groped at her belly. It was flat,
the skin still creased with flaccid folds. She looked wildly
to Anne-Marie. "Did I—?"

"A fine boy, madame. Hale and sound."

"Last night?"

"Near three weeks agone, madame."

She touched her breasts, shrunken now to their nor-
mal size. "And did I nurse it—him—all that time?"

Anne-Marie shook her head. "Not a drop, madame.
You were so sick with fever that twice Monsieur
Despreaux had to send for the priests to give the last
sacraments. It was a blessing that the cook's sister has
only just been delivered of a child herself—a mite who
needs so little that Berthe has milk enough for both
infants. And of course Monsieur Despreaux has promised
to pay her generously for as long as she must nurse the
child. But—what is it, madame?" she cried as Delphine
moaned softly. "Would you like aught to drink or eat?
Shall I have Berthe bring your child to you?"

"No—no. I am so weary. Let me sleep a little." She
closed her eyes and turned her head away that Anne-
Marie might not see the bitter tears that seeped from
beneath her lashes. *Ah Dieu!* She was unworthy to call
herself a woman that could not even suckle her own
child! Endless grief, to be a woman. For a man—for
André—a moment's pleasure soon forgotten. Curling up
on her side, she filled her pillow with scalding tears.

March blew into sweet April, while Delphine slept and
ate, her strength increasing each day, her lithe figure
growing slender and supple once again. The child was a

joy, his little tufts of hair as blond as her own, his tiny face well-formed and beautiful. She spent hours holding him, crooning to him, delighting in his perfection. When she had carried him in her belly, she had sometimes felt anger, bitterness toward the burden in her womb— because of André. But the sweet babe she now held was hers alone; André had no part of him. She suffered only when she had to surrender him to Berthe's nurturing breast, feeling again her deficiency as a woman. They christened him Robert, after Gilles's grandfather; Delphine was secretly pleased at the choice because it had been Copain's name.

Gilles was still cool and distant to her, a strange contrast to his generosity in the hiring of Berthe. He could hardly have let the child starve; still it was one of the few expenses he did not complain about. Or perhaps he was aware that his servants gossiped regularly with the servants of his friends; it would have been unseemly to begrudge his own child. When they supped together, Delphine was careful to mind her manners, reluctant to draw Gilles's attention to her, to antagonize him. She was content to spend her days in the solitude of her room— with her son, her books, the sweet illusion of a life without Gilles. She did not go to the shop, not wishing to know of his dishonesty, and they spoke of the weather, or the latest gossip in Dieppe—or not at all.

She sat one morning at her window, the casement thrown wide to the sunny day. It was warm for early April, and the sweetness of the air filled her with contentment. It was a lovely crystallized moment, and the bars of her cage seemed to melt away. Her father would come at the end of the month, or the beginning of May, and release his wolf cub.

She was combing her hair. She had thrown a little combing jacket, a *casaque,* over her nightdress, but her hair had grown so long, well below her shoulders, that the large-toothed comb kept snagging the ruffles. Impatiently she snatched off the *casaque,* then, feeling lighthearted and fanciful, she stood up and pulled off her nightdress as well. She tossed her head back and forth. How lovely it was to feel the silkiness of her long hair stroking her bare shoulders. She tilted up her chin to see how far down on her back the tresses reached; the feeling was exquisite. She felt beautiful, free. The April breeze caressed her bare flesh, and the golden curtain of her hair brushing against her stirred her senses. She kicked off her slippers and began to dance about the room, moving her head so her hair swirled around her face, her body swaying and turning sensuously. She looked up. Gilles was standing in the doorway, his face red with embarrassment and distress.

"Forgive me," he stammered, "I had not meant—I should have knocked—" He frowned and cleared his throat. "Are you alone?"

What a prig! she thought. "Of course." Unselfconsciously she stooped down and picked up her nightdress, wrapping it modestly about her shoulders like a cloak so Gilles would not be so uncomfortable. "What did you want of me?"

"I cannot find the bill for the last hogshead of wine you bought of Monsieur Moillon. And now with the new currency that was introduced last month, he wishes to be paid in louis d'or instead of écus. I think he wishes to cheat me in the conversion. Have you the bill?"

Delphine rummaged in her writing table. "Yes. Here. Twenty crowns is what he charged." She handed the paper to Gilles.

"*Mon Dieu!* Twenty écus. What a thief. Well, he shall have to give me a discount if he wishes to be paid in louis d'or." He turned and made for the door, then stopped, looking back at her with contemptuous eyes. "Name of God, clothe yourself. Sometimes I think you are still a wild colt!"

He was very quiet at supper, glancing surreptitiously at her when he did not think she noticed. He seemed calm, his face betraying nothing, but she noted the way he toyed with his knife, tapping it repeatedly against his wine goblet, seeming unaware of his agitated fingers. When she rose to leave the table, he put his hand on her sleeve and would not let her go. His eyes were burning, and when he spoke it seemed as though the words were torn from him.

"Are you well enough to receive me in your bedchamber this evening?"

She hesitated. It was strange. The look on his face—haunted, tormented—seemed almost to be begging her to decline. Still—

"Anne-Marie says you are well enough," he growled. "Is it so?"

She sighed. She was still his wife, and it was her duty. "Yes," she murmured.

"Then wait for me," he said, and poured himself another glass of wine.

There had been several more glasses of wine before he appeared in her room. That was apparent—even in the light of the single candle—from the way his face was flushed and his dressing gown was carelessly tied on. He was usually so fastidious about his clothing. Has it come to this, she thought, that he must be drunk to take me? She sat on the bed, in the shadow of the draperies, watching him, waiting for him to announce his pleasure. She felt strangely numb, indifferent. Only a few more weeks until her father came home. What did it matter?

"Get up," he said, leaning against the closed door, "and take off your nightdress. I would see your body again."

Dutifully she did as he asked, dropping her gown to the floor, seeing the hungry flicker in his eyes. She nearly laughed aloud. Who would have thought it? He had used her sensuality against her, to torment her; now he burned with desire, burned despite his obvious wish to be indifferent. The lust-ridden whoreson! Let him drink his fill! Deliberately she pirouetted in front of him, enjoying the agony on his face.

"Unpin your hair," he ordered, his voice a hoarse croak in his throat, "as you did this morning!" She shook her tresses about her shoulders; he ran his fingers through their silken smoothness, then pulled her to him and crushed her mouth with his. Not even his kiss had the power to arouse her anymore. When he pulled her onto the bed and began to caress her body she felt nothing at all, as though he had long since forfeited the right to stir her senses. Have done, she thought. Have done and leave me in peace. He threw off his dressing gown and entered her; she watched in loathing as he labored above her, his face twisted with the effort. *Ah Dieu!* she thought, closing her eyes against the sight of him. She had never loved him. Now she realized with a start that she did not even *like* him! There was no pleasure in his company, no satisfaction from his selfish lovemaking, nothing but disgust.

He had finished with her and withdrawn, but he still knelt between her wide-spread knees. She opened her eyes—cold amber—and stared at him. He was peering intently at her face, his jaw set, his face black with anger. He raised his hand and slapped her violently across the face, with such force that she thought her neck would snap. She was too stunned even to cry out, not even when he slapped her again, and yet a third time. He scrambled from the bed, tossing on his dressing gown, and hurried from her room.

She raised shaking hands to her burning cheeks. She could not even cry. He had a right. She had left his manhood in tatters, had ripped up his pride and left him bleeding.

The caged wolf cub had become a feral beast.

Chapter Eleven

IN THE MORNING HE BEHAVED AS THOUGH NOTHING HAD happened, but he made a point of going out in the evening and telling Anne-Marie in Delphine's presence that she was not to expect him home until very late. There was no need for any servants to wait up for him, nor to hold supper; he was dining with a friend. The next day he sent Anne-Marie to the mercer's to buy a lace falling band and a fan that he took with him when he went out. After nearly a week of late evenings and gifts, Anne-Marie could hardly bear to look Delphine in the eye, so mortified was she on her mistress's behalf. The cook, with far less nicety, opined as how Monsieur Despreaux must be seeing that slut Lucie again.

Delphine was indifferent. Let him do as he wished, so long as he left her in peace. She had nothing with which to reproach herself; *she* would not betray her marriage vows, whatever her feelings for him. She supped alone in her room each night, and kissed and petted her sweet Robert. She put a candle beside her bed and sat and read her books, blowing out the candle only when her eyes were too tired to read another line. But one night she drifted off in the midst of turning a page and awoke to the sound of the wick end sputtering in its dish, the candle having burned to the bottom. Even as she watched, it flickered and went out, plunging the room into darkness. She groped on the table for the tinder and flint, meaning to find another candle, then cursed as her hand jostled the candleholder, spilling the hot tallow over her fingers. Rot and damnation! She would need light just to remove the tallow from her hand, and she suddenly remembered that this had been the last candle in her room tonight. It seemed to be very late and the house was still, but if that whoreson Gilles was yet riding his doxy in some tavern, there would be a lighted candle or two waiting for him in the corridor. She slipped out of bed and opened her door. The passageway was dark, but Gilles's door was ajar and there was a light coming from within. She hesitated, wondering if her appearance in his room at this hour would give him mistaken ideas, then shrugged. If he had spent the evening with Lucie, he would scarcely be interested in her. And besides, her hand had begun to itch and sting, despite her efforts to scrape off the wax; the sooner she could clean it properly, the less the risk of festering sores.

She was surprised to hear laughter coming from Gilles's room. Softly she pushed open the door, standing transfixed at the sight before her. Gilles sat in a large armchair in the center of the room, his arms folded imperiously across his chest, a makeshift wreath of leaves—like a king's crown—perched on his brown curls. His bearing was regal, but he grinned evilly like a devil out of hell. Before him stood a young woman, naked as Eve, with tousled black hair that she pushed out of her eyes from time to time. Gilles murmured something to her, and they both laughed; then she began to dance in front of him, gyrating obscenely while he gazed in rapt fascination. He clapped his hands together and she curtsied, holding wide an imaginary skirt. He spoke another command and she leaned over and kissed him, running her hands across his body, probing beneath his open shirt, his breeches. Again he clapped his hands and she curtsied, doing honor to her "king," but laughing vulgarly all the while. She pressed her breasts together, inviting him, her eyes smoldering as she backed up toward the waiting bed.

"Damn your poxy soul!" shrieked Delphine, bursting into the room. The girl's clothing lay in a heap on the floor; Delphine swept up the jacket and began to beat Lucie with it. The girl cringed and tried to back away, letting out a small yelp each time a button of the jacket struck her and left a little red mark on her bare skin.

"*Nom de Dieu*, Delphine! Stop it!" Gilles grabbed at her arm, wresting the jacket from her, struggling to keep her from the now-whimpering Lucie. Delphine fought like a tiger, tearing at his hair, kicking at him with her bare feet. She was itching to sink her nails into the girl's face. Sobbing and trembling, Lucie hastily donned her clothes, anxious to be gone. Delphine broke free of Gilles and went for the girl again; Gilles took hold of her arm and flung her against the wall. The shock of it took her breath away for a second; in that moment Gilles snatched up the armchair and pinned her against the wall with it, imprisoned between its legs.

"Get out!" he gasped at Lucie. The girl fled.

Delphine struggled against the chair. "How dare you!" she screeched. "How dare you bring that slut into this house!"

He bared his teeth, his face twisted in an ugly grimace. "I brought *you* into this house, didn't I?"

She felt her knees go weak beneath her. "What—what do you mean?"

"Do you think I am a fool? That child was not too

soon, for all your pretense! Less than seven months! A seven-month babe would be stillborn, or sicken and die. But that child—strong and hearty! Seven months—bah!"

"But Gilles—" she protested, then stopped, the lie dying in her throat. She was weary of lies, hungry for the fresh air of truth, clean and sweet like the breezes at sea. "Why did you have him christened with your name?" she asked tiredly.

"It were better my friends think you played the whore for *me* before our wedding. I shall not be a cuckold for their amusement! Did you know, I wonder, when you married me, that you carried another man's seed? Filthy strumpet! You *must* have known! 'No, Gilles, not for any man!'" he mimicked, then laughed bitterly. He set the chair upright, releasing her, and sat down heavily.

"Please, Gilles," she whispered, overcome with remorse. "Forgive me, I—" She reached out a conciliatory hand but he slapped her fingers away, jumping up to confront her with fresh anger.

"And who was the father?" he growled. "Is he the one you dreamed of when you lay with me? He was not a seaman—you swore you never slept with any of *Olympie*'s crew." He sneered, his lip curling in disgust. "Lying whore! For aught I know, you slept with them all!"

"Blasted dungheap! You are not worth my remorse! I have not dandled a lover for all the months of our marriage as you have that trollop! Look to your own sins ere you chide me!"

"No," he said, his voice suddenly quiet and deadly. "I shall do as I choose. If I wish to take Lucie in this house—in your very bed!—I shall do so. And you will hold your tongue, my sweet. Else Berthe will be sent packing, and you and your brat will find yourselves out on the streets begging." His eyes raked her body contemptuously. "A whore you were—a whore you shall become again if I turn you out. If you spread your legs often enough, you can earn food for yourself. But how shall you feed your child with your useless breasts?"

She reeled back, her hand to her mouth, staggering as though he had struck her. Without a word she stumbled to her room, there to fall on her knees before her bed and pray *le bon Dieu* to bring *Olympie* home quickly, filled with gold from a successful voyage.

It was several days later that he stopped her in the kitchen garden, as she helped the cook to plant early peas (an empty gesture, for she would be with her father long before the vines flowered). She had not seen him since the night in his room: twice he had stayed out all night, and once Charretier had come to supper and the two men had sat in the kitchen until nearly dawn, drinking and whispering and laughing.

On her knees before the furrows, Delphine looked up in surprise as Gilles's shadow fell across the rich earth. She eyed him carefully, gauging his temper, unsure of his mood after all that had happened.

He nodded brusquely. "I shall come to your bedchamber tonight for supper. There is something I must discuss with you, far from prying servants." Delphine rose to her feet, brushing the loam from her skirts, and frowned at him, half minded to refuse. Gilles smiled sourly. "Think of Robert, *ma chère*, and then mayhap you will receive me with civility."

She inclined her head. "For Robert's sake, I think I may endure your company for an hour or two."

"At seven," he said, and left her to her garden.

She scarcely ate at supper, watching him like a caged beast, fearful that he might insist on taking her to bed, knowing she must submit because of Robert. She thought briefly of putting her sea knife under the pillow, then changed her mind. Who would raise her darling child if she were in prison or hanged?

When the last dishes had been cleared and Gilles had waved the servants away, he poured himself another cup of wine and leaned back in his chair. "Dieppe has had a distinguished visitor these last few months. Monsieur le Duc de Janequin. His estates are in Auvergne, but his late sister, who died—alas—of the ague December last, was widow to the Marquis de Courtan, *seigneur* of the district to the west of Dieppe. You may know it." Delphine nodded; there were many fine estates surrounding Dieppe, and the townspeople had often spoken highly of Monsieur de Courtan. Gilles continued. "Monsieur le Duc came to Dieppe to settle his sister's affairs, and has been living in a charming house on the hill overlooking the Hôtel de Ville."

Delphine sneered. "And does he need furniture? Does he own fine treasures that you covet?"

"He owns, through his late sister's generosity, a magnificent diamond necklace worth a quarter of a million livres."

She threw back her head and laughed scornfully. "Were I to dance naked in front of him—like your harlot Lucie—I could scarcely distract him well enough for you to do your thieving work! A diamond necklace is not a tobacco box!"

He glared at her with icy eyes. "Monsieur le Duc brought the necklace to Monsieur Charretier to be cleaned and repaired. My friend the *bijoutier* had the good sense to copy the piece in glass."

"Mother of God! What a fool! When he gives back the imitation he will be found out immediately!"

"And so I told him. Monsieur de Janequin has taken the care to bring from Paris a very shrewd lawyer. Sure enough, so soon as Charretier returned the real necklace, Monsieur Braudel, the lawyer, had another jeweler testify as to its genuineness."

"And there's an end to it," she shrugged.

"No. Charretier still has the imitation. And we have devised a scheme whereby Monsieur de Janequin will be so cleverly duped that he will not think to authenticate the necklace this time. There will be an—exchange—at a time when he does not expect it, and so smoothly done that it might be years before he discovers his necklace is false—at which time he will be hard pressed to recall at what moment he might have been deceived."

"Knowing you, I have no doubt that the plan will be devilishly clever."

"Indeed. But for its execution, my lovely, we need you."

She leaped up from the table. "The devil you do!"

He sipped at his wine—cool, in control. Delphine shuddered at the mockery of a smile on his face, so evil, so smugly confident. "But you see, my love, it needs a woman."

"Then ask Lucie!"

"Lucie is a lusty wench between the sheets—but she is a common slut. We need a woman who is—who can *pretend* to be—" he amended, and watched her flinch, "a lady."

"By the horn of Satan, I shall take no part in your wicked schemes! When they burn the brand of thief on your forehead, I shall glory in your downfall!"

"If you are not dead of starvation long since—you and your whelp!" The threat was unmistakable.

She thrust out her chin proudly. "Better to be a whore and a beggar than a thief! Shall I send for Anne-Marie to pack my few belongings?" She thought quickly, her mind spinning with alternatives. The weather was growing warmer; if she could not find humble lodgings, there might be a cozy barn to shelter her and Robert. It was only a few more weeks until *Olympie*'s return, and since the night with Lucie she had managed to salt away a few extra coins from her household accounts, contriving even to falsify the ledgers so Gilles would not notice. He had taught her well!

And she *would* be a whore, if need be! She had endured Gilles—could she not endure the restless aristocrats and hungry sailors who prowled the waterfront seeking a doxy? She had seen scores of the slatterns in every port of the globe—not an enviable lot, but they earned their own way. All she needed was enough money to hire a wet nurse for Robert.

"Before you hasten to leave me, sweet Delphine, you might consider this. That bastard child of yours was baptised with my name. I have formally acknowledged him. If you leave here—more especially if you leave as a deserting wife—you leave alone, without the child. There is no court in the land that would deny me the right to my own son."

"It cannot be! There are laws—I bore the child!"

"You may consult a lawyer, of course, but I hardly think you have the finances to oppose me."

She clasped her hands together, her face twisted in pain. "You could not do it, Gilles. Please! I beg you!"

"I am quite prepared to turn you out—alone—unless you do exactly as I direct. Foolish woman," the voice unexpectedly gentle, "did you never think, while you swooned in your lover's arms, that—sooner or later—you would have to pay for your stolen pleasures?" He laughed harshly, enjoying his total mastery of her. "And the price, sweet love—one diamond necklace! Now, sit down. Take a glass of wine; you look pale. And listen carefully. You will insinuate yourself into Monsieur de

Janequin's favor. I have a plan as to how this may be accomplished. And make no mistake about it, my charming whore, you *will* go down for him if the man desires you!" Carefully he laid out his plan, then rose to leave, signaling the end of their discourse. At the door he turned—Lucie's "king."

Delphine's "king."

"You will do all that I command," he said softly, "or you will no longer have a child."

Chapter Twelve

THE DRIVING RAIN PELTED DELPHINE'S FACE. SHE PULLED the hood of her mantle lower over her forehead and wiped the drops from her eyes, peering through the gloom at the heavy carriage making its way up the hill toward her. Leaning into the high hedge that surrounded the manor house, she knew she could not be seen by the coachman. Soon now the carriage would crest the hill and, picking up speed again, would swing into the muddy lane that led to the gates and the long drive of the house. That would be the best place, where it swung wide into the curve. Less risk of falling under the horses' hooves. It must be timed just so, so that she could fling herself away as the wheels caught her, and not be pulled beneath the carriage. Thanks be to her years on *Olympie* she was agile; still, her heart beat madly at the foolhardiness of the whole scheme.

Now! She stepped into the lane, shoulders hunched against the rain, walking quickly despite the mud that dragged at her feet and fouled her skirts. As he maneuvered the turn, the coachman saw her and shouted frantically for her to get out of the way. She looked up in pretended alarm, steeling herself to keep from leaping to safety until the last possible moment. She had planned to scream ("There is nothing so heartrending as the cry of a distressed woman!" Gilles had advised), but the force of the heavy wheel striking her shoulder and spinning her away so violently that she felt a wrenching pain in her ankle, tore an involuntary cry from her lips. The mud oozed about her as she fell, gasping, dazed with pain. Damn Gilles! Small wonder the bastard had suggested this plan. That streak of cruelty in him enjoyed the sufferings of others.

Up ahead, the carriage had stopped. The coachman leaped from his box, and hurried to help her up, while his passenger, an elderly man with snow white hair, leaned out of the window, frowning in concern. *Dieu du ciel!* thought Delphine. God in heaven! I cannot lie here with the mud seeping into my clothes until the man reaches me! As the coachman neared her she struggled to rise, then cried out as her ankle gave way under her and the pain ripped through her leg. There was the buzzing of a thousand bees and the world closing in on her—then blackness.

When she awoke, she was in a handsomely appointed bedchamber and gentle hands were stripping her filthy clothes from her, washing the mud from her feet, toweling her rain-drenched hair. She was bundled into a warm nightdress and carried with care to the large bed by the two robust servant girls who had been assisting the old housekeeper. They tucked her in and plumped up her pillows; then, with much curtsying and bobbing they left her alone.

"Are you feeling better now, mademoiselle?"

"Thank you, yes, monsieur." Delphine nodded at the man who had just entered the room. She judged him to be in his late fifties or early sixties, his white hair almost to his shoulders, his trim moustache and spade beard neatly cut. He was clad in a splendid brocade doublet and breeches, though the style was somewhat out-of-date. The sleeves of the doublet were slashed to reveal silk undersleeves. The breeches were in the Spanish style, ballooning out, then fastening tightly at the knees, instead of the wide-legged breeches favored by the younger dandies and cavaliers, or the narrow knee breeches that Gilles had. He wore silk stockings and low shoes adorned with shoe roses, and though he limped slightly, his carriage and bearing were so noble as to make the irregularity of his step an attribute. His face was kind, his eyes were gentle, and the sweetness of his smile made her conscience ache.

"You will find this *clairet* most agreeable," he said, handing her the goblet he had carried into the room. He drew up a small chair to the side of the bed, settled himself comfortably in it, and smiled at her again. "My housekeeper says your shoulder is grievously bruised, but she does not think your ankle is broken. If you cannot walk in the morning, mayhap I shall send for a physician."

"In the morning?" Delphine pushed at her coverlet, pretending to get up. "But I cannot stay until morning!"

"Nonsense, mademoiselle! It is a dreary evening, your clothes will not be dry for hours—and you must at least enjoy my hospitality for a little, more especially since my coach was the cause of your pain and distress! No, mademoiselle, I shall not hear of your leaving tonight."

She cast her eyes down modestly. "It is not mademoiselle. It—it is madame. And my husband will be expecting me."

"Then you must allow me to send a message to him

this evening, telling him his wife is safe and will remain under my care, if it pleases him, until she is well enough to return home."

She dimpled prettily at him. "And who is my benefactor, monsieur?"

"Ah, forgive me!" He rose and bowed grandly to her, catching her fingers to his lips with such elegance that she felt like a queen. "I am Bernard de Chagny, Duc de Janequin."

"I am honored, Monsieur de Janequin."

"The honor is mine, madame, to have such a charming guest. Now, you will wish me to notify your husband. Yes?"

She hesitated for a moment, a shadow crossing her face. "Yes. Monsieur Gilles Despreaux. The upholsterer's shop on the Rue des Saintes."

"Ah, Madame Despreaux. May one venture to suggest that Monsieur Gilles is a bit of a fool for allowing his lovely wife to be abroad on such a dismal evening?"

"He—he did not—allow it. He does not know I went out."

A gentle smile. "Your troubled eyes tell me it was not an assignation in the rain."

"No. I—I wished to be alone for a little."

"A lovers' quarrel, n'est-ce pas?"

There was no need to feign the hurt in her eyes. "Lovers quarrel, but husbands and wives bring grief to one another."

"My wife and I were supremely happy. There were few quarrels and no infidelities, though the temptation was strong at times! But she was a blessing to me until the day she died."

"Then you are most fortunate, Monsieur de Janequin," she sighed.

"Come! Let me bring a smile to your face, madame.

We shall sup together here in your room, and I shall tell you amusing little stories until your gloom is quite dispelled! Fortunately my house guest Monsieur Braudel is dining elsewhere tonight. He is a dour and suspicious man, but perhaps that is the nature of lawyers. Finish your *clairet* while I arrange our supper and send a message to your husband. If you have quarreled"—and here his eyes twinkled warmly— "mayhap this enforced separation will make him more appreciative of your virtues!"

They dined on partridges and goose pâté and fresh strawberries, while Monsieur de Janequin regaled her with stories of life at court and Delphine laughed gaily, forgetting for awhile the ugly part she must play. But after the dishes were cleared away, a cozy fire lit in the fireplace, and two chairs drawn up in front of the hearth (Monsieur de Janequin, despite his own limp, helped her hobble out of bed and into a chair), the mood turned pensive and somber. They sat, side by side, sipping the last of their wine and gazing into the flames. He told her of his wife, his two daughters, his son—all dead, wiped out by the plague four years before, while he was away fighting at Corbie.

"I left them safe at home," he said softly, "while I marched off into the jaws of hell. I returned with naught but this shattered leg—to an empty château. Death's great jest—a bitter irony."

"Ah Dieu. How lonely you must be."

"I have my memories. Ours was a great and wondrous love, my wife's and mine. It is the children I mourn, cut off in their prime. My daughter Laure would be almost your age now. You are—what? Seventeen? Eighteen?"

"Nineteen for a month now."

"Laure would have been sixteen." He sighed. "She might have been a wife, even as you." Delphine turned her head away, seeming to fight back tears. The gesture was not lost on Janequin. He put a gentle hand on hers. "Are you so unhappy, my child?"

"My father warned me. But I was headstrong and would not listen. His was a fine family of the nobility, with titles and honors. But he was the fourth son, and there was never enough money as I was growing up. And though I was raised in the traditions of our class, I could never forget that my mother—of equally fine lineage— was always ashamed of my father's slender means. Gilles was rich, and he seemed devoted to me. I thought my father's warnings were mere snobbery, the aristocrat's disdain of the bourgeoisie. Alas! It did not take me long to understand his misgivings. Gilles is—" She shook her head. "No. It is not your concern. You have been more than kind to me. Why should I burden you with my unhappiness?"

He took her hand in his own two. "It is a sweet burden for a lonely man. I can pretend for a little that—you are my daughter. Please go on."

"What can I say of Gilles? He is so far from being a gentleman, so— What can I say? Yet it is *he* who seems ashamed of *me.* I am kept almost a prisoner, denied the right to be *châtelaine* of my own household. The house-keeper holds the keys and only gives them to me when he instructs her to do so. If I am thrifty, I can manage to save a coin or two from the household accounts, but if I spend them in an indulgence he curses me for an extravagant aristocrat and reduces my allowance accordingly. And he keeps me only that he may flaunt me before his friends, while he gives his attentions to other women." She stopped, overcome with emotion. It was not difficult to persuade him of her misery with Gilles, but she did not want her feelings to carry her away to the point where she might forget to keep her wits about her.

She took a deep breath, and waited until she felt more in control of herself.

"And your parents?"

"My mother died, long before I met Gilles. My father spurned me after my marriage and went away to America to seek his fortune."

"And now you are quite alone, poor child." Janequin's words were full of understanding, but he frowned slightly to himself, wondering if the girl intended to take advantage of his sympathy and ask for money. He would probably give it to her—God knows he had more than enough for himself, and no heirs—but he fervently prayed she would not do so. He would not like to be disappointed in her.

She laughed softly. "I am drowning in gloom tonight, and there is no need for it! See? I have made you unhappy as well. And yet my heart is filled with hope. I have had a letter from my father. He has a plantation in Guadeloupe and has met with great success. He is coming home. He forgives me."

"And then?"

"And then I shall settle my accounts with Gilles and leave him."

"Are there children?"

She hesitated. Gilles had given her free rein in the telling of her tale—at least in the details that did not matter—but she wished Robert to remain untouched by the corrupting poison of her lies. "No," she said.

She spent nearly a week with Monsieur le Duc de Janequin, deliberately grimacing each time she tried to stand, so that he waggled his finger like a knowing father and insisted she must stay another day, and then another. She met his lawyer Monsieur Braudel, and though the man treated her with suspicion at first, she managed at length to charm him with an ease that surprised even

herself. Janequin dutifully sent letters to Gilles keeping
him apprised of his wife's health, and secretly wondered
that the man never bothered to visit her. And though
Delphine missed her sweet Robert, she took great joy in
Janequin's company, feeling again a pang of guilt that he
must be deceived. They read Descartes together, and
Corneille and Ronsard; they played cards and trictrac,
though Delphine was hard pressed to hold her tongue
each time a sea oath sprang to her lips. When she left,
Janequin presented her with a small volume of poetry as
a memento of her visit.

It was a week later that a note arrived from Monsieur le
Duc, begging her to take supper with him. Gilles was
delighted, and accepted for her, urging her to advance
the scheme as quickly as possible. She ignored his
malicious parting shot ("Has the old fool asked you to go
down for him yet?"), and went forth into the sweet spring
night.

This time they dined with Monsieur Braudel. Delphine
cursed silently. It would be far more difficult to set the
plan in motion with him present! Then she reconsidered.
Perhaps in the long run it would be better. If *he* believed
her, surely Janequin would, and it would prove to them
both that she had nothing to hide.

She sighed and put down her soup spoon. "I should
not have come tonight. I fear I am poor company." The
men hastened to reassure her.

"What troubles you, madame?" Janequin reached
across the table and patted her hand.

"I am sick with worry. My father still has not returned,
and I fear I shall need money soon. For—someone
else."

Braudel's face was hard, but a light of triumph glowed
in his eyes. Had he not warned Janequin to be on his
guard? "For a lover?" he asked harshly.

Janequin banged down his fist loudly. *"Nom de Dieu,* Braudel! You shall not insult my guests at my table!" He looked kindly to Delphine, now sitting shamefaced, as though Braudel's words might have hit the mark. "If you need a loan until your father comes home, I shall be happy to oblige. Not a word, monsieur," he warned Braudel, who had begun to huff and sputter. "I know you are my adviser. But it is my money, and if I choose to loan it—or *give* it even—I will do so. For *whatever* reason madame needs the money."

"No!" she said with asperity. "I have my pride, monsieur! I shall not presume on your kindness so much as to take a single sou from you! You may rest easy, Monsieur Braudel," she said, drawing herself up with dignity, "I am not a common mountebank who would defraud your client!" Braudel blushed furiously and mumbled an apology, and no more was said of the matter for the rest of the evening.

But three days later she composed a careful message to Janequin. She wished to see him on an important matter. Her mind was made up, but she wished to talk to him, simply as a friend. It would be helpful if Monsieur Braudel would attend the interview as well, though she knew he would not be happy with what he might hear. Still, she welcomed his advice.

When they were settled comfortably in a cozy salon in Janequin's house, she turned first to the lawyer.

"Do not scold me, Monsieur Braudel," she began. "I know that what I propose is contrary to the law, but it is only a small thing, and where's the harm? I beg your understanding. To begin: I found, among my mother's papers, deeds to some properties in Brittany. They were part of my dowry to Gilles, and quite properly belong to him now. I know that I must, by law, turn them over to my husband, and I may not sell them. But I can use two or three of them as collateral on a loan, to be repaid when my father returns."

Braudel frowned and shook his head. "Not if they belong to your husband!"

"But they are in my mother's name—Madame la Vicomtesse de Fresnel."

"But if your mother is dead—?"

"Yes, child," said Janequin gently. "The deeds belong to your husband."

Delphine took a deep breath. "Not if the moneylender thinks that *I* am the Vicomtesse de Fresnel."

"Mon Dieu! You cannot!"

"I told you, my mind is made up. But oh, messieurs," the amber eyes filled with tears, "is it such a dreadful thing I would do? When my father returns, the money will be paid back, the deeds will be returned to Gilles— though he will never have missed them—and I shall be free. It is only a little amount, two thousand livres."

"A-a-ah!" Monsieur Braudel leaped from his chair in exasperation, pacing the room like a man who knows he is beaten.

Janequin laughed softly. "There are times, Braudel, when the heart is worth more than the head. But tell me, my child, if you were minded to do it—willy-nilly—why did you come here?"

"For your blessing, mayhap," she whispered.

"You have that—hush, Braudel!—and I shall accompany you to the moneylender if it will give you courage."

She thought for a moment. "Yes—perhaps. He is so suspicious. As though he thought the deeds were stolen or counterfeit. I must do everything I can to persuade him that I am Madame la Vicomtesse. I shall wear my best gown. *Ah Dieu!"*—she put a delicate hand to her bosom—"had I a jewel or two, to appear rich and important—"

"My late wife's jewels are in the bank in Paris, but I have here in Dieppe a necklace which belonged to my sister the Marquise de Courtan. You shall wear it."

"Nom de Dieu!" Braudel was beside himself.

"I cannot, monsieur. No."

"I insist upon it."

"How can I?" she asked, "when Monsieur Braudel looks at me as if he were seeing a thief!"

Janequin smiled. "But I shall be with you—and the necklace. Will that not suffice?"

Her lip trembled with injured pride. "No. I shall not wear the necklace unless Monsieur Braudel accompanies us as well, and never lets the necklace out of his sight!"

Janequin nodded. "Agreed. Braudel?" Reluctantly the lawyer assented.

Delphine wrung her hands. "I'm afraid. It is in a vile part of town, and I have agreed to meet the man at night. Could we not have one or two armed men as well, to guard the necklace?"

"I shall see that they guard *you*, for you are far more precious than cold stones."

"God bless you, Monsieur," she whispered.

Gilles was overjoyed to hear the plan was proceeding so well, that Delphine had so easily led Janequin into offering the necklace. They arranged for the "loan" to take place the following night, in a small warehouse, dimly lit but reached through a wide lane that would allay Monsieur Braudel's fears of cutpurses lying in wait. Gilles, in a long black wig, with heavy spectacles on his nose, his voice deliberately lowered and guttural, played the moneylender. He growled suspiciously at Delphine, even after she had nonchalantly thrown back her cloak to reveal the sparkling necklace at her throat. But Monsieur Braudel harrumphed angrily, and Monsieur de Janequin folded his arms across his chest and insisted that the moneylender honor his promise. Still grumbling, Gilles examined the "deeds" and counted out two thousand livres for Delphine.

As soon as they had regained the Duc de Janequin's coach, Delphine pulled the jewels from her neck and thrust the piece into Braudel's hand. "There, monsieur! Not for another moment would I wear them, feeling your eyes on me!"

"Forgive me, Madame Despreaux, I—" Braudel looked shamefaced, though more than a little pleased. The jewels were safe, and this ridiculous scheme of the deeds had not, after all, been a plot to defraud the *duc*. He was growing quite fond of the girl; how nice to be reassured of her basic goodness.

Glad to have the whole matter done, Janequin laughed aloud. "It is I who merit your apology, Braudel! That you should think me a fool who must be governed in all my affairs! But come. Wine. Supper. And then we shall bring madame to her home before her errant husband returns from his wanderings!"

It was several days later that Monsieur de Janequin appeared at Gilles's workshop. Delphine was in a panic that the *duc* would recognize her husband, but Despreaux bowed low and chatted pleasantly with the man, thanking him in person for all the kindnesses he had extended to his wife. When at last the *duc* had departed, promising to send an invitation soon to Monsieur Despreaux and his charming wife, Gilles laughed uproariously at the look of anxiety on Delphine's face. "Are you sure you have not let him bed you, my sweet? The man can scarcely be parted from you for a day or so!"

"Damn your black soul," she said. "He is a dear man who looks upon me as a daughter. It breaks my heart to see how he trusts in me."

An ugly laugh. "But then he does not know you as well as I! Let us make an end to this charade as soon as possible. The sheep is waiting to be sheared. Thursday next, I think. Can it be managed?"

She nodded, hating him, hating herself.

On Thursday morning she went again to Monsieur de Janequin. She found him in the garden, admiring the first of his Holland tulips—pink-streaked and feather-edged—that danced in the gentle spring breeze. He smiled. "I have not known May to shine so sweetly for me in a long time. Is it the flowers? Or your presence in my garden that warms my old heart?"

She gave a heavy sigh. "You will not be so glad to see me when I tell you why I have come. I have—debts—I do not wish Gilles to know. There is one more deed, and the moneylender has agreed to loan me another five hundred livres. But I am afraid. If you and Monsieur Braudel—Ah, I have no right to ask it of you again!"

"When?"

"Tonight. I was ashamed to come and tell you before this."

"*Dommage!* Braudel has returned to Paris for a day or two. How he will howl to find I have gone on this venture without him!"

Delphine hesitated. She had counted on Braudel's presence. He was skeptical and shrewd—if he could be fooled, they had nothing to fear. But when Braudel returned, might he not be suspicious of a meeting that had taken place without him? Now she was forced to play a reckless game and hope that Monsieur le Duc would respond as she wished him to. "If Monsieur Braudel is not here, I shall not take the necklace," she announced firmly.

"Nonsense! Of course you shall."

She shook her head. "No. I cannot."

"*Nom de Dieu!* Do you agree with Monsieur Braudel that I am a fool?"

"Of course not!"

"Then listen to me. I shall give you the necklace in the carriage and watch it carefully until the transaction is done and you have handed it back to me. If Braudel asks me, I shall tell him with perfect truth that the necklace never left my sight." He smiled, his eyes twinkling. "If he doubts me still, I shall toss the rascal on his ear! What say you to that?"

Delphine buried her face in her hands, overcome with remorse. Then the thought of losing Robert to Gilles crowded out everything else, and she lifted her head and smiled, wiping away her tears. "I think—I think you are the kindest man I have ever known."

It was almost too easy. This time Delphine asked that Janequin's two men at arms stand inside the door of the warehouse rather than waiting at the coach as they had before. It was too dim for them truly to see anything, but they would help to maintain the illusion in Janequin's eyes (and later in Braudel's, when he heard of it) that the necklace was never in any danger. Delphine and Janequin sat facing Gilles across the rickety table, the single large candle sputtering in front of them. Again Gilles grumbled about the transaction, questioning the authenticity of the deed, the genuineness of the signature, the honesty of the lady herself.

"How am I to know," he burst out, "that you are Madame de Fresnel? You look like a great lady, with your jewels and all, but how am I to know you did not steal the deed, that your sparkling diamonds are not false?"

She drew herself up haughtily. "How dare you! Look!" She snatched the necklace from her throat. "See for yourself!" She dropped it into Gilles's hand; he held it to the light of the candle, squinting at it through his thick glasses, then turned his hand over and dropped it back into her palm. It had been done so smoothly, so quickly, that she almost thought he had not made the exchange; it was only when she put the necklace on again and had to keep from flinching at the cold metal against her skin that she knew he had shaken the imitation necklace out of his sleeve in that moment when he had put it in her hand.

"They're real enough," he growled, and completed the transaction in silence, exchanging the deed for five hundred livres. In the carriage, Delphine urged Monsieur le Duc to put the necklace in a safe place as soon as possible: even if she needed money again she would not go through another such scene. It was too difficult, she assured him, to play the false role for the moneylender.

They celebrated long into the night, Gilles and Charretier, and a reluctant Delphine—eating and drinking, planning how they would spend a quarter of a million livres. Charretier was in no hurry to break up the necklace. If he waited for awhile—and especially since Monsieur le Duc was reported to be returning to Paris at the end of May—he might be able to sell it, intact, almost openly in Rouen, substituting an emerald or ruby for a few of the diamonds to change the look of the piece.

Gilles was ecstatic, bragging to Charretier of Delphine's coolness, his own adroitness in making the switch. In a sudden burst of emotion—or satisfied greed—he threw his arms around Delphine and kissed her resoundingly.

"I shall leave you to your joy," she said, and pushed him away. She went tiredly up the stairs to her room, then stopped as she heard faint stirrings from the nursery. Tiptoeing in, she saw that Robert had kicked off his coverlet; she bent over the cradle and tucked him in again, crooning softly as she rocked him back to sleep. His busy mouth found his thumb at last, and he closed his eyes and slept.

How blue his eyes were becoming. More and more like André's. She was too weary for hatred tonight, only an overwhelming sadness. Oh André, she thought. Because you came into my life, I have lied, and I have stolen. She wiped Gilles's kiss from her mouth.

Because of you, shall I kill as well—someday?

Chapter Thirteen

MAY BLOSSOMED WITH TULIPS AND PEONIES, PINK AND white apple trees, green willows that cast their swaying branches to the soft breezes. The nights were sweet and moon-filled, the days golden with sunshine. But Delphine's heart was as cold as winter, heavy with black dread. Such a long time, and no sighting of *Olympie;* no word, even, though she had questioned the sailors in the harbor as their ships came in to port. She tried to keep busy, to still the anxiety, the panic that threatened to overwhelm her.

She could not break off abruptly with Janequin for fear of rousing his suspicions (and perhaps she did not want to lose his company before his departure for Paris made it necessary), and so she spent several afternoons strolling with him in his gardens. She and Gilles were invited to supper; Gilles maintained the role of cruel husband that had been fashioned for him—though he seemed to glory in it—scolding Delphine in front of Braudel and Janequin until she turned red with humiliation.

But at home he had become kinder to her, looking at her with new eyes as though her skill at handling the affair of the necklace had made him aware of her value to him, her attributes as a woman. As far as she knew, he had not visited Lucie in weeks. No more was said of taking Robert from her, but she was not put off her guard. When her father returned, he would know how to hire and pay for a lawyer. If need be, she would have Michel swear in open court that he had lain with Delphine and the child was his.

Only let *Olympie* return! Delphine sat at her dressing table, gazing into her mirror by the light of the candle. It was late; she had sent Anne-Marie to bed hours ago. But she could not sleep, and she had not the patience for reading tonight. She took out her brazier and curling iron; perhaps such a simple and mindless task as curling the wisps about her face would help to still her nerves. Outside her window she could hear the rumblings of thunder far off. There was a storm brewing—like the storm she sensed was building in Gilles. She shivered, feeling strangely fearful, wondering if she should lock her door.

He had stared in fascination at her bosom during supper last night, a small muscle working in his jaw; this morning he had slipped his arm about her waist as she carried flowers from the garden. She had put down her basket and scissors and pushed his hand away.

"You had best visit Lucie," she said with contempt.

"Should I?"

"Indeed yes. You would—regret Delphine."

He had blanched at that and turned away, clearly recalling the humiliation of their last encounter. She had picked up her flowers and gone about her work, sure that she had cooled whatever ardor he had begun to feel again. Still, he did not like to be powerless—she knew that—and she stirred uneasily, remembering the look in his eyes.

She finished her hair and left the curling iron in the brazier. Anne-Marie could put it away in the morning, when the embers had smoldered out. She combed out her chignon, letting the back of her hair hang straight and loose, then went to the window, opening it to the night air, sniffing the tinge of moisture that blew from the sea, that promised a night of storm and fury. Even as she stood at the window the wind freshened, rattling the leaded panes of the casement, and a jagged knife of lightning ripped through the black sky. *Nom de Dieu!* Why did she feel such misgivings? Idly she began to plait her hair into a long braid, then jumped as a crash of thunder rent the air. She slammed the casement shut and turned, shaking, to see Gilles silhouetted in her doorway. In his hand he held a bottle of wine; when he closed the door and came toward her, staggering, she saw that the bottle was already nearly empty.

"Bitch," he said softly, the word thick and slurred.

"*Nom de Dieu,* Gilles," she snapped. "Have you come to torment me tonight?"

"And wherefore not? Do you not torment me? You are my wife—yet never mine! Never! In all these months, never mine. There is passion in you. There is fire! But not for me!"

"Go and find Lucie," she said tiredly. "She will please you more than ever I could."

"Bitch!" he said again, catching her wrist in a steellike grip. "Why not for me?"

"Because you disgust me!" she cried, tearing away from his grasp. "Because you are cruel and vicious and dishonest! Because you lie and cheat and make me steal for you. Because there is not one breath of goodness in your soul!" Her voice rose in fury, all the anger and hatred spilling out in a torrent, like the rain that had begun to beat furiously against the window. "Drunken pig—I spit on you!"

He pointed an accusing finger. "Look at you! Is that the only passion that can be aroused? Your foul rages?"

Her lip curled. "For you—yes. Always!" The shrieking wind echoed her fury.

He gulped the last of the wine and smashed the bottle into the empty fireplace, wiping his mouth carelessly across his sleeve. "And for him? Was there passion for him?"

"Go to the devil."

His eyes were blazing. "What did he do? Did he kiss you—like this?" His arms shot out to imprison hers, dragging her roughly to him.

She tossed her head from side to side, avoiding the mouth that would take hers. "Damn your eyes! Let me go! I warn you, Gilles—"

He laughed drunkenly, holding her squirming body tightly against his own. "What will you do? Will you claw me, you tiger? Will you fight me, and struggle and cry out? Will you make me know at last that I married a woman of fire?" With a sideways wrench that upset her balance, he dragged her down to the floor and straddled her knees so she bucked helplessly beneath him, her nightdress riding up to her thighs. Then he held her wrists together over her rib cage.

"I shall make you wish you had never been born a man!" she panted, still struggling.

"No, my sweet. Not tonight." With his free hand he pulled up the nightdress to her waist, wrapping it about her shoulders and arms, twisting it tightly so she lay entwined and entrapped in the folds of fabric, her upper torso imprisoned and helpless, her lower body bare. "Tonight you shall know I am more the man than he ever was—that villain I saw in your eyes each time you lay with me!"

"You dungheap! You filthy whoreson!" she cursed through clenched teeth, straining her muscles against the determined hands that had begun to pry her legs apart. With a cry she felt her strength give way as he forced his knee between her legs. She struggled to sit up, but it was almost impossible with her arms folded helplessly before her and her knees spread wide. She went limp, overcome with disgust and lassitude. "You will never be the man that he was."

"Bitch!" He slapped her face. She grunted in pain as the back of her head banged against the hard tiles of the floor. Outside, the thunder crashed and the wind howled. "What was he like?" he growled. "Was he handsome? Was he strong?" His voice rose in jealous fury, eyes glowing with a light that was almost madness. "Do you see him still in your dreams?" His glance went wildly about the room and stopped at the curling iron in its brazier on the vanity near him, in reach of his hand. He snatched it down and held it close to her face; she could feel the heat of the iron above her flesh. "Shall I burn him out of your eyes?" he whispered. She looked at him steadily, trying to keep from trembling, knowing he was drunk enough—and angry enough—to do her harm. He laughed, an ugly sound, and touched the hot iron for a second to her neck. She flinched, but bit her tongue to keep from crying out; she eyed him sternly, her voice the strong voice of reason.

"You are drunk, Gilles. In God's name, go to your bed. This is folly. This is madness. You can only earn my hatred."

"Not your eyes," he said, as though he had not heard her. "They are too lovely. But, mayhap," his hand dropped to her loins, the hot iron passing dangerously near her belly, "so he may never give you pleasure again—"

Delphine held her breath, steeling herself, praying he was only bluffing. To her relief Gilles tossed aside the curling iron and began to weep and blubber, his words thick between sobs. "You'll forget him tonight. You'll see. Tonight—only Gilles—only Gilles—" He sniffled loudly and began to fumble with his breeches; then he leaned down and kissed her, his mouth wet on hers, reeking with wine. She stared at him open eyed, choking with disgust, knowing he'd rape her anyway, and hoping only that he would have done with her quickly. "Don't look at me like that," he said. "Close your eyes. Close your eyes."

She laughed contemptuously. "I shall watch you make a fool of yourself."

A great flash of lightning illuminated his haggard face. "Damn you! Close your eyes!" He clutched at the curls that hung over her forehead, lifting her head and banging it back onto the hard floor—once, twice. Her eyelids fluttered for a moment, then closed, and she lay very still. He frowned and stood up, swaying slightly. Stooping, he lifted her in gentle arms and carried her to the bed, tenderly unwrapping the twisted nightdress and pulling it off her, stroking her naked limbs, spreading her hair like a golden halo on the pillow where she lay. Bending over her, he kissed her unconscious lips, then lifted her limp hand, guiding it to caress his cheeks, his mouth, while tears of pain streamed down his face. Then his visage darkened, his jaws clenched with remembered humiliation. He let go her flaccid arm and threw himself off the bed, glowing eyes darting furiously about the room to rest at last on the discarded nightdress. His hands tore savagely at it, ripping and rending in mad fury, as though the soft fabric were a living thing.

"Bitch!" he hissed, while the carpet before him filled with shreds of linen. "Bitch! Bitch! Bitch!"

Delphine stirred in her bed, passing her hand across her eyes. Why did her head throb so, just behind her closed lids? She opened her eyes, blinking at the bright sunshine that streamed into the room. She tried to sit up, then groaned aloud at the hammer-beats within her brain. She closed her eyes again, unable to think, and rubbed at her face and neck. *"Dieu du ciel!"* she gasped aloud, her eyes springing open as her fingers touched the small raw blister on her neck. Gilles! Last night! Oh God, why could she not think clearly? Gingerly she touched the back of her head, feeling the tender swelling, the crusted blood on her scalp. That villain! It hurt too much to think. She closed her eyes again and let her mind drift, absorbing reality in small doses only as she could cope with it: the pounding in her head that clamored for supremacy, the twittering of birds beyond her window, the feel of the sheets against her naked skin. Her eyes flew open. But she had been wearing her nightdress last night! In dread she ran her hands over her body, exhaling in relief to find herself unviolated. *Ah Dieu!* She shuddered in horror that the thought had even crossed her mind. But—the whisper of a tiny voice—Gilles was capable of it, however much she had closed her eyes to the evil of the man.

She lifted her pounding head from the pillow and gasped at the sight of her torn nightdress. Dear Mother of God! She clutched her arms about her bosom, feeling Gilles's hatred—so manifest in the shreds of her garment —like a pulsing wave of poison that was almost harder to endure than if he *had* raped her. She could not bear to look at them another moment. She struggled to sit up, the gorge rising in her throat, and staggered out of bed, clutching at the bedhangings for support. With shaking hands she gathered up every bit and piece of fabric—all her horror, all her shame in those tattered shreds—and hid them in a drawer of her vanity. Her head splitting, she barely tottered back to her bed, falling across it without the strength even to crawl between the sheets. Sweet Jesu! She could not stay another minute, another hour with such a monster! If only she could think. Perhaps if she closed her eyes for a little—Sighing, she pulled the coverlet around her and drifted off.

It was thus that Anne-Marie found her, curled up in the coverlet at the foot of her bed. "Madame!" She gasped in shock, holding up the bloody pillow. "What has happened?"

"Help me back to bed, Anne-Marie, and bring me a cup of wine. It is nothing. Monsieur and I—quarreled last night. I fell and struck my head. It is nothing."

"Nothing?" Anne-Marie frowned, her fingers probing among the bloody tresses to find the still-oozing wound, her eyes noting the small burn on the tender flesh, the broken bottle in the hearth. Had it come to this? She had always found him a good master, though she was aware of his harshness to the apprentices. But that was natural —they were headstrong lads and needed to be molded. But his wife? A man had a right to beat his wife, of course—a few slaps on the rump to keep her in line—but not to brutalize her! Anne-Marie sighed. Well, it was none of her concern. She was too old to start looking for another position.

Clad in a fresh nightdress, Delphine leaned back against a clean pillow and sipped at the wine Anne-Marie had brought, feeling a bit of her strength returning. "Where—where is Monsieur Despreaux this morning?"

"I know not, Madame. He woke the stableboy in the midst of the storm last night—it was very late, and the wind howling like Satan, the boy said—and rode out into the tempest. He has not returned." Her brow creased with concern. "Will you sleep again now, madame? Please. You look so pale."

Delphine hesitated. She was safe so long as Gilles had not returned. Still—

"I shall wake you should monsieur come home," said Anne-Marie quickly.

Delphine nodded gratefully and closed her eyes. But when the old housekeeper had gone, she got out of bed and crossed to a small cabinet. Rummaging in a drawer, she withdrew her sheathed sea knife; only when it was tucked safely under her pillow did she allow herself to drift into defenseless sleep.

By afternoon she was feeling a little better, her headache subsiding, and she sat patiently while Anne-Marie cleaned the blood from her golden hair, and helped her to dress. But her brain was churning with thoughts. As long as Gilles remained away, there was time to decide what she must do. She could not stay—she would kill him if she did. But if she left with Robert, she would have to hide so Gilles could not find them, stay in seclusion until her father came home. She had not seen the cottage since the fire—there might be a corner of it yet standing. She would have to be careful about lighting a fire to cook or keep warm, lest someone see the smoke from afar and run and tell Gilles. The coins that she had would buy enough milk for Robert for a few weeks. As for herself, she would steal as much of Gilles's food as she could carry away; she thought she could persuade Anne-Marie to give her the keys to the larder. It was a desperate plan, but she was desperate. Tucking her sea knife into her waist beneath her bodice (she would never go without it again, so long as Gilles lived), she set out for the cottage.

The beach bore the ravages of the storm, bits of

seaweed and driftwood flung about, dead fish and washed-up mussels beginning already to stink under the warm sun. With eyes that had spent years gazing out over the vastnesses of the ocean, Delphine could see from far away that there was nothing but one or two charred timbers left standing of her father's cottage. But she plodded on across the dunes, refusing to accept the testimony of her eyes until she stood before the scattered ashes that had once been home to her. Heavyhearted, she turned about and returned to Gilles's house, deliberately avoiding the harbor of Dieppe. She could not bear to see that *Olympie* still had not returned.

Anne-Marie met her at the door. Monsieur was still away, but there was a man come to see her. She had left him in the garden.

"A gentleman?"

"No, Madame. One of the men who came last fall with Monsieur Fresnel your father."

"Ah Dieu!" With a glad cry Delphine rushed to the garden, her heart filling with joy at the red-faced giant who turned to greet her. "Gunner!" she squealed, throwing herself into his arms. She kissed him joyously again and again until his rosy face darkened to crimson, then stepped back, grinning, her words tumbling over themselves in a rush to get out. "Did you come on *Olympie?* When did you make landfall? Where is my father? Is Michel well, that lazy lout? Have you missed me?"

"We—we landed yesterday morning and—"

"Rot and damnation!" she burst out, interrupting him. "Yesterday morning? And no word to me?" She stamped her foot angrily. "God's blood! How could you—" then stopped, seeing his face. "Where is my father?" she whispered.

He rubbed his eyes. "I could not come to see you until we had settled our accounts with Monsieur Ramy."

"Where is my father?"

"I told Master Fresnel the barrels were too big, but he thought there would be more profit, and he needed the money. The repairs in September were more than he had bargained for."

"What happened?" Her blood had run to ice.

"We were five days out of Martinique. The ship was riding low. The barrels were filled with tobacco and tortoise oil—the hold was crammed gunwale to gunwale —and furs we had bartered for in New France. And then the squall struck—a great gale blowing out of the north—"

Delphine's eyes were almost pleading. "*Olympie* is a worthy ship! She could ride out any storm. Is it not so?"

He shook his head. "She was overloaded, and riding the swells badly. We prayed to God she would not capsize. Master Fresnel decided to jettison some of the barrels. We untied a few and tossed them over the side. But the lashings gave way—one rope snapped, and then another—and the barrels broke loose—every lubbardly one of 'em—rolling with every pitch of the sea—crashing into the hull till some of the planks cracked and the water gushed in. Be hanged if we did not think it was the end of us and *Olympie* too. We lashed them down at last— thanks be to God—or old Gunner would not be here now to tell the tale. Brise cracked his pate, and Michel broke a leg—"

She felt numb and cold. "And my father?"

"Crushed by a barrel. He lingered for a day, then went peacefullike, be hanged if he didn't, and sending his blessings to his Gosse."

"I was always his good luck, wasn't I, Gunner?"

"That you were, Gosse."

"I heard the crew—before you sailed last June—
talking among themselves. It was bad luck, they said,
because I was not with them. Did I do it, Gunner, letting
Olympie go without me?"

Gunner crossed himself hurriedly. "Now, Gosse. You
know as well as I that *Olympie* wasn't cursed by you
staying ashore! Else why was the voyage to the Levant
safe? Aye, and profitable too! It was just God's will, this
time."

"Thank you for telling me, Gunner." She took a deep
breath, feeling no pain. She must think clearly. She must
think of Robert—the living, not the dead. "The cargo is
gone?"

"We lost some over the side, and some of the tobacco
was spoiled by the seawater, but we salvaged a little."

"Enough to pay back the moneylenders for the supplies?"

"Not quite enough."

"Well, we'll pay them back double from the profits of
the next voyage."

"Monsieur Ramy has already paid them back. Out of
respect for your father. He did not want to leave Master
Fresnel's debts as a burden to you."

"How kind of him. Then we can plan the next voyage
with no drag-sail to hinder us."

"No."

"What do you mean? I shall name you master, or
become *Olympie's* master myself."

Gunner looked shamefaced. "Begging your pardon,
Gosse, but *Olympie* is not yours anymore. I told you. The
repairs last fall—more than the master thought. He—he
borrowed of Monsieur Ramy against her ownership—"

"It cannot be!"

"I have spent two days with Monsieur Ramy's lawyers

and clerks. I am a simple man, but I know they did not cheat Master Fresnel. Ramy is swallowing the loss himself, but *Olympie* is his now. He has asked me to stay on as master, with Michel for bosun's mate when he can walk again."

"There—there is nothing—nothing left?"

"Master Fresnel's sea chest is still aboard with all his belongings, and yours as well. If you want to send someone 'round to fetch them."

She nodded wordlessly, numb with shock, and ushered Gunner to the gate of the garden that led to the street. She shook his hand, and kissed him on the cheek, then turned to go into the house.

"Gossé!" he burst out. "If—if you want it, be hanged if there won't always be a berth for you aboard *Olympie*, so long as I am master! We're away for the coast of Africa in a month or two."

"Thank you." She stumbled into the house and up the stairs to the nursery, taking Robert in her arms and rocking him gently to soothe the panic that threatened to drown her. She could not weep; her grief was replaced by desperation. She had relied on her father, on *Olympie's* profit, to rescue her from Gilles.

"What shall I do?" she whispered. And the caged wolf cub beat in terror against its prison bars.

Chapter Fourteen

GILLES STILL HAD NOT RETURNED THE FOLLOWING MORN-
ing. Delphine spent hours in his bedchamber, ransacking
drawers and cabinets. Damn! She did not even know
where he kept his money! His writing table was locked,
and she contemplated breaking it open, then changed
her mind. If there was no gold there, and Gilles should
return before she had quite decided what to do, she did
not want him to guess her intentions, lest he spirit Robert
away from her. She racked her brain. She must at all
costs keep Gilles from taking her child. It meant hiding, or
going far away where he could not find them. She
remembered Gunner's words. Why *not* go to sea? She
had been raised on shipboard—would it not be a good
life for Robert? They could settle in America someday;
she had always liked Quebec. She smiled with relief,
recalling the happy innocence of her life aboard *Olympie*.
Yes. She would go to sea again.

It was well into the afternoon when she hurried up the
gangplank to *Olympie*'s deck, clutching the robe handrail
to maneuver the steep incline. She flinched as the rough
line scraped her palm, and looked at her hand, surprised

to see a red welt already forming. After nearly a year ashore her hands had lost their work calluses.

"Here's a pretty doxy!"

Delphine turned at the voice. It was one of the seamen she remembered had signed on at the beginning of her last voyage, but now he was leering at her, his snag-toothed face split in a wide grin. "Don't you recognize me, Jean?" she said.

"Gosse! By all the saints—is it you?" He let his eyes travel the length of her body in open lechery, his glance lingering at her full bosom. "Sink me, Gosse, but if I'd known what you were hiding, I should have taken you on my lap the other way 'round, not like that Monsieur André! Eh?" He laughed and slapped his hands together.

"Where's Gunner?" she asked coldly.

He looked shamefaced and tugged at his forelock. "I meant no disrespect, Gosse. We were all sorry about Master Fresnel—a fine captain he was to serve under. Gunner's in the Great Cabin aft."

"Thank you. I shall find my way." She swept past him, daintily lifting her skirts to keep them from catching on the coiled lines on deck. Climbing the stairs to the quarterdeck, she resolved to cut her hair and put on her breeches again as soon as possible. Though Jean had apologized for his bawdiness, she did not like the look in his eyes, and the voyage to Africa would be long, with empty stretches that gave a man time to think. As she entered the dim passageway she could hear, from far below, the sounds of the bilge pumps in operation. Sweet Jesu, how the place stank! She covered her mouth and nose with her hand, feeling as though she would gag from nausea. Had it always been as bad as this? She blinked in the gloom and peered down the companion-way to the galley deck below. She could hear the soft squeak of a rat as it scurried from its hiding place. God's blood! she thought. Why can they not keep a cat aboard ship as we do at home? She knocked softly at the door of the Great Cabin, entering at Gunner's command.

He greeted her warmly and they chatted about Michel and Brise laid up in a tavern ashore until they should mend, while she tried not to let her eyes stray around the cabin and to the bunk that had belonged to André. She did not tell Gunner she had decided to ship aboard—there would be time for that after she had settled the matter of the sea chests.

"In the roundhouse, Gosse," said Gunner. "I have put most of Master Fresnel's things away, but you must check to see that I have not missed anything. Your chest is in there as well. We needed your cabin for storage last voyage out."

She mounted the companionway to the roundhouse, retrieving a pipe tucked away on a shelf, a small chart tacked to the bulkhead—the few small items that Gunner had overlooked. A quick look told her that her own things were intact; closing both chests she returned to the quarterdeck to arrange with Gunner for the transport of the trunks to Gilles's house at least until she and Robert should be permanently aboard *Olympie,* and out of Gilles's clutches. She passed her old cabin. On a sudden whim she pushed open the door and went inside. *Mon Dieu!* How small it was! Dark and gloomy, dank and airless—suffocating after the cheeriness of her large room at home. And the stench! She shuddered at the fetid odors of rancid oil and tallow, bilge water and sweat, stepping carefully around an empty crate to sink to the narrow bunk. Three large roaches skittered out of the straw pallet to seek refuge elsewhere. Sweet Mother, she thought, feeling her revulsion growing, I don't belong here anymore! How could she live like this for months at a time—even if she did not have Robert with her? She was used to clean floors, and sweet air in her nostrils, and food that did not crawl with vermin. Gosse, *Olympie,* her carefree days with Michel—they belonged to a part of her life that was gone, vanished like a dream, as dead as Copain and her father. I don't belong here, she thought again, her heart filled with despair. Damn you, André! I might have sailed with *Olympie,* I might have saved my father! But for you, this might still be my life! Sick at heart, she hurried back to the Great Cabin and Gunner.

"If you're ready to leave, Gosse," he said, "I'll have a mate take the sea chests and follow you home."

"Thank you. Wait! No. Have someone trundle them around in a wheelbarrow whenever he can. I am not going home just yet. I have—another errand." She hugged him tightly, wondering if she would ever see him again, ever laugh with this gentle giant who had been father and mother to her, friend and teacher.

It was twilight before she reached the hill and Monsieur de Janequin's manor house. She prayed that Braudel would not be in—it would be difficult enough to deal with Janequin without the accusing eyes of the lawyer upon her.

"Madame Despreaux!" The *duc* greeted her warmly, bringing her fingers to his lips. "What a charming surprise!" He led her into a small room, indicating a chair. "Come. Sit. Braudel will be sorry he missed you. He is making final arrangements for our return to Paris next week. Let me send for wine. Will you take supper? What a pleasure to see you!"

"No! No wine. And I wish to stand." She looked at him with pain-filled eyes. "God knows I should kneel at your feet!"

"What nonsense is this?"

She took a deep breath. "I am a thief and a cheat. I lied to you. All that I told you was lies! My 'noble' birth, the deeds, the loan, all of it. But you have lost nothing. Charretier still has the diamond necklace."

He shook his head in disbelief. "*I* have the necklace!"

"No. Charretier made a copy."

"It cannot be. I had it authenticated when Charretier returned it."

"He returned the original. It was I who—" She stumbled and could not go on.

"But how?"

"The moneylender. My—my husband Gilles. In disguise."

"*Nom de Dieu!* He only looked at it for a second! I myself saw him return it to you in plain sight!"

"He had—the other—tucked in his sleeve. You were not looking for it, so why should you have seen it?"

"Why did you do it?"

She turned away, unwilling to look in his eyes. "I have no excuses. I did it. That is all."

"And now you come to tell me how I may recover the necklace. Wherefore?"

"I need your help. I must get away from him and there is nowhere else to turn. I need money, but I need your influence—and the services of Monsieur Braudel as well. I thought—if I confessed all, saw that your jewels were returned, you might be merciful to me and give me your help."

He put his hands on her shoulders, frowning sternly down at her. "Why should you trust me? I could have you imprisoned, branded for a thief and a swindler." His voice rumbled angrily, clearly disappointed in her.

She laughed bitterly. "I am branded for being his wife," and indicated the mark of the curling iron on her neck.

"Nom de Dieu! Why do you stay with him?"

"Yes. I could leave him, beg in the streets. Earn my way somehow—"

"Indeed!" he interrupted, a sardonic smile twisting his fine features. His eyes swept her body. "There is much you could do to earn money, as well you must know! So why do you risk my wrath? Have I given you cause to believe I'm a fool? *Why* do you come to me?"

"Because—there is someone else—very dear to me— whom I must care for, and I fear Gilles would use the law to—track us down and harm us."

"Ah! The someone else! Then they were not *all* lies after all?"

"No."

"The villainous husband, the someone who is dear to you—?"

"No. Not lies."

"And the father in America, who was to return some-day to pay back the 'loans'—was he a lie?"

She stared at him, stricken. "I was waiting for him to return that I might be free of Gilles."

"And—?"

She gulped, fighting back the tears she had denied for two days. "He will never come home. I have only just learned—" She turned away, clutching her arms to herself to keep from trembling, from crying out her grief to the heavens.

"Poor child," he murmured, reaching out to pull her into his embrace. "My poor child—"

"No!" She choked back her tears and broke away

from him. "I am unworthy of your kindness. I am a wicked woman. But—there is nowhere else to turn."

"You did not need to tell me of the necklace. I should have helped you in any event." He laughed softly. "I did not tell Braudel of our second visit to the moneylender. I did not want his suspicions poisoning my thoughts of you. My dear child. Jewels are but empty trifles, gold is—" He shrugged. "What is their glow next to the warmth of a human heart? You could have come to me at the very first. Did you not know that? Now go home and put your mind at rest. I must think about what is to be done, and smooth Braudel's ruffled feathers, though I have no doubt he will be pleased to be confirmed in his low opinion of people's honesty! I have no wish to see you in prison. I would have my sister's diamonds, of course, but not if you must suffer. Let me think on it. Take my carriage—it has grown quite dark. I will send a message around to you in the morning."

For the first time in days she felt heartened, riding through the dark streets to Gilles's house. So soon she would be free! She felt it in her soul.

She was met at the door by Anne-Marie. "Madame!"

Ah Dieu! she thought, seeing the housekeeper's face. Gilles has returned! She hurried up the stairs, hand poised at the ready above her sea knife, then stopped on the landing, eyes wide with shock, to see Lucie flouncing toward her. "Whore!" she hissed. "Would you flaunt yourself in my house?"

A simpering smile. "I've brought your husband back to you. Is that all the thanks I get?"

"Be grateful I do not tear your hair out!"

"Your husband is dying, madame! It was only my

Christian charity that led me to bring him home to die in his own bed."

"How dying? What happened?"

"He came to me, the other night, in the midst of that frightful storm. He has not been constant of late. I was—entertaining another gentleman. There was a fight. Your husband is not so prudent when he has been drinking. Monsieur Despreaux was stabbed."

"Mother of God."

"I paid for the doctor out of my own pocket, but when he told me today that monsieur was lost, I thought it wise to bring him to his wife's arms to die."

A sardonic laugh. "More especially as it would not look well for him to die in your—establishment!"

"I do have a certain reputation to maintain!" said Lucie haughtily, and swept out of the house.

Gilles lay propped against his pillows, his face gray and ashen, his breath heavy and labored. His shirt was mottled with dried blood, great crimson gouts that soiled the white linen; just beneath his heart the wound still oozed bright vermillion. "Is that you, Delphine?" he said softly, then coughed and groaned, the sound ending in a wheeze that was torn from his chest.

She hurried quickly to his side. He was Gilles—but he *was* a dying man. "Rest quietly," she said, with a certain sympathy. "I shall send for the doctor again."

"No. There is no hope. And I would speak to you."

"Name of God, Gilles—hush!"

"I would speak to you—I would curse you with my dying breath. Were you with your lover tonight? Ungrateful woman! I created you. I took a crude savage," he gasped for breath, "and made a beautiful woman. I gave you your dream. And you have repaid me by killing me—"

"Please. Rest!"

"No! You poisoned our marriage from the first! You—and that—" he coughed, and a thin trickle of blood appeared at the corner of his mouth "—that lover you dreamed of, that you compared to me, every day of our lives together. I curse you—you faithless bitch—I curse you—I curse you—I—" He lapsed into unconsciousness, his head lolling to one side.

Trembling, Delphine left his room. "See to monsieur, Anne-Marie," she said, her voice shaky, and made for the refuge of her own room. The two sea chests had been brought from *Olympie* and left in the middle of her room. In a daze she dropped to her knees and lifted the lid on her own trunk, rummaging about distractedly among possessions that no longer seemed a part of her. She found Gosse's red mariner's cap and stood up, clutching it to her bosom. Without her willing it, her feet carried her down the stairs and out into the garden. It was true, what Gilles had said. She had killed him. She had poisoned their marriage. Had he been a saint, even, she would have tormented him, the memory of André always between them. She sat down on the garden bench and gazed up at the night sky, brilliant with stars. Gosse had gloried in those stars, filled with wonder and joy. Now they were just cold lights that shone upon her guilt and remorse.

That was what André had done. She could almost forgive him the unhappiness of her marriage, his abandonment of her, even the death of her father. But when she searched her heart she could not find Gosse anywhere. Delphine had killed her, had plunged the knife into her heart, had let the vital spirit drain away. And wherefore? For blue eyes that had imprisoned her, strong arms that had beckoned to her, lips that had whispered a siren song. Now Gosse was dead, and Gilles was dying because of her, and André was gone. She had nothing.

She shook the red cap skyward. "If it takes a lifetime, André," she sobbed, her tears overwhelming her at last, "there will be a reckoning as will shake the pillars of God's heaven!"

Chapter Fifteen

"UPON MY WORD, ANDRÉ, BUT YOU HAVE TAUGHT YOUR boys to ride well!"

André laughed and sat up, settling his back against the sun-warmed tree trunk on the bank of the Loire. He smiled and waved at the two boys who raced their horses in the open meadow that fronted the river—a blond lad about nine, a chestnut-haired boy perhaps two years younger. They shouted something and wheeled about, making for the far side of the meadow, their voices loud and boisterous in the soft spring air. His face twisted in a mock grimace, André turned to his companion, a man of about his own age with a pleasant face and a remarkable head of flowing red curls. "But I fear they will frighten the fish away with their noise, Jean-Auguste." He poked lazily at the fishing pole propped against a small rock, stirring the line in the water.

Jean-Auguste, Vicomte de Narbaux, grinned and popped a ripe strawberry into his mouth, then handed the basket of fruit to André. "On such a beautiful day, *mon ami,* one does not go fishing to catch fish. Only to find tranquillity."

"Indeed? Then why has no one told that to my lads?"

"It is happy noise, André, my friend. Be grateful!" Jean-Auguste tugged at the fishing pole that had jerked suddenly in his hand, then swore as the line went slack again.

"Tranquillity, Jean-Auguste. Tranquillity!"

Jean-Auguste gave him a withering stare and ate another strawberry. "Oh! By the by," he said suddenly, "did I tell you I had a letter from my cousin Georges de Mersenne in Quebec?"

"No. He is well?"

Jean-Auguste laughed. "Well—Aunt Marguerite may say he has taken leave of his reason. It will be amusing to hear what she has to say about her grandson when she visits us this summer. She has never been at a loss for words. And it seems that Georges has married a savage! Some Huron woman he has been living with."

"I remember her," said André. "A charming girl. And if he is happy—?" He shrugged.

"But Georges is Marguerite's only heir. When she dies, her estate in Poitou will fall to him. What will he do? Abandon his wife and come home?"

"No," said André, remembering. "I think New France is his home now. He would miss it grievously if he came here."

"Do you miss it?"

André shook his head. "No. It was like a dream, a time of healing—no more." He looked thoughtful. "Do you realize it is more than two years since I have been there? It was the middle of April—in '39—when we sailed for home—and what is it today? The fourth of May?"

"The fifth, I think."

André helped himself to another berry. "Thirty-nine. That was a year for battles! Do you remember the fighting in Salces in July?"

"I remember we lost it again in December! That was

why, when we took Arras last summer, I volunteered to stay on through the winter to hold it. And with the end of the war in sight—God willing!—and fewer battles being fought, my winter duty has discharged this summer's obligation. I intend to fish and laze about until the snow falls!"

André sighed. "I would volunteer if I could this summer, but Richelieu will not hear of it."

"And a wise decision it was," said Jean-Auguste sharply. "That fever you came down with on the Italian front last year—*Nom de Dieu!* You know as well as I that your lung has never healed fully since your injuries at La Forêt! And you are far more valuable to the king as an adviser on New France, with your knowledge of the Huron ways and language."

"But how am I to fill my days, if I cannot go to war again?"

Jean-Auguste laughed. "I don't remember your being so enamored of battle in the past!"

"That was when Marielle waited at home in Vilmorin."

"Oh, my friend. Is it so hard for you still?"

"It is three years since—" he could not say the words. "I am forty-three, the years are passing, and I feel dead and old—empty and lonely—"

"But what about Clémence de Vignon? Lysette was so sure you would enjoy her company. She is a sweet woman, widowed far too young—not yet thirty, I think. She seems much like Marielle—gracious, serene, quiet—"

"I shall tell you, Jean-Auguste, but you must not breathe a word to that lovely wife of yours. Lysette is very kind to play matchmaker, to concern herself with my lonely days—and nights—but—I spent a week in Clémence's company last fall when the court was at Fontainebleau."

"In her bed?"

"No. She is very chaste and proper."

"As was Marielle, I think," said Jean-Auguste defensively.

"Yes, but—" André plucked absently at a blade of grass, his blue eyes deep with remembrance. "As I said," he continued at last, "I spent a week with Clémence at Court, and a week with her at Chimère, with you and Lysette—and I shall tell you, my friend, the woman bores me to tears! God knows, if I wanted her I could have seduced her long since. But I would rather go to Paris and pay a call on Marion de Lorme. She's expensive, but at least she does not put me to sleep!"

"*Ah Dieu!* And since Marielle—no one to stir your heart?"

André laughed sardonically, the sound barely hiding the pain in his voice. "The tavern wench in Vouvray is madly in love with me. She lifts her skirts before I come in the door." He rubbed his eyes tiredly, the humor suddenly empty and flat. "There was a girl—two years ago—she haunts me still." He leaned forward, arms around his knees, gazing into the rippling current of the river. "She was so young, so full of joy and life. Her sunshine filled my cold heart, awakened my soul. And even when she angered me—which was often, *mon Dieu!*—the anger made me feel alive. Is that foolish, *mon ami?*"

Jean-Auguste shook his head in understanding. "No. How old was she?"

"Very young, in more than years. A child-woman, but as much woman as child. Yet more fearless and brave than many a man. And her laughter—I hear it in my dreams still—rich and deep, caressing my senses even in memory—"

"Merde! And you let her go?" Jean-Auguste's gray eyes were wide with disbelief.

"She was like a young bird, wild and free. Did you ever break a stallion and watch the light die in its eyes? I think it would be so with her." He sighed. "But her flame warmed these old bones for a spell."

"You are a fool for not seeking her out!"

"I am too old to play the panting swain."

"Pah! *I* don't feel old! And I am scarce five years your junior!"

"I think it is because Lysette keeps you young. She never ceases to surprise me. A changeable flower. *That* would keep a man young."

Jean-Auguste laughed ruefully, thinking of his wife. "And make him old at the same time! But—yes. Lysette tries me often, but her freshness is a joy. I would have her no other way."

"And so it was with her, though I did not know her worth until long after we were parted."

"Then seek her out!"

"I did at last—as best I could—when I could no longer bear the emptiness of my days, the sound of her voice in my dreams. I sent a man to where I thought she might be, to where there might be those who knew her. Alas! He found a cottage burned to the ground, no word of her father, no trace of her. My bright bird had flown."

Jean-Auguste was silent for a long time. "Why not go to Paris? The court is at the Louvre Palace, and Louis would be delighted to see you. He is growing tired at last of his favorite, Henri de Cinq-Mars."

"Yes. I've met him. Arrogant little popinjay. Too young to have found such favor as the king's tender companion."

"I think he will not have that favor much longer. When the dog forces the master to bark—But Louis will be restless, and as a consequence the court will sparkle with gaiety, trying to amuse him. Why not go? There was a time when André, Comte du Crillon, could have any woman in Paris he wanted, married or unmarried! Are you too old for that anymore?" Jean-Auguste grinned wickedly, his baiting that of one old friend to another. "I give you a challenge, *mon ami!* Marion de Lorme. You have enjoyed her favors in the past?"

"For a price. That particular courtesan comes dear. But I have found her worth it."

"Well then. They say she has attached herself to Cinq-Mars. With his position and prestige at court, he makes a worthy patron. It would take a—remarkable man to turn her head at this time. And with no remuneration, mind you! Are you—equal to the challenge?"

André chuckled deep in his throat, contemplating the dare, half minded to take up the gauntlet. "Why not?" he said at last. "And I shall send you the lady's garter as proof. I only pray that Clémence does not decide to come to Paris this month! She has invited me to her château several times, and I have declined on the pretense that I was too busy with my vineyards at Vilmorin. By my faith, I am feeling much bedeviled and pursued by that lady!"

"I fear that Lysette has her heart set on Clémence as a neighbor! The moment my wife finds that you have gone to Paris, she will want to follow at once, and bring Clémence with her. Well, I shall try to forestall her plans. In the meantime, I should be starting for home." Jean-Auguste stood up and stretched. "'Tis a pleasant hour's ride, but Lysette will pout if I am late, and I shall be forced to forfeit a new fan or a mirror to coax a smile from her!"

"Come back to Vilmorin, then," said André, indicating the large golden-stoned château set at some distance from the river. "I shall fortify you with a cup of good Crillon wine whilst the grooms bring your horse around."

"Ha! That vinegar?" Jean-Auguste grinned and slapped André on the back. "Well, I shall drink it anyway. It will be a humbling experience, to know how fortunate I am that *le bon Dieu* has seen fit to make *my* wine so much finer than yours!" Laughing, the two men crossed the grassy meadow.

Jean-Auguste raised himself up on his elbows to contemplate the woman who lay beneath him. In the light of the single candle Lysette's eyes, heavy with sated passion, were as black as the raven curls that tumbled in disarray about her head. But he knew it was an illusion of the dark night; the color of those eyes—the rich purple of wood violets—was as familiar to him as the elfin face and the full mouth that smiled seductively at him. He leaned down and kissed her again. Five years, and still his heart swelled with love and joy for this woman who shared his bed, who gave him the sons he had wanted—and in full measure! He nearly laughed aloud, thinking of it, the wonder of it. He had wanted a son to name after his dead brother Gabriel; three years ago Lysette had presented him with two sons, as alike as two peas—Jean-Gabriel, Pierre-Gabriel. They had hair that flamed as red as his own, gray eyes—like his own—and the glint of the devil in their smiles that could only have come from their mother! Sighing contentedly, he eased his weight off Lysette's form and lay back on his own pillow, beaming absently at the canopy above the bed. Lysette grumbled at being abandoned and snuggled into the warmth of his arm, idly tracing patterns on his chest with a delicate forefinger until he found himself beginning to want her again.

"How handsome you are," she murmured. "Do you know how proud I am to be seen with you when we go out?"

His mouth twitched in a crooked smile. "Go out where?"

"Oh, just out! To visit friends, to a party."

"What do you want?"

"Why should I want anything? *Dieu du ciel*, Jean-Auguste, why should I want anything?"

He sat up and frowned down at her. "I shall never understand why you must play your little games!" An edge of exasperation entered his voice. "I am not deceived, and you know it. Sometimes I think you do it for the joy of it, but it seems an unnecessary bother to me! Now, where are we going?"

She looked shamefaced. "You remember—I told you. Wednesday next. Madame d'Hiver's birthday."

"Ah. Yes. And what do you want? A new gown?"

"Yes—no—I—"

"Hum. You have bought it already, and now you are afraid to tell me."

"Oh, Jean-Auguste," she said, smiling meekly. "It is a lovely gown, the yellow of primroses—"

"I have no doubt you will look charming in it. Why could you not simply have told me of it to begin with?"

"It cost so much—I did not think, when I ordered the fabric, of the new taxes—one sol per livre!—and the finished gown was far more than—I did not mean to spend so much—I promise you, the next time—"

"Enough!" he said, laughing. "We can afford it this year." His eyes twinkled. "When the grape harvest comes, I shall set you into the vat to tread the grapes—that way you may earn your keep!"

"Pooh!" she said, pushing him down onto the pillow

and leaning over him. "If I must earn my keep, I shall do it in my own way!" She kissed him resoundingly on the mouth and grinned in satisfaction.

"Only assuming I find you more valuable in the bedchamber than in the vineyards!" He dodged aside as she pummeled him with her pillow. After a brief battle, during which he tickled her unmercifully and she battered him with the pillow, she settled once again into his arms.

She sighed. "How did you find André?"

"Well."

"He is so lonely, the poor man. And his motherless children—"

"Louise is good to them."

"But Louise is a housekeeper, not a mother, and far too old. And André is so alone. Do you think he would come to Madame d'Hiver's birthday next week? I'm sure I could persuade her to invite him. And Clémence will be there—"

Jean-Auguste hesitated. "He—will be off to Paris in a day or two. The change will do him good."

"Paris? *Nom de Dieu!* Let me see if I can arrange it. I shall send our regrets to Madame d'Hiver, and notify Clémence at once—"

"No."

"But Jean-Auguste—if André will be in Paris—"

"We shall *not* go! And certainly not with Clémence de Vignon."

"But he needs someone like Clémence. The boys need her. She is so like Marielle—" Lysette's voice was wistful. "She was such a dear friend, was she not? We had so little time. Do you remember how she visited me all that winter, as I grew large with the twins in my womb? How kind she was to me, easing my fears—"

"Is it for André—or yourself—that you promote Clémence's cause?"

"What do you mean?"

"I grieve for André as well, *ma chère,* but you can no more bring Marielle back than André can. Leave him alone."

"Are you forbidding me?" she said petulantly.

"I refuse to treat you like a child, with rules and commands."

She wriggled contentedly in his arms. "Then may I do as I please in this matter?"

"No!" he exploded. "We shall not follow André to Paris, dragging Clémence with us! Name of God! Heaven alone knows why I do not beat you every single day of our lives together! Sometimes I think you are the same willful, stubborn, impossible—"

"Yes?" she said, sitting up and folding her arms across her bare bosom.

He shook his head, softening. "The same stubborn, willful, adorable woman that I loved when we married, that I love now." He pulled her down into his embrace, filled with desire. "Not another word tonight, wench! Earn your keep!"

"Not another word," she murmured, and wrapped her arms around his neck, abandoning herself to his passion.

But a small voice still whispered in her ear. Perhaps in a week or two it would be time again to talk about going to Paris. She would see Clémence installed in Vilmorin yet! For André's good, the foolish man!

Chapter Sixteen

"COME ALONG, ANDRÉ, I HAVE A BARGE WAITING."

André nodded and followed his companion through the long corridor of the Louvre Palace, down a marble staircase, and into the May twilight. When they stood at last on the edge of the stone *quai* that kept the floodwaters of the Seine from inundating the city every spring, his companion, René, Duc de Rannel, waved his arm daintily in the air, signaling to a small boat waiting on the placid river. André threw on his cloak, adjusting it so it lay over one shoulder and swept diagonally across his back; it was a slightly more flamboyant style than he usually affected, but Rannel was such a peacock that he, André, felt positively plain in the man's presence. In truth, he was not overly fond of Rannel, with his beribboned doublet and his plumes and lappets and fussy manners. One of the younger dandies, he had never learned that the measure of a man was in his sword and his wit, not in the skill of his tailor. Even his hair was carefully dressed in that seeming offhand manner adapted by many of the courtiers: the long flowing curls purposely tousled, except for one piece, longer than the rest, combed over one shoulder and tied with a ribbon bow. A lovelock, they called it, and it was to signify that the wearer burned with a secret love.

But André had been feeling lonely, and it was too sweet a night to stay in his apartments in the Louvre and fret. There were to be no royal receptions this evening, as the queen was at Saint-Germain and Louis was dining privately with Cardinal Richelieu. André had seen the latest play in the Hôtel de Bourgogne, many of his friends were off fighting at the front, and he had never enjoyed the gambling houses of Le Marais. Moreover, Mademoiselle Marion de Lorme, whose garter had been sent to Jean-Auguste barely a week after André's arrival in Paris, was entertaining Monsieur de Cinq-Mars tonight. And so when Rannel had invited him to accompany him, promising an enchanting evening, André had agreed.

They settled into the small boat, sitting back comfortably on cushions while the oarsmen pulled on their long sweeps. The night was soft, the spring sky still light, with a fine mist beginning to rise on the river; a silver crescent moon hung in the pale heavens just over the Pont Neuf.

"Where are we going?" said André.

"The Place Royale."

André nodded. He knew it well. It was a fine address, with magnificent town houses that fronted on an open square. Houses there were difficult to come by, because of their desirability, and they were expensive to maintain. "Our host is a wealthy gentleman, then?"

Rannel hesitated. "Our hostess," he said at last. "Frankly, *mon vieux,* I was not sure whether I wished your company tonight."

"Indeed?"

"She is a charming lady, very dear to my heart." He indicated his lovelock, tied with a length of blue silk. "I begged this ribbon of her, that she might always know the constancy of my devotion."

"What have *I* to do with her?"

"I am—not unmindful of your reputation, André. If Monsieur de Crillon can steal Mademoiselle de Lorme from under the very nose of Cinq-Mars—and he the reigning favorite—"

"Nonsense! I did not steal her away. She is an old friend. I merely renewed a past acquaintance. And she has not abandoned Cinq-Mars, so what have you to fear?" By now the boat had reached the Île de la Cité and was following the right bank of the Seine, passing under bridges that joined the island to the mainland. Up ahead the bell tower of Notre Dame chimed out a solemn carillon, sending a flock of pigeons into the evening sky. "But tell me of our hostess."

"What is there to tell? She is proud, beautiful beyond measure. I adore her! It is enough."

"You have a lover's soul—but surely there is more!"

"Well then—she has the liveliest salon in all of Paris, because of the fineness of her mind. All the great wits and men of letters are to be found at her *hôtel*. I have met Corneille there, and the philosopher Pierre Gassendi with his pupil, a remarkable man by the name of Cyrano de Bergerac. Even Madame de Rambouillet has been known to leave her own salon and pay her court."

"How odd that I have not even heard of this new star in the social firmament!"

"But you have not been in Paris for almost a year, *n'est-ce pas?* She burst upon the scene this past winter, and has been the talk of Paris ever since. There is news of her in the *Gazette* every week—the parties she attends, the guests she has received, even the gowns she wears!"

André sighed, filled with the old lassitude. He was so out of touch with court affairs since Marielle's death, and—what was worse—he no longer seemed to care. He had pursued Marion de Lorme (an easy conquest) merely to flatter his vanity, to prove to himself that he had lost none of his virility nor power to charm the opposite sex. But there was little joy in it. "What does she look like, this glorification of womanhood?" he asked idly, wondering if she would be worth the chase.

"She is—magnificent! Her face, her form, the swell of her bosom near breaks my heart. Ah! Exquisite! Her voice is music, and when she smiles I am transported to heaven!"

"Have you—enjoyed her favors?" asked André delicately.

"She has never even allowed me to kiss her sweet lips, but I dream on it."

André burst into laughter. "Not even a kiss? Small wonder you fear my usurpation! But surely there is someone—another admirer, mayhap—a charming courtesan rarely sleeps alone!"

The Duc de Rannel drew himself up haughtily. "You offend me, monsieur, when you mock the lady. There is not a man who does not languish at her feet, yet I'll wager not a one has seen her bedchamber! I pray it may be so." He sighed, the besotted lover, filled with thoughts of his beloved. "But she refuses so sweetly that the very words of denial seem a blessing from her honeyed lips."

Mon Dieu! thought André. The man is not only a peacock, he is most assuredly an ass, to let a woman turn his head so! "But who *is* she?" he said.

"No one knows. A woman of mystery—a sweet enigma—"

"Good God!" cried André impatiently. "But—her name? Perhaps I know the family."

"Her name—oh—undistinguished—there is no *de* in it to indicate nobility. She is simply Madame—" He stopped, misty-eyed once again. "No. She is 'La Déesse,' the Goddess, since the day that Simon Vouet painted her as Diana, goddess of the hunt. She owns the portrait herself, but Cardinal Richelieu—that old reprobate—is enchanted with her beauty, and would like to buy the painting for himself.''

"She begins to interest me more and more. She is wise, she is beautiful. What more could a man want?''

"She's a devil as well! Playful and amusing. I promised you a lively evening; you shall not be disappointed. She delights in clever jokes. I am minded of a time at Versailles when Monsieur de Deplan had spent the evening moaning about his expanding girth and the bother of outgrowing his breeches, though it did not prevent him from eating more than anyone else there! La Déesse contrived to have his breeches spirited from his bedchamber whilst he slept, and set her seamstress to work all the night, taking in the seams by several inches! Gasping from the snugness of the fit the next morning, Monsieur de Deplan swore a solemn oath then and there to eat in moderation if *le bon Dieu* would only let his breeches fit again!''

André laughed heartily. "A benign joke, and one that taught the man a lesson, I'll wager!''

"Sometimes the deviltry is less benign, but only when it is well deserved. Monsieur l'Abbé Gontier will not soon forget La Déesse!''

"I know the man slightly. Sanctimonious old cleric.''

"Yes. Championing his chastity, his celibacy at every turn. And spreading slanderous rumors about La Déesse's virtue.''

"If she is as discreet as you say, she had every right to be angry.''

"But I told you, she is clever. She delights in playing a role—there are those who think she has been in the theater. She dressed as a chambermaid and went to Monsieur l'Abbé's apartments in the Louvre—with half the court and King Louis himself hiding and listening from the antechamber. By the time we burst into the bedchamber Gontier was dandling her on his knee, his hand under her skirts, while he entreated her to look to her soul, in God's name. It was a rare joke, more especially when Gontier found out she was the woman he had presumed to judge. But Louis was furious at the Abbé's lechery and lack of Christian virtue, and banished him from court for a year."

André stirred impatiently in the boat, more and more anxious to meet this fascinating creature called La Déesse. "But if she is not nobility, who—or what is she?"

Rannel shrugged. *"Qui sait?* Who knows? The unacknowledged child of royalty? The mistress of some well-placed noble? A foreign princess? She is seen frequently with one of the older gentlemen of the court. There are those who say she is his illegitimate daughter. But she is surely highborn. Her sensitivity, her refinement can only come from noble parents, whatever the answer to the mystery."

"And what do you think?"

"I neither think, nor care. I worship her. That is enough! Ah! Here we are at last!" The boat had pulled alongside the stone bulwark just beyond Île St. Louis, and the two men climbed the steps to the top of the *quai*. At Rannel's command, one of the boatmen lit a torch and, following where the *duc* indicated, made his way down a narrow street to the Place Royale, André and René close behind. When they emerged into the wide square, Rannel turned to the torchbearer, placing several gold coins in his hand. "Wait here until the evening is over. We will need a ride back to the Louvre Palace—so inform your companion in the barge. There will be double this recompense on the return journey."

The *hôtel* of La Déesse was on the corner of the row of

town houses, so it enjoyed the advantage of both the
high windows that faced the square, and the airy case-
ments and balconies that looked out over the side street.
A footman in livery took their cloaks and led them up a
wide staircase to the large salon that blazed with lights
and echoed with the sound of laughter. Some thirty or so
men and women, in their best finery, milled about the
room, chatting gaily with one another. Several musicians,
busy tuning reeds and lutes and violins, now struck up a
galliard and the couples began to drift into the center of
the room to pick up the steps of the dance.

Rannel had been frantically scanning the salon. "There
she is!" he exclaimed. "La Déesse," he explained,
pointing to the far side of the room.

André did not need to be told. Even at this distance,
and with her back to them, her presence commanded the
room. A tall and stately woman, with an elegant carriage,
her slim-fingered hands moving gracefully as she talked
to the circle of admirers who surrounded her. Her blond
hair was twisted into a chignon at the back of her head,
the chignon encircled by a braid. At the nape of her neck
and along the edge of her face—the tantalizing corner of
which André could just see—the hair had been allowed
to spring free from her coiffure, and curled in beguiling
ringlets. Her pale blue silk dress was fitted snugly over a
waist so slender and dainty that it begged a man's
encircling arm. The bodice of the gown was cut quite low
in back, even with its lace falling band; the velvety skin
and the swanlike neck thus presented made André's
senses stir. Fortunate the man who planted kisses on that
neck, those soft shoulders!

He and Rannel edged their way past the dancers to La
Déesse. At Rannel's greeting she turned, her smile
dazzling. André went white.

"Gosse?" he whispered, frowning.

Her amber eyes flickered for a second, the smile frozen upon her face; then she lowered her glance. "I am Madame Despreaux," she said, holding out her hand to him. In a daze, he took her fingers. "René, *mon cher,*" she murmured, turning to Rannel, "will you present your friend?"

"I am delighted. André, Comte de Crillon, madame."

André stared in disbelief. It could not be Gosse—and yet it must be Gosse, or someone as alike as Gosse to be her kin! Unsure of himself, he waited for her to speak.

She laughed, her voice rich and musical. (Surely no one but Gosse could laugh like that!) "Ah, Monsieur de Crillon," she said. "I thought you did not come to Paris anymore. Can you be tired at last of war? But then, they say you fight your best battles in the bedchamber." She let her eyes scan his form and linger brazenly at his groin. "Is your—sword—as devastating as they say?"

As several of the guests laughed at this sally, André smiled uneasily. *Was* it Gosse? And were her words meant to be insulting, or merely amusing? He opened his mouth to reply, then thought better of it and brought her hand to his lips. Just as he was about to kiss her fingers she laughed, and in one smooth gesture she pulled her hand away and turned to Rannel.

"René, my dearest, I have not yet greeted you!" She bent Rannel's head down and kissed him gently on the mouth.

André felt his face flaming red with anger and humiliation. There was no mistaking the intended slight *this* time! Gosse or Despreaux, the woman was a bitch! Furiously he turned on his heel and made for the door.

Rannel hurried to join him. "Surely you are not leaving!"

André stopped. He had never been driven from a battlefield by such a small salvo before. "No, of course not," he said. "I shall stay for a little—to see if our hostess can be as fascinating as she is rude!"

Rannel chuckled. "I had not thought a woman alive could discompose the great André de Crillon! And to think I feared to introduce you. I am in your debt: because of you, I won a kiss! But did I not tell you she was divine?"

André nodded his head stiffly, then excused himself. He was languishing for a cup of wine, he said, and he had seen an old acquaintance in an alcove. And surely Monsieur de Rannel would wish to return to their hostess and pursue an association that had begun so well this evening. Rannel was delighted to pay court to La Déesse, and André was relieved to be quit of his company for a little. But though he chatted with several friends, and ate and drank, he could not take his eyes from La Déesse. She could not be Gosse, and yet—At last, unable to bear it any longer, he strode to her and, bowing deeply, invited her to dance the sarabande that the musicians had just begun to play. She curtsied and gave him her hand, allowing him to lead her to the center of the floor. They danced in silence for a few moments, while he felt his senses quickening at the woman's allure. Her fingers were soft in his, her waist yielding to his embrace, and once, as she moved past him in the graceful pattern of the dance, she brushed against him so he caught the delicate scent of her perfumed hair.

"Have we not met before, madame?" he said at length.

"I scarce think so, monsieur." She smiled wickedly, her amber eyes sparkling. "You are a soldier, and I am—not!"

"But Rannel says you are new to Paris, n'est-ce pas?"

"Yes."

"And before Paris—?"

"Ah monsieur! That is an indiscreet question! A woman is allowed to have secrets." She laughed aloud at the look of consternation on his face. A deep laugh, with a vibrant ring.

"It *is* Gosse, isn't it!" he burst out.

"Gosse?" she said coldly. "Is that supposed to be a name?" Before he could reply, she let out a little shriek so the other dancers stopped and stared at them. "Have a care, monsieur!" she said sharply. "You have stamped upon my foot! By my faith, can you not dance with more grace?"

"Forgive me," he stammered, "I was not aware—"

She smiled magnanimously. "Of course, monsieur." And they resumed the dance once again. But when she let out another cry a moment later he frowned. This time—damn the contrary baggage!—he was sure he had not stepped on her foot.

"Now, madame," he growled, "why do you make sport of me?"

"I, monsieur? I only wished to oblige you by dancing with you, but you are too clumsy by half. And now, having crushed my poor toes, you accuse me of making sport of you!" She sighed, her mouth an unhappy pout. "Since I cannot please you, I shall leave you to find another partner!" So saying, she turned away from him and limped off the floor. He stood there, feeling like a fool, half minded to storm after her and wring her neck. He was aware that several of the guests were snickering at his abandonment; with as much pride as he could muster, he marched to a sideboard and helped himself to a cup of wine.

An old friend of his, an aging *comtesse*, sailed up to him, fanning herself briskly and grinning with delight. "Upon my word, André! What have you done to Delphine to earn such scorn?"

"Delphine? Her name is *Delphine?*"

"Of course. Delphine Despreaux. Did you not know?"

He shook his head. "No—no—" and moved away distractedly. Then it *was* Gosse! He looked to where she was laughing gaily with admirers, seeing her with new eyes. *Mon Dieu!* How beautiful she was become, graceful and elegant, polished and refined. It seemed too good to be true, to find Gosse again, after he thought he had lost her forever. Then he frowned. He was overjoyed to see her again—why did she not share that joy? Why did she pretend not to know him, and deliberately humiliate him? He looked at her again. Under the beauty, the grace, there was a coldness that had not been there before. Her guests admired her; she accepted their praise with modesty. But where was Gosse's fire?

He watched her for a while, following her at a distance as she moved among her guests, drifted in and out of small rooms that adjoined the large salon, stopped for a glass of wine and a bite of food in a fine chamber that had been set aside for dining. Finally, seeing her alone for a few moments, he moved quickly to her and took her by the elbow.

"I must talk to you," he said.

She laughed merrily, but the sound had a hollow ring to it. "What can you possibly have to say to me, monsieur?"

"Shall we talk in front of your guests, Delphine?" The name deliberately stressed.

She shrugged and led him into a small room that appeared to be a library, the walls lined with books. Above the mantel was a magnificent portrait of Delphine, regal and beautiful in flowing magenta draperies. Simon Vouet's goddess. "Well?" she said, closing the door behind her and tapping one dainty foot impatiently on the floor.

"It is Gosse, of course," he said.

She stared at him, her eyes like cold amber. "Gosse is gone."

"And Master Fresnel?"

She looked stricken and turned away. "An accident at sea," she said softly.

He touched her arm in sympathy. "Gosse—"

"There *is* no Gosse!" she said fiercely, swirling away from him. "I am Delphine!"

He shook his head. "I cannot believe such a change in you."

"How so changed?" she said with a sneer. "I did not like you then—I do not like you now! Where is the change?"

"Gosse would have shown her anger, not hidden behind sweet smiles and a tongue like a sword."

"Gosse was a fool!"

"Gosse was an *honest* fool, then. Far more appealing than the celebrated Madame Despreaux who bewitches half the men in Paris and publicly insults and humiliates those she does not like! I wonder if Monsieur l'Abbé Gontier says a prayer for you now and again?"

She eyed him coldly. "Are you trying to goad me into a temper?"

He frowned, thinking about it. "Yes," he said at last, "perhaps I am. To see what remains of Gosse." He strode to her and took her roughly by the shoulders, then smiled sheepishly, softening. *"Nom de Dieu!* Don't you know how glad I am to see you? I have thought of you often these past two years."

"Have you?" she asked. Her expression was unreadable.

"Yes. And now that I have found you again, I shall not let you go!" He held her at arms' length, shaking his head in delighted wonder, his eyes appraising and approving.

"Who would have thought—little Gosse—" He lifted he
fingers to his lips, inclined his head in a courtly nod. "B
your leave, Madame Despreaux, I would spend ever
waking hour with you!"

She smiled up at him, her eyes half closed an
seductive. "And would you like to kiss me?" she mur
mured.

He gazed deeply at her, feeling the blood pounding i
his temples. Her lips were sweetly enticing, her heavin
bosom—peeping immodestly above her low-cut bodic
—invited his burning lips. "By my faith," he whispered
"but you are a beautiful woman," and bent his mouth t
hers.

"Wait!" she said, pushing him away. "Come!" Sh
groped for his hand. While he yet wondered what wa
amiss, she led him back to the large salon. She clappe
her hands and the musicians stopped their playing
"Listen!" she cried to her guests, who gathered aroun
wondering what new surprise the always delightful L
Déesse had in store for them. "I have a riddle," she sai
"You must name the game and the player. Now. Th
player collects four hearts—though two are undisclose
to the player—captures a king, and discards a knave
Who is the player? What is the game?"

"Name of God, Delphine, what is this?" growle
André.

"Piquet!" cried one of the guests. "The game i
piquet!"

Delphine shook her head. "No. Not piquet. The gam
is not a game of cards."

"There was a king," said another, "Chess?"

"Not with hearts, *mon Dieu!*" There were various call
and suggestions, while Delphine smiled benignly an
André scowled.

At last Delphine held up her hands to still her guests. "

shall tell you," she said. "The player is myself—the game is love. Look you," she said to the chorus of surprised voices. "There is Louis—he is the king, by the grace of God. He has been captured by Monsieur de Cinq-Mars who, in his turn, has been captured by Mademoiselle Marion de Lorme. I have met neither Cinq-Mars nor Mademoiselle de Lorme—the two undisclosed hearts, n'est-ce pas? De Lorme, that charming woman, has—as all of Paris must know by now!—been captured by the gentleman here, Monsieur le Comte de Crillon." She counted on her fingers. "Louis, Cinq-Mars, de Lorme, Crillon. That makes four captured hearts, two of which are unknown to me."

"But how have you collected them?"

"Why—Monsieur de Crillon, of course! I have conquered him at our first meeting." And here she smiled sweetly at André. "How flattering of you to say such charming things to me, mon cher. In so doing you have helped me to capture all four hearts, so to speak, since it is an unbroken chain of love from Crillon to Louis! And there you have the answer to the riddle!"

There was delighted applause and cries of bravo, and several guests kissed Delphine's hand and complimented her on her cleverness.

"A moment," said André through clenched teeth. "The riddle is not quite done! Am I also the knave that you have discarded?"

She reached up and patted him on the cheek, charming and patronizing all at the same time. "Perhaps not. The game is up to you, knave."

"By my faith!" he said, his eyes burning in fury. "You are, without a doubt, madame, the most—"

"Tut, tut, monsieur! Will you insult my hospitality by an unseemly show of bad temper? For shame! You have eaten my food and drunk my wine, and now you would rail at me for a simple jest. Has no one ever taught you manners? René, my love," turning to Rannel, who had joined the group, "take Monsieur le Comte home. He bores me." She did not wait for a rejoinder from André, but snapped her fingers to the musicians and stepped out to the center of the room, choosing a dancing partner and smiling dazzlingly at him as they went through their paces. The smile held even as André stormed from the room, and the dances were finished and the last guests had mercifully departed; only then did she sag, dropping her face tiredly into her hands, massaging her throbbing temples.

"Have I not told you half a score of times that you cannot forever drive yourself at this frenzied pace?"

Delphine turned to the Duc de Janequin. "Bernard! I thought you had gone home long since."

"I fell asleep," he said, shamefaced. "I cannot keep up with your lively doings. Nor can you, from the look on your face! I shall leave, and let you get to sleep."

"Wait. I—I need a little extra money this month, if you would be so kind—"

"The country house again?"

She nodded.

"When shall I ever see it? What do you do there, I wonder, when you leave Paris for days at a time?" He laughed ruefully. "Methinks I knew more about you in the old days when you were telling me lies and half truths than I do now when I may call you friend! You are almost as much a mystery to me as you are to the court gossips. I know nothing of your family, your background, your life before you met Gilles."

"Forgive me, Bernard. There is so much I would forget."

"And much that is not the concern of a prying old man?" He smiled warmly. "I shall send Braudel around in the morning with money for you. He will rage as usual, but I think he is getting quite used to the arrangement. And after all, there are no heirs to protect. Go to your country house, your—someone else, and with my blessing."

"You never ask where I go, who I see. Why?"

"I think I do not wish to know if it is a lover. And besides, when you return you are a little more at peace, mayhap, your soul a little less tormented."

"I owe you so much," she said, going to stand by the window. "I should have saved Gilles's money when he died last year, and managed my own affairs like a good little bourgeoise."

"What do you owe me? I reclaimed my sister's diamonds—and it would please me if you would wear them more often—and I have a sweet and charming companion who is delightful company, who brightens my days and shares with me the theater and good books, who lets me see life through her young eyes. You are wife and daughter and tender friend all at once. You owe me nothing."

She turned from the window, wringing her hands. "Do you want me?" she burst out.

"Mon Dieu! You never asked before. Why now?"

"And you have never done more than kiss my hand. Why? Am I—undesirable? Less a woman than you would want?"

"Oh, my dear. You must be bedeviled tonight to ask such a question. I am an old man. My passions have long since cooled. But you—you cannot truly think yourself unwomanly! There have been too many fevered swains around you for you to doubt yourself. And yet—and I would take an oath on it—I judge you to be as chaste and untouched, for all your coquetry, as you were when first we met."

She laughed bitterly. "I was scarcely a virgin!"

"But I think you were a virtuous wife, despite your unhappiness with Gilles. So I ask you yet again—why do you now offer yourself to me?"

"Damn it!" she burst out. *"Do* you want me?"

He smiled gently. "Do you want *me?*" Delphine turned away, her lip trembling. "My dear child," he went on, "if I need a woman to spread her legs for me, I can find one! But I would not have you for gratitude's sake, nor out of duty and obligation."

"Ah Dieu," she sighed, near tears. "I feel so old sometimes."

"And filled with torment—"

"Yes."

"And never more so than tonight?"

"Yes."

"Why?"

"Because—vengeance is mine—at last. Because my enemy is delivered to me at last!"

"And who is your enemy?" he asked gently.

She turned to him, her eyes blazing. She opened her mouth to speak, to say the hated name of André de Crillon, then found that she could not. The fury in her eyes faded to pain, and she turned to stare out the window. When at last she spoke, it was an anguished whisper torn from her throat.

"Love," she said softly. "My enemy is love."

Chapter Seventeen

THEY MET AT THE THEATER TWO DAYS LATER, THOUGH IT was not truly an accident. André had discovered that the Duc de Rannel was taking Delphine to the Hôtel de Bourgogne to see a play by Corneille. He had bought himself a seat on the stage, and from there he could look out over the audience on the open floor below and the curtained boxes above. It was not difficult to guess where Delphine was—the stir of cavaliers in a side box made it clear. At the intermission, when most of the gentlemen had come downstairs seeking refreshments, André waited until Rannel had left to fetch wine for Delphine, then slipped quietly into her box. Rannel would not return soon—André had already paid a charming *soubrette* a lordly sum to waylay the *duc* and keep him from returning.

"Delphine," he said softly, and was surprised to see her wince as she turned and spied him in the shadow of the curtains. He had thought her imperturbable, totally in control of her life, her feelings.

"André! *Mon cher!* How delightful to see you again." She smiled, the smile as false as her words.

"Don't," he said wearily. "René says you enjoy playing a role. I beg you—can you just be Delphine for a little while?" Frowning, he sat in the chair opposite her.

"La! André," she laughed, "the play is serious enough! Must you gaze at me so solemnly when I would have joy?"

He sighed in exasperation. "Gosse would not have played so falsely with me."

"I shall tell you yet again—" the golden eyes cold and distant "—Gosse is gone. No one knows of her. I—I should prefer it to remain so."

His mouth twitched in mockery. "The creature of mystery? The noblewoman in disguise?"

"Yes, if you will. I play the part well, do I not?"

"Indeed," he said uncomfortably, remembering her triumph over him in her salon. "And the *Despreaux*? Is as artificial as the rest of you?" He had meant it to be cruel, hoping to find a spark of passion in her, if only in anger.

But she eyed him coldly. "The name is my own. Despreaux was my husband."

He swallowed his surprise. "Was? Did you cast him aside like a discarded knave, to be treated with scorn when you meet again? To be mocked and taunted?"

She sighed. "The man is dead. *Mon Dieu*, how tiresome you can be—like a petulant child! Is it so difficult for the great Crillon to be bested by a woman?"

He took a deep breath, willing his anger to cool. Gosse's temper might be gone, but she had not lost her power to infuriate him. Now it was her words, not her behavior, that rankled, and in some ways it was harder to deal with her. If she went to strike him, he could hold her, keep her from assaulting him, even (if his fury got the better of him) strike her back; when her words attacked him behind her benign smile, he could scarcely retaliate without seeming the brute. "Listen to me," he said gently, taking her hand in his. "I do not know how I have offended you. I beg your forgiveness, whatever the cause of your anger. But we were friends, you and I. We laughed together on *Olympie*. I would have it so again between us."

"*Olympie* is a long time ago. I can scarce remember it."

He lifted her fingers to his lips, kissing the soft flesh delicately scented with orange-water, then smiled warmly at her. "And have you forgotten the night in my cabin? I have not."

She shrugged. "It was just—what it was, and nothing more. A bit of deviltry. Gosse was a devil, a savage who tormented you with her games—you said so yourself, many a time!"

He stood up, his face drained of color. "A game? A *game?* The woman in my bed that night was a creature of passion and fire! Is it my memory that is faulty—or yours? *Nom de Dieu!* Why did you come to my cabin that night?"

She laughed, the deep timbre harsh with contempt. "Curiosity." He glared at her, his eyes blazing in fury. But his pride was in tatters and she knew it. Does it hurt, André? she thought. Does it hurt to suffer? She delivered the final knife thrust. "Yes. Curiosity. But I might have saved myself the bother."

He growled under his breath and made for the door. It opened before he reached it, and René de Rannel entered. The *duc* glanced from André's face to Delphine's and laughed nervously. "Have I interrupted a—rendezvous?" he asked, the sharp edge of jealousy in his voice.

"Don't be a fool, René my sweet. I should be blushing if you had."

Rannel glanced at André's face, the grim mouth, the angry flush that darkened his bronzed skin. "Monsieur le Comte, then. Has he been importuning you?"

"Of course not! Why should André want to seduce me into his bed? No. We were having a pleasant chat, that was all. You see? The words did not even stir my heart." She stood up and crossed to Rannel, lifting his hand and placing it deliberately on her bosom. He blushed and beamed, embarrassed and delighted at the same time.

André inhaled through his teeth. "By my faith," he said coldly, "you are—endlessly curious, madame. I wish you well," and turned and strode from the box.

The weather turned hot in the middle of May, and King Louis arranged for the court to be moved to Saint-Germain-en-Laye, some four or five leagues to the west of Paris. It was a small town, situated on a high promontory above the river Seine, and surrounded by a forest. The royal château, built in 1370, boasted a terrace and promenade that commanded a magnificent view of the river and the rolling hills beyond. The air was cool and sweet, the breezes marvelously refreshing after the heat of Paris. It had been a favorite retreat of the French kings for centuries; indeed, Queen Anne had spent her confinement there and had been delivered of the Dauphin Louis at Saint-Germain.

Delphine was pleased to receive an invitation to join the court there. She only hoped André would be invited as well. She spent her days conjuring up ways to be revenged upon him, to make him suffer for all the wrongs she had suffered in the past two years. She knew he was still bewildered by her rebuff of him; she knew as well that he was drawn to her, attracted like a moth to a candle, and she smiled in satisfaction. She would play with him, humiliate him, humble him—until he begged her for mercy. And then—? She shook her head. No. She did not like to think about it. For two years her anger and bitterness had sustained her, but when at last André was humbled, destroyed, what would she have to live for? She had never allowed herself to think beyond her vengeance.

"The petticoat is a trifle long, Charlotte. Can something be done about it?" She glanced down at the servant kneeling in front of her. She lifted the top skirt—*la friponne*, the hussy—so Charlotte could reach the petticoat beneath, then turned her head to scan herself once again in the large Venetian mirror. The gown was a lovely shade of pink, clear and strong, accenting her own high coloring. The underbodice was white satin, and the sleeves, from shoulder to mid-forearm, were wide strips of pink ribbon, joined only at top and bottom, so the satin showed through. There were rosettes of pink ribbon at her waist, and the unexpected flash of silver braid trimming the front of the bodice and the hemline of *la secret*, the underskirt. The wide white falling band and deep cuffs were edged with lace scallops. On her feet were rose silk stockings and dainty brocaded shoes with high cork heels. *Mon Dieu!* she thought, eyeing herself, what a contrast to the somber dresses she had worn as Gilles's wife! *This* gown would turn André's head! She tugged at the bodice. "And can you make this a bit lower, Charlotte?" She smiled disarmingly. "I wish to appear a little more—wicked!"

There was a knock on the door. Charlotte rose to her feet and ushered in Monsieur de Janequin. He limped slowly toward Delphine, beaming his approval of her costume. "Have you decided after all to buy a new dress for your stay at Saint-Germain?"

Delphine motioned Charlotte away. Standing on tip-toe, she kissed Janequin softly on the cheek. "Good morrow, Bernard. Why do you delight in spending so much money on me?"

"That I may bask in your radiance!" he said.

"Do you think, when we are at Saint-Germain together, that all the court will say," and here she affected a pompous tone, " 'That is a glorious gown that Monsieur de Janequin has paid for?' "

"Indeed, yes," he said solemnly, but his eyes twinkled, enjoying their banter.

"Then you may not come with me to Saint-Germain, for this gown has been given to me for nothing by Mademoiselle Bijou, the dressmaker in the Place Dauphine, on condition that I make a point of telling all my friends where the gown has come from."

"All doors open to youth and beauty." He sighed in mock dismay. "Very well, I shall not go with you to Saint-Germain!"

She laughed. "I hear that Louis is planning fireworks. You must show me the best place on the promenade to watch them from."

"No," he said. "Truly, I shall not be going to Saint-Germain. I came to tell you so."

She frowned. "I shall miss your sweet company, Bernard. But why?"

"Do you remember I told you about that dear lady of my younger days, Louise de Trémont?" He beamed. "I met her the other evening at a supper Braudel took me to. I think it must be twenty years—we were both married, but—it was a brief moment of joy—"

"And you have met her again! Oh Bernard! How glad I am for you."

"And she is widowed. She will not come to Saint-Germain. She must stay in Paris to conclude some business."

"Then stay as well—and court your charming Louise."

"You don't mind?"

"Of course not!" And how could she tell him that she had counted on him at Saint-Germain? René was off in Bordeaux visiting a cousin, and several of her most devoted followers were fighting in the Netherlands. She would have no shield against André. Are you afraid of him? Copain had asked her that once. And she feared that beyond the sophisticated Parisienne, the Delphine in command of herself and her life, the woman who would be revenged, lurked the vulnerable innocent who trembled in his presence. Stay with me! she nearly cried aloud to Janequin. Stay with me!

The persistent rain beat against the leaded panes of the château at Saint-Germain. For two days now it had rained, and the court, bored with one another, with the confinement, had grown restless. Louis had quarreled with Cinq-Mars and sent him back to Paris in disgrace, then retired to his own apartments to sulk.

Only Delphine was glad of the enforced captivity; there was no way André could avoid her. And he was suffering, that was plain. He wanted her. He ached for her. Where once—on *Olympie*—his presence had tormented her with longing, now it was he who burned with desire, his eyes hungry and tortured each time they dined in the same room, or passed one another in a dim corridor, or gathered with the rest of the courtiers and their ladies to play the countless games that helped the rainy hours to pass more quickly.

They had just finished a game of charades. Delphine, glowing in her pink gown, was basking in the compliments her clever imitations had elicited. She allowed one of the gentlemen to kiss her hand and slip his arm about her waist, knowing André was watching, his brow furrowed in anger and jealousy. Several of the company began to murmur in discontent. What were they to play now? It was too warm for dancing, and too early in the evening to play the kinds of games with kisses that would inevitably lead to alternative pairings in the bedchambers later on that night.

Delphine smiled brightly. "I have a game!" she said. "The children play it, but it might be amusing." Quickly she outlined the game. One person was to stand with his hands behind his back; his chosen partner was to take his place behind him and slip his arms through the opening thus created. As the person in front improvised a monologue, his "hands" would act it out. There were nods of approval from the company. It sounded amusing, and there would be opportunities for ribaldry never dreamed of by children.

"But we must have rules," said Delphine. "Each player is to be allowed to choose his next partner to be his hands, then the 'hands' becomes the 'body,' and chooses a new player. And the one who uses his hands must obey *all* that the speaker commands! At the end, we shall decide who has been the most clever."

The game began innocently enough, with a red-faced *comtesse* standing behind a gentleman in green brocade. As he complained of fleas, she scratched his beard and nose, then retied his falling band strings at his command. When they were finished, there was a polite smattering of applause and the *comtesse* chose her husband to be her hands, feigning sleepiness with much stretching and stifled yawns. But after a few more players, the gestures called for became a great deal more crude, and the company was laughing merrily. One young cavalier, a buxom *duchesse* pressed up against his back, complained of the need to relieve himself, while the lady's hands explored his groin. Since everyone but her husband knew that the two were lovers, the joke was doubly

delicious. At last Delphine was called to partner a shy
young man; she kissed him sweetly on the cheek before
going to stand behind him and slip her arms through his.
His improvisation was not particularly witty, but she
made so much of it, unbuttoning his doublet, scratching
his ear, propping up his head with her hands, that the
company applauded long and loudly when they were
done, and the young man beamed with delight, thinking
himself the cleverest man in the room.

Delphine scanned the faces of the eager men, all
desirous of being her partner; her glance focused on
André leaning against a wall, arms folded across his
chest, his handsome face twisted in obvious disapproval.
"I choose—Monsieur de Crillon. Perhaps we can make
him smile tonight."

André shook his head in protest, but several voices
urged him on, and the gentleman in green brocade took
the opportunity to push him toward Delphine in the
center of the room. Reluctantly he stood behind her,
aware of the fragrance of her hair, the warmth of her
back against his chest. She twisted her head around to
peer at him over one shoulder, and grinned wickedly, her
golden eyes twinkling. "Remember," she said, "you
must do everything I say!" She turned back to the
company and began her monologue. "Oh, dear," she
said, tilting her head to one side, "I wonder when my
lover will come to see me?" Worriedly, her "hand"
scratched at her chin. "Will he find me beautiful?" André
patted her cheeks, then fussed with the curls about her
face. "How the blood throbs in my temples waiting for
him!" The action was suited to the words, her "hands"
pressing against her forehead. "And my heart—how it
beats in my bosom—" André had not moved. "My
heart," she said pointedly. "I can *feel* it beating in my
bosom!"

"Vixen!" he hissed in her ear, and put a reluctant hand on her breast. One of the women giggled.

"I shall wear my pearl earrings," Delphine continued. André's hands went to her earlobes. "*Ah, Dieu—*" the fingers covering her mouth in dismay "—I have lost my earring!" André clutched at one ear. "My *right* earring." He switched hands quickly and the company laughed in delight.

Delphine smiled to herself. He was beginning to enjoy the game, thinking it harmless deviltry. She had lulled him, led him on, like a skillful fencer. How do you like my *passado*, André? she thought, and let out a little shriek. "I have lost the earring in the bodice of my gown! I must search for it!" The men guffawed loudly and the women whispered among themselves, each longing to be in the clutches of the handsome Comte de Crillon. How clever was La Déesse! She could have any man she wanted.

Delphine peered over her shoulder. André's face had gone red, and a small muscle worked in his jaw. "I shall never find my earring unless I search in my bodice!" André glared at her, his eyes like blue fire. Delphine turned back to the company. "What shall I do if my hands do not do my bidding?" she asked, amber eyes wide in innocence.

André growled and pushed her away. "'Tis a foolish game!"

The shy young man leaped forward and bowed before Delphine. "Sweet goddess, let me be your hands!"

She smiled gently at him. "*You,* at least, are not a coward. But alas—you are not my hands." She turned to André, her eyes cold. "Yes. Coward, monsieur, that could not even play a simple game. Coward!"

He flinched at that, feeling helpless. If she were a man he could have struck her down, left his challenging glove in her face. Without a word he whirled about and strode from the room. Behind him, he could hear the sound of her mocking laughter.

"Excuse me, madame, but there is a gentleman who wishes to see you."

About to unpin her chignon, Delphine stopped and turned away from her mirror, frowning at the chambermaid. "Do you know who he is?"

"It is Monsieur de Crillon, I think. I have seen him here at Saint-Germain in the past. Will you receive him in your antechamber?"

Delphine smiled. There was hardly a need to plot against André. He invited his own destruction. "No. Here in my bedchamber. Show him in and then leave me for the night." As the maid left the room, she bent to retrieve her peignoir from a chair, then changed her mind. She would receive André in her nightdress alone; it would be great fun to see him struggle to keep from noticing how the thin lawn clung to her curves.

He strode purposefully into the room, nodded at her, and began to speak at once, his words calm and reasonable—and seemingly rehearsed. "I do not know why you hate me, Delphine. I bear you no ill will. Truly, I had thought we were friends. But that is neither here nor there. It is you I am concerned about. Master Fresnel would be ashamed to see what you have become. You flirt with all the men, you practice deception, you hide your malice behind honeyed words—would you want your father to know you flaunt yourself like a common trumpet, your bosom exposed shamelessly?"

"You shall not provoke me with your ugly words. Gosse's rages have vanished with Gosse."

"Even your coldness is an affront to the memory of Gosse. But heed me, Delphine. I have only your best interests at heart. As a father—and I *am* old enough to be

your father—I beg you to recall the warmth that wa
Gosse, and the modesty that was Gosse, and the honesty
that was Gosse."

She threw back her head and laughed, that rich
melody that stirred his senses. "A father? No. You may
pretend so to yourself, but your eyes tell a different
story." She indicated her large bed, shadowy behind it
heavy draperies. "Tell me, 'father,' if I lay down and
spread my legs for you, would you commit incest?" She
laughed again as his face purpled in sudden anger.

"You whelp!" he said through clenched teeth. "You
foul—"

"Tut, tut!" she interrupted. "Can you not control your
temper? By my faith, *I* do not find it difficult!"

He took a deep breath, struggling to recover his
aplomb. "I do not desire you. Your father was my friend
I think of you merely as a child—his child—who need
my guidance."

"Indeed?" With graceful fingers she unpinned her
chignon, shaking out the blond tresses so they fell about
her shoulders and rippled down her back. André seemed
almost to flinch at the sight of that golden glory, finding i
suddenly hard to breathe. Delphine laughed softly. "And
I say you want me. That you were afraid to touch me
when we played the game tonight."

"Nonsense."

"Then touch me now."

"What? Are you mad?"

"Touch me now. If you are as a father to me, it wil
mean nothing." She put her hands behind her back—a
she had in the game—and stood in front of him
presenting her back. "Touch me now."

Reluctantly André slipped his arms through hers, an
reached up to cup her breasts in his firm hands, hi
fingers stroking her through the thin fabric. She ha

steeled herself against his touch, and was surprised to realize that it had not been necessary. Thanks be to God, she had no feelings left. It was Gilles's legacy, and she blessed him. Her sensuality had been her weakness; without it, she was invincible.

André pressed her more tightly against his chest, and buried his face in the silken tresses that curtained her neck and shoulders. "Delphine," he whispered.

"André, *mon cher,* do you want me?" she asked, her voice inviting and husky in her throat.

"Mother of God, you know I do!" He turned her in his embrace and bent to kiss her. Then he saw the eyes like amber ice and drew away, frowning in disbelief.

She laughed under her breath, an ugly, guttural sound. "But perhaps I do not want you!"

He grabbed her fiercely by the shoulders. "By my faith, I ought to—" His eyes burned in fury. "Gosse was more woman than you, for all her crude ways! God knows she was a creature of passion and spirit—not a cold, scheming whore!"

"Will you leave?" she said, her voice frosty. "Or shall I send for a footman and have you thrown out?"

He stormed from the bedchamber, slamming the door behind him. She stared at the closed door for a minute, then, with a shriek, she picked up a small bench and hurled it violently against the panels, so it shattered and fell to the floor in splinters.

Chapter Eighteen

THE BRIGHT ROCKET BURST HIGH ABOVE THE TERRACE OF Saint-Germain, sending dazzling pink showers into the night sky. There was a loud explosion, and a golden starburst joined the pink sparkles. Lysette gasped in delight and clutched Jean-Auguste's arm.

"Was it not a happy circumstance, Jean-Auguste, that I had occasion to write to Madame Séguier, the wife of the chancellor? Else we would not have thought to visit her here at Saint-Germain."

"Indeed, a happy circumstance," he said, his mouth twitching. "I have no doubt, my charming wife, that you would *never* have found André but for Madame Séguier!"

"I never know when you're laughing at me," she said sharply. "I was not seeking André! It was merely a fortunate accident that Clémence de Vignon was able to accompany us." She indicated with her fan where André and Clémence were leaning over the parapet, watching the glittering catherine wheels set far below on the slopes of the embankment. "And you see, André is delighted with Clémence. He has scarce left her side all the evening, fussing over her like a devoted husband."

Jean-Auguste watched the path of a green rocket as it climbed to the heavens and exploded in a shower of red, then turned to Lysette, his gray eyes thoughtful. "I've known André long enough," he said. "And despite the attentions he has paid to Clémence since we arrived, I would swear his real interest lies with the woman they call La Déesse."

"Nonsense! He has been very cold to her, and she to him. They have not exchanged half a dozen words all day, I'll wager—indeed, they seem to be avoiding one another."

"Precisely. I have never known André to be cold to a woman. He is naturally gallant and courtly, though the woman be plain or tedious. It is his nature. So why should he be cold to La Déesse? Unless the coldness masks the fire within."

"Have you asked him of his sentiments toward La Déesse?"

Jean-Auguste tweaked her nose. "What an inquisitive imp you are, my love. I have no doubt that if André wished to share his inclinations with me—or you!—he would do so!"

"Really, Jean-Auguste!" She flounced away from him, then sidled back as Delphine swept the length of the terrace, trailing worshipful admirers in her wake. "I do not like her," Lysette announced, the mother hen aroused. "She cannot possibly care for André. She is treating him shamefully, flaunting her cavaliers before him! And surely you are mistaken about André's feelings! I have never seen him so attentive to Clémence!"

Jean-Auguste laughed sardonically. "And more especially when Madame Despreaux is nearby to see!"

"Don't be silly! He is attentive because he knows that Clémence is the perfect woman for him. She will make him a proper wife, eminently suitable to his needs."

"*Mon Dieu,* Lysette!" he said, an edge of exasperation in his voice. "We seldom fall in love with suitable types!"

"What do you mean?" Her dainty chin outthrust in injured pride.

"Rest content, my sweet. I still adore you. But if I had chosen a suitable wife, she would try me less than you do! And as for you—you would have profited more from a husband who was easily duped. You would not have had to work so hard to convince him of things that are not so!"

She pouted and swirled away from him, going to join André who now stood alone on the promenade, seeming absorbed in the dazzling fireworks display.

"Poor André! Has Clémence abandoned you?"

"Not at all, Lysette. She went to fetch a shawl."

"Charming woman, is she not?"

"Indeed."

Lysette sighed. "I always thought it a pity that *le bon Dieu* did not bless her marriage with children. I watch her sometimes with my twins. What a sweet mother she would make!"

"Perhaps a trifle old, now. Near thirty, I believe?"

"How ungallant of you, André! If she were to marry a—a widower, mayhap—"

"One with children, no doubt."

"It would be a great joy for her. And an—older woman—is far more suited to a man of years. More faithful—less skittish and apt to bring him woe." She smiled brightly, indicating Delphine who had just greeted her shy young suitor with a kiss. "What think you of Madame Despreaux?"

"A handsome woman."

"Pooh! A child! Not yet twenty, I vow."

"Only just twenty, I believe."

"And still a child! Did you know—" and here Lysette leaned forward, a conspirator's smile on her face "—that she is seen often in the company of Monsieur le Duc de Janequin? Such a disgrace for a man to go about with a woman young enough to be his daughter! Well, there's no fool like an old fool, n'est-ce pas? She will lead him a merry chase ere she's done with him!" She smiled again and moved back to stand with Jean-Auguste, confident that she had set André on the path to wisdom.

André frowned, staring at Delphine. How she bedeviled him! He had been cold to her all the day, his pride still rankling at the way she had humiliated him. Yet try as he might he could not hate her. He could only suffer to watch her play the coquette with every man who came within her orbit, wanting nothing more than to drag her away, unpin that golden hair, take her in his arms. Name of God! He turned away from the sight of her, his brain exploding with fire like the rockets that lit up the night sky.

"André, have you missed me?" Clémence came hurrying toward him, smiling sweetly. "I could not find my shawl," she said, the edge of a whine in her voice. Ah Dieu, he thought, will this tormenting evening never end? Clémence was gentle and gracious—as Marielle had been. But sweet Mother of God, he could not remember a moment's boredom with Marielle! And surely that complaining tone in Clémence's voice—heard all too frequently—had been foreign to Marielle. Mechanically he tucked Clémence's hand under his arm and led her inside the château to seek the missing shawl.

Tomorrow, he thought. He would go back to Paris tomorrow and seek out Marion de Lorme. She did not make him feel old, nor bore him to death.

Nor drive him mad with desire.

*   *   *

Marion de Lorme carelessly pinned up her disheveled hair and handed André his sword. He buckled it on and stooped to kiss her once again, feeling her yielding body beneath the thin chemise. She stepped away from him and began to don the petticoats and gown so hastily cast aside an hour before.

"André," she said, her eyes gentle, "you are charming and I adore you, but pray do not come again."

He frowned. "Have I displeased you, Marion?"

"Not at all, *mon cher*. Never. But I do not want you to visit me. Not while your thoughts are filled with someone else!"

"What foolishness is this?" he growled.

She put a sympathetic hand on his. "Oh, my dear! You do everything but call me by her name! It is quite disconcerting, you know!"

He laughed nervously. "I did not think—is it so plain?"

"Yes, my love, it is. But—it is very odd. I cannot decide whether you desire her—or despise her."

"*Nom de Dieu.* I scarce know myself. I only know she torments me."

Marion smiled and handed him his gauntlets and hat. "To bed her, or to beat her. Is that your dilemma? Methinks, sweet André, you had better go to her and find out!"

So it was that he found himself back on the highroad to Saint-Germain barely two days after he had left. This time, he told himself, he would not let Delphine get the better of him. As much as he desired her, he would not let her beguiling ways seduce him. She meant only to lead him on, that she might humble him. He would be cold, distant, reasonable, seeking the crack in her icy façade, the why of her animosity. And if she proved to be the cold bitch she seemed, he might at last be free of her spell.

But oh, how he longed for Gosse, sweet, wild Gosse!

Just outside the walls of Saint-Germain, he looked up to see a cavalcade of mounted riders and carriages hurtling toward him. He jerked his horse aside to avoid the onrush, then waved frantically at Jean-Auguste and Lysette in the midst of the throng. They guided their horses to where he waited at the side of the road, and leaned forward in their saddles to shake his hand warmly.

"Well met, André!" cried Jean-Auguste. "I thought you were staying in Paris!"

"Paris was—tiresome."

"Then join us today!" Lysette bubbled. "We're off on a gallop through the woods, then by boat to a little island on the river. Louis has sent the cook there, and we shall picnic and play games like happy children all the day!"

"Yes, do come, André. The whole of the court has come on this outing, as you can see."

"Not I! I have spent enough hours in the saddle. There would be no joy in a gallop for me!"

"Ride in a carriage then," said Lysette, indicating the half dozen heavy coaches that lumbered down the hill from the château, picking up speed as they reached the path into the woods.

André laughed. "With the ladies who are fearful of mounting a horse? Heaven protect me! They would mock me with *softling* then!"

Lysette pouted in disappointment and he nearly relented; then a carriage bore down on them and Clémence de Vignon leaned out, waving happily to him as she passed. "No," he said decisively. "I shall enjoy a few hours of solitude and join you at supper. Think what a pleasure it will be to have someone to listen to the day's adventures!" And wheeling his horse about, he made his way up the road to the château and the stables.

Delphine hurried down the wide marble staircase, holding fast to the blue velvet hat that matched her riding costume. Bother the foolish shoe! It had pinched so badly, and the cobbler she had sent for had worked at a snail's pace until she thought she would shriek at him in impatience. And now she was late! She sped into the bright sunshine, dashing through a shadowy portal to the inner courtyard where the party was assembling. It was empty. She spied a groom brushing down a horse in one of the stables, and called to him. He was sorry, he said, but everyone was gone. There was not another carriage to be had, he said, unless madame wished to take the dogcart.

"Never mind," she said, turning about unhappily. It would be a long, boring afternoon, but it could not be helped. The only bright spot was the letter she had received this morning from Bernard de Janequin. His affair with Louise de Trémont—his old love—had gone badly. Though the lady seemed pleased enough with him, he was dismayed to find her far different from the woman he had remembered. They had quarreled frequently, her jealousy at his past liaisons poisoning their every meeting. Consequently, he was joining Delphine at Saint-Germain as soon as he could make the final break from Louise.

She looked up. André was riding into the courtyard. *Ah Dieu!* she thought, feeling her heart leap in her breast. How beautiful he was, handsome and self-assured, strong and masculine. She nearly groaned aloud. No! Sweet Jesu, it could not be happening again! She had locked her fragile heart to him, had deadened her emotions—and now the sight of him had set her to trembling again. She turned desperately to the groom. "Is there not another carriage? Are you sure?"

André rode up and swung himself easily out of the saddle, allowing the groom to lead his horse away. "Has Madame Despreaux been abandoned?" The blue eyes twinkling devilishly. "What will you do all afternoon, with no man to entice?"

Her face twisted in disgust. "As I recall, I found you an easy mark. Twice!"

He smiled blandly. "But alas, not a third time! I can no longer avoid the realization that you do not like me; knowing that, it is plain to me that whatever warmth you show is a snare. By my faith, I am not a complete fool—and you are scarcely *that* desirable!" He folded his arms across his chest, eyeing her, wondering why she seemed agitated. "But I shall keep you company this afternoon," he went on. "I find it amusing to watch you, to see how artificial you have become!"

She whirled to him, her fists clenched, then took a deep breath and lowered her eyes. But not before he had caught the angry spark in their amber depths.

He roared with laughter, almost seeming relieved. "What? Is it still there after all? That hellion's temper? Madame Despreaux is not completely civilized after all, n'est-ce pas?"

She turned away, feeling her defenses crumbling. "Go to the devil," she muttered.

He grinned. "Come!" he said, pressing his advantage. "May I suggest a game of trictrac? It will be amusing to see if the cold and icy Delphine can lose with grace!" He was delighted to see another flash of fury sweep across her face. "How fortunate for me that there is not a single coach left!"

"Damn you," she hissed, then called out to the groom. "Fetch me a horse! At once!" She glared at André. "I would rather die than spend the afternoon with you!" When the horse was brought, she mounted it from the block and sat stiffly in the sidesaddle until the groom had handed her the reins; then she kicked its flank fiercely with her heel and galloped out of the courtyard.

The groom shook his head. "I did not think the lady could ride."

"What do you mean?"

"Begging your pardon, monsieur, but that particular lady *always* rides in a coach."

André frowned, remembering how stiffly she had sat on the horse, how awkward her hands had been on the reins, as though it was strange to her. *Mon Dieu!* The little fool! Where would she have learned to ride a horse aboard ship? He paced impatiently while the groom resaddled his horse, then leaped into the saddle and raced off in the direction of the woods.

He found her some half a mile into the forest and at a distance from the path. The blue of her riding habit, vivid against the green trees, caught his eye and he followed it until he found where she lay, crumpled pitifully beneath a large tree, her hat gone, her hair wild and loose about her face. As he leaped from his horse, she groaned and opened her eyes, then closed them again. Scooping her up in his arms, he carried her to a small stream nearby and set her down gently on a patch of soft grass. He moistened his handkerchief in the water and knelt beside her, propping her up with one arm about her shoulders and dabbing at her temples. Her eyelids fluttered; she stared at him blankly, then managed to focus on his face.

"Foolish child," he whispered tenderly, "do you hate me so much that you would risk life and limb to flee from me?" She murmured and stirred in his embrace. "I beg you, Delphine, tell me what I have done! Let me make amends. By my faith, I do not wish to be your enemy! *What* have I done?"

She held her breath, seeing the face that bent so close: the sapphire eyes that pierced her heart; the lips that had kissed her, that she ached to feel again on hers. No! I hate him! she thought. Only hatred drives away the pain! She took a deep breath, feeling her strength returning, then shook herself free of his encircling arm. "Your concern is touching, Monsieur le Comte, but the ground is damp and I shall soon be soaked through! Let me go."

He sighed in exasperation and stood up to fetch his horse. Behind him, she struggled to her feet, wincing at the ache in her bones, and began to limp toward the path.

"No!" he said. "You must ride with me."

She drew herself up coldly. "I shall walk."

He frowned, his eyes narrowing. "Gosse's stubbornness has not vanished! You shall ride before me like a lady, or you shall ride trussed up like a sheep to market and slung across the rump of my horse. But you shall *not* walk!"

Her angry glance faltered at the determination in his face; she shrugged, feigning unconcern, and indicated the horse. "If you will help me up, monsieur—"

The ride back was an agony. His arm around her waist burned her with its touch, and each time the horse moved and she swayed against André, her back against his muscular chest, she thought she would die. She cursed the weakness of her body, the door to sensitivity that she had thought was locked for good. It had brought her nothing but grief with Gilles. Would it betray her again?

* * *

Delphine dipped her quill into the inkpot and drew a sheet of paper from her writing desk. "My dear Anne-Marie," she began. "I send you my warmest greetings. I arrived back in Paris two days ago and found your letter waiting for me. Be assured if the roof of the cottage needs repairs, you may have them done, and I shall forward the necessary funds as soon as I receive an accounting from the carpenter. I am glad to hear my sweet Robert has another tooth; I wish I had been there to ease his sufferings and pain. The weather continues warm in Paris, though not so irksome as it was last month. I am still planning to visit you for much of the month of July; you must save all your tender little stories of Robert to tell and retell to me when I arrive. God keep you. Madame D."

She folded it and, heating the sealing wax at a small candle, fastened the letter with a dab of wax pressed down with a plain seal. She was surprised when Charlotte announced Monsieur de Janequin; it was late in the evening for Bernard, who liked to retire early.

"My dear!" she said, rising to greet him warmly. "What brings you here at such an hour?" She smiled fondly at him. What a godsend he had been, arriving at Saint-Germain just when she thought she could not bear another second in André's presence. She had given Janequin all her attention for the rest of their stay, ignoring André, content to spend her hours in the safety of Bernard's company. When King Louis had decided to return to the Louvre Palace, she had breathed a sigh of relief and gone back to her house in the Place Royale. She knew André was now installed at the Louvre with the rest of the courtiers, and she had carefully declined all invitations from the king. But Janequin had been at the palace tonight. "Was there such delicious gossip that you could not wait until morning?"

"There was gossip," he said, and now she saw the tight lines around his mouth, the pained look in his eyes.

"Bernard. Come and sit. What is it?" She took his hand in hers.

"It—it was about you."

"I'm used to rumors and silly gossip! What am I supposed to have done now? Driven my carriage through the *Grand Galerie* of the Louvre?" She smiled wickedly. "I've always wanted to, you know!"

"The rumors were about you and me."

"La! Do they think us lovers? How flattering for us both!"

"They think us father and daughter. That you are my bastard."

"They have thought so in the past." She shrugged in unconcern.

"The gossip names us father and daughter—and lovers as well."

She gasped, her hand flying to her mouth. *"Dieu du ciel!* How vile!"

He wrung his hands together. "There was much more, so ugly and obscene that I do not wish to cause you distress by telling it. And it is more than merely harmless gossip. Whoever began it has taken the trouble to discover that—I am keeping you—paying your bills—"

"What is to be done?"

"I should like you to marry me."

"No, Bernard, I—"

He cleared his throat, his delicate features coloring slightly. "I would not expect you to—fulfill a wife's—obligations, unless you wished it. But I cannot bear to think of you besmirched by such filth, and I the cause of

it. Marriage between us would set the ugly rumors to rest.
And I am—very fond of you."

She closed her eyes, feeling the tears burning behind
her lids, moved beyond measure by the kindness of the
man. Through all her pain and grief, he had been her
salvation. He had rescued her from Gilles, and now, God
be praised, he would save her from André—and her own
weakness. The passions that once again were stirring
within her—to rise up and destroy her—could be buried
for good, soothed, quieted, by Bernard's tender sentiments. She would be safe at last. She opened her eyes,
the tears sparkling in her lashes. "My dearest," she said,
"if you want me, I should be honored to be your wife."
He beamed in pleasure and kissed her fingertips. "Now,"
she said brightly, brushing away her tears, "I shall give a
great *soirée!* Let the gossipmongers come and see how
happy we are together! Will that please you?"

"Indeed," he said, "if it pleases you."

"Go home now," she said tenderly. "You look so tired.
Come and have breakfast with me in the morning, and I
shall tell you all about the plans for the *soirée!*"

"Nom de Dieu," he laughed, rising and making for the
door. "Go to sleep yourself!"

"Not I! I must compile my guest list!" She bid him
good-night and returned to her writing table, frowning as
she picked up the letter to Anne-Marie. Sooner or later
she would have to tell Bernard about Robert. If she was
going to be the Duchesse de Janequin, and live in a fine
château, she would want to have Robert with her.
Perhaps Bernard would agree to adopt him, even leave
him a title and lands as an inheritance. Yes, she would
have to tell him about Robert. But how much else should
she tell? The name of Robert's father? Certainly not. Yet
the thought of him assuming Robert was Gilles's child
made her sick. And could she tell the story of Gosse, and

her own background? No. Janequin was a fine nobleman, from an aristocratic family, cultured and proud.
How could she shame him by telling him his *duchesse*
was the daughter of a common sea captain? Let him
continue to think she had a bourgeois background—it
still was not aristocracy, but it was better than the
common peasant clay from which she sprang. But to be
dishonest with such a dear man. *Ah Dieu!* She sighed.
Best to say nothing until she had decided on her story.
Best to think of more immediate concerns: her guest
list. Drawing a fresh paper toward her, she put quill to
ink, shaking off the superfluous drop of ink onto a blotter.
She frowned and tapped the pen against her teeth. One
more bit of revenge. One more proof to show herself she
was free of him, once and for all. With a flourish, she
wrote the name of her first guest on the top of the paper:
André, Comte de Crillon.

Chapter Nineteen

THE DUC DE RANNEL POUTED UNHAPPILY AND HANDED THE blue ribbon to Delphine. "I shall never wear another woman's favor, now that you have broken my heart!"

"René, my dear, will you not keep it as a memento of my great affection for you?"

He brightened. "Do you mean that after you are wed to Bernard de Janequin I may still entertain—some—small—hope?"

Gently she cuffed the side of his head. "You are very wicked. And—no—you may not!"

"Then I intend to get very drunk tonight!"

"If you spend the night in misery, I will regret having invited you to my *soirée!* In sooth, René," she said, more seriously, "are you not happy for me?" He hung his head, shamefaced. "Then enjoy yourself this evening—it will please me greatly. And I shall know you truly love me."

He smiled and kissed her hand. "Why is it that a tender rebuke from you fills my heart with more warmth than the sighing devotion of twenty silly women?"

She laughed. "I challenge you to find twenty silly

women here tonight. I expect to see them sighing over you before the evening is done!"

"Pah! They are not silly. They are so—*common!* There is none to match you in breeding."

She smiled thinly. "What a snob you are, René. Would you love me the less if you thought me common?"

He laughed. "How you enjoy your mystery! But I am not deceived."

"Time will tell. Now go and find your sighing women."

"I shall begin at once," he said, frowning. "I see Monsieur de Janequin bearing down on us. I have not the grace to wish him well." With a sigh he moved toward a group of women chatting in an alcove.

"*Nom de Dieu*, Bernard," said Delphine, as Janequin hurried toward her, his face creased in an unhappy scowl. "What is amiss?"

"Louise de Trémont has just arrived. I had hoped she would not come—"

"Then why did you have me invite her?"

"She—almost begged an invitation—"

"And you could not refuse—dear, kind Bernard! Well, she is welcome here."

"I fear she means you no good will. She was—quite put out when she heard of our betrothal."

"I shall win her over with my charm," said Delphine, holding out her hand as Louise de Trémont came sailing toward them. "Madame de Trémont! How nice to meet you at last!"

Louise de Trémont was a large, imposing woman with a haughty manner and stiff carriage. There might have been a time—in her youth—when she was considered handsome, but years of discontent had taken their toll, and now the lines around her mouth and nose were set in a permanent sneer of disapproval, as though the world around her had a disagreeable odor.

"Madame Despreaux. *Enchanté!*" The voice had a
high pitch, grating to the ear. "What a surprise it was to
hear that Bernard had chosen you for his bride! But you
are a sweet child—I can tell it at a glance. And sometimes
a man will abandon old friends for—a last fling with
youth. I'm sure Bernard will not regret it." She smiled
tightly, her mouth a thin line, reminding Delphine of a
large snake that had slithered aboard *Olympie* once as
she lay in the harbor of some tropical port.

"How kind of you to wish us well," said Delphine. She
indicated the milling guests in her glittering salon. "It
brings great joy to Bernard and me to be surrounded by
dear friends who hold only the tenderest thoughts for
us." Deftly she slipped her hand under Louise de
Trémont's elbow and guided her to a laughing group of
people, leaving a relieved Janequin behind to greet
latecomers.

As the evening progressed, Delphine circulated among
her guests, pleased with the way things were going.
Everyone seemed to be enjoying himself—except the
one guest who had been invited for the very purpose
of suffering. André had arrived late, slinking in like
a reluctant thief, moving up the great staircase to
the salon as though pulled against his will. He had
watched Delphine with mournful eyes, his chin sunk to
his chest, declining the invitations of every hopeful
female who tried to drag him into the merriment
and dancing. It warmed Delphine's heart to see his
agony.

Foulon, her steward, was now moving among the
guests to announce supper. A large room had been set
up off the grand salon with long trestle tables arranged in
a U-shape and covered with snowy cloths and fine gold
plate and delicate crystal goblets from Venice. Janequin
had been lavish in his budget for the *soirée* (despite

Braudel's bleats of protest), and Delphine had planned a sumptuous repast.

Watching her guests file into the dining room, Delphine massaged her earlobe absently, then winced in annoyance. Damn! Her earring had begun to pinch and chafe; there was a rough spur of metal that would have to be rasped smooth. Well, perhaps there was time to put on new earrings now—it would be several minutes before all the guests had found their seats. She hurried up the stairs to her own chamber on the floor above and exchanged her jewels, then sped back to her guests. As she passed the library, she glanced in and was surprised to see André standing before the cold fireplace and gazing morosely up at the Vouet portrait of her above the mantel.

"La! André!" she laughed gaily, her voice a silver bell. "Will you not come to supper?" And turned to leave.

But he crossed the room in several long strides, clutching her arm as she would have gone out the door, and pulling her savagely back into the room. He swung her around to face him, his hands tight on her shoulders, his blue eyes burning with fierce intensity.

"Let me go," she said coldly.

"I cannot believe you would do this," he said bitterly. *"Nom de Dieu,* Delphine, he is an old man!"

"And a very dear one."

"And when he takes you to bed—can there be any joy for you?"

"That's scarcely your concern! Will you let me go?"

He released her and turned away, running his fingers impatiently through his hair. "Don't be a fool," he said quietly. "I speak to you as a friend. There is passion in you—for all your banked fires. How long can an old man satisfy you?"

"That remains to be seen. Are you so young and—virile—yourself, that you can speak ill of Bernard?"

His face went white, as though she had struck him in the pit of his stomach. "You viper!" he spat at last, his chest heaving in anger. "I wonder if Bernard knows what a savage he is really marrying!" And turning, he strode from the room.

In the dining salon he took a seat just where the main table turned a corner, and where he could stare at Delphine with a resentful frown. She stirred uncomfortably as the meal progressed, seeing the anger, the naked desire in his face. Several times she sent a servant to offer him a particularly succulent dish, but he waved it aside impatiently and called for more wine. He was drinking a great deal of wine, and though she guessed that as a soldier he was used to it, it still made her uneasy. She smiled and chatted with forced gaiety, but the strain taxed her nerves. Bernard was of little use to her. Louise de Trémont had insinuated herself next to him and was clinging to his arm, demanding every moment of his time. And Rannel, seated to her left, had already found a new love; even as Delphine watched, the young woman untied a bow of pink ribbon from her bodice and looped it shyly about René's lovelock. Delphine sighed. So much for love. She had always known the shallowness of her admirers' affections for her; she had been indifferent in the past, but now she felt an unexpected twinge of pain. Copain, Gunner, Michel. They had loved her honestly, truly, deeply. Now she had Bernard's sense of decency that would not allow her honor to be stained, René's fickle love—a thing of shadow with little substance, and André's lust. It was an ill-matched exchange.

As the evening wore on, the wine flowed and tongues were loosened; wit gave way to ribaldry and eventually to calumny, particularly in the case of Louise de Trémont. She took great delight in maligning courtiers who were not present, and passing on choice bits of malicious gossip, choosing as her victims those who seemed to be held in low esteem by the majority of the guests. After all, who would chide her and her wicked tongue who secretly agreed with her slanders?

At last Janequin had had enough. Louise was talking about Madame de Chevreuse who was in exile in England. Since the woman had often been involved in treasonous activities against the crown, the company felt free to heap scorn upon her, attributing to her the most scandalous behavior, all to the accompaniment of great hilarity. Janequin set down his wineglass quietly. "There is much commendable in La Chevreuse," he said.

"Commendable?" Louise's voice rose in a horrified shriek, her nose twitching in sanctimonious disapproval. "The woman encouraged the queen to write letters to her brother the king of Spain—in cipher, *mon Dieu!*—and in time of war! But for the queen's warning to her confidante, your 'commendable' Chevreuse might have been arrested!"

Janequin sighed. "She was misguided, perhaps, but she is a woman of great beauty and intelligence—and bravery. She scarce deserves your mockery."

"How so brave?" asked a guest.

"With little aid from her friends, the woman escaped to Spain alone. And on horseback."

"On horseback? The entire journey?" There was an awed silence.

"But my dears!" gushed a fat *duchesse*, popping a piece of marchpane into her mouth. "Do you not know the story? It is quite delicious! Chevreuse escaped dressed as a man!"

"No! In breeches?"

"Yes. And she rode astride!"

"*Mon Dieu*," giggled one of the women. "I would not spread my legs for a horse."

"A horse would not petition you, my love," said her husband sourly.

A thin-faced *comtesse* sniffed. "But to wear breeches! Only harlots wear breeches, and then only under their petticoats! Father Joseph, my confessor, often says that a woman of virtue should allow nothing between her legs."

"My dear, we are speaking of Chevreuse," said Louise, "not a woman of virtue." This was followed by much laughter and snickered asides by the men.

"Well, I never heard of such a thing before," said the thin *comtesse* primly. "A woman dressed as a man!"

"*Au contraire,*" said André suddenly, draining the last of his wine. "I have a better story to tell." Delphine froze, feeling her heart begin to thump in her breast. It was obvious from his slurred voice that he had drunk too much and was feeling reckless. "I knew a woman who not only dressed as a man, but played the part as well."

"I should think it a tedious story," said Delphine tightly.

"No, no! Let Monsieur le Comte tell it!"

"It was on my journey home from New France. She was the daughter of the captain."

"*Nom de Dieu,*" said Rannel, fanning himself with delicate fingers. "A ship's brat."

"Yes. But a ship's brat who thought herself a lad, and could climb the rigging and handle a rapier with a skill that you might envy, *mon ami*. And swear—? Sweet Mother of God! Every curse I ever heard on the battle-field, and more besides, poured from her lips."

"How distasteful," said a courtier with a sneer. "I should have ignored the brat."

André poured himself another glass of wine. His face was bland, his expression unreadable. His eyes might have given him away, but Delphine had not the courage to look him full in the face. "And so I thought to do," he responded to the man. "But she was a devilish savage besides, with a fiery temper, always tormenting me with her foul ways."

"She sounds so—ill-bred," said Rannel with contempt.

"Come, René," said Delphine sharply, finding her voice at last. "Merely because she was lowborn?"

"My dear goddess, I wonder André can even speak of such a creature in your divine presence!" At these words, a small smile twitched at André's lips.

"It must have been a tiresome voyage," said the *duchesse.*

André stared at Delphine. "Say, rather, dangerous! This—boy-girl would rage and fight. I bore more than one bruise and scar on the voyage!"

"Mon Dieu! I would have thrashed her soundly!"

The smirk had become a grin, the blue eyes twinkling wickedly at Delphine. "And so I did, with much satisfaction!" There was an outburst of laughter.

Delphine's face was stiff, and a pulse beat in her temple, but when she spoke her words were measured and controlled. "I had thought you a civilized man, Monsieur le Comte. Had you not the wit or the wisdom to deal with the woman without behaving like a savage yourself?"

"Would you have me reason with a viper?" he asked. "No. One must pluck out the scorpion's sting."

The *duchesse* giggled. "But a scorpion's sting is in its tail!"

"Indeed. You might say I—hit upon the seat of the problem!"

"Bravo, André. Well done." A compliment to his wit.

"Tell me," piped up another guest. "Do they call that a *spanking* breeze at sea?" Again there was laughter and

murmurs of approval at the speaker's cleverness. In a
moment, everyone was laughing and talking, each trying
to outdo his fellows with graphic imagery.

As though Gosse was a faceless creature meant only
for their amusement, thought Delphine bitterly. She had
begun to tremble—in fury, in fear that André would
reveal all. Nervously she jumped up from her chair. Her
sleeve caught and overturned a large ewer of wine on the
table, spilling the bright ruby liquid across the pristine
cloth. Snatching up a napkin, she began to blot at the
stain, but her hands were shaking so badly that her labors
were wasted. "Forgive me," she murmured, and turned
to Bernard, her eyes almost pleading.

"My dear," he said softly, and rose to stand beside her,
holding out a silencing hand to the guests. "Mesdames,
messieurs. My poor Delphine is languishing with weariness. Had I noted before how tired she is, I should have
most kindly asked you all to depart long since. I beg you
now, for the love you hold for her, to take your leave."

Delphine smiled her gratitude as the guests, with many
polite nods to her, rose from their chairs. She led them
down the great staircase, standing on the landing to bid
her farewells, while Janequin descended to the vestibule
and moved about the milling throng who waited for
torches to be lit outside to see them home.

André was the last. He waited until the landing was
empty, then came unsteadily down the stairs and took
Delphine's hand in his, smirking like a sly fox as he
brought her fingers to his lips. "I had not realized what
sport it was to bait you, *ma chère*. I must have learned
the trick from that imp Gosse!"

She drew herself up haughtily. "Fool! Drunken fool!"
she sneered. "Even sober you're scarce a match for me!"
She swept past him and sailed down the steps to stand
beside Janequin and her departing guests.

André frowned. Bending down, he reached into his boot and pulled out his knife; aiming carefully he hurled it so it was impaled in the floor just to one side of Delphine's skirts.

Startled, she whirled to him, the flicker of sudden fear in her eyes turning to rage. "Damned bilge rat!" she shrieked. There was dead silence. Delphine saw the look of shock on the faces around her, and began to laugh. *"Ma foi!* My faith, did I fool you all?" she asked.

Rannel exhaled slowly. *"Nom de Dieu,* goddess, your wit is so quick it takes my breath away! There is not another woman—no, not even the actresses of the Hôtel de Bourgogne—who could improvise so cleverly!"

"Yes," said Louise de Trémont, her eyes like glittering jets. "You did that so naturally one would almost think you could be the creature of whom André spoke!"

"If I were she," laughed Delphine, "I should have plucked forth the blade and slit his throat by now." She looked down in mock horror at the knife still quivering at her feet. "André, you wicked man, come and take your knife away. I shall not soon forgive you for trying to frighten me!"

Shamefaced, André retrieved his blade, while the guests chided him for tormenting poor, tired Delphine. It was only her fine breeding, they said, that had turned his deliberate rudeness into a moment of frivolity. A lesser woman would not have played a role for the amusement of her guests; a lesser woman would have banished him from her company forever.

Finally they were gone, André at the last, looking as though he would beg her forgiveness for his behavior. Only Janequin remained to take her hand in his and wish her a good-night. "Stay abed in the morning, my dear," he said. "You look so tired. If the day is fine, I shall send a message to you and we shall meet in the Palais Cardinal.

There was an exquisite fan I saw in a shop there. I should like you to have it, if it pleases you." He kissed her softly on the forehead and went out to his waiting carriage.

The smile remained on Delphine's face until the door had closed behind them. Then, snarling, she strode to a small table and picked up a porcelain bowl that rested there, holding it high above her head and dashing it to the floor so it smashed into a thousand pieces. She shrieked in outrage and kicked furiously at the legs of the table, then swirled about the room, tearing at her hair, her rage almost beyond containing.

"Foulon!" she screamed at last. "Foulon, you lazy lout, where are you?"

"Madame." Her steward came hurrying into the vestibule. He bowed politely, but his eyes flicked to the smashed bowl and back to Delphine, astonished to see his mistress in such a state.

Delphine took a steadying breath. "Foulon," she said. "Do you know Monsieur le Comte de Crillon? He was a guest here tonight."

"Certainly, madame. I have seen the gentleman often in Paris."

"The—gentleman," her voice heavy with contempt, "is staying at the Louvre Palace. He will have taken a barge to return there. Take as many men as you need, and go through the streets—you will arrive at the *quai* long before he does—and bring the blackguard to me!"

"Madame? Do you—wish us to—invite the gentleman to accompany us?"

"Damn his black heart! I wish you to bring him to me in a sack—bound and trussed like a chicken! I would have no swordplay. Take enough men so you may waylay him with impunity. But *bring him back!*"

She stormed up the two flights of stairs to her bedchamber where Charlotte was waiting to help her out of her gown and into a silk nightdress and peignoir. She felt distracted, impatient, stopping her toilette every few moments to pace the chamber and curse softly under her breath. Charlotte's solicitude only set her more on edge. "Go to bed, Charlotte!" she snapped at last. "Leave my hair. I shall unpin it myself."

The maid curtsied and fled. Delphine shook out her chignon and began to plait her hair into a long braid, then abandoned the task, feeling too restless to concentrate. Damn! What was keeping them? She poured herself a large goblet of wine from a sideboard, gulping the first few mouthfuls to feel the soothing warmth in her belly. At length she heard a noise on the stairs. There was a knock on her door. At her command, Foulon and several of her grooms and footmen entered, carrying with some difficulty a large burlap sack that writhed and twisted with a life of its own. From within came muffled sounds. At Delphine's nod, the contents of the sack were dumped unceremoniously to the floor. André lay in a heap, his hands bound behind his back, mouth gagged, eyes covered. He struggled to his feet, swaying, his arms working furiously at the rope that bound them. Delphine saw that, in the skirmish, the locket with Marielle's portrait had slipped from beneath his shirt and now rested on top of his doublet; the sight only sharpened her hatred toward him. She motioned Foulon to remove his gag; he was cursing before the steward had finished untying the knots.

"Damn you!" he said. "Filthy coward, whoever you are! Let me see my adversary. Give me my sword! I shall run it through your craven heart! You dunghill! You son of Satan!" His voice was clear and harsh—fury had burned out the last traces of the wine. At Delphine's signal, Foulon pulled the blindfold from his eyes; André shook his head and blinked, then gasped in astonishment as his eyes found Delphine. "You!" he said, scarcely believing his senses.

She looked beyond him to Foulon and the other men. "Give me his sword," she said coldly, "and then begone. I have no more need of you this night; I shall let the villain go when I'm through with him. You have done your work well." When the door had closed behind them, she unsheathed André's sword and went to stand in front of him.

"Delphine—" he began quietly, still mystified.

She lifted the rapier point to his throat. "Hold your tongue," she said through clenched teeth, "and heed me well! I have earned the right to a good life! I will not live in fear of your loose words. If ever you tell aught of what you know of *Olympie* and Gosse—I shall kill you!"

His lip curled in contempt. "So that's it. The brave Gosse has clothed herself in deception and now fears the light of day!"

"Damn you, hold your tongue!"

The blue eyes glittered angrily. "Will you run me through? Will you slit my throat whilst my hands are bound? Is La Déesse a coward as well as a sham? *Mon Dieu!* Give me Gosse!"

The fury broke then. The hatred and bitterness and grief that had lain like a festering sore on her soul, poisoning her every waking moment, burst forth. "Gosse is dead!" she shrieked. "You killed her long since!" She threw down the sword and strode to him, fists upraised, striking savagely at him again and again—while he tried to duck the blows—until his face was red and a thin trickle of blood seeped from the corner of his mouth.

He staggered back, panting, his tongue searching for the cut on his lip, his bound arms working furiously behind him. "Only Gosse's goodness is dead," he spat.

"The vile child remains!" He stuck his chin out belligerently. "Will you strike me again? Come—have at me!"

With a curse she leaped for him; this time he was ready for her. He sidestepped and thrust out a booted foot; she fell forward onto her face, her hands breaking the fall at the last minute. He threw himself on top of her, his weight pinning her to the floor, and hissed in her ear. "I beat you once before, you devil! This time you'll feel the sting of a rope end!"

"Pig!" she gasped, trying desperately to wriggle from under him. He could feel the rope cutting into his wrists as he struggled against his bindings. As he freed his arms at last, she squirmed out from under him, sliding forward on her belly. He grabbed at her legs, holding them fast; with a savage grunt she wriggled and kicked backward until she had freed his hold for a second, then scrambled to her feet, making for his sword to defend herself. In a moment he was up, standing before her, blocking her way. One long arm shot out and clamped about her wrist; stooping, he scooped up the rope from the floor and began to drag her to the bed.

"No!" she shrieked in panic, fighting desperately against the superior strength that was pulling her inexorably to the bed. Flinging her forward with one sweep of his arm, he cast her face downward upon the pillows. In terror that he would strike her, she rolled over and away from him. He fell upon her, the rope held in both hands and pressing on her windpipe; she struggled for a moment, nearly choking, and then lay still.

In the sudden quiet they stared at each other, gasping for breath, hair awry, clothing askew. André tongued his cut lip again, his sapphire eyes burning. "Damn you," he growled, "why do you haunt me?" And he crushed her mouth with his.

Delphine trembled, feeling his lips, his hard body on hers. All that she had thought dead, buried with the past, gone forever, flamed into life at his kiss. She tangled her fingers in his hair, her mouth parted in surrender, her body arching upward to press against his in fevered anticipation. He kissed her eyelids, her neck, her throat, murmuring "Delphine" over and over. She pushed him from her with an impatient cry and began to pull at his clothing, wanting nothing so much as the feel of his sleek body on hers. He sat up and tore off his doublet and shirt, flinging aside the intimidating locket, then removed boots and hose and breeches. With shaking hands she pulled off her nightclothes and lay back, waiting for him, hungering for him, until she thought she would die. She groaned in pleasure when he took her at once, sliding his hands down her flanks to press her body more tightly to his heaving loins. She clung to him, her hands kneading the muscles of his back with every spasm that permeated her body. She was floating, she was soaring, she was consumed by a white-hot flame—

"*Ah Dieu*—André?" she gasped. Her eyes flew open. He had withdrawn so abruptly that she still floated in the void, her passion not yet sated.

"I want to hear you say it," he said, his voice low and intense. "Am I young enough? Am I—virile enough to satisfy you?"

"Damn you, don't torment me!"

"Am I?"

"Yes! Oh, yes," she breathed, pulling his mouth down to hers. He kissed her resoundingly, his mouth hot and possessive, then thrust into her again so she cried out and abandoned herself once more to her ecstasy.

When he left her chamber an hour later, she lay quietly for a long time, staring up at the paneled canopy of her bed, feeling the waves of contentment wash over her body. She had nodded in agreement at his parting words—"Tomorrow night. At the hour of nine."—knowing that she would be waiting, trembling in anticipation. And after all, what did it matter? Nothing had changed. She still intended to marry Bernard, but until André's lust for her was sated, what harm was there in pleasuring herself as well? She had spent enough time trying to deny her body's needs—why not a little self-indulgence, before she became a virtuous wife and buried for good and all this sensuality that threatened to get out of control?

André had brought it to life. Let it end with André.

Chapter Twenty

DELPHINE PERCHED ON ALL FOURS IN THE CANOPIED BED, leaning over André. Her unbound hair hung like a curtain around them, shutting out everything save lips that yearned for one another, eyes that smoldered with desire. André reached up a languid hand to stroke that golden glory, then caught his fingers at her nape and pulled her mouth down to his.

She shook her head free and sat up, her eyes glinting wickedly. "No," she said. "You promised to bring me a copy of l'Hermite's *Marianne.*"

"It was a dull play," he said, his hands caressing the soft roundness of her breasts.

"But you promised!" she pouted, pushing his hands away.

"Will you come here, you tormenting devil?" He reached up to take hold of her; suppressing a smile, she wriggled beyond his grasp.

"Where is my book?"

"Mon Dieu! I only promised yesterday!"

"You promised the day before! I have welcomed you into my bed for nearly a week now. And what have I to show for it?"

"By my faith," he growled, dragging her down to the pillows and rolling over to pin her body with his own, "I'll show you what you have to show for it!"

She allowed him to kiss her, and then giggled, "I think—old man—" but here he kissed her mercilessly, his mouth strong on hers until, gasping, she was forced to retract the insult. "I think," she went on at last, a little breathless, "that you are too exhausted from your labors to take the time to buy me the book!"

He sat up and folded his arms across his chest. "You are a very taxing woman—and not only in bed! Small wonder Janequin escaped to Auvergne!"

She sat up in her turn, mocking his gesture with her own. "He went because I asked him to! Though you have been very discreet, I did not wish him to be hurt by—rumors. And then, his château must be prepared for our wedding."

He frowned, the lighthearted mood forgotten. "I must talk to you about that."

"Indeed, no. Not tonight. Tonight is for frivolity, and for—other things, if you can persuade me!" Laughing, she skipped out of bed and danced about her chamber, flaunting her naked body before him. "La!" she said airily. "I am perishing for a cup of wine!" She filled a goblet to the brim and seated herself primly in a large armchair at some distance from the bed and André.

He beckoned to her with one slim forefinger. "Come here."

She shook her head no and took a drink of the wine, eyes shining with mischief.

"You wicked tease," he said.

She nodded her head yes.

"Well, then," he sighed, easing himself out of the bed as though he had not a care in the world. He circled her chair slowly while she sipped at her wine and waited for the attack she knew must come. But instead of a frontal assault the soldier had chosen a furtive invasion. Delphine shivered as his hands came from behind to rest on her bare shoulders and then slid down to cup her heaving breasts. He leaned over her shoulder, his mouth finding her neck, his teeth nipping playfully at her earlobe. She trembled in sensuous delight at his touch, abandoning herself to her feelings, the warmth that flooded her being.

"Now," he whispered in her ear, "will you come to bed?"

She smiled like a cat with a secret. "No."

He laughed. "You will regret it, madame!" He moved around to stand in front of her, and gently took the goblet from her fingers, setting it aside on a small table. He knelt before her and took one dainty foot in his hands, stroking her ankle, then letting his fingers travel upward to caress her knee, her thigh—and beyond.

"*Ah, Dieu!*" she gasped, and leaned her head back, closing her eyes to keep her brain from spinning dizzily. When he gathered her up at last in tender arms and carried her to the bed, she lay there trembling, her senses stretched to the limits of endurance, consumed by her hunger, her need of him.

He was very quiet, making no movement to touch her, to take her. Surprised, she opened her eyes to see him grinning above her, waiting to play his trump card. He moved toward the edge of the bed, as though he would leave her. "I thought I'd have a cup of wine," he said. "By my faith, but all this toil is wearying for an—old man!"

"Sink me," she hissed through clenched teeth. "If I had my sea knife now I'd slit your gizzard!"

"Do you think you are the only one who can play the tease?" He threw back his head and laughed, his teeth dazzling against his copper skin. Delphine's heart caught at the beauty of the man, the wonder of making love to him. Gilles had withheld himself to torment her, to mock her sensuality; André withheld himself that her final ecstasy be all the sweeter. Dear Mother of God, what was happening to her? She had meant this only to be a pleasant interlude before her marriage to Janequin, resolving to keep the wall of injured pride, the last vestiges of her hatred, always between them. Then why did she keep remembering that he could be dear and good and kind, when she meant only to satisfy her body's cravings?

He saw the sudden change of her mood. "Delphine," he said gently, and kissed her with such sweetness that her heart nearly broke and her brain spun in confusion. He made love to her tenderly, until she wanted to weep and hold him forever, feeling warmed and protected, for all the passionate intensity of her body's responses.

After they had lain quietly for some time, he propped himself up on one elbow and gazed down at her. She smiled brightly, trying to recapture their earlier playfulness, feeling herself vulnerable and weak for allowing herself such thoughts about André even for a moment. Don't be a fool, Delphine, she thought. Think of Gosse and her grief. Your heart has played you false before. He is a man consumed with passion, and nothing more. But wasn't Gilles? Yes. Best only to think of her senses, to satisfy her body, and forbid aught else. And when this brief flame with André had burned out, she would bank her fires with snow, and settle in for the simplicity of a long winter with Bernard.

André did not return her smile. "Where is your heart?" he asked softly.

She laughed. "What a foolish thing to say!"

"Is it? I know where your senses are. But a part of you—is it your heart? your thoughts?—drifts away from me at times."

"Does it matter to you?"

He hesitated, then sat up, turning away from her. "No, indeed not. Why should it?" The answer too quickly given.

"Then why ask?" she said, her voice suddenly frosty, feeling unexpectedly disappointed in his answer.

"What of Bernard?" he said. "I cannot believe that you still intend to marry him."

"And wherefore not?"

"This is the why and wherefore," he said angrily, bending down to crush her lips with his. He lifted his head, seeing her tremble beneath him. "Can you live without passion, Delphine?"

She turned her head away, lips pressed tight in annoyance. "You had better go, André. My life is my own. I owe you no accounting. Let us be as we are, and nothing more." She watched in silence as he rose from the bed and donned his garments, putting on the locket at the last. He held it in his palm for a moment, as though he were drawing strength from Marielle—that ghostly presence who haunted Delphine every moment she lay in André's arms—then slipped it beneath his shirt and doublet. At the door he stopped and turned, his hand on the latch.

"Tomorrow night?" he said.

She smiled and threw him a kiss. "Of course, *mon cher,*" she said lightly. "Never fret, André. After my marriage to Bernard, I will keep you as my lover, if you so desire!"

He smiled thinly and left her room. In the barge back to the Louvre Palace he sat bent over the bow, his hand across his eyes, his soul deeply troubled.

André awoke to cold splashes of water in his face. Damn the rain! He grumbled and groped for his heavy cloak, surprised that it did not seem to be about his shoulders; then he opened his eyes to find himself—not in the field as he had dreamed—but in his own bedchamber at the Louvre, with Jean-Auguste grinning above him and sprinkling water on his head from a small pitcher. "Jean-Auguste! *Ma foi!* What brings you to Paris again?"

"Get up," said Jean-Auguste, striding to the curtains and throwing them wide to the soft June morning. "I've taken the liberty of having an enormous breakfast brought in, and I cannot possibly eat it all!"

"But why are you here?" André swung his legs over the side of the bed and drew on his dressing gown. "I thought when you and Lysette and Clémence left Saint-Germain I had seen the last of you this summer!"

"We did not leave. We—retreated—according to Lysette! She is very put out with you for your treatment of Clémence."

"I was perfectly civil to the woman at all times!"

"Precisely! Lysette seems to think, with your experience—and how, by the way, did you manage to acquire such a reputation with my wife?—that you should have tried to seduce Clémence long since! She's scarcely a blushing virgin, after all!"

André sat at the table of food the servants had laid out, pouring himself a large mug of ale and taking a ravenous bite from a fat quail roasted and glazed with honey. "Have you come to Paris to badger me, then? Go back to Chimère and your vineyards and your glasshouse—how

is the glassworks managing, by the way?—and leave me
in peace."

"The glasshouse is prospering. Rondini has had many
commissions in Vouvray and Tours—his goblets are
exquisite, as well you know—and will soon pay back my
loan. In the meantime, the wine bottles that he makes for
me grow more faultless each day, until I fear Chimère's
wines will be noted for the vessels, not the nectar within!"

"I can suggest a remedy. I shall sell you Vilmorin wine,
that the contents may outshine the containers!"

Jean-Auguste ignored the gibe and took a bite of
cherry tart. "In truth, *mon ami*," he said wryly, "it is the
success of my ventures that has brought me to Paris.
Lysette has taken it into her head that we must have a
town house for when we are here. My coffers are bursting
with coins, and my sweet wife has restrained herself
somewhat in the matter of gowns and jewels—so how
can I refuse? I have seen three or four promising *hôtels*."
And here he rattled off a few addresses to André's
approval. "I should settle the matter before the week is
out."

"But with time for a ride in the Bois de Boulogne, and
a fencing match or two?"

"But certainly, my friend! And will you join me at the
Marais Theater this evening? I hear the play is bawdy,
and the actress is divine!"

André hesitated. "No. I have—an engagement."

"Tomorrow night, then."

"No. Forgive me."

"Ah," said Jean-Auguste quietly. "La Déesse, I think."

"*Mon Dieu!* How did you know? I had thought myself
discreet—"

"Name of God, André! I heard no gossip. But can you
keep a secret from an old friend? I saw you at Saint-
Germain, sighing in her presence. And now you stay in

Paris. You who love your vineyards. And for what, I ask myself. *Voilà!* The pursuit of La Déesse!"

André threw down his napkin and strode to the window, gazing through the leaded panes to the Seine below. "I am consumed by the woman," he said.

"Then why do you suffer so? And do not deny it. I see it in your eyes. Is the goddess cold, a marble beauty and nothing more?"

"She is a woman of fire and passion, she—"

Jean-Auguste laughed and held up a restraining hand. "Spare me, my friend! I am a married man! But then, your joy should be complete!"

"Ah Dieu!" groaned André, returning from the window and staring at Jean-Auguste with stricken eyes. "She is so young! Less than half my age—it is madness!"

"What has age to do with the heart?"

"No. Lysette was right. I am an old fool—and the world would mock me."

"Name of God!" said Jean-Auguste in exasperation. "Lysette means you well, but she can be meddlesome! She truly believes that Clémence would be the best wife for you. But you must follow your own heart! Tell me," he said, putting his hand on André's sleeve, "do you love her?"

André frowned in concern. "Would I betray Marielle's memory if I said yes?"

"Why should that be a betrayal? You loved Marielle truly while she lived. You can give her no more. But what of your own happiness, your boys? How betray Marielle by taking a new wife?"

"They are so different, one from another. Is that not a betrayal of my love for Marielle? They are so different!"

Jean-Auguste gazed at him, his gray eyes thoughtful. "Are they?"

"Mon Dieu! Marielle was sweet, gentle, and serene—"

"Yes. As the years went on. She had her home, her husband, her children. It was enough. But I remember a different Marielle, in the beginning, when I near fell in love with her myself." He chuckled. "Do you remember the picnic we had on the river, that hot summer day?"

André smiled. "And the water fight! I had forgotten! She was young and fresh and innocent." He stared sightlessly into space, as though he were seeing Marielle with new eyes. "There was a sun spark within her that flashed out sometimes to challenge the soft serenity of her outward show. The beauty, the elegance that came with maturity—all that I loved. But it was her innocence and spirit that first won my love—and kept it."

"And La Déesse? Is she so different?"

André shook his head in wonder, recalling Gosse's youthful fire, Delphine's passion that turned a moment of love into exquisite pleasure. As it had been with Marielle. Always.

"Then why do you need advice of me? Take her for your wife!"

"She is betrothed to Bernard de Janequin."

"Who is older than you."

"Who is older than I. I tell you, the woman torments me. Sometimes I think I see love in her eyes, but sometimes—" he shivered at the memory, downing the last of his ale "—such—hatred, though I may misread it. It has kept me from pouring out my heart to her. *Mon Dieu!* I had thought, when a man grew older, he no longer suffered if a maiden spurned him. But—I fear, my friend, I fear. And that fear has kept me silent."

The sound of a rooster crowing somewhere beyond the open casement woke Delphine. She yawned and stretched. It would be hot today, and with July only a week or so away, Paris would soon become unbearable.

The court had already retired to the coolness of Fontainebleau; Delphine was to leave this afternoon and join
Bernard there. Even if André followed, there would be
less gossip if Delphine was with Janequin. She sighed,
her body sated from a night of lovemaking (and if a small
finger of discontent scratched at her heart, what matter?),
and rolled over in her bed, nearly colliding with a sleeping
André. *Mon Dieu!* What was to be done about him? He
never remained until morning, but last night, after the
rapture, she had stayed curled in his embrace, wanting
his warmth. They had neither of them intended to drift
off to sleep. She could count on Foulon and Charlotte to
be discreet and keep her confidences, but what of the rest
of the servants? There would be gossip if anyone saw him
leave her house at this hour—and the court dined on
gossip! It was one of the reasons she had so jealously
guarded her own identity, and the secret of Robert,
even from Janequin. Better to be a woman of mystery, with speculation swirling around her name, than
have each small detail of her past on the lips of every
courtier. Well, André would think of a way to leave un-
seen.

She smiled down at his sleeping form. How young he
looked in repose, like a lad, his face sweet and innocent.
Like Robert. How alike they were. She sighed. Robert. It
had been weeks since she had seen him. Anne-Marie
said that he was walking now—so many changes every
day in a sixteen-month-old child, and she not there to see
them. She had meant to visit while Janequin was away,
and now, with the trip to Fontainebleau, it might be
weeks more until she could see Robert. Watching the
sleeping André, her heart swelled with unexpected tenderness. She was almost tempted to wake him, tell him of
Robert, share with him the joy of their son. She shook
her head. No! She could not afford weakness or senti-

ment. It must be her secret forever. It would be best for Robert, best for Bernard.

She slipped quietly from the bed and threw her peignoir around her, enjoying the slide of the silk on her bare flesh. She padded to the window and looked out onto the square below, where the early-morning peddlers were beginning to set up their carts and tables. A flower seller arranged several baskets of bright blue and lavender flowers, the colors rich and glowing. She must remember to send Charlotte down this morning to fetch up an armful of the blossoms. She inhaled the sweet scents of June, then turned back into the room. André's clothes were strewn about where he had cast them off last night. She picked them up and smoothed them out before laying them carefully across the back of the armchair. Like a good little wife, she thought resentfully. Had his Marielle laid out his clothing for him? Her eye was caught by the locket. She picked it up, fingering the ribbon that had grown frayed from constant wearing. She felt her hands trembling. Dared she look at the portrait within, and see the woman whose presence she had felt so often? She hesitated, then flicked open the hinged lid. How strange. On *Olympie* she had looked at the picture and seen a queen, a woman beyond compare, matchless in her perfection. Now she saw merely the painting of a beautiful woman, the pigments fading, the gown and coiffure out of date—a sad and musty echo of the past. She sighed and closed the locket, meaning to set it on the table, then frowned, turning it over in her hand. She had not noticed it at first, but there seemed to be a leaf added at the back, the new piece so skillfully blended in with the old that only the worn patina of the older metal showed the difference. She swung out the leaf and gasped, then sank to the chair, her eyes filling with tears.

She was gazing upon her own face. Someone had

copied the portrait of her by Vouet—the same smile, the same look in the eyes, but in miniature. Only where Vouet had painted her hair in golden swirls about her face, in this picture her hair was short and straight, as Gosse's had been. She began to cry, muffling her sobs in her hands.

"Delphine." André was before her, kneeling at her feet. "What is it?"

She looked up, holding out the locket with shaking fingers. "But—why?" she whispered.

He cleared his throat and stood up, turning away to pull on his breeches and slip his shirt over his head. When at last he spoke, his back still toward her, his voice was muffled. "Because I love you."

She stood up, unsure of what to say, then sat down again, wiping nervously at her tears. She looked at the locket again. "Don't you like my curls? My long hair?"

He turned to her and smiled. "Your hair is beautiful."

"But—then—the picture—"

"I had Monsieur Vouet paint it from his sketches when I first met you again. I wanted the hair short—as a remembrance—because I thought that my dear Gosse had vanished."

"And now? Am I Gosse or Delphine?"

"A little of both, I think. And everything I love." He pulled her up into his arms and held her close, covering her face with kisses.

She threw her arms around his neck, clinging to him, her heart bursting with the wonder of it. He loved her! She was as dear to him as his Marielle, that woman whose memory she had never dared hope to supplant.

"Delphine. My love," he said. "Forget Janequin, forget the past—only be my wife and fill my days with your sunshine." She smiled lovingly at him, her eyes still sparkling with tears. He kissed the tears away and grinned. "I have two sons, you know. Will you mind being mother to two boys?"

She laughed softly, enjoying her secret. Not two. Three. "I shall not mind," she said, filled with joy that her sweet Robert would grow up knowing his own father. She danced away from him, wondering how she was to tell him of the child who had been conceived on that magical night aboard *Olympie*. Then she felt the memory of pain tug at her heart. No. Not yet. She would not tell him yet. There was something she had to know first, the canker that had gnawed at her for two long years. "André," she said softly, "why did you leave *Olympie* that morning with no word to me?"

He frowned, searching his memory, as though it were of so little importance that he had long since forgotten it. "I was—impatient to see my home and children—" (Yes, she thought, almost relieved, she had expected that was so.) "And then, fool that I was, I did not prize Gosse until long after I had lost her." Delphine began to breathe more freely. It was as she had guessed. Why had she feared to ask the question? André laughed ruefully. "And then, of course, I knew that it meant little to you, that night. And a man's pride is fragile."

"What do you mean—it meant little to me?"

"I was not unmindful of the men you lived with aboard *Olympie*! As I recall, you compared my body with theirs—thanks be to God you did not compare my abilities!—it was very disconcerting, my love!"

"Are you mad?" Her voice rose to a shriek. "I was a virgin!"

"Delphine, *ma chère*," he said soothingly, pulling her into his arms. "What matter now? I love you. Let it be."

"No!" She pushed him away savagely. "You pig! You whoreson! I was a virgin!"

"Oh, come now!" he said, his voice sharp with

annoyance. "The woman who came to my bed that night was a woman of experience!"

"Curse you! She was a child! Eager to learn what had been shared—in words, damn you, in *words!*—with her shipmates for years! Damn your eyes! You thought me a whore?"

"Not a whore, surely, but—"

"But a 'woman of experience?'" she said bitterly. "And now? What of now? Do you think that Madame Despreaux, La Déesse, has bestowed her favors on half of Paris?"

"I know not. I care not. It is not for me to judge."

"But you think it, don't you? *Don't you?*"

He thrust out a belligerent chin. "Why does Janequin pay for all your needs? Your clothes, your jewels, this house? I am scarcely deaf to the rumors!"

"And you think I am his mistress?"

"Are you?"

She drew herself up coldly. "I have known but two men in my life. And *one* of them—Despreaux—had no right to me! And you, you villain, how many women have you had?" Her voice grew more strident as her fury mounted. She snatched up the rest of his belongings—cloak and sword and hat—and threw them savagely in his direction. "Get out of my house and don't ever come back! I would not marry you now if the king commanded me on pain of death! You pig—that think so vile of me!" She stormed about the room while he finished dressing, stifling the urge to shriek her outrage to the heavens.

He buckled on his sword, then caught at her, shaking her violently by the shoulders. "Delphine! Please! Will you be reasonable?"

Her lip curled with contempt. "Was she a virgin, your sweet Marielle, when you took her?"

He recoiled, his face going pale. "She was a lady."

"And she was a fool to go down for the likes of you!"

He glared at her as though he would strike her, then, whirling, strode to the door.

"Wait!" she cried. "Mark me well. Do you love me? Do you desire me? Well, mark me! Bernard would marry me without the rewards of the bedchamber. But now, to spite you, I shall take him to my bed as often as he is able! I shall dance naked to stir his blood, and tease his poor prickle into a hardness. And for every night that he makes love to me, I shall send you a thorn from a yew tree! For each thorn that I send—may it pierce your flesh!—you will know that I have let my husband pierce me! And so I will be revenged!"

His eyes burning in anger, André stormed from the room. Delphine watched him go, her fists clamped tight to her sides, her body shaking with fury. But when he had gone, her face crumpled in anguish. With a mournful cry, she threw herself onto her bed and gave way to her grief.

Chapter Twenty-one

THE PALACE OF FONTAINEBLEAU WAS LOCATED SOME TEN leagues to the south of Paris, in a small town of the same name, and surrounded by a magnificent forest. The palace, built of local sandstone in the Italian manner—severe and classical and unadorned—had been constructed near an older château by King Francis I a century before, when Italian craftsmen and artists (not the least of whom was the great Leonardo) had been welcomed in the French court. It was a grand and sprawling palace, with great open courtyards: the Cour du Cheval Blanc, with its statue of a prancing white horse, the Cour de la Fontaine—the splashing fountain—from which, some said, the town and palace had first derived its name. The main door was reached by a sweeping, horseshoe-shaped staircase that the present king had built, and the whole of the palace was surrounded by formal gardens and artificial lakes. Beyond the front gate was a long avenue which stretched into the vast forest of Fontainbleau, with its picturesque mounds of antediluvian rocks and its lush vegetation.

The courtiers, in that summer of 1641, had come to enjoy a respite from the heat of Paris, and to escape the

wearying talk of the war with Spain. Dragging on for
some six years now, the war had begun to stir up bitter
resentment, not only among the overtaxed peasants and
bourgeoisie, but among the nobility as well. To forget
their cares, they amused themselves with riding and
hunting through the woods, leisurely boating on the lakes
and the river Seine which flowed nearby, and bowls and
court tennis on the vast lawns of the palace.

But only this morning, reality had intruded on their
pleasures. The king had received word that the Comte de
Soissons, a prince of the blood, had joined forces with
Spain to bring the war to an end. Soissons had crossed
the French frontier from the Spanish Netherlands, leading his army of revolt. There were even rumors—
according to Richelieu's spies—that Cinq-Mars had been
involved in the treasonous plot. Louis had left Fontainebleau at once to lead an army already in the field; those
who remained in this bucolic retreat enjoyed their last few
weeks of pleasure before they, too, might be called upon
to mobilize their own forces.

Delphine had managed to shun André since they had
been at Fontainebleau, throwing herself into the whirl of
activities with false gaiety; with the king away there would
be few *divertissements* to keep them from the confronta-
tion she wished to avoid. She even considered renewing
her flirtation with René de Rannel; Bernard had not been
jealous of it before, and since their marriage plans
proceeded apace, where was the harm in it?

Still, Janequin seemed strangely quiet and distracted, a
morose companion these last few days. Perhaps it was
because of Louise de Trémont, who had continued to
pursue him despite the announcement of his betrothal to
Delphine.

With a sigh Janequin limped to a stone bench beneath
a tree, sitting in the cool shadows and mopping at his

brow with a lace-edged handkerchief. "I cannot take another step, my dear," he said, smiling sheepishly up at Delphine. "I shall enjoy the beauty of the day from this bench, and leave the strenuous activities to the young."

"Of course," she said, sitting beside him.

He frowned, and sighed again. "To the young—" he murmured.

"Is something troubling you, Bernard?"

He hesitated. "Will you be happy married to an old man? I cannot dance with this leg of mine, I tire of long walks—"

"What has that to do with age? Many a young limb has been rendered useless because of war. We have always enjoyed one another's company—the theater, the books we share—why are you troubled now?"

He looked down at his hands, nervously twisting the signet ring on his finger. "Forgive me, but—I have heard rumors—whilst I was in Auvergne, and you in Paris—they did not say the—gentleman's name—but—"

She stood up and turned away from him. "I give you my oath, Bernard, I—shall be a chaste and virtuous wife—you shall have no cause to doubt my fidelity—"

"I understand," he said quietly, wondering if she had deliberately avoided the answering of his question. "I have arranged everything with the mayor of Bellerive. We shall sign the marriage contract and exchange the forms of consent on the same day. The nuptial mass will be celebrated on the following day. I had thought we would stay here at Fontainebleau for another week or so, then travel to my château together. The marriage has been planned for the twenty-fifth of July. Does that suit you?"

Delphine looked up. André had just alit from a small boat on the nearby canal, and was now walking toward them. *Dieu!* she thought, feeling herself trembling. "Bernard!" The name shot out so forcefully that Janequin stared at her in surprise. "Can we not go to Paris this week?"

"*Dieu du ciel.* Whatever for? You know Paris is stifling in July! If there are things you need from your *hôtel,* I shall have them brought to Auvergne by carriage."

"But must we stay here?" She felt the panic rising within her.

"My château is not prepared properly as yet, *ma chère.* I would not have you see your new home dusty with plaster and ringing with the sound of hammers! Let the sound of wedding bells be your welcome."

She sighed in resignation. "Of course." André was now striding purposefully down the garden path in their direction. Would he dare to make a scene in front of Bernard? "Do you mind," she said, turning to Janequin, "if I escape this warm day for a little? The palace is so cool. I shall join you later on the lawn for a game of bowls."

He laughed. "*I* find the day pleasant. And you wished to return to the heat of Paris?"

She stood up quickly, poised for flight. "You must forgive a woman her inconstancy!" she said brightly. "Now, here comes Monsieur de Crillon. He looks bored. You must be a dear, Bernard, and speak to the man. I shall see you anon." She hurried to the palace, slipping inside the first door she came upon. She had made her way through two narrow corridors and a small sitting room before she realized she had lost her way. Opening a door that looked promising, she found herself at last in the long Galerie François I, and breathed a sigh of relief. At the far end, she knew, was the door and the staircase that led to her apartments. She hurried down the long room, past alcoves crowded with marble statues and paintings that lined the walls, pausing ever so briefly to admire her favorite: the portrait of the Italian woman, La Joconde, the madonna Lisa, that King Francis had bought of Leonardo. At the last alcove at the end of the gallery she stopped, peering through the window to see if she could observe Bernard and André in the garden, but the tree blocked her view. She turned around. André was standing there, between her and the door, between her and escape.

"I thought you might come this way," he said quietly.

"Get out of my way."

"You have sent back every one of my notes unanswered—"

"Unread!" she spat.

"Please, Delphine! Hear me out. I beg your forgiveness; I hurt you grievously with my words. I had not meant to be cruel, I swear it to you. They were foolish words and foolish thoughts. I should have guessed you were a virgin, seeing the innocent Gosse who hid behind manly trappings and show. I suppose I—was jealous, thinking it so—that my dear Gosse—"

"Sweet Jesu!" she swore. "I am sick unto death to hear you talk of Gosse as though she were some sainted memory! She is gone! I am Delphine now, no more able to man a ship now than you yourself! You treated Gosse vilely then! And now that she is gone—never to return— you mock Delphine and yearn for Gosse! And yet I mark that two long years have passed since those days on *Olympie!* And never a word from you. A-a-h!" With an impatient cry, she turned her back on him.

He was silent for a long time. And then "I looked for you," he said softly.

She felt the tears spring to her eyes. "Did you?" she whispered, her lips trembling.

"Yes," he said, turning her into his embrace. "But when I sent to find you, there was only a burned-out cottage, and the sailors in port who said that Gunner was master of *Olympie*. It near broke my heart. Delphine. I love you more than life itself. I cannot have us parted because of a foolish quarrel."

Ah Dieu, she thought, her brain whirling with confusion, what am I to do? "No!" she cried, pushing him away. "You thought me a whore. How am I to forgive that? Do you think I have no pride?" She fought back her tears. "Leave me alone! Let me marry Bernard. It is so much easier, so much—" She took a deep shuddering breath.

"So much—what?" he growled.

She drew herself up, pulling the cloak of ice around her heart. So much safer, she thought. "It is over between us. I should be pleased if you did not trouble me again." Stepping past him, she hurried to the door and from there to the gardens and the safety, the heart's tranquillity of Bernard.

Janequin smiled at her coming, then froze for a moment, his eyes flickering to see André following close behind. Then he smiled again, shaking off his suspicions. "We have all been waiting for you, Delphine." Tucking his hand under her elbow, he led her to the smooth lawn where the bowlers and half a score of spectators were assembled. "I must warn you, *ma chère,*" he laughed, "there are several wagers already today that the gentlemen will defeat the ladies!"

She feigned astonishment. "What? Is it so? René?" She turned to Rannel, who stood with a young *duchesse.* "Would you wager against me?"

"Goddess," he bowed, "in the game of love you are peerless; the game of bowls is another matter!"

"For shame!"

"I will put ten crowns on you, Madame Despreaux."

She turned stiffly. "Monsieur de Crillon. I am flattered!"

"Is there any game you cannot play well?" There was more sadness than malice in André's voice.

Louise de Trémont smiled primly at Janequin. "I must betray my sex and wager for Monsieur de Janequin. You were always an accomplished bowler, Bernard. Do you remember that summer in Blois?"

"I remember I was young," he said dryly. "Save your coins, Louise! Come, gentlemen, shall we decide who is to roll first?"

Just then a booming voice shouted from across the gardens. "Sink and scuttle me, Gosse! Is it you? Be hanged, Michel, but it *is* our Gosse!"

Delphine whirled at the voice. Lumbering toward her across the lawn was Gunner, his hair more grizzled than ever, his rolling gait strange and out of keeping amid the manicured gardens and neat paths. Michel, a little less gangly now, strode along beside him.

"Gosse!" he shouted, and ran to Delphine to pick her up and sweep her around in a joyous circle.

"Put me down," she said, barely able to find her voice.

"Be hanged if ever I thought to see you again in this world!" laughed Gunner. "Come and give us a kiss!"

Delphine ran a hand nervously across her mouth. "What are you doing here?" she hissed.

Gunner frowned, his open face creased in dismay. "Be you ashamed of your shipmates, Gosse?"

"Gosse? Brat?" Louise's sharp voice cut the air like a knife. "*Nom de Dieu*, André! Why did you never tell us Delphine was your famous—sailing companion?"

"Goddess! You?" Rannel's voice was deep with shock and disappointment. "A common—"

"Common—what?" she spat, her eyes burning.

"Mother of God! Am I less a woman because of my birth?"

"La, André!" laughed the *duchesse*. "Is that the temper you spoke of?"

"I cannot believe it," said Rannel, tugging nervously at his lovelock. "You!" he said to Michel. "Who is this woman?"

"But that's our Gosse! The best shipmate a sailor ever had!" At this several of the women began to laugh in derision.

"Did she dress as a man?"

"How else climb the rigging?" said Michel, mystified at the laughter.

"And the swearing?" sneered Rannel.

"Rot and damnation," growled Gunner. "What sailor doesn't?"

A fat *marquis* began to chuckle, his belly bobbing up and down. "The famous—and mysterious—oh, what a jest!—Madame Despreaux—nothing but a—"

"A ship's brat!" shrieked the *duchesse* in delight, and they laughed uproariously.

"André, you should have told us long since," chided Louise. "The joke is too delicious to keep to yourself!"

Like a cornered animal, Delphine turned around and around, seeking a spark of warmth among the smirks of derision, the sneers of contempt. Gunner and Michel stared in unhappy confusion and Janequin's face was stiff with shock. André stepped toward her and put a hand on her arm.

"Delphine—" he said softly.

She shook him off. "Are you revenged at last, André? Have you waited until now to destroy me? Listen!" she cried, whirling to the guests. "You shall see Despreaux in her best role—ship's brat! Will that please you, you poxy dungheap, Rannel? And yes, Madame la Duchesse—I wore breeches! And had more between my legs than you shall ever have with that pisspoor husband of yours! Look you now!" She bent over and reached between her legs, pulling the back of her skirt forward and up and tucking the fabric firmly in her waist to form a kind of loose pantaloons. Then she rolled up the sleeves of her bodice. "Come, Monsieur le Marquis, you fat whoreson, lend me your sword! Will you not see the whole of the show? Lend me your sword, that I may deal with this son of a dog Crillon!" She snatched the *marquis's* rapier from its scabbard and slashed the air with it. "A lousy blade for a lousy coward," she sneered. "No balance, no heft— but it will serve. Now, André, you scurvy knave, will you see what new tricks I have learned?" She made a pass at André. "Draw your sword, you stinking bilge rat!"

"Delphine, please—" he said quietly.

"Curse your eyes!" she cried, her fury mounting. "I am Gosse! The ship's brat! Now draw your sword!"

He shook his head. "No."

"Delphine. *Ma chère,*" said Janequin. "Come away."

She was almost beside herself now, her anguish and humiliation mixing with her rage. "Don't you want to see what you nearly married, Bernard? Damn you, Crillon! Draw your sword!" She lunged forward, the point of her blade just touching André's wrist. A small spot of crimson appeared on his skin.

"Don't, Delphine."

"Gosse, you scum!" she shrieked, and attacked. This time he flinched as the blade pierced the soft flesh of his thigh. When she lunged again, her rapier flashing, he sidestepped and held up his elbow to ward off the blow; the slashing blade tore through his doublet and shirt and bit into his skin.

"Damn you!" he said, and drew his sword, parrying her next thrust. "Will you come to your senses? I have no

wish to—*Merde!*" he swore, as she broke through his
defense, her sword point tearing the front of his doublet.

She was weeping tears of helpless rage now. "I'll kill
you!" she screamed. "I'll kill you!" Again and again she
thrust at him, her fury driving her, until he was forced to
fight for his very life against that murderous blade. At last,
with a great sob she lowered her arm, her fury giving way
to grief.

André dropped his sword and took a step toward her,
his eyes warm with understanding. "My poor Gosse—"

She stared at him, the bitter tears pouring down her
cheeks, seeing the handsome face, the deep blue eyes
that had haunted her, destroyed her marriage, destroyed
her peace of mind for two long years now. "Be damned
to hell!" she cried and, lifting her blade, slashed at that
beautiful face.

André clutched at his cheek as the knife point ripped
open the flesh, and sank to one knee, blood gushing
from between his fingers. Louise shrieked in terror and
the *duchesse* gasped aloud, fanning herself with trembling fingers. André sat down heavily on the grass, feeling
his head spinning. Gunner and Michel were suddenly
beside him, easing him down, pressing on the cut edges
of the flesh to stanch the flow of blood. Gunner looked as
though he were about to cry.

"Did we do wrong, André? We were so longing to see
our old Gosse. Be hanged, but she's a fine wench that
Master Fresnel would be proud of—" He stopped to wipe
away a tear. "Did we do wrong?" he said again, his face
twisted in grief.

Janequin knelt in front of André. "I've sent for a
surgeon, monsieur."

André nodded his thanks, feeling unexpectedly weak
and closed his eyes, drifting through a haze of pain and
light-headedness, barely conscious save for a nagging

gadfly of a thought that would not quit his spinning brain. "Gosse," he mumbled, and opened his eyes, struggling to sit up despite Gunner's restraining hands.

But when he looked around the circle of concerned faces that bent over him, wide-eyed with horror and shock, he could not see the one dear face he sought.

Gosse was not to be found.

Chapter Twenty-two

THE SEA GULLS WHEELED AND SHRIEKED OVERHEAD, swooping down to pluck their supper from ocean and shore, dropping the mussels on the sharp rocks again and again until the shells cracked and disgorged their tender morsels. The sun hung like a scarlet disk on the edge of the sea, turning the sky and the waves a glowing pink. After the heat of the day, the breezes blew fresh and cool from the ocean, whipping up little whitecaps that broke softly against the sand.

André threaded his horse through the dune grass and reeds to the top of the rise. He would be able to see much of the coastline from here. The tavern keeper in Honfleur had said the cottage was isolated, set on a promontory, a high point of land projecting into the sea beyond the coastline. It would be what Delphine would have chosen.

He reined in his horse for a moment and took off his plumed hat, rubbing his sweaty forehead across his sleeve. Replacing the hat, he touched his cheek gingerly, feeling the strip of adhesive plaster that protected the silk sutures which bound up the cut edges of his wound. Damn! he thought in annoyance. Already it was beginning to itch. It was little more than a week, and the cu would heal without corruption—thanks be to God—but the desire to scratch at the puckering flesh was driving him mad. Urging his mount on once again, he sighted the cottage at last, where the coast swung out into a rocky headland. The beach on either side of the promontory was wider than the rest of the stretch—two pale, sandy crescents that seemed to bracket the spit of land.

He sighed. He was fortunate to have found the cottage so easily. He had hardly waited for the surgeon at Fontainebleau to finish his work before he and the Duc de Janequin were off and away for Paris. But it was too late. Delphine had already fled.

He had paced the vestibule of her *hôtel*, looking impatiently at Janequin, while a distressed Charlotte had wrung her hands in alarm at these two madmen who had invaded her lady's home.

"Where could she have gone?" he asked Janequin.

"She goes away oftentimes. There is a house—in the country—"

"Where?"

"I know not."

"Name of God!" cried André . "You pay her bills, you are betrothed to her—and you know not where she goes when she is away from Paris?"

"You are perhaps bolder than I, my friend. I never wanted to ask. I feared she journeyed to see a lover."

André looked shamefaced. "Forgive me. I can scarcely reproach you for that. But have you no idea where she went?"

"It was on the coast, I know that for a certainty."

André turned to Charlotte. "Do you know where madame goes?"

She bobbed nervously. "No, monsieur. She was very —discreet about her dealings—as well you know." The caustic innuendo was not lost on André. "Only the coachman knows the place, and he always stays with her until she returns."

André frowned. "Dieppe?" he said, half to himself. "It was where she lived with her father. Could it be Dieppe?" he asked Charlotte.

"I know not. It was *near* to Dieppe, I think, for the coachman talked of a—lady friend—he had there. Madame often received letters. I think they came from Normandy, but I cannot be sure."

André turned to Janequin. "Honfleur? Saint Valéry-en-Caux? They are close by."

Janequin shook his head. "No. It could not be."

"What makes you so sure?"

"I—have—sent inquiry once or twice, when—jealousy got the better of me—to Honfleur and Saint Valéry and Dieppe—and half a dozen other towns in the district. There was no Delphine Despreaux."

André looked thoughtful. "Tell me, did she—love Despreaux?"

"No. I think she despised him. I could never understand why she had married him. He treated her damnably, as far as I could tell. And he was a thief besides."

"Then I'll wager if she is to be found in Saint Valéry or Honfleur or any other village nearby, it will be a Delphine Fresnel, or even Copain. She would choose a name that was dear to her."

"Would it then be Crillon?" said Janequin softly.

"I know not." André sighed. "I have brought her so much grief, I think she would choose the devil's name before mine."

"I pray that it be so," said Janequin, "for my sake." He clasped his hands together. "Bring her back—to me, you can."

André moved along the top of the rise, looking for a break in the dunes that would lead him easily to th

beach. His intuition had been right. Honfleur had been
only the second village he had visited, asking for a
Madame Fresnel, a Madame Copain. Yes, the tavern
keeper had said, there was a Madame Fresnel who had
bought a house near the shore. Kept to herself. No one
saw her very much. Went away a great deal, though
someone lived in the house, it was said. Maybe a servant.
He had given André directions, then beamed in pleasure
at the coins that were pressed into his hand.

André frowned, recalling his conversation with Janequin. Why had Delphine married Despreaux if he had
been such a villain? Gosse had loved the sea. Why had
she left it? She said her father had died in an accident at
sea—did the reason lie there? But surely Gunner, as the
new master of *Olympie*, would have been delighted to
welcome her aboard. He shook his head. What had
turned the happy and open Gosse into the artificial,
angry, suspicious Delphine? She had not seemed like a
creature who needed worldly goods for her happiness.
Perhaps the answer lay here, in this desolate stretch of
coastland.

His heart leaped in his breast. On the strip of beach
beyond the cottage a figure was pacing slowly back and
forth. Even from here, with her sweet body clothed in
somber garments, it was impossible to mistake Delphine.
She seemed deep in thought, her golden head bent, her
shoulders drooping with unhappiness.

The horse descended noiselessly to the beach; it was
not until André was level with Delphine, and at some
hundred yards, that she glanced up and saw him. A look
of panic crossed her face and she turned away from him,
fleeing across the sand, her hands clutching at her skirts
to speed her escape.

"Delphine!" he called, spurring his horse forward.

She looked over her shoulder for a moment, her eyes

wide with dismay, then continued her flight. But though
she was fleet of foot, he had soon bridged the gap;
tossing off his hat, he leaped from his horse and tackled
her, so they fell together onto the warm sand.

"Let me go!" she shrieked, struggling furiously. "You
vile—you—let me go!" She bucked and kicked, pushing
up with tight-clenched fists against his chest, twisting
and writhing to pull away. Grunting, he managed at
last to straddle her body, which kept her in one place at
least; with some difficulty he grabbed at one wrist and
then the other, pinning her hands to the sand beside her
head.

"Damn it," he gasped, fighting for breath, "I am too
old for these incessant battles! Will you be still and listen
to me?"

Knowing that further struggle was hopeless, she lay still
beneath him, her body going limp in resignation. Her
mouth twisted with bitterness, angry tears filling her eyes.
"Will you not leave me one corner of the world where I
may belong?"

"Delphine—"

She closed her eyes, letting the tears flow, giving way
to her grief and despair. "Go away," she sobbed, her
voice shaking. "I can no longer call the sea my home. I
cannot return to Paris. Go away and forget Delphine.
Leave me a shred of dignity. Leave me a last refuge!"

"Delphine. My dearest Delphine, look at me." He
waited until she had opened her eyes, then released one
of her hands and gently dabbed at her wet cheeks, his
fingers soft and loving. "I did not bring Gunner and
Michel to Fontainebleau. I would not hurt you so. It was
Louise de Trémont, filled with jealousy and envy, who
meant to disgrace you and gain Bernard for herself." He
moved off her body and got to his knees, helping
Delphine to sit up beside him. *"Nom de Dieu!* Did I no

tell you I searched for you and could find no trace? But I searched for Gosse. Louise, knowing I had sailed on *Olympie,* searched for the ship and found the truth. Poor Gunner is heartbroken, thinking he has brought you grief."

She buried her face in her hands. "What does it matter? I am ruined in any event."

"No. Come back to Paris. Marry Janequin, if that is your wish."

"He would not see me again, I'll wager."

"No. His last words to me were to bring you back. I was to tell you that—Delphine or Gosse—he wants you as his bride. He loves you very dearly, you know."

"Ah Dieu!" she cried. "And he would suffer every moment that the court mocked his *duchesse!"*

André began to laugh. Delphine looked at him in shocked surprise. Scowling, she rose to her feet and would have stalked off, but he stood up in his turn, clasping her hand in his so she could not flee. "You will return to Paris in triumph," he said, smiling. "Monsieur le Cardinal Richelieu has heard of your skill with a rapier, and is most anxious to see a demonstration of your talent." He touched at his wound. "With less—disastrous results this time, God willing!"

She gaped in astonishment, wiping the tears from her face. "I cannot believe it!"

"The court is fickle, but a woman of beauty and spirit is always to be admired. Even that popinjay Rannel— having recovered from his initial surprise—"

"The snobbish prig!" she hissed.

"Indeed. But now he is telling the whole court that he divined all along that the matchless La Déesse was a more extraordinary creature than anyone else suspect- ed!"

"Damn his hide! I shall hang him by his lovelock!" said

Delphine, then smiled sheepishly at the ferocity of her own words.

He held both her hands. "How gladsome to see you smile again. Go back to Paris and your triumph. Marry Janequin. Marry Rannel, for aught I care! Only be happy. I see such pain in your eyes, and I suffer to think that—all unknowing—I may have put it there. If marrying Janequin will take the grief away, then I would see you as his bride, though it break my own heart. My dear love, I long to see Gosse again—free, untamed, joyous. Do as you wish, only be happy. Let me know you are happy."

He turned away, feeling suddenly vulnerable. He had poured out his heart to her, handed her his naked soul. He was not brave enough to stay and watch her tear it to pieces. He went over to his hat, lying on the beach where he had tossed it, and, scooping it up, banged it against his leg to dislodge the sand. Setting it firmly upon his head, he whistled to his horse and waited, his back resolutely to Delphine, until the steed should make its way to him. He gasped aloud as a piece of driftwood, hurled through the air, tumbled his hat from his head and knocked it to the sand. Whirling, he saw Delphine standing there, legs spread wide, hands on hips, her jaw set in defiance.

"Sink and scuttle me, landlubber! But how am I to be happy without you?"

He grinned. "Gosse, you devil! Will you cost me every hat I own?" And he opened his arms to her.

She flew to his embrace, to the kiss that set her heart on fire, the arms that welcomed her home. He kissed her over and over again, murmuring her name, swearing his devotion forever until her head spun with the wonder of being loved so deeply, so dearly.

She stirred uneasily in his embrace. "Am I such a—devil? Such a savage, as you were wont to call me?"

He laughed and kissed her again. "You are a delight, and everything I prize in a woman!"

She bit her lip nervously. "And your—serene and gentle Marielle?"

He chuckled. "Marielle once crowned me with a boot! I had forgotten that!"

"I have no doubt you deserved it," she said dryly.

"Indeed, yes, as I recall. But if you promise not to do the same, my love, I swear I shall do all in my power to make you happy." He bent to her mouth, suddenly serious, and kissed her gently, his mouth sweet on hers.

She broke from his embrace and turned away, feeling overwhelmed by the old pain, the old grief. "The happiest—and most miserable day of my life—" she said softly, stumbling over the words "—was the dawn in the harbor of Dieppe. I put on a gown—and smoothed my hair—to greet my love in the morning," the bitter tears flowed, "and the villain had fled—"

"Ah, Dieu!" he cried, turning her into his embrace and cradling her in his arms. "Not only a villain, but a fool as well! My poor Gosse. Did you love me then?"

"Then—and always," she whispered.

"And I wondered at your hatred when we met again! Nom de Dieu. Can you forgive me?" His voice was heavy with remorse. "You said once that I had killed Gosse. God save me, you were right."

She shook her head. "No—no. I thought so then, but—Copain said it, a long time ago. We cannot hold back time. It had to happen as it did. Gosse was so young, so trusting—how could there be aught but pain to find the world ugly and cruel?"

He stroked her hair with tender fingers. "And yet Gosse came sometimes to bedevil me, and gladden this old heart with her youth and joy—"

She touched the plaster on his cheek. "What have I done to your beautiful face?"

"If my eyes may see you, my lips kiss you, I am content. And if I may take you to wed, what more shall I need to make my life complete?"

"But your face!"

"It will heal."

"But it will leave a dreadful scar."

He laughed, his eyes twinkling. "Then, mayhap, the women will leave me in peace! If I am scarred, you need not fear other women!"

She tossed her head. "Pah! What care I? I have never concerned myself with your—other women. If you are attracted to that slut Marion de Lorme, if you find that whining Clémence de Vignon interesting—"

He roared with laughter. "But you never noticed or cared—of course!"

She snapped her fingers. "Not a whit!"

"I think . . . to keep you out of mischief—I shall keep your belly fat with children!' He kissed her firmly then stepped back, his blue eyes warm and serious. "Will you bear my children, Delphine?" he whispered.

She laughed, that deep, musical sound that bubbled from her throat and filled his senses. Without a word she pulled him by the hand, guiding him across the beach and to a narrow path that led up to the cottage. It perched on a small hill, looking out over the ocean, a solid building of rubble masonry with pale gray-green stones that echoed the color of the waves. Delphine pulled him inside and through a spacious sitting room glowing with the last light of day. She led him up the stairs and pushed open a door off the landing. In the dimming light, André saw an elderly woman standing by the casement, holding a small bundle in her arms. At their entrance, the woman turned around.

"Light the candles, Anne-Marie," said Delphine. "We shall have supper."

Anne-Marie put down her bundle, curtsied, and left the room, glancing curiously at André as she passed. He saw now that her bundle was, in point of fact, a small child, not much more than a year old, he guessed, with rosy cheeks and hair as yellow as hay on a midsummer's day.

Delphine knelt and held out her arms. "Robert," she said gently. The child gurgled and toddled toward her, his pink fists reaching for her. She swept him into her arms, kissing his forehead and rounded cheeks before handing him to a startled André. He gaped, looking into eyes as blue as sapphires, as blue as his own. He stared questioningly at Delphine.

"Monsieur le Comte," she said, laughing softly, "your son."

Tapestry

HISTORICAL ROMANCES

Breathtaking New Tales

of love and adventure set against history's most exciting time and places. Featuring two novels by the finest authors in the field of romantic fiction—<u>every</u> <u>month</u>.

Next Month From Tapestry Romances

SNOW PRINCESS
by Victoria Foote

FLETCHER'S WOMAN
by Linda Lael Miller

617